THE DEATH
OF IVAN ILYCH AND
OTHER STORIES

Leo Tolstoy

With an Introduction and Notes
by David Goldfarb

George Stade
Consulting Editorial Director

BARNES & NOBLE CLASSICS
NEW YORK

ЛВ
BARNES & NOBLE CLASSICS
NEW YORK

Published by Barnes & Noble Books
122 Fifth Avenue
New York, NY 10011

www.barnesandnoble.com/classics

The present anonymous translation of *The Kreutzer Sonata* first appeared in 1899.
Alymer Maude's translation of *Hadji Murád* was first published in 1912.
Constance Garnett's translations of *The Death of Ivan Ilych* and
Family Happiness first appeared in 1915.

Published in 2004 by Barnes & Noble Classics with new Introduction, Notes,
Biography, Chronology, Inspired By, Comments & Questions,
and For Further Reading.

The Death of Ivan Ilych and Other Stories
ISBN-13: 978-1-59308-069-3
ISBN-10: 1-59308-069-7
LC Control Number 2003109509

Produced and published in conjunction with:
Fine Creative Media, Inc.
322 Eighth Avenue
New York, NY 10001

Michael J. Fine, President and Publisher

Printed in the United States of America

QM

11 13 15 17 19 20 18 16 14 12

LEO TOLSTOY

Frail and exhausted by familial unhappiness, Leo Tolstoy, at age eighty-two, quietly stole away from his home one evening in late October 1910, aided by his youngest daughter, Alexandra, and his doctor. The greatest living figure in Russia had no planned destination as he boarded a late-night train, but hours later his journey was cut short when pneumonia forced him to disembark at Astapovo. A media frenzy of international proportions ensued as Tolstoy lay dying in the stationmaster's house, and days later the world grieved to learn that the literary giant had reached his final destination.

Tolstoy's life was much like his novels—expansive, complex, ambiguous, profound. Born into an aristocratic family on August 28, 1828, at their estate Yasnaya Polyana, Count Leo Nikolayevich Tolstoy lost both his parents when he was a child, a fact that instilled in him a deep and lasting awareness of death. Educated by tutors and raised by aunts, young Leo revered Charles Dickens, Voltaire, Georg Hegel, and especially Jean-Jacques Rousseau. After a short time studying languages and law at the University of Kazan, he left school and returned to his estate, determined to improve the lives of the peasants who lived there.

Tolstoy's efforts at Yasnaya Polyana were not entirely successful, and the severe mental and physical rigors he imposed on himself were relieved by periods of debauchery in the gambling salons and brothels of Moscow. Wanting something more than a life of philistinism, Tolstoy joined the military and devoted himself with great seriousness to his writing. His first novel, *Childhood*, and *Sevastopol Stories*, a collection of short fiction based on his experiences in the Crimean War, earned him the respect of both Czar Alexander II and the writer Ivan Turgenev, as well as a place among the leading writers of his day. The brilliant young author hardly courted his admirers, however. Outspoken, wild, and difficult, Tolstoy offended many with his radical contrariness and criticism of the Russian status quo. Love mellowed some of his legendary appetites, and in 1862 Tolstoy wed

Sophia Behrs, who would bear him thirteen children and handwrite thousands of pages of his manuscripts.

Over the next decade Tolstoy published two of the world's greatest novels, *War and Peace* and *Anna Karenina*, which earned him the highest acclaim among his countrymen and secured him a reputation equal to that of other masters of the modern novel—George Eliot, Gustave Flaubert, Fyodor Dostoevsky, Thomas Hardy, Henry James. His later stories "The Death of Ivan Ilych" and "The Kreutzer Sonata" are also considered to be masterpieces. But while Tolstoy's reputation grew, his private life degenerated. Neither philosophy nor organized religion could soothe his ennui or lead him to understand how he could live a meaningful life. In his long essay *A Confession*, Tolstoy states that during one period he was forced to abandon his favorite hobby of hunting for fear he would be tempted to turn his gun on himself: "At the very time that I was writing and finishing my book *Anna Karenina*, this despair reached the point that I could do nothing but only think, think about the dreadful situation that I was in." Sophia, overextended from perpetual pregnancies and wifely duties, responded to her husband's increasing spiritual unrest with incomprehension. The marriage suffered terribly and never quite recovered from that period of unhappiness. Tolstoy's writing suffered as well. In the years following his conversion, he renounced his earlier masterpieces as worldly trash and devoted his talents to hortatory essays and revisions of the New Testament. His public was appalled at this turn of events, and a dying Ivan Turgenev begged Tolstoy to fulfill his deathbed wish and take up his pen once more.

During the time he spent educating the Russian peasants, Tolstoy came to believe that a literal interpretation of Christ's teachings, stripped of church doctrine, gave meaning to their lives. Following similar principles, he determined to improve his own spiritual well-being by signing over his property and following the minimalist program outlined in the biblical book of Matthew—decisions that permanently alienated him from most of his family. In his essays *A Confession, What Then Must We Do?, The Kingdom of God Is Within You*, and *What I Believe*, Tolstoy presented his philosophy of simplicity and nonresistance to evil—an outlook that inspired Mahatma Gandhi, among many others. Leo Tolstoy died on November 7, 1910.

TABLE OF CONTENTS

THE WORLD OF LEO TOLSTOY AND THE DEATH OF IVAN ILYCH AND OTHER STORIES

1828   On August 28 Leo Nikolayevich Tolstoy is born into a noble family at Yasnaya Polyana, the family estate.

1830   Leo's mother dies.

1833   Aleksandr Pushkin's *Eugene Onegin* is published.

1837   The family moves to Moscow. Leo's father dies.

1840   The Tolstoy children are taken in by their Aunt Alexandra. Leo loves stories, and is captivated by his brother Sergei's tale of a small green stick buried in the neighboring woods; on it, his brother claims, is written the secret to uniting all of humanity in mutual love. Mikhail Lermontov's *A Hero of Our Time* is published.

1841   Aunt Alexandra dies. Leo comes under the care of his beloved Aunt Tatiana in Kazan and is educated by tutors. A sensitive and precocious child, Leo displays the keen awareness of death that will haunt him throughout his life. He also reveals his attraction to extremes—he forces himself to adhere to grueling physical exercises, including self-inflicted back-lashing, only to be overcome by bouts of self-indulgence and laziness.

1842   Nikolai Gogol's *Dead Souls* is published.

1844   Tolstoy enters Kazan University, where he studies Oriental languages in preparation for a career in diplomacy.

1845   Tolstoy decides to study law. While in school, he takes up a rigorous program of self-betterment, which includes physical exercise, exhaustive study, and the painstaking documentation of his moral development in a diary some have considered to be his writer's laboratory. The works of Georg Hegel, Charles Dickens, Voltaire, William Shakespeare, and Jean-Jacques Rousseau are among his favorites.

1847–   Tolstoy quits his studies and returns to the family estate,
1850   which he has inherited. He dedicates himself to bettering the life of the local peasants with education and practical assistance. He is not completely successful, but his experience only

increases his commitment to a lifelong struggle on behalf of the impoverished. True to his divided nature, Tolstoy counterbalances these noble efforts with gambling binges and sexual escapades in St. Petersburg and Moscow.

1851   He begins to write an autobiographical novel, Childhood, and joins the military with his brother.

1852   Childhood is published to great acclaim.

1853–   Tolstoy fights in the Crimean War. He completes another
1856   novel, Boyhood (1854), which is the sequel to Childhood, and a collection of short fiction based on his wartime experience, Sevastopol Stories (1855–1856). Czar Alexander II, the writer Ivan Turgenev, and many other readers embrace Tolstoy as an important writer. The author manages to offend some followers with his eccentric views and arrogant self-righteousness.

1857   Tolstoy publishes Youth, the third novel in his autobiographical trilogy. He travels throughout Europe and is repulsed by the barbarity of a public execution he witnesses.

1859   Tolstoy publishes "Family Happiness," a short novel. He devotes more energy to public education by lecturing and founding a school for peasant students.

1861   The serfs are freed by the Emancipation Manifesto. Tolstoy's brother, Nikolai, dies of tuberculosis, and Tolstoy experiences a profound depression.

1862   After much indecision, Tolstoy marries Sophia Behrs. As a condition of their union, Tolstoy demands that Sophia read journal descriptions of his past sexual promiscuity. Ivan Turgenev publishes Fathers and Sons.

1863   Tolstoy publishes The Cossacks, a novel, begins his research for War and Peace, and publishes the first of the epic work's six volumes. Sophia becomes her husband's secretary; over the course of their forty-eight-year marriage she will handwrite thousands of his manuscript pages.

1866   Fyodor Dostoevsky publishes Crime and Punishment.

1869   The last of the six volumes of War and Peace is published.

1870   Vladimir Lenin, who will lead the Russian Revolution of 1917, is born.

1872   Tolstoy views the corpse of Anna Pirogova, a young woman who has committed suicide by throwing herself beneath the wheels of a train after learning her lover planned to abandon her in order to marry another woman. Karl Marx's *Das Kapital*, an analysis of capitalistic politics, circulates throughout Russia.

1875 *Anna Karenina* begins to be published in installments and is overwhelmingly popular. Nevertheless, three deaths—the extreme suffering and death of his baby son, the premature birth and death of a daughter, and the death of his Aunt Tatiana—plunge Tolstoy into a serious depression and contemplation of suicide. Continuing his search for a new philosophy of life, he studies the ancient philosophers, numerous religions, and the culture of the Russian peasantry.

1878 Although Tolstoy has submitted the final chapters of *Anna Karenina* to his publisher, the outbreak of war in the Balkans inspires him to write what he calls an epilogue to the novel. The publisher refuses to issue it, and Tolstoy brings it out at his own expense, in the form of a brochure. In conversation with Sophia, Tolstoy agonizes that he is incapable of continuing to live with the spiritual and philosophical questions that absorb him and that are articulated in the final, rejected pages of his novel.

1879– Fyodor Dostoevsky's *The Brothers Karamazov* is published.
1880

1881 Czar Alexander II is assassinated.

1882 Tolstoy publishes *A Confession*, an essay, banned in Russia, on religion and the meaning of life; in this work, he embraces a philosophy of Christian love and nonviolence unfettered by organized religion.

1883 Tolstoy meets Vladimir Chertkov, who becomes his disciple and a source of anger and resentment between Tolstoy and his wife. The Russian government becomes increasingly watchful of Tolstoy and his antigovernment sentiments.

1886 "The Death of Ivan Ilych," a story considered to be another Tolstoy masterpiece, is published.

1889 Tolstoy writes "The Kreutzer Sonata," an account of sexuality and wife murder so scandalous it cannot be published and must circulate in manuscript form. It is read aloud at social gatherings throughout Russia—sometimes by Tolstoy himself—and provokes extensive debate.

INTRODUCTION

The continued popularity of Leo Tolstoy's story "The Death of Ivan Ilych" perhaps owes as much to the author's ability to sympathize with the bad choices his eponymous hero makes as to the fact that this protagonist represents a class still in existence to this day—an upwardly mobile middle class whose members will attend the university and read stories by Tolstoy and will recognize Ivan Ilych as a character they have met, perhaps in their own circle of acquaintances, in their family, or even within themselves. Tolstoy's success in conveying the psychological reality of his characters is not exclusive to his portrayal of Ivan Ilych. It is not uncommon to hear male readers say that they feel they know Anna Karenina as well as they know their own wives, or for contemporary female readers to say that they sympathize with Anna and identify with her in some ways. Though many readers would ascribe genius to Tolstoy, this acuity of psychological perception did not develop without practice.

The forms of the short story, novella, letter, and diary, which offered Tolstoy the possibility for greater narrative experimentation than did long works like *Anna Karenina* or *War and Peace*, provided a field for this practice. Written throughout his life, the stories offer some insight into the development of Tolstoy's ideas over time, while the long works, though broad in scope, provide only two snapshots of Tolstoy's evolution as a thinker and writer of fiction. The nineteenth century was generally a very dynamic period in the development of Russian prose forms, as writers reacted to the neoclassicism of the late eighteenth century and attempted to create a prose style that was modern and European but still distinctively Russian and not simply derivative. In an age dominated by realism, experimentation was not merely about style, but about truth in the representation of reality and in the critique of social reality. Where direct political criticism was stifled by tsarist censorship, literature and literary criticism often took its place. For Tolstoy it might be said that this critique is manifested in both the content and in the practice of writing fiction and in his ever-present question "How to live?" The process of writing for Tolstoy provides a means of understanding the subjective feeling of the reality of another person's existence and conveying that feeling to readers, thus creating a bond between the character and readers through the words of the author. Tolstoy's practice of psychological observation and the practice of fiction constitute a spiritual and social practice of forging unity among individuals.

The axis of the most pervasive disunity among individuals in nineteenth-century Russia and beyond is that of gender. Of Tolstoy's stories, the early "Family Happiness" and the late "The Kreutzer Sonata," provide distinct perspectives from which to evaluate Tolstoy's views on "the woman question." "Family Happiness" appeared in 1859, only four years before Nikolai Chernyshevsky's Fourierist novel, *What Is to Be Done?* This radical, utopian novel proposed the abolition of marriage and the establishment of communes, envisioned a future in which happiness would be guaranteed by technology, and regarded material comfort as the basis for human motivation. By this time Russian women pursued education and had even begun to enter medical school, first by traveling abroad and eventually in Russia itself. Science introduced new methods of contraception and abortion and new views on human sexuality that did not always coincide with traditional religious teachings.

In order to best understand modern life as a woman might experience it, in "Family Happiness" Tolstoy takes the bold step of attempting a first-person narrative in a woman's voice—the story is his only work in this form. As the family was then still the main sphere of women's activity, the problem of "domestic happiness" (as the title may alternately be translated) provides an avenue to most of the issues associated with the woman question, as well as questions about love, the nature of happiness, and what it means to "live for others," which will recur in all of Tolstoy's work. The prose, which evolved from letters between Tolstoy and his friend Valeriya Vladimirovna Arseneva, resembles that of a letter written from the perspective of a woman who has been married and had her first child—written perhaps to a younger woman of the age that the narrator is at the beginning of the story. The letters to Arseneva, which contain a fictional account of a romance between two invented characters, gave the author an opportunity not only to debate important social questions, but to test his ear, to write in a woman's voice that a woman would find believable. The choice of a quasi-epistolary voice is significant in that the sentimental romances that Tolstoy frequently criticizes were often written in the epistolary form or as a narrative in which letters played a significant role. The challenge for Tolstoy here is to write a kind of epistle that is believable and neither sentimental nor a parody of the sentimental epistolary novel in the manner of Dostoevsky's *Poor Folk*.

We meet Masha as a girl of seventeen living with her sister, Sonya, and their governess, Katya, on a country estate after the death of their mother. The girls' father has died some years before and their future is entrusted to his younger friend, Sergei Mikhailych. The tale that unfolds is that of Masha's falling in love with Sergei, the evolution of their marriage, and their changing definition of love and happiness in the domestic sphere.

Masha has grown up in the country, and her first ideas about love derive from sentimental romance novels, in which dashing characters experience dramatic shifts of passion and are rewarded in moments of "wild delight"—a catch phrase, the content of which is left to the reader's imagination. Early in her romance with Sergei, Masha often compares her experience with what she has read and awaits the "wild delight" she has read about, but nothing in real life can fill that perfectly open category. With its attractive lack of specificity, "wild delight" refers to individual happiness in accord with the reader's personal desire, rather than the communal happiness of the family or of fulfillment in genuine self-sacrifice.

The idea of "living for others" (p. 32) is Masha's answer to the question of "how to live," but at first it is a facile answer, pervaded by an egoistic and sentimental idea of self-sacrifice. She anonymously gives money to a poor family, prays fervently, and tearfully begs for forgiveness from persons she has not injured or has wronged in trivial ways. Like the "wild delight" she has read about in novels, "living for others" is at this point in the story an empty phrase filled by self-indulgent fantasies. This egoistic idea of self-sacrifice becomes poisonous to the marriage when Masha, still in search of "wild delight," and Sergei move to St. Petersburg to escape the boredom of the country. At first Masha takes pleasure at being the center of attention as a new face at fashionable society balls, where her husband's jealousy is aroused. But eventually she takes even greater joy in denying herself the pleasures of flirtation, which only leads to further conflict, because it puts Sergei in the position of feeling he is oppressing her by causing her to sacrifice her pleasure for his sake. Even without the benefit of a psychological theory of "passive aggression," Tolstoy well understands the concept of sacrifice that has more to do with the vanity of the person making the sacrifice than it does with true recognition of the human needs of the other.

"Living for others" becomes truly meaningful for Masha only in motherhood, when the sacrifice is genuine and there can be no confusion between real life and "playing at life" (p. 53), as there is before their move to St. Petersburg. Masha's concern about "playing at life" is a gendered one, arising from her observation that Sergei is managing all the important affairs of their estate, and she has no real sphere of activity in which she can effect change in the world. Her concern is real, and while the content of Masha's desire to be a fully human agent exercising her free will in the world is as yet unformed, Sergei's response—"But in what way are you not on equal terms with me? . . . Is it because I, and not you, have to deal with the police captain and drunken peasants?" (p. 53)—is clearly evasive and patronizing. Their solution in moving to the city, though, will prove unsatisfying as a means to providing a sphere of productive female activity; the novelty and ability to effect change that Masha can attain in St. Petersburg is meaningful only within the world of society balls and the opera. On the other hand, Tolstoy presents motherhood as being grounded in nature. When Masha looks at her little Vanya, she can say, "Mine, mine, mine!" without any doubts or questions. Vanya's birth "ended my love-story with my husband," Masha concludes (p. 83). This "love-story" is the sentimental narrative of "wild delight" that substitutes for the real life that can no longer be avoided.

"The Kreutzer Sonata" is another narrative that takes place largely in the first person—this time in the voice of Pozdnyshev, a man who has murdered his wife—framed by an outer narrator who relays the main narrator's tale to the reader. It is important to remember that Pozdnyshev is not Tolstoy, but a narrative persona, and like Masha's, his voice is unique in Tolstoy's oeuvre. Pozdnyshev's voice is full of verbal ticks, his peculiar sound, his self-contradiction and crude language. It bears a closer resemblance to the narrator of Fyodor Dostoevsky's *Notes from Underground* than to any other Tolstoyan character, and we might even read "The Kreutzer Sonata" as an experiment in writing in a Dostoevskian voice or in creating a Dostoevskian character. Perhaps the reason that more such characters are not found in Tolstoy is that, while Tolstoy had encountered some rough characters and radical types and had his own period of youthful dissolution, he was not of the world of the Underground Man or Raskolnikov from *Crime and Punishment* in the sense that Dostoevsky was. Unlike Dostoevsky, Tolstoy spent much of his life on his estate at Yasnaya Polyana rather than in the city; he was never exiled to Siberia; and he was not implicated as a member of subversive underground circles—yet such people played an important role in the Russian intellectual and political landscape of his day. Imagining the voice of Pozdnyshev was a means toward understanding a voice that was certainly in the air, but on a profound level must have been radically alien to Tolstoy's experience.

In the tight structural device of a voyage by train—in which the time of narration is determined by the distance between two points on a map, and the number of characters is restricted by the number of seats in a compartment—Tolstoy frames Pozdnyshev's narrative with a conversation on marriage and divorce among a group composed of a modern woman of somewhat masculine bearing; her companion, who is a lawyer very much in favor of Europeanization; an elderly merchant of the old school, who believes that things were better when marriages were arranged; a young clerk, who has come from a fair with the merchant; and the narrator. Yet another perspective is squeezed into the train compartment by way of Tolstoy's epigraph from the gospel of Matthew (19:10–12): "The disciples say unto him, If the case of the man is so with his wife, it is not expedient to marry. But he said unto them, All men cannot receive this saying, but they to whom it is given. For there are some eunuchs. . . ." This passage suggests the possibility of celibacy, which Russian readers of the day would have read as an allusion to the *skoptsi* ("eunuchs"), a religious sect not unlike the Shakers in certain respects, who practiced celibacy and in some cases castration, lived communally, and extolled the values of manual labor.

Pozdnyshev describes a marriage that begins much like those of Masha and Sergei or Ivan Ilych and Praskovya Fyodorovna. It is defined to some degree by social circumstances, and there are balls, moments of jealousy, quarrels, children, and middle-class economic striving. The children, rather than affirming the virtues of motherhood as they do in Masha's case, serve more often as proxies for disputes between the parents and as troublesome hosts for illnesses requiring attention. A violinist, Trukhachevsky, emerges from their circle in high society and begins to play music regularly with Pozdnyshev's unnamed wife, who, like Masha and all young ladies groomed for society, has learned to play the piano. It is not clear that anything other than music happens between the two, but Pozdnyshev's jealousy is aroused, sometimes to the point of rage. Like Dostoevsky's Underground Man, Pozdnyshev takes ecstatic pleasure in this rage (p. 224), which Tolstoy describes with the same word (*vostorgi*) that he uses to describe the "wild delight" of Masha's sentimental fantasies of love.

Pozdnyshev's rage leads to murder, which comes about in a situation in which it is socially ordained for a husband to murder his wife, just as it is socially ordained for Ivan Ilych to propose marriage to Praskovya Fyodorovna when they have been seated alone in a room for a suitable interval, while the family sits in the hall awaiting the happy news. Trukhachevsky has come for a visit while Pozdnyshev is away on business. The husband returns early, hears the voices of his wife and her alleged lover, confronts them with a dagger, and stabs his wife as the violinist escapes. He would chase after Trukhachevsky, but he realizes that he has removed his shoes so that he could approach the supposed scene of adultery with the element of surprise, and he considers that the image of a husband in his stocking feet chasing after his wife's lover with a knife bears more of a resemblance to comedy than to the heroic tragedy he has scripted since Trukhachevsky's arrival.

Pozdnyshev's fervent views on marriage and women's emancipation come from the realization that, like Masha's, his view of love is sentimental and egoistic. He does not blame his wife but his lust. He recognizes their original courtship as a sentimental cover for sexual desire and comes to see his jealousy as an effect of that desire in conjunction with his self-centeredness. Marriage as a lifelong attachment is something "true only in novels" (p. 154). He compares the honeymoon to a circus sideshow, where patrons exiting the booth are expected to vouch for their amazement upon witnessing a bearded lady, so as not to spoil the excitement for those who have yet to purchase a ticket.

But what would be the alternative to marriage for Pozdnyshev? He gives us one hint in his statement that marriages "have existed and exist for people who see in marriage something sacred—a sacrament which is entered into before God—for such people it exists. Among us, people get married, seeing nothing in marriage except copulation, and the result is either deception or violence" (p. 155). The possibility of chaste marriage suggested by the epigraph from the Bible, Matthew 19:10–12, might be one option, but it almost seems like a confession of defeat—we know from "Family Happiness" that Tolstoy could imagine motherhood as a positive value and purpose in life. The alternative would be a change in perception and intention rather than in action, as Tolstoy suggests with his first epigraph to the story, also from the Bible, Matthew 5:28: "But I say unto you that every one that looketh on a woman to lust after her hath committed adultery with her already in his heart." Here Tolstoy seems to be suggesting a form of union in which a man does not look at a woman with lust in his heart.

It would be easy to view Tolstoy's critique of women's education and valorization of motherhood and domestic life as antifeminist, but it is important to understand these views in their full context and to recognize the conditions under which these issues were being raised in the latter half of the nineteenth century in Russia. For Masha, the twenty-first-century choice of a career over motherhood is just barely emerging as a revolutionary possibility in 1859. The only socially acceptable alternative to motherhood in the country for a woman of Masha's status would be a life in St. Petersburg society. The problem for Tolstoy is not women's education in itself, but education merely for the sake of raising a woman's value in a marketplace in which she is objectified. Pozdnyshev rants:

> Well, and now they emancipate woman, they give her all rights the same as to men, but they still continue to look on her as an instrument of enjoyment, and so they educate her with this end in view, both in childhood and by public opinion. But all the time she is just the same

kind of dissolute slave as before, and her husband is just the same kind
of a dissolute slave-owner. (p. 182)

The key line here is that "they still continue to look on her as an
instrument of enjoyment," invoking rhetoric of the biblical epigraph
from Matthew 5:28. Pozdnyshev's criticism rejects the women's
emancipation movement at the surface, but it affirms its goals on a
deeper level. The measure of emancipation cannot be gauged only by
the degree of legal access to education or birth control or abortion—
each of which may be used to affirm or to subvert patriarchy. True
emancipation in Pozdnyshev's view will happen when men and
women can look on each other in mutual recognition as ends in
themselves and not as instruments of enjoyment or profit.

In the sexual economy of St. Petersburg or Moscow high society, a
fashionable woman who can also play the piano or knows something
about science becomes a more valuable commodity. By contrast, an
intelligent yet unfashionable woman such as Marya Dmitrievna
Akhrosimova—a domineering intellectual known as "the Dragon" in
War and Peace (a character based on a historical personage)—can only
appear as something of a sideshow attraction. The problem here is
not women's education and intellectual development per se, but a
system of objectification in which all activity, including education, is
subverted for the sake of that system.

In "The Death of Ivan Ilych" Tolstoy moves the stage for an examination of the family to the city and shows how the ethos of bureaucracy infects every aspect of life for the administrative class in
nineteenth-century Russia, from personal friendships to marriage
and the family. Ivan Ilych quickly learns that "conjugal life, though
providing certain comforts, was in reality a very intricate and difficult
business towards which one must, if one is to do one's duty, that is,
lead the decorous life approved by society, work out for oneself a definite line, just as in the government service" (p. 101). Ivan Ilych acts
from a sense of duty, but not the duty that Immanuel Kant—the
philosopher par excellence of duty—argues for in The Groundwork of
the Metaphysic of Morals (1785): "Act on that maxim which can at the
same time have for its object itself as a universal law of nature" Rather,
for Ivan Ilych "[h]is duty he considered whatever was so considered
by those persons who were set in authority over him" (p. 96). For

Kant, duty is discerned by looking inward and asking to what maxims would one submit, even if they were to result in one's personal destruction. For Ivan Ilych, the source of duty is an external set of maxims and conventions accepted without consideration, which would hardly be willful action in accord with duty. Kant's theory of duty is based in a conception of the ultimate free will of any rational being. Ivan Ilych squanders that freedom by failing to consider his own actions, allowing important choices to be made for him by those "in authority" and their arbitrary system of rules.

In the course of Ivan Ilych's death, which begins at birth and continues until the demise of his body, Ivan Ilych never becomes a mature human agent. Even his marriage does not involve a clear discrete act on his part. Rather, he is paired with a woman who would make a good match from the perspective of society, and the marriage becomes inevitable. They are seated alone in a parlor—a situation in which a marriage proposal might be offered—and without it actually being offered, the happy couple is congratulated and the wedding takes place around them. There is no decisive moment in this course of events. Even if Ivan Ilych had uttered a formal proposal, it would not have been an act of will, because it would merely confirm what the conventions of the administrative class had ordained.

This inability to will as a free agent is a central theme in nineteenth-century Russian literature, known from Turgenev's phrase as the problem of the "superfluous man." The most characteristic of such men is the eponymous hero of Ivan Goncharov's novel, *Oblomov* (1859). Oblomov is a nobleman living in the city on credit while his estate falls into ruin, and he is entirely unmotivated to do anything about it. The first quarter of the novel—more than a hundred pages—takes place in Oblomov's sitting room, where he can barely get up from his couch or change out of his dressing gown, and he comically refuses to shake hands with any of his visitors for fear of contracting some miasma from the cold street. In an influential essay that was probably more widely read than the novel itself, "What Is Oblomovitis?" The progressive critic Nikolai Dobrolyubov characterized Oblomov's disease thus:

> [A] normal man always wants to do only what he can do; that is why he immediately does all that he wants to do. . . . But Oblomov . . . is

not accustomed to do anything; consequently, he cannot really deter-
mine what he can do and what he cannot do—and consequently, he
cannot seriously, *actively*, want anything. . . . His wishes always assume
the form: "how good it would be if this were done," but how this can
be done he does not know (p. 185; see "For Further Reading").

Oblomov is a gross caricature of the Russian nobility, but he becomes
a symbol of the stagnancy of Russian society—a theme that would
return many times during the Soviet period and would be synony-
mous with excessive bureaucratization. This absolute surrendering of
the will produces a bureaucratization not only of society, but of the
soul as well. Ivan Ilych is more like the majority of Tolstoy's readers,
leading thoroughly unremarkable lives for never having fully exercised their human agency, for never having asked the Tolstoyan question "How to live?"

Ivan Ilych, like most of the men in his circle, seems to find his only
moments of happiness at the bridge table. The card game might be seen
as an analogue to the sentimental romance in "Family Happiness" and
music in "The Kreutzer Sonata," in that all serve as substitutes for and
escapes from "real life." In a life that is otherwise regulated by administrative ritual, the game provides an illusion of activity, where choices
are made, chance is confronted, and results can be clearly measured in
rubles. The events that happen in the card game, however, are pseudo-
events with no real content, like the transports of "wild delight" that
Masha reads about in novels or passionate music played as spectacle "in
a drawing-room before ladies dressed *décolletées*" (p. 211).

In "The Kreutzer Sonata" Pozdnyshev rails against this ability of
music to produce empty emotion in the listener. Like a coquette,
"music excites and does not bring to any conclusion" (p. 211), Pozdnyshev says. The complaint is similar in some respects to Tolstoy's
complaints about the claims of the sentimental romance "to elevate
the soul," or more precisely, the confusion of "excitement" with ele-
vation of the soul.

Pozdnyshev also articulates a positive theory of art that is not so
different from Tolstoy's. This music was, after all, clearly powerful to
Pozdnyshev and to Tolstoy as well, who heard his son Sergei and
the violinist Lysoto play the Kreutzer Sonata in the spring of 1888.
Tolstoy writes in *What Is Art?*:

> To evoke in oneself a feeling one has experienced, and having evoked
> it in oneself, then, by means of movements, lines, colors, sounds, or
> forms expressed in words, so to transmit that feeling that others may
> experience the same feeling—this is the activity of art.
>
> Art is a human activity consisting in this, that one man con-
> sciously, by means of certain external signs, hands on to others feel-
> ings he has lived through, and that other people are infected by these
> feelings and also experience them (p. 51).

This seems to be precisely what Pozdnyshev hates about hearing
Beethoven. The Kreutzer Sonata hijacks his emotions. Music causes
him to feel something that he is not entitled to feel. He says,
"Beethoven . . . knew why he was in that mood. That mood impelled
him to do certain things, and therefore that mood meant something
for him, but it means nothing for me" (p. 211). We might ask how
this is different from what Anna Karenina feels when she is reading
an English novel on the train from Moscow to St. Petersburg, imagining that she might be giving a speech in Parliament or running with
the hounds (p. 94). In both cases the artistic work is effective because
of its ability to "infect" the listener or reader with the emotions of
the artist, although Pozdnyshev and Anna have not lived through the
experiences that would have inspired the artist, and the circumstances of reception—the drawing room musicale or the train compartment—are wholly inappropriate to such feelings.

So does this mean that Tolstoy thought that "The Kreutzer Sonata"
was bad art? Perhaps, similar to his views on women's education, his
opinion would depend on the context in which it is performed. The
drawing room with ladies dressed *décolletées* might devalue anything
performed in its midst, as far as Tolstoy is concerned, but such music
might be appropriate to "grave, significant conditions" (p. 211). The
context seems to have distorted the power of Beethoven's sonata to
achieve its complete power of "infection," which is the measure of
true art expressed in *What Is Art?*: "However poetical, realistic, effect-
ful, or interesting a work may be, it is not a work of art if it does not
evoke that feeling (quite distinct from all other feelings) of joy and of
spiritual union with another (the author) and with others (those
who are also infected by it)" (p. 139). Ironically, this idea of "spiritual union" or "Christian brotherhood," in which individuals are

united "with God and with one another" (*What Is Art?*, p. 149), or *sobornost* in the broader terms of Russian religious thought, may be consistent with Beethoven's intention as expressed in Schiller's words to the famous "Ode to Joy" in the final movement of the Ninth Symphony, in which all people are called upon to be united as brothers in spiritual joy.

Tolstoy's late work "Hadji Murád," set in the war-ridden Caucasus region, offers a testing ground for Tolstoy to explore the possibility of universal brotherhood among military enemies separated by politics, religion, language, and culture. Russian expansion southward and eastward in search of warm-water ports, taxes, and territory began with Peter the Great's incursions through Georgia into Armenia and continued with Russian involvement in the European conflict with the Ottoman Empire during the 1820s, the Russo-Persian War, and a push into the Caucasus toward Chechnya during the 1840s and 1850s, the time represented in "Hadji Murád." The problem of peace for Tolstoy would rest on the question of whether "unity with God and with one another" is possible between people with such a history of enmity.

"Hadji Murád" might be considered a historical novella that Tolstoy approached in the manner of *War and Peace*, fleshing out historical events and personages he researched in memoirs and accounts of the Caucasian conflict and adding fictional material and the occasional polemic on the role of the individual in history. From 1844 to 1847 Tolstoy studied at the University of Kazan, where he began in Oriental languages, with the idea of entering diplomatic service, and later studied law, but he did not complete a degree. These studies required knowledge of Latin, French, German, and English, and elementary knowledge of Arabic and Turko-Tatar. The last of these would serve him well during his military service in the port city of Sevastopol during the Crimean War of 1854–1855 (which became the basis of his *Sevastopol Sketches*) and facilitated the research and writing of "Hadji Murád" many years later, from 1896 to 1904.

While Tolstoy makes clear efforts to portray Hadji Murád in a realistic light, attributing to him rational and believable motivations for action, this portrayal is not without its own sentimental idealization of the kind we see in Romantic Orientalist works such as Byron's poem "The Giaour" (1812), wherein a Turkish warrior, Hassan, meets a similar fate. It would seem that the Western archetype of the rugged, wise, pious, and noble Oriental warrior has survived into the twenty-first century. One only has to compare essential details of "Hadji Murád" to journalistic accounts of "The Lion of the Panjshir," Ahmed Shah Massoud, the leader of the Afghan Northern Alliance who was assassinated on September 9, 2001, immediately before the attacks on the World Trade Center and the Pentagon. This particular species of "Orientalism" might be seen as an extension of Tolstoy's more general idealization of peasant culture and art, visible in his portrayal of peasant characters like Gerasim in "The Death of Ivan Ilych" and in his decision to emulate peasant life in his later years.

Even as Tolstoy participates to some degree in this romantic master narrative, he applies to all characters the principles he argues for in *War and Peace*—that the vast majority of people act out of self-interest, and that history is not controlled by "great men" but is the sum of so many individual self-interested actions. Hadji Murád may switch between serving the Russians and Shamil's forces, but his motivations are personal. Vengeance for the death of his brother Osman drove him to side with the Russians against Shamil at first, until a conflict with Akhmet Khan—also serving the Russians—drove him to Shamil, who later turned against him, taking Hadji Murád's family hostage, pushing him again over to the Russians.

While Tolstoy, like Pushkin, Lermontov, Byron, and others before him, is stereotyping the Caucasian mountaineers as unruly, hot-blooded savages unable to set aside personal feuds for the sake of the order of civil society, at the same time he is exposing the Russian military and civil bureaucracy as a mask for its own forms of tribalism and personal feuding. Vorontsóv's power derives from his aristocratic background and wealth, rather than military experience or rank. This first presents a potential conflict with General Meller-Zakomelsky, who properly should have accepted Hadji Murád's surrender; but the dispute is mediated through the friendship of the wives of Meller-Zakomelsky and Vorontsov, who invoke the general's respect, rather than by any respect for military protocol. The minister of war, Chernyshov, of lesser tribal status, resents Vorontsov's success, taking every opportunity to diminish him in the eyes of his superiors, much as Akhmet Khan did to Hadji Murád. Tsar Nicholas I—who is subjected to the most cutting political lampoon in all of Tolstoy's work—sides with Vorontsov's wealth and nobility over Chernyshov's experience and bureaucratic rank, meanwhile taking credit for so called "plans" that in fact were never made or acted upon. Hadji Murád, despite his lack of Russian, can tell through body language and tone of voice that Vorontsov is really the chief of this Russian clan, and puts his fate in his hands. It would take Tolstoy's effort of empathy, as imperfect as that effort may have been, to feel some kind of *sobornost* even with Hadji Murád, in order to imagine how Russian society might look to someone on the outside, and to discover that it may be ruled as much by the mysterious force of *mana* as by a complex system of arcane laws and rules. Even as Tolstoy partakes of certain "orientalist" stereotypes, this tribalization of the Russian social order represents a positive step toward self-criticism and a questioning of what had become a well-established dynamic of racial opposition.

Tolstoy's version of realism in fiction offers an approach to moral knowledge, an answer to his question "How to live?" Tolstoy's method of character development is a sincere effort at empathy and recognition of the other, and involves an attempt to become infected with the feelings of his characters—a young woman from a rural estate who marries an older friend of the family, a conformist, upwardly mobile bureaucrat, a wife murderer, or a Tatar warrior (or even a dog or a horse, if we consider some of Tolstoy's most extravagant examples of psychologically omniscient narration in *War and Peace*). By inhabiting the character's voice through the practice of writing, Tolstoy transmits this infection to the reader through words. He often manages this act of empathy in presenting the character's views in a convincing and challenging light so successfully that it is easy to confuse the character's views with the author's, despite the fact that his characters may contradict each other or even themselves as their lives unfold.

Perhaps the answer to the question of how to "live for others" is revealed in Tolstoy's epistemological method of full recognition of the other through an effort of empathy, even when the other seems unknowable or unworthy of empathy. Sentimentalism was particularly focused on "the movements of the heart" or the philosophically skeptical view that subjective experience is the only reality and subjective pleasure the only value, and Romanticism emphasized the work of art that sprang fully formed from the mind of genius. But Tolstoy's realism is about the author's interaction with the world and with persons different from himself. Even as Tolstoy seemed to withdraw from the world, removing himself from his family in his later years to live what some might regard as a sentimental imitation of peasant life, writing stories that were more and more like fables, late works like "The Kreutzer Sonata" and "Hadji Murád" still reveal this striving to test the unknown through narrative experimentation, to experience brotherhood with the radically other.

In the post-modern age readers might view this striving for universal unity as yet another sentimental meta-narrative concealing a deeper ideology of imperialism, wherein "universal unity" is a euphemism for "unity under a Eurocentric conception of human nature." Tolstoy was certainly an optimist to have believed in the possibility of universal brotherhood. A test of the sentimentality of this idea might be to ask how much one is willing to sacrifice of oneself "for others": Are there "infections" that would destroy the organism, and is one willing to accept the possibility of being profoundly changed by such an infection? In Dostoevsky we might point to Prince Myshkin in the Idiot as such a character perfectly willing to receive all infections. As readers of Tolstoy, we might ask whether any of Tolstoy's characters could suffer such exposure.

David Goldfarb is an assistant professor in the Department of Slavic Languages at Barnard College, Columbia University, and holds a doctorate in Comparative Literature from the Graduate Center of the City University of New York; an M.A. in Slavic, specializing in Polish Literature, from the University of Toronto; and a B.A. in Philosophy from Cornell University and Deep Springs College. His doctoral dissertation is entitled *The Discourse of the "Primitive" in Western European and Polish Modernism*. He has published articles on Bruno Schulz, Zbigniew Herbert, Stanislaw Ignacy Witkiewicz, Mikhail Lermontov and narratology, Nikolai Gogol and Giuseppe Arcimboldo, and East European cinema in *East European Politics and Societies, Indiana Slavic Studies, Philosophy* and Literature, Prooftexts, The Polish Review, and Slavic and East European Performance, and book chapters on Jozef Wittlin and Witold Gombrowicz. He is writing a book on the Marquis de Sade, Leopold von Sacher-Masoch, and the genre of the pornosophic novel.

A NOTE ON THE TEXTS

The translations of the stories in this edition were selected for their readability and accuracy. Constance Garnett translated "The Death of Ivan Ilych" and "Family Happiness"; "The Kreutzer Sonata" is an anonymous translation from 1899; and Alymer Maude translated "Hadji Murád." For the benefit of the contemporary reader many revisions have been made to these early translations. Names have been re-transliterated where appropriate using more common English spellings or the Library of Congress system favored by most translators today. Translations that appeared imprecise, archaic, awkward, or misleading have been corrected in many places, and important key words have been rendered more consistently across the different texts.

—David Goldfarb
July 2003

THE DEATH
OF IVAN ILYCH AND
OTHER STORIES

FAMILY HAPPINESS

PART I

I

We were in mourning for my mother, who had died in the autumn, and we spent the whole winter in the country—Katya, Sonya, and I. Katya was an old friend of the family, the governess who had brought us up, and whom I had known and loved ever since I had known anything. Sonya was my younger sister. We passed a gloomy and sorrowful winter in our old house at Pokrovskoe. The weather was cold and windy, so that the snowdrifts were heaped up higher than our windows; the windows were almost always frozen over and dimmed; and almost the whole winter we neither walked nor drove out anywhere. It was not often that any one came to see us, and the few visitors who did come did not add to the gaiety and cheerfulness in our house. They all had mournful faces; they all talked in subdued tones as though afraid of waking someone; never laughed, but sighed, and often shed tears, when they looked at me, and still more at little Sonya, in her black frock. There seemed still a feeling of death in the house; the gloom and horror of death were still in the air. Mamma's room was kept shut up, and an uncanny feeling came upon me, and something impelled me to peep into that cold empty room when I passed it on my way up to bed.

I was at that time seventeen; and the very year of her death mamma had intended moving to town for me to come out. The loss of my mother was a great grief to me; but I must confess that behind this grief there was a feeling too that I was young and pretty, as every one told me, and that here I was wasting a second winter in solitude in the country. Before the end of the winter this sense of depression and loneliness, of boredom, in fact, became so intense that I hardly left my room, did not open the piano, and did not look at a book. When Katya tried to persuade me to take up either occupation, I answered, 'I don't care to, I can't,' while in my soul something said to me, 'What for?' What reason was there to do anything while my best time was being lost, wasted like this? What for? And to the question 'What for?' there was no answer but tears.

They told me I was growing thinner and losing my looks in those days, but even that did not interest me. What did it matter? For whom? . . . It seemed to me that all my life was to be passed like this in this remote solitude and helpless dreariness, from which by myself, all alone, I had not the force, nor even the will, to escape. Towards the end of the winter Katya began to be uneasy about me, and made up her mind that come what might she would take me abroad. But to do this we must have money, and we hardly knew what was left us after my mother's death, and every day we were expecting her executor, who was to come and go into our affairs.

In March the executor came.

'Well, thank God!' Katya said to me one day as I wandered aimlessly about like a shadow, with nothing to do, no thought, no wish in my mind. 'Sergei Mikhailych has come home again; he has sent to inquire after us, and is coming to dinner. You must pull yourself together, my little Masha,' she added, 'or what will he think of you? He was so fond of you all.'

Sergei Mikhailych was a near neighbour of ours, and had been a friend of my father's, though he was many years younger. Apart from the effect of his arrival on our plans, and the possibility through it of our getting away from the country, I had been used from a child to love and respect him; and Katya in advising me to rouse myself had guessed rightly that of all my acquaintances I should most dislike to appear to disadvantage before Sergei Mikhailych. Like every one in the house, from Katya and Sonya, his godchild, down to the humblest coachman, I liked him from habit; but apart from that, he had a peculiar importance in my eyes from a word my mother had once dropped in my presence. She had said that he was the sort of husband she would be glad of for me. At the time this had seemed to me amazing and positively unpleasant; the hero of my dreams was utterly different. My hero was delicate, slender, pale, and melancholy. Sergei Mikhailych was a man no longer youthful, tall, squarely built, and, as I fancied, always cheerful. But in spite of that, these words of mamma's had made a deep impression on my imagination; and even six years before, when I was only eleven, and he used to address me by my pet name and play with me, and used to call me 'little-girl-violet,' I sometimes wondered, not without dismay, what I should do if he were suddenly to want to marry me.

Before dinner, to which Katya added a cream tart and spinach sauce, Sergei Mikhailych arrived. From the window I saw how he drove up in a little sledge; but as soon as he drove round the corner, I hastened to the drawing-room and tried to pretend that I was not in the least expecting him. But hearing the tramp of feet in the hall, his loud voice and Katya's footsteps, I could not restrain myself, and went out to meet him. He was talking loudly, holding Katya's hand and smiling. Catching sight of me, he stopped short, and for a little while gazed at me, without greeting me. I was disconcerted, and I felt that I was blushing.

'Ah, is it really you?' he said in his unhesitating direct manner, gesticulating with his hands and coming up to me. 'Can any one change so? How you have grown up! So this is the little violet! You've become quite a rose!'

He took my hand in his big one and squeezed it so warmly, so heartily, that it almost hurt. I expected he would kiss my hand, and was bending towards him, but he pressed my hand once more, and looked me straight in the face with his resolute, good-humoured eyes.

It was six years since I had seen him. He was very much altered; he looked older, darker, and had grown whiskers, which did not suit him at all. But he had just the same direct manner, the same open honest face with large features, the same shrewd, bright eyes and friendly, as it were, childlike smile.

In five minutes he was no longer a visitor; he became like one of the family to all of us, even to the servants, who, as could be seen by their eagerness to please him, were delighted at his arrival. He behaved quite differently from the other neighbours who had called on us since my mother's death, and had thought it necessary to sit in silence or shed tears while they were with us. He was, on the contrary, very talkative and cheerful, and did not say a word about my mother, so that at first such callousness struck me as strange, and even unseemly, in so intimate a friend of the family. But afterwards I felt that it was not callousness, but sincerity, and was grateful for it. In the evening Katya sat down to pour out tea in the old place in the drawing-room, just as she used to do in mamma's lifetime. Sonya and I sat down near her. Old Grigory brought him a pipe he had sought out, that had been papa's, and he fell to walking up and down the room just as in old days.

'What terrible changes there have been in this house when one thinks of it!' he said, stopping short.

'Yes,' said Katya with a sigh, and, putting the lid on the samovar, she looked at him, already on the point of tears.

'You remember your father, I suppose?' he said, turning to me.

'A little,' I answered.

'And how happy you would have been with him now!' he said softly, and dreamily, gazing at my head above my eyes. 'I was very fond of your father,' he added still more softly, and it seemed to me that his eyes were brighter.

'And now God has taken her too!' said Katya, and immediately she put the dinner napkin down on the teapot, took out her handkerchief, and began to cry.

'Yes, there have been terrible changes in this house,' he repeated, turning away. 'Sonya, show me your playthings,' he added a few instants later, and he went into the parlour. With eyes full of tears I looked at Katya when he had gone out.

'He is such a good friend!' she said. And certainly I felt a sort of warmth and comfort from the sympathy of this good-hearted man from the outside world.

From the drawing-room we could hear Sonya's shrieks and his romping games with her. I sent him some tea into the parlour, and we could hear him sitting down to the piano and striking the keys with Sonya's little hands.

'Marya Alexandrovna!' I heard him call: 'come here and play me something.'

I liked his addressing me so simply in this tone of affectionate peremptoriness; I got up and went to him.

'Here, play this,' he said, opening a volume of Beethoven at the adagio of the sonata *quasi una fantasia*. 'Let me see how you play,' he added, and walked away with his glass of tea to a corner of the parlour.

I somehow felt it impossible with him to refuse and make excuses for playing badly; I seated myself obediently at the piano, and began to play as best I could, though I was afraid of his criticism, knowing that he understood music and loved it. The adagio was in harmony with that feeling of reminiscence that had been called up by the conversation at tea, and I played it, I think, decently. But the scherzo he would not let me play.

'No, that you don't play well,' he said, coming up to me, 'let it be. But the first thing wasn't bad. You've a notion of music, I see.' This measured praise so delighted me that I positively blushed. It was so new and agreeable to me that he, the friend and equal of my father, was talking to me by ourselves seriously, and not treating me as a child, as in old days. Katya went upstairs to put Sonya to bed, and we remained alone together in the parlour.

He talked to me of my father, told me how he had come to know him, and what good times they had had together while I was still busy with my lessons and my playthings. And in what he told me I saw my father for the first time as a simple, lovable man, such as I had never known him till then.

He questioned me too about my tastes, my reading, my plans, and gave me advice. He was not now for me the lighthearted friend, full of jokes, who used to tease me and make playthings for me, but a serious man, frank and affectionate, for whom I felt an instinctive respect and liking. I was at ease and happy, and yet at the same time I could not help feeling a certain constraint as I talked to him. I was apprehensive over every word I uttered; I had such a longing to deserve, on my own account, the love that was bestowed on me now merely as the daughter of my father.

After putting Sonya to bed, Katya joined us and complained to him of my apathy, of which I had said nothing to him.

'The most important thing she didn't tell me,' he said, smiling and shaking his head at me reproachfully.

'What was there to tell?' I said; 'that's very dull, and besides it's passing off.' It actually did seem to me now that my depression was not merely passing away, but had passed away already, or in fact had never been at all.

'It's bad to be unable to stand solitude,' he said; 'surely you're not a young lady.'

'Of course I'm a young lady,' I answered, laughing.

'No, it's a bad sort of young lady who's only alive when she's being admired, and as soon as she's alone lets herself go altogether and finds no charm in anything—who's all for show, and nothing for herself.'

'You've a nice opinion of me,' I said, in order to say something.

'No,' he said after a brief pause, 'it's not for nothing you're so like your father; there's *something in* you,' and his kindly, intent eyes again flattered me and put me to joyful confusion.

Only now I noticed in his face, the first impression of which was cheerfulness, that look in the eyes, peculiar to him, at first bright, then growing more and more intent, and rather mournful.

'You ought not to be and can't be bored,' he said. 'You have music, which you understand, books, and study. You have a whole life before you, for which you can only prepare yourself now so as not to feel regret later. In a year even it will be getting too late.'

He talked to me like a father or an uncle, and I felt that he was continually putting a check on himself so as to keep on my level. I felt both offended at his considering me on a lower level, and pleased that he should think it necessary to try and adapt himself simply on my account.

The rest of the evening he talked about business with Katya.

'Well, good-bye, dear friends,' he said, getting up, and coming up to me, he took my hand.

'When shall we see you again?' asked Katya.

'In the spring,' he answered, still keeping hold of my hand. 'Now I'm going to Danilovka' (our other estate). 'I'll look into things there and arrange what I can, then I'm going on to Moscow to see to my own business, and in the summer we shall meet again.'

'Oh, how is it you are staying such a little while?' I said, with extreme mournfulness; and indeed I had been hoping to see him every day, and I felt suddenly so miserable and afraid that my depression would come back again. This must have been apparent in my eyes and my tone.

'But you must try and work a little more; don't give way to depression,' he said, in a tone, as I thought, too coolly direct, 'and in the spring I shall put you through an examination,' he added, letting go my hand and not looking at me.

In the hall where we stood seeing him off he made haste to put on his fur coat, and again his eyes looked past me. 'He needn't trouble himself,' I thought. 'Does he suppose I'm so pleased at his looking at me? He's a nice man, very nice, but . . . that's all.'

That evening, however, Katya and I sat up talking a long while, not about him, but of how we would spend the summer, and where and how we would stay for the winter. The terrible question—What for?—did not occur to me. It seemed to me very simple and evident that we must live to be happy, and a great deal of happiness seemed lying before me in the future. It seemed as though our dark old house at Pokrovskoe were suddenly full of life and light.

II

Spring had come. My former depression had completely gone, and was replaced by the dreamy spring melancholy of vague hopes and desires. Though I did not spend my time as I had done at the beginning of the winter, but was busily occupied with Sonya and music and reading, I often went off into the garden and spent long, long hours wandering alone about the garden walks or sitting on a garden seat. God only knows what I was dreaming of, what I was hoping and longing for. Sometimes, especially when there was moonlight, I would sit the whole night long till dawn at my bedroom window. Sometimes with nothing on but my dressing-gown I would slip out into the garden, unnoticed by Katya, and run through the dew as far as the pond; once I went as far as the open fields, and alone at night made the round of the whole garden.

I find it hard to recall now the dreams that filled my imagination then. Even when I do remember them, I can hardly believe that those were really my dreams, so strange they were and remote from real life.

At the end of May, Sergei Mikhailych came back, as he had promised, from his travels. The first time he came to see us was in the evening, when we did not at all expect him. We were sitting in the verandah, just going to have tea. The garden was already all in green, and among the overgrown shrubs the nightingales had been building all through St. Peter's fast. The leafy lilac bushes looked as though they had been sprinkled at the top with something white and lilac, where the flowers were just going to come out. The foliage of the birch avenue was all transparent in the setting sun. It was cool and shady in the verandah. There must have been a heavy evening dew on the grass. From the yard behind the garden came the last sounds of the day, the noise of the herd being brought home. The half-witted Nikon, passed along the path before the verandah with a water-barrel, and a cool trickle of water from the watering-hose made dark rings on the loose earth round the stems of the dahlias and the sticks that held them up. On the white cloth set before us on the verandah stood the brilliantly polished samovar boiling, cream, and biscuits and cakes. Katya, like a careful housewife, was rinsing the cups with her plump hands. I was hungry after bathing; and without waiting for the tea to be ready, I was eating some bread heaped with thick, fresh cream. I had on a linen blouse with open sleeves, and had tied a kerchief over my wet hair. Katya was the first to see him from the verandah window.

'Ah, Sergei Mikhailych!' she cried; 'why, we were only just talking about you.'

I got up, and would have retreated to change my dress, but he came upon me just as I was in the doorway.

'Come, why stand on ceremony in the country? Where's the need of being so proper?' he said, looking at my head in the kerchief and smiling. 'Why, you don't mind Grigory, and I'm the same as Grigory to you really.' But precisely at that moment I fancied he was looking at me not at all as Grigory might have done, and I felt awkward.

'I'll be back in a minute,' I said, moving away.

'What's amiss with that?' he called after me. 'You look like a peasant-girl.'

'How queerly he looked at me!' I thought, as I hurriedly changed my dress upstairs. 'Well, thank God, he's come; things will be more lively now.' After looking at myself in the glass I ran gaily downstairs, and not disguising my haste, I went panting out on to the verandah. He was sitting at the table and telling Katya about our affairs. He glanced at me, smiled, and went on talking. Our affairs were, to judge by his account, going very favourably. Now we had only to spend the summer in the country, and then to go either to Petersburg for Sonya's education or abroad.

'Now if only you could come abroad with us,' said Katya. 'We shall be utterly lost there by ourselves.'

'Ah, I should like to go round the world with you!' he said, half in jest, half in earnest.

'Well, do then,' I said; 'let's go round the world.'

He smiled and shook his head.

'What about my mother? and business?' he said. 'Well, that's not the question. Tell me how you've been getting on all this time. Not depressed again, surely?'

When I told him that I had been working hard in his absence and had not been dull, and Katya confirmed my words, he praised me, and in words and looks caressed me like a child, as though he had a right to do so. I felt bound to tell him in detail and with peculiar sincerity all that I had done right, and to acknowledge, as though at confessional, all that he might be displeased at. The evening was so fine that after they had taken away the tea-things we stayed out on the verandah, and the conversation was so interesting to me that I did not notice that gradually all sounds of human life were hushed. The scent of flowers from all round us grew stronger, a thick dew drenched the grass, a nightingale trilled not far off in a lilac bush, and ceased when it heard our voices. The starlit sky seemed sinking over our heads.

I became aware that it was getting dark, because a bat suddenly flew noiselessly under the awning of the verandah and fluttered about my white dress. I shrank back against the wall, and should have liked to scream, but the bat just as swiftly and noiselessly darted out again from under the awnings and disappeared in the dusk of the garden.

'How I love your Pokrovskoe,' he said, breaking off from the conversation; 'I could sit all my life here on the verandah.'

'Well, do then, sit still,' said Katya.

'Sit still, indeed,' said he; 'life doesn't sit still.'

'How is it you don't get married?' said Katya. 'You would make such a good husband!'

'Just because I like sitting still,' and he laughed. 'No, Katerina Karlovna, marriage is not for you and me. Every one's long ago given up looking upon me as a man who might marry. And I've given it up myself for some time past too, and I've felt so comfortable since then really.'

It seemed to me that it was with a sort of unnatural vehemence that he said this.

'What nonsense; thirty-six years old, and done with life already!' said Katya.

'I should think I have done with life!' he went on; 'why, all I want is to sit still. But you want something very different for marriage. You should ask her now,' he added, with a motion of his head towards me. 'It's they who've to think of getting married, while you and I will look on and rejoice in them.'

In his tone there was a suppressed melancholy and constraint which did not escape me. He paused for a while; neither I nor Katya said anything.

'Just imagine,' he went on, turning round on his chair, 'if I were all of a sudden to get married by some unhappy chance to a girl of seventeen like Mash—Marya Alexandrovna.[1] That's an excellent example, I'm very glad it has happened to come up, and it's the best example possible.'

I laughed, and was unable to comprehend what he was glad of, and what it was that had come up.

'Come, tell me the truth, with your hand on your heart,' he said, turning jestingly to me, 'would it not be misery for you to bind your life up with someone elderly, who had lived his life, whose only wish was to sit still, while God only knows what's working in you, what you are longing for?'

I felt uncomfortable; I was silent, not knowing what to answer.

'Oh, it's not an offer I'm making you!' he said, laughing; 'but tell me truly, it's not of such a husband that you dream when you wander about the garden in the evening, and it would be misery for you, wouldn't it?'

'Not misery,' I began.

'Not the right thing, though,' he finished for me.

'Yes; but of course I may be mistaken.'

But again he interrupted me.

'There, you see, and she's perfectly right, and I'm grateful to her for her sincerity, and very glad we have had this conversation! And what's more, it would be the greatest calamity for me too,' he added.

'What a queer fellow you are, you're not changed a bit!' said Katya, and she went in from the verandah to order supper.

We were both silent after Katya had gone, and all was still around us. Only the nightingale was flooding all the garden with melody, not now the jerky faltering notes of evening, but the serene, unhurried song of the night. And another nightingale, from the ravine below, for the first time that evening answered him in the distance. The nearer one ceased, seemed listening for a moment, and then still more shrilly, more intensely, poured out drop by drop his melodious trill. And with sovereign calm these voices rang out in their night world, so remote from us. The gardener went by on his way to sleep in the greenhouse; his steps in thick boots echoed retreating along the path. Twice someone uttered a shrill whistle at the bottom of the hill, and all was silence again. Scarcely audibly the leaves rustled, the curtain of the verandah fluttered, and some sweet fragrance hovering in the air was wafted into the verandah and flooded it. I felt awkward at being silent after what had been said, but what to say I did not know. I looked at him. His shining eyes in the dusk looked round at me.

'It's good to be alive!' he said.

For some reason I sighed.

'Eh?'

'It's good to be alive!' I repeated.

And again we were silent, and again I felt ill at ease. I was haunted by the thought that I had wounded him by agreeing with him that he was elderly, and I wanted to soothe him, but I didn't know how to do it.

'I must say good-bye, though,' he said, getting up, 'mother expects me back to supper. I've hardly seen her today.'

'And I wanted to play you a new sonata,' I said.

'Another time,' he said, coldly I thought. 'Good-bye.'

It seemed to me now more than ever that I had wounded him, and I felt sorry. Katya and I went with him as far as the steps, and stood in the courtyard looking down the road along which he had vanished. When the thud of his horse's hoofs had died away, I went round to the verandah, and again I fell to gazing into the garden; and in the dewy darkness, where the night sounds now were still, for a long while yet I saw and heard all that I longed to see and hear.

He came a second time and a third, and the awkwardness arising from the strange conversation that had passed between us had completely disappeared, and was never renewed again. During the whole summer he used to come two or three times a week to see us; and I became so used to him, that when he did not come for some time I felt it strange to be going on with life by myself, and I was angry with him, and considered he was behaving badly in deserting me. He treated me like some favourite young comrade, asked me questions, drew me into frankness on the deepest subjects, gave me advice and encouragement, sometimes scolded me and checked me. But in spite of his continual efforts to put himself on my level, I felt that behind what I understood in him there remained a whole unknown world into which he did not think fit to initiate me, and this somehow more than anything increased my respect for him and attracted me to him. I knew from Katya and from the neighbours that besides his care of his old mother, with whom he lived, besides looking after his property and ours, he had a great deal to do with the public affairs of the provincial nobility, and that he had much vexatious opposition to encounter in it. But what was his attitude to all this, what were his convictions, his plans, his hopes, I could never find out from him. Whenever I turned the conversation on his affairs, he wrinkled his brows in his peculiar way that seemed to say, 'Stop that, please, what's that to do with you?' and changed the subject. At first this used to offend me, but later on I got so used to our always talking only of what concerned me that I thought it quite natural.

What I disliked too at first, though afterwards it pleased me, was his complete indifference and, as it were, contempt for my appearance. Never by a glance or a word did he hint that he thought me pretty; on the contrary, he wrinkled his brows and laughed when people called me pretty before him. He took a positive pleasure in finding defects in my appearance and teasing me about them. The fashionable dresses and elaborate coiffure in which Katya liked to make me elegant on festive occasions only called forth jeers from him, mortifying kind-hearted Katya, and at first disconcerting me. Katya, who had made up her mind that he thought me attractive, could never make out his not liking to see the girl he admired shown off to the best advantage. I soon saw what he wanted. He was eager to feel sure that I had no frivolous vanity. And as soon as I saw that, there actually was not left in me a trace of vanity in regard to what I wore, how I did my hair, and how I moved. But in place of that there was transparently obvious an affectation of simplicity, just at the moment when I had ceased to be able to be simple. I knew that he loved me; but how, whether as a child or as a woman, I had not as yet asked myself. I prized his love; and feeling that he considered me the best girl in the world, I could not help wishing to keep up this delusion in him. And involuntarily I deceived him. But while deceiving him, I did myself become better. I felt how much better and more dignified it

was for me to show off the finer side of my soul than of my body. My
hair, my hands, my face, my ways, whatever they might be, bad or
good, it seemed to me that he had summed up once for all, and knew
so well that I could add nothing—except a desire to deceive—to his
estimate by attention to my looks. My soul he did not know, because
he loved it, because at this very time it was growing and developing,
and there I could deceive him, and I did deceive him. And how safe I
felt with him when I clearly perceived this! All my causeless bashful-
ness, my awkwardness in moving, disappeared completely. I felt that
whether he saw me full face, or in profile, sitting or standing, with
my hair done up high or hanging low, he knew all of me, and I fancied was satisfied with me as I was. I think that if, contrary to his
practice, he had suddenly told me, as others did, that I had a fine face,
I should really have been anything but pleased. But, on the other
hand, what comfort and gladness there was in my soul when, after
some word I had uttered, he gazed intently at me, and in a voice of
emotion, to which he tried to give a jesting tone, said—

'Yes, yes, there's *something* in you. . . . You're a splendid girl, that I
must tell you.' And what was it for which I received such a reward,
filling my heart with pride and gladness? For saying that I felt so for
old Grigory's love for his little grandchild, or for being moved to
tears by some poem or story I had read, or for preferring Mozart to
Schulhoff.* And it's marvellous, when I think of it, the extraordinary
instinct by which I guessed at that time what was fine and what I
ought to like, though in those days I had not really the least notion of
what was fine and what was to be liked. The greater number of my
old habits and tastes were not to his liking; and he had but by the
twitching of an eyebrow, by a glance, to show that he did not like
what I was going to say, to make his peculiar grimace of commiseration and faint contempt, and it seemed to me already that I didn't
care for what I had liked till then. Sometimes when he had hardly
begun to give me some piece of advice, it seemed to me that I knew
already what he was saying. He would question me, looking into my
eyes, and his eyes drew from me the thought he wanted to find in
me. All my ideas at that time, all my feelings were not mine; but his

---

*Julius Schulhoff (1825–1898), Czech pianist and composer.

ideas and feelings, which had suddenly become mine, passed into my life and lighted it up. Quite unconsciously I had come to look at everything with different eyes—at Katya, at our servants, and at Sonya and at myself and my pursuits. Books which I used to read simply to escape from ennui suddenly became one of the greatest pleasures of my life; and all simply because we talked together about books, read them together, and he brought them to me. Before this time looking after Sonya and giving her lessons had been a burdensome task which I forced myself to perform simply from a sense of duty. He sat by during the lessons, and to watch over Sonya's progress became a delight to me. To learn a piece of music all through thoroughly had seemed to me hitherto an impossible feat; but now, knowing that he would hear and perhaps praise it, I would play the same passage forty times over, till poor Katya stuffed her ears up with cotton wool, while I was still unwearied. The same old sonatas were played somehow quite differently now, and sounded quite different and far finer. Even Katya, whom I knew and loved like another self—even she was transformed in my eyes. Only now I understood for the first time that she was under no compulsion to be the mother, the friend, the slave that she was to us. I grasped all the self-sacrifice and devotion of this loving nature, felt all that I owed to her, and learned to love her more than ever. He taught me to look at our people—peasants, house-serfs, and serf-girls—quite differently from how I had done. It sounds an absurd thing to say, but I had grown up to seventeen among these people more remote from them than from people I had never seen. I had never once reflected that these people had their loves, desires, and regrets just as I had. Our garden, our copses, our fields, which I had known so long, had suddenly become new and beautiful in my eyes. It was not for nothing that he said that in life there is only one certain happiness—living for others. At the time this seemed to me strange, I did not understand it; but this conviction without conscious thought had already come into my heart. He opened to me a whole world of pleasures in the present, without changing anything in my daily existence, without adding anything except himself to any impression. Everything that from my childhood had been voiceless around suddenly blossomed into life. He had but to come into it for all to become speaking, rushing headlong into my soul and flooding it with happiness.

Often during that summer I would go upstairs to my own room, lie down on my bed; and instead of the melancholy of spring, the hopes and longings for the future that had absorbed me, a thrill of happiness in the present took possession of me. I could not sleep, got up, sat on Katya's bed, and told her that I was perfectly happy, which, as now I recall, it was utterly unnecessary to tell her—she could see it for herself. But she told me that she too had nothing to wish for, and that she too was very happy, and kissed me. I believed her—it seemed so right and inevitable that every one should be happy. But Katya could think of sleep too, and even pretending to be angry, sometimes drove me away from her bed and fell asleep, while I would spend long hours going over all that made me so happy. Sometimes I got up and said my prayers a second time, praying in my own words to thank God for all the happiness He had given me.

And in the room all was still; only Katya breathed drowsily and evenly, the clock ticked by her side, and I turned from side to side, murmuring words, or crossing myself and kissing the cross on my neck. The doors were closed, the shutters were on the windows, some fly or gnat buzzed, stirring continually in the same spot. And I would have liked never to leave this room; I did not want morning to come, I did not want the spiritual atmosphere that enfolded me ever to be dissipated. It seemed to me that my dreams, my thoughts, and prayers were live things, living with me in the darkness, flying about my bed, hovering over me. And every idea was his idea, and every feeling was his feeling. I did not know then that this was love—I thought that this might always be so, that of itself, for no other end, this feeling had come to me.

III

One day during harvest-time Katya and Sonya and I had gone after dinner out into the garden to our favourite seat in the shade of the lime-trees above the ravine, beyond which stretched a view of forest and fields. Sergei Mikhailych had not been to see us for three days, and that day we were expecting him, especially as our bailiff told us he had promised to come to the fields. About two o'clock we saw him on horseback riding towards the ryefield. Katya, glancing with a smile at me, sent for some peaches and cherries, of which he was very fond, lay down on the seat, and began to doze. I tore off a flat, crooked branch of lime-tree with juicy leaves and sappy bark that moistened my hand; and waving it over Katya, I went on reading, breaking off continually to look towards the field track by which he would come. Sonya was rigging up an arbour for her dolls at the root of an old lime-tree. The day was hot, windless, steamy, the clouds kept packing closer and growing blacker, a storm had been brewing since the morning. I was excited, as always before a storm. But after midday the clouds began to break up at the edges, the sun floated out into clear sky, and only on one edge there was grumbling thunder; and from a lowering storm-cloud that hung over the horizon and melted into the dust of the fields, pale zigzags of lightning now and then cleft their way through to the earth. It was evident that the storm had passed off for that day, from us at least. Along the road that could be seen in parts beyond the garden there was a continual slow string of high creaking waggons laden with sheaves, and rapidly rattling to meet them a line of the unladen carts returning, with legs swinging and skirts fluttering in them. The thick dust did not fly away nor settle, but hung in the air behind the hedge between the transparent foliage of the garden trees. Further away at the threshing-floor the same voices could be heard and the same creaking of wheels; and the same yellow sheaves, after slowly making their way past the fence, were there flying in the air, and before my eyes the oval stacks were growing up, the pointed roofs were taking shape, and the figures of peasants swarmed bustling about them. In front, too, in the dusty fields, carts were moving and yellow sheaves were to be seen, and the sounds of carts, of voices, and of singing floated across from far away. On one side the stubble was growing more and more bare, with lines of hedge overgrown with wormwood. More to the right, below, all about the cut field that lay in unseemly confusion, were dotted the bright gowns of the peasant women tying sheaves, bending down and spreading out their arms, and the untidy field was being put in order, and handsome sheaves were ranged close about it. It was as though straightway before my eyes summer was turning into autumn. The dust and the sultry heat hung over all except our favourite nook in the garden. On every side in this dust and sultry heat, in the scalding sunshine, the labouring peasants were talking, noisily working and moving.

But Katya was so sweetly snoring under her white cambric hand-kerchief, on our cool garden seat, the cherries glistened with such juicy blackness on the plate, our dresses were so cool and fresh, the water in the jug sparkled with such rainbow-coloured brightness in the sun, and all was so well with me. 'I can't help it,' I thought; 'am I to blame for being happy? But how share my happiness, how and to whom am I to give up all myself and all my happiness? . . .'

The sun had already gone down behind the tree-tops of the birch avenue, the dust was settling in the fields, the distance showed clearer and more distinct in the slanting sunshine, the storm-clouds had quite disappeared, at the threshing-floor behind the trees three new stacks could be seen, and the peasants had gone away from them. Carts went trotting by with loud shouts, clearly making their last journey; peasant-women with rakes on their shoulders and sheaf-ties stuck in their girdles were strolling homewards singing loudly, and still Sergei Mikhailych did not come, although I had long ago seen him ride off under the hill. Suddenly his figure appeared in the avenue, from the direction in which I had not at all looked for him (he had gone round the ravine). Taking off his hat, with a good-humoured beaming face, he was coming with rapid steps towards me. Seeing that Katya was asleep, he bit his lip, shut his eyes, and advanced on tiptoe. I saw at once that he was in that characteristic mood of irrational gaiety which I liked extremely in him, and we used to call 'wild delight.' He was like a schoolboy playing truant; the whole of him, from his face down to his feet, was radiant with con-tent, happiness, and childlike frolic.

'Well, good day, young violet! How are you? quite well?' he said in a whisper, coming up to me and pressing my hand. 'Oh, I'm first-rate!' he said in answer to my inquiry; 'today I'm thirteen; should like to play horses and climb trees.'

'Wild delight!' I said, looking at his laughing eyes, and feeling that this *wild delight* was infecting me too.

'Yes,' he answered, winking and keeping back a smile. 'But why beat Katerina Karlovna on the nose?'

I had not noticed as I looked at him, and went on waving the branch, that I had twitched the handkerchief off Katya and was stroking her face with the leaves. I laughed.

'And she will say she has not been asleep,' I whispered, as though to avoid waking Katya; but really not for that—it was simply that I enjoyed whispering with him.

He moved his lips, mimicking me, pretending I had spoken so softly that he could hear nothing. Seeing the plate of cherries, he snatched it, as it were, slily, walked off to Sonya under the lime-tree, and sat on her dolls. Sonya was angry at first, but he soon made peace with her, starting a game in which he was to race her in eating the cherries.

'Would you like me to send for some more?' I said. 'Or shall we go and get some ourselves?'

He took the plate, sat the dolls in it, and we all three walked to the walled-in garden. Sonya ran laughing after us, tugging at his coat to make him give up the dolls. He gave her them and turned seriously to me.

'Yes, there is no doubt you are a violet,' he said to me still as softly, though there was no one here to be afraid of waking; 'as I came near you, after all that dust and heat and work, there was the scent of violets. Not the scented violet, but you know . . . that early, dark, little one that smells of the thawing snow and the spring grass.'

'Oh, and is everything going well in the fields?' I asked him, to disguise the blissful confusion produced by his words.

'Splendidly! The peasants are everywhere so splendid. . . . The more one knows of them, the better one likes them.'

'Yes,' I said, 'today, before you came, I looked from the garden at their work, and I felt all at once so ashamed that they should be working, while I was so comfortable, that——'

'No affectation on that subject, my dear!' he interrupted me, with sudden seriousness, but glancing affectionately into my face, 'that's a holy thing. God forbid you should trifle with that.'

'But it's only to you I say it.'

'Oh yes, I know. Well, how about the cherries?'

The walled-in garden was shut up, and there were no gardeners about (they had all been sent off to the harvest). Sonya ran off to get the key; but without waiting for her to come back, he climbed up at a corner, lifted the netting, and jumped down on the other side.

'Like some?' I heard him asking from there; 'pass the plate.'

'No, I want to pick them myself too; I'll go for the key,' I said. 'Sonya won't find it.'

But at the same time I longed to look at what he was doing there, how he was looking, how he was moving, supposing that no one could see him. It simply was that at that time I did not want to lose sight of him for a minute. I ran on tiptoe through the nettles round the enclosure to the other side where the wall was lower, and standing on an empty barrel, so that the wall did not reach to my bosom, I leant over. I scanned the enclosure with its old gnarled trees and its broad saw-edged leaves, behind which the heavy juicy black fruit hung down straight; and poking my head under the net, I saw Sergei Mikhailych under the knotted branches of an old cherry-tree. He undoubtedly thought I had gone away, and that no one was seeing him. With his hat off and his eyes closed, he was sitting on a broken-down old cherry-tree, carefully rolling a bit of cherry gum into a ball. Suddenly he shrugged his shoulders, opened his eyes, and saying something, he smiled. So unlike him was that word and that smile that I felt ashamed of having spied on him. I fancied the word was 'Masha.' 'It can't be!' I thought. 'Darling Masha!' he repeated, still more softly and tenderly. But this time I distinctly heard those two words. My heart throbbed so violently, and such an agitating, as it were forbidden, joy suddenly took possession of me, that I clutched at the wall with both hands that I might not fall and betray myself. He heard my movement, looked round in alarm, and suddenly looking down, he flushed, crimsoned like a child. He tried to say something to me, but could not, and more and more hotly his face flamed. He smiled, though, looking at me. I smiled too. His whole face beamed with delight. He was not now like an old uncle, petting and instructing me, but a man equal with me, who loved and feared me, and whom I feared and loved. We said nothing, and simply gazed at each other. But suddenly he frowned, the smile and the light in his eyes died away, and coldly, in his fatherly way again, he addressed me, as though we were doing something wrong, and he had come to his senses and advised me to do the same.

'Get down, you'll hurt yourself,' he said. 'And put your hair straight. What do you look like?'

'Why is he pretending? Why does he want to hurt me?' I thought with vexation. And at the same instant I felt an irresistible desire to confuse him once more and to try my power over him.

'No, I want to pick some myself,' I said, and clutching hold of the nearest branch, I swung my feet up on to the wall. Before he had time to assist me, I had jumped down on to the ground inside the enclosure.

'What silly things you do!' he said, flushing again, and trying to conceal his confusion under the guise of anger. 'Why, you might have hurt yourself. And how are you to get out from here?'

He was even more confused than before, but now this confusion did not rejoice, but dismayed me. It infected me; I blushed, and avoiding him and not knowing what to say, I began picking cherries though I had nowhere to put them. I blamed myself, I felt remorseful and frightened, and it seemed to me that I had ruined myself for ever in his esteem. We were both mute, and both were wretched. Sonya running up with the key rescued us from this painful position. For long after this we said nothing to one another, but both addressed Sonya. When we got back to Katya, who declared she had not been asleep, but had heard all we said, I regained my composure. He tried to drop back into his fatherly, patronising tone, but he did not quite succeed with it, and did not impose on me. I vividly recalled now a conversation that had taken place between us a few days before.

Katya was saying how much easier it was for a man to love and to express his love than for a woman.

'A man can say that he loves, but a woman can't,' she said.

'But it seems to me that a man cannot and ought not to say that he loves,' he said.

'Why not?' I asked.

'Because it will always be a lie. As though it were a strange sort of discovery that someone is in love! Just as if, as soon as he says that, something went snap-bang—he loves. Just as if, when he utters that word, something extraordinary is bound to happen, with signs and portents, and all the cannons firing at once. It seems to me,' he went on, 'that people who solemnly utter those words, "I love you," either deceive themselves, or what's still worse, deceive others.'

'Then how is a woman to find out that she is loved when she's not told it?' asked Katya.

'That I can't say,' he answered. 'Every man has his own way of telling things. And where there's feeling it finds expression. When I read novels I always fancy the perplexed countenance that Lieutenant Strelsky or Alfred must have when he says, "I love thee, Eleonora!" imagining that something extraordinary will suddenly happen; and nothing is changed in either her or him—the same eyes and nose and everything!'[2]

Even at the time I felt instinctively in this jesting saying something serious relating to me, but Katya could not tolerate such irreverent treatment of the heroines of romance.

'Your everlasting paradoxes!' she said. 'Come, tell us the truth, do you mean to say you have never told a woman that you loved her?'

'I never said such a thing, and never fell on one knee,' he answered, laughing, 'and I'm not going to.'

'Yes, he has no need to tell me he loves me,' I thought now, vividly recalling that conversation. 'He loves me, I know it, and his efforts to seem indifferent will not alter my conviction.'

All that evening he spoke little to me, but in every word he said to Katya and to Sonya, in every gesture and glance of his, I saw love, and had no doubt of it. I only felt sore and angry with him for thinking it necessary to go on being reserved and affecting coldness, when everything was now so clear, and when it might have been so easy and simple to be so incredibly happy. But what tormented me like a crime was my having jumped down into the cherry garden to him. I was continually thinking that through this he had lost all respect for me and was angry with me.

After tea I went towards the piano, and he followed me.

'Play something; it's a long while since I've heard you,' he said, overtaking me in the drawing-room.

'Yes, I wanted to . . . Sergei Mikhailych!' I said suddenly, looking him straight in the face. 'You are not angry with me?'

'What for?' he asked.

'For not minding what you said this afternoon,' I said, reddening.

He understood, shook his head, and smiled. His face said that he ought to scold me, but he could not find it in his heart to do so.

'It didn't matter, we're friends again?' I said, sitting down to the piano.

'I should hope so!' he said.

In the big lofty hall there were only two candles on the piano; the rest of the room was in half-darkness. The clear summer night looked in at the open windows. Everything was still except Katya's footsteps creaking at intervals in the dark drawing-room; and his horse, tied up under the window, snorting and stamping his hoofs on the burdocks. He was sitting behind me so that I could not see him; but every-where—in the half-dark of this room, in the sounds of the night, in myself—I felt his presence. Every glance, every movement of his, though I did not see them, was echoed in my heart. I played a sonata fantasia of Mozart's, which he had brought me, and I had practised in his presence and for him. I was not thinking at all of what I was playing, but I fancy I played it well, and it seemed to me that he liked it. I felt the pleasure he was feeling in it; and without looking at him, I felt his eyes fastened on me from behind. Quite involuntarily, while still moving my fingers unconsciously, I looked round at him. His head stood out against the light background of the clear night. He was sitting leaning on his elbow with his head in his hands, and looking intently at me with shining eyes. I smiled, seeing the look on his face, and stopped playing. He smiled too, and shook his head reproachfully at the music for me to go on. When I had finished the moon was higher and shone brightly, and now besides the dim light of the candles a different silvery light came in at the window and was cast on the floor. Katya said that it was beyond everything, how I had stopped in the finest passage, and how badly I had played. But he said, on the contrary, I had never played so well as today, and began walking up and down the rooms, across the hall into the dark drawing-room, and back again into the hall, every time looking round at me and smiling. And I smiled, I wanted to laugh indeed for no reason—so glad I was at something that was happening today, just now. As soon as he had disappeared through the doorway I embraced Katya, with whom I was standing at the piano, and began kissing her in my favourite spot, in the plump neck under her chin. As soon as he returned, I put on a serious face, and with difficulty kept myself from laughing.

'What has come to her today?' Katya said to him.

But he did not answer, he simply looked at me and laughed. He knew what had come to me.

'Look what a night!' he said front the drawing-room, stopping before the balcony window that opened on to the garden.

We went up to him, and truly it was a night such as I have never seen since. The full moon stood over the house behind us so that it could not be seen; and half the shadow of the roof, of the columns and the verandah awning, lay slanting *en raccourci** on the sandy path

---

*Foreshortened (French).

and the circular lawn. All the rest was light, and bathed in silver dew and moonlight. The broad flowery path, all bright and cold, with shadows of the dahlias and their sticks lying slanting on one edge, and its rough gravel glistening, ran into the mist in the distance. Behind the trees there gleamed the roof of the conservatory, and below the ravine rose the gathering mist. The lilac bushes, already beginning to lose their leaves, were bright all over in every twig. The flowers, all drenched with dew, could be distinguished from one another. In the avenues the light and shade were so mingled that they seemed not trees and little paths between, but transparent, quivering, and trembling houses. To the right of the house all was black, indistinct, and weird. All the more brilliant rising up out of this darkness was the fantastically-shaped top of the poplar, which seemed as though, for some strange inexplicable cause, it had halted near the house, in the dazzling brightness above it, instead of flying far, far away into the distant dark-blue sky.

'Let us go for a walk,' said I.

Katya agreed, but said I must put on my goloshes.

'Oh no, Katya,' I said. 'Sergei Mikhailych will give me his arm.'

As though that could save me from getting my feet wet! But at the time, that was to all three of us quite intelligible and not at all strange. He never did offer me his arm, but now I took it of myself, and he did not think it strange. We all three went out of the verandah. All that world, that sky, that garden, that air, were not the same as I had known.

When I looked ahead down the avenue, along which we were walking, it seemed to me continually that over there further we could not go; that there the world of the possible ended, that it must all be crystallised for ever in its beauty. But we moved on, and the magic wall of beauty parted, admitted us, and there too it seemed was our old familiar garden with the trees and paths and dry leaves. And we did actually walk along the paths, stepped into the rings of light and shadow, and there were real dry leaves that rustled under our feet, and a real fresh twig that struck me in the face. And this was really he, walking gently and smoothly beside me, carefully supporting my arm, and it was really Katya who walked with creaking shoes beside us. And doubtless that was the moon in the sky that gleamed at us through the motionless twigs.

But at every step the magic wall closed up again before us and behind us, and I could not believe that it was possible to walk further, could not believe in all as it really was.

'Ah, a frog!' said Katya.

'Who's saying that, what for?' I thought. But then I recollected that it was Katya, that she was afraid of frogs, and I looked down at my feet. A little frog hopped and stopped motionless before me, and its little shadow could be seen in the light on the clay of the path.

'But you're not afraid,' he said.

I looked round at him. One lime-tree was missing in the part of the avenue we were passing—I could see his face clearly. It was so handsome and happy.

He said, 'You're not afraid'; but I heard him saying, 'I love you, sweet girl! I love you, I love you!' repeated his eyes, his arm; and the light and the shadow and the air, everything repeated the same.

We walked round the whole garden. Katya walked beside us with her little steps, breathing heavily from fatigue. She said it was time to turn back, and I felt sorry, so sorry for her, poor thing. 'Why isn't she feeling the same as we?' I thought. 'Why isn't every one young and every one happy like this night, and me and him?'

We went home, but for a long while yet he stayed on though the cocks were crowing, every one in the house was asleep, and his horse more and more often stamped on the weeds and snorted under the window. Katya did not remind us that it was late, and we sat on chatting of the most trivial things, unaware of the time till past two o'clock. The cocks were crowing for the third time, and the dawn was beginning when he went away. He said good-bye as usual, saying nothing special; but I knew that from that day he was mine, and that now I should not lose him. As soon as I had owned to myself that I loved him, I told Katya too all about it. She was glad and touched by my telling her, though she, poor thing, could go to sleep that night; but I, for a long, long while yet, walked up and down the verandah, and out into the garden, and recalling every word, every gesture, I walked along the garden paths along which I had walked with him. I did not sleep all that night, and for the first time in my life I saw the sun rise and the early morning. And such a night and such a morning I have never seen again. 'Only why doesn't he tell me simply that he loves me?' I mused. 'Why does he invent some sort of difficulties, and call himself old, when it's all so simple and so splendid? Why does he waste the precious time which may be will never return? Only let him say, "I love," say it in words; let him take my hand in his, bend his head over it, and say, "I love you." Let him blush and drop his eyes before me, and then I will tell him all. Not tell him even, but embrace him, clasp him to me, and weep. But what if I'm mistaken, if he does not love me?' suddenly occurred to me.

I was frightened at my own feeling. God knows what lengths it might lead me to, and his and my confusion in the orchard when I had jumped over to him came back to my mind, and my heart ached and ached. Tears streamed from my eyes, and I began to pray. And there came to me a strange reassuring thought and hope. I resolved to fast and prepare myself from that day to take the sacrament on my birthday and the same day to be betrothed.

By what means, in what way, how this could come to pass, I knew not, but from that minute I believed and knew it would be so. It was broad daylight, and the peasants had begun getting up when I went back to my room.

IV

It was the time of the Fast of the Assumption,* so no one in the house was surprised at my intention of fasting during these days.

During the whole of that week he did not once come to see us; and far from wondering, being disturbed and angry with him, I was glad he did not come, and looked for him only on my birthday. All that week I got up early every day; and while they were putting the horses in, I walked alone about the garden, going over in my mind the sins of the previous day, and considering what I had to do today to be satisfied with the day and not once to fall into sin. It seemed to me at that time so easy to be perfectly sinless—it only needed trying a little, it seemed. The horses were brought round, and with Katya or the maid I got into the trap and drove three miles to the church. As I entered church I always recalled the prayer for all 'who enter in the fear of God,' and tried with that feeling in my heart to mount the two steps of the porch overgrown with grass. In the church there were

---

*In the Orthodox tradition also known as the Fast of Dormition.

usually at that time not more than some ten persons, peasant-women and house-serfs, keeping the fast. With studied meekness I tried to respond to their low bows, and walked myself—it seemed to me a great achievement—to the candle drawer to take candles from the old elder, a soldier, and placed them myself in the sockets. Through the doors could be seen the altar cover, embroidered by mamma; above the holy picture-stand were two angels with stars, who used to seem to me so huge when I was little, and a dove with a yellow halo which used to attract my attention in early days. Behind the choir one could see the font where I had assisted at the christening of so many children of our house-serfs and had been christened myself. The old priest came out wearing a stole made out of my father's pall, and officiated in the same voice in which ever since I remember anything I had heard the church service in our house, and Sonya's christening and the last mass for my father and my mother's burial service. And the same jarring voice of the deacon rang out in the choir, and the same old woman whom I always remember in church at every service stood bent over at the wall, gazed with tearful eyes at the icon in the choir, pressed her cramped fingers to her faded kerchief, and mumbled something in her toothless mouth. And all this seemed no longer curious, nor through a single memory familiar to me; it was all now grand and holy in my eyes, and seemed to me full of profound significance. I listened to every word of the prayer, tried to respond in feeling to it; and if I could not understand it, I prayed inwardly to God to enlighten me, or made a prayer of my own in place of the one I could not follow. When the Confessions were read, I thought of my past, and that childish innocent past seemed to me so black in comparison with the pure condition of my soul now that I wept and was horrified at myself. But at the same time I felt that it would all be forgiven, and that if there had been even more sin in me, sweeter still would have been my repentance. When the priest at the end of the service said, 'The blessing of God be with you,' it seemed to me that I felt instantly passing into me a physical sensation of well-being, as though a sort of light and warmth had rushed into my heart. The service was over, the good father came up to me and inquired should he not come to us for the all-night service and when; but I touchingly thanked him for what he wished, as I imagined, to do for my sake, and said that I would myself walk or drive over.

'You want to put yourself to that trouble?' he said.

And I did not know what to answer for fear of falling into the sin of pride.

I always let the horses go back from the service if I were without Katya, and walked home alone, bowing low and meekly to all who met me, and trying to find opportunities to help, to advise, to sacrifice myself for someone, to assist in lifting a load, to dandle a baby, to make way by stepping into the mud. One evening I heard the bailiff, in giving his account to Katya, say that the peasant Semyon had come to beg some planks for his daughter's coffin and a rouble for the funeral service, and that he'd given it him.

'Are they really so poor?' I asked.

'Very poor, madam, not a pinch of salt in the house,' answered the bailiff.

I felt a pang at my heart, and at the same time I felt a sort of joy at hearing this. Deluding Katya with the pretext that I was going for a walk, I ran upstairs, and got out all my money (it was very little, but all that I had). Crossing myself, I went alone through the verandah and the garden to the village to Semyon's hut. It was at the edge of the village, and unseen by any one I ran up to the window, laid the money in the window, and tapped on it. A door creaked, someone came out of the hut and called after me. Shaking and chill with panic like a guilty creature, I ran home. Katya asked me where I had been, what was the matter with me, but I did not even understand what she said to me, and made no answer. Everything seemed all at once so worthless and petty to me. I locked myself in my own room and walked up and down a long while alone, unable to do anything, unable to think, to get a clear idea of my own feelings. I thought of the joy of all the family, of the words they would say of the person who had brought the money, and I felt sorry too that I had not given it myself. I thought of what Sergei Mikhailych would say when he heard of it, and at the same time rejoiced that no one would ever hear of it. And I was full of joy, and all people and I myself seemed so bad to me, and so tenderly I looked on myself and every one, that the thought of death came to me like a dream of bliss. I smiled and prayed and wept; and with such passionate fervour I loved every one in the world, and myself too at that moment. Between the services I read the gospel, and more and more comprehensible it had become to me, and more and more touching and simple the history of that divine life, and more awful and inconceivable the depths of feeling and thought I found in its teaching. But, on the other hand, how clear and simple everything seemed to me when getting up from that book I looked into my heart and pondered on the life surrounding me. It seemed so difficult to be bad, and so simple to love every one and be loved by them. Every one was so kind and gentle with me; even Sonya, whose lessons I still went on with, was quite different, tried to understand, to please me and not to vex me. As I was, so were all of them to me. Going over my enemies, of whom I had to beg forgiveness before making my confession, I could only remember one young lady, whom I had a year ago made ridiculous in the presence of guests, and who had given up coming to see us. I wrote a letter to her, confessing my fault, and begging her forgiveness. She answered with a letter, in which she too begged my forgiveness, and forgave me. I wept with joy, reading those simple lines, in which at that time I saw such deep and touching feeling. My old nurse cried when I begged her forgiveness. 'Why were they all so good to me? How had I deserved such love?' I asked myself. And I could not help thinking of Sergei Mikhailych, and for a long while I thought of him. I could not help it, and did not even look on it as a sin. But I thought of him now not at all as I had done on the night when I first knew that I loved him. I thought of him as of myself, unconsciously associating him with every thought of my future. The overwhelming influence of which I was conscious in his presence had entirely disappeared in my imagination. I felt myself now his equal, and from the height of my present spiritual condition I completely understood him. What had hitherto seemed strange in him was quite clear to me now. Only now I understood why he had said that happiness is only to be found in living for others, and now I perfectly agreed with him. It seemed to me that we should be so endlessly and calmly happy. And I pictured to myself not tours abroad, not society, and a brilliant life, but something quite different, a quiet family life in the country with continual self-sacrifice, continual love for one another, and a continual sense in all things of a kind and beneficent Providence.

I took the sacrament, as I had intended, on my birthday. In my heart there was such complete happiness when I came home that day from church that I was afraid of life, afraid of every impression, of anything that could disturb that happiness. But we had hardly got out of the trap at the steps when a familiar vehicle rattled on the bridge, and I caught sight of Sergei Mikhailych. He congratulated me, and we went together into the drawing-room. Never since I had known him had I been as calm and self-possessed as that morning. I felt that there was a whole new world in me which he did not understand, which was above him. I did not feel the slightest embarrassment with him. He must have understood what this was due to, and there was a peculiar tender gentleness and reverent consideration in his manner to me. I was going to the piano, but he locked it and put the key in his pocket.

'Don't spoil your mood,' he said. 'There is music now in your soul, better than any in the world.'

I was grateful to him for this, and at the same time I rather disliked his so easily and clearly understanding all that should have been hidden from all in my soul. At dinner he said he had come to congratulate me on my birthday, and at the same time to say good-bye, as he was going next day to Moscow. As he said this he looked at Katya, but then glanced stealthily at me, and I saw that he was afraid he would detect emotion in my face. But I was not surprised nor agitated. I did not even ask whether he were going for long. I knew he would say this, and I knew he would not go. How I knew it I cannot explain to this day; but on that memorable day it seemed to me that I knew everything that had been and would be. I was as though in a happy dream when whatever happens seems as though it has been already, and that one has known it long ago, and it all seems, too, as though it were to come, and one knows that it will come.

He had meant to leave soon after dinner; but Katya, tired after the service, had gone to lie down, and he was obliged to wait till she waked up to say good-bye to her. The hall was hot with the sun on it. We went out into the verandah. As soon as we had sat down, I began with perfect composure speaking of what was bound to decide the fate of my love. And I began to speak neither too soon nor too late, but the very moment we were seated, before anything had been said, before there had been a conversation of some tone or character that might have hindered what I wanted to say. I can't understand how I came by such composure, such decision, and such exactness in my phrases. It was as though it were not I, but something apart from my own will was speaking in me. He sat opposite me, his elbow leaning on the rail, and drawing a branch of lilac to him, he was stripping off its leaves. When I began to speak, he let the branch go, and leaned his head on his hand. It might be the attitude of a man in perfect repose or in great agitation.

'What are you going away for?' I asked deliberately and significantly, looking him straight in the face.

He did not at once answer.

'Business!' he said, dropping his eyes.

I saw that it was not easy for him to lie to me, and in answer to a question put to him so frankly.

'Listen,' I said. 'You know what today is for me. For many reasons this day is very important to me. If I ask you this, it is not to show my interest (you know how well I know you, and how I care for you), I ask because I must know. . . . What are you going for?'

'It's very difficult for me to tell you the true reason why I am going away,' he said. 'During this week I have been thinking a great deal about you and myself, and have decided that I ought to go. You understand why, and if you care for me you will not ask.' He passed his hand over his forehead, and covered his eyes with it. 'It's painful to me. . . . And easy for you to understand.'

My heart began to beat violently.

'I can't understand,' I said; 'I can't; but you—do tell me, for God's sake, for the sake of today, tell me—I can hear anything calmly,' I said.

He shifted his position, glanced at me, and again drew the branch to him.

'Well,' he said, after a brief pause, in a voice that tried in vain to be steady, 'though it's absurd and impossible to put it into words, though it's painful even, I will try and explain to you . . .' he added, pausing as though in physical pain.

'Well?' said I.

'Imagine that there was a certain Monsieur A., let us say,' he said, 'elderly and blasé, and a Mademoiselle B., young and happy, knowing nothing of men or of life. Through various family circumstances he loved her as a daughter, and was not afraid of loving her in any other way.'

He paused, but I did not interrupt.

'But he forgot that B. was so young, that life was still a plaything for her,' he went on, with sudden swiftness and determination, not looking at me, 'and that it was easy to love her in a different way, and that that would be an amusement to her. And he made a mistake, and suddenly was aware that another feeling, as bitter as remorse, had forced its way into his soul, and he was afraid. He was afraid of destroying their old affectionate relations, and resolved to go away rather than destroy those relations.' As he said this, again as it were carelessly, he passed his hand over his eyes and hid them.

'Why was he afraid of loving in another way?' I said, scarcely audibly, suppressing my emotion, and my voice was steady; to him it probably seemed playful. He answered in a tone, as it were, of offence.

'You are young,' he said. 'I am not young. You want to amuse yourself, but I want something else. Amuse yourself, only not with me, or I shall believe in it, and it will do me harm, and you will be sorry for it. That was what A. said,' he added. 'Oh, well, that's all nonsense, but you understand why I'm going. And we won't talk any more about it. Please don't.'

'No, no, we will talk about it,' I said, and there was a quiver of tears in my voice. 'Did he love her, or not?'

He did not answer.

'And if he didn't love her, why did he play with her as if she were a baby?' I said.

'Yes, yes, A. was to blame,' he answered, hurriedly interrupting me, 'but it was all over, and they parted . . . friends.'

'But that's awful! And could there be no other ending? . . .' I uttered faintly, and was terrified at what I had said.

'Yes, there is,' he said, uncovering his agitated face and looking straight at me. 'There are two different endings. Only, for God's sake, don't interrupt, and listen to me quietly. Some say,' he began, standing up and smiling a sickly, bitter smile, 'some say that A. went out of his mind, fell madly in love with B., and told her so. And she only laughed. For her it was a jest, but for him it was the question of his whole life.'

I started, and would have interrupted him to say that he must not speak for me, but he laid his hand on mine, restraining me.

'Wait a minute,' he said in a shaking voice. 'Others say that she took pity on him; fancied, poor girl, having seen no one else, that she really could love him, and consented to become his wife. And he in his madness believed it—believed that life would begin over again for him—but she saw herself that she had deceived him, and that he was deceiving her. . . . We won't talk any more about it,' he concluded, apparently unable to go on, and he began walking up and down facing me.

He had said, 'We won't talk of it,' but I saw that with all the strength of his soul he was waiting for my words. I tried to speak, but couldn't—something ached poignantly in my bosom. I glanced at him; he was pale, and his lower lip was quivering. I felt sorry for him. I made an effort, and suddenly, bursting through the spell of silence that seemed enchaining me, I began speaking in a subdued inner voice, which I feared every second would break.

'There's a third ending,' I said, and stopped, but he did not speak, 'a third ending, that he did not love her, but he hurt her, hurt her, and thought he was right, and went away, and seemed proud too for some reason. It's you, not I, you, that it's a jest to; from the first day I've loved you—loved!' I repeated, and at that word 'loved' my voice involuntarily passed from a soft murmur into a wild shriek that frightened me myself.

He stood facing me, his lips quivering more and more, and two tears stood out on his pale cheeks.

'It's a shame!' I almost screamed, feeling that I was choking with angry, unshed tears. 'What's it for?' I articulated, and stood up to get away from him.

But he did not let me go. His head lay on my knees, his lips were kissing my trembling hands, and his tears wetted them.

'My God! if I had known,' he said.

'What for? what for?' I was still repeating, but my soul was full of happiness, happiness that seemed to have gone for ever and was coming back to me.

Five minutes later Sonya was running upstairs to Katya and shouting to all the household that Masha was going to marry Sergei Mikhailych.

V

There was no reason for delaying our marriage, and neither of us desired to do so. Katya would indeed have liked us to go to Moscow to purchase and order the trousseau, and his mother urged his providing himself with a new carriage and furniture, and having the house repapered, before he was married. But we both insisted that all this should be done afterwards if it really were so necessary, and that we should be married a fortnight after my birthday, quite quietly, without a trousseau, without guests and bridesmen, without a wedding supper, champagne, and all the conventional accompaniments of a wedding. He told me how disappointed his mother was that his wedding was to take place without music, without mountains of boxes, and without the complete redecoration of the whole house (like her own wedding, which had cost thirty thousand roubles), and how seriously and surreptitiously she was turning out her chest of stores and consulting with her housekeeper, Maryushka, about certain rugs, curtains, and tea-trays essential to our happiness. Katya too, on my behalf, was busy in the same way with my old nurse, Kuzminishna, and it did not do to speak lightly of it to her. She was firmly persuaded that when we were talking of our future together we were simply babbling the lovers' nonsense peculiar to persons in our position; but that our real future happiness would depend entirely on the correct cutting and careful stitching of chemises and the hemming of tablecloths and dinner-napkins. Mysterious communications on the progress of the preparations passed several times a day between Nikolskoe and Pokrovskoe; and though the relations between Katya and his mother appeared on the surface to be of the tenderest, one had a sense of a somewhat antagonistic but most delicate diplomacy in their intercourse. Tatyana Semyonovna, his mother, with whom I now became more intimately acquainted, was a ceremonious, old-fashioned lady, very correct in the management of her household. He loved her not simply as a son, from duty, but as a man, from feeling, considering her as the best, the wisest, the kindest, and most loving woman in the world. Tatyana Semyonovna was always kind to us, to me particularly so, and she was glad her son should marry; but when I was with her as her future daughter-in-law, it seemed to me that she tried to make me feel that as a match for her son I might have been better, and that it would not be amiss for me to keep that in mind, and I perfectly understood her and agreed with her.

During that fortnight we saw each other every day. He used to come to dinner and to stay on till midnight; but although he said—and

I knew he spoke the truth—that he had no life apart from me, he never spent the whole day with me, and tried to go on with his usual work. Our external relations remained the same as before right up to our wedding. We still addressed each other formally by our full names; he did not kiss even my hand; and far from seeking opportunities of being alone with me, seemed positively to avoid them. It was as though he feared the too violent, disquieting tenderness that was within him. I don't know whether he or I had changed, but now I felt completely on an equality with him, saw no trace in him of that effort after simplicity that I had once disliked in him; and often, to my satisfaction, I seemed to see before me, instead of a man inspiring respect and awe, a soft-hearted child dazed with happiness. 'So that was all there was in him,' I often thought. 'He's just the same sort of person as I am, nothing more.' Now it seemed to me that the whole of him was before my eyes, and that I had learned to know him fully, and all that I had learned was so simple and so perfectly in harmony with me. Even his plans for our life together in the future were just my plans, only better and more clearly defined in his words.

The weather was bad during those days, and the greater part of the time we spent indoors. Our best, most intimate talks took place in the corner between the piano and the little window. The light of the candles was reflected on the black window close by, and on the glistening pane there was often the patter and drip of raindrops. On the roof the rain beat, and in the pool below there was the splash of water; there was a damp draught from the window under the eaves, and it made it seem all the brighter, warmer, and more joyful in our corner.

'Do you know, I've long been wanting to say one thing to you,' he said late one evening when we were sitting alone together in our corner. 'When you were playing, I thought of it.'

'You need not tell me; I know all about it,' I said.

'Yes, that's true. We won't talk of it.'

'No, tell me, what is it?' I asked.

'Why, do you remember when I told you the story of A. and B.?'

'I should think you'd better not recall that silly story! It's a good thing it ended as it did.'

'Yes, a little more, and all my happiness would have been shattered by my own hand. You saved me. But the thing is, I was always telling lies then, and it's on my conscience. I want to speak out now.'

'Oh, please, you needn't.'

'Don't be afraid,' he said, smiling. 'I only want to justify myself. When I began to speak I was trying to be reasonable.'

'Why be reasonable?' I said. 'You never ought to.'

'Yes, I was wrong in my reasoning. After all my disappointments and mistakes in life, when I came this year into the country I said to myself so resolutely that love was over for me; that all that was left me was the duties of the decline of life; that for a long while I failed to recognise what my feeling for you was, and what it might lead me to. I hoped and did not hope. At one time it seemed to me you were flirting, at another I had faith—and I didn't know myself what I was going to do. But after that evening—do you remember, when we walked in the garden at night?—I was frightened; my present happiness seemed too great and impossible. Think what it would have been if I had let myself hope and in vain? But, of course, I thought only of myself, because I'm a sickening egoist.'

He paused, looking at me.

'But still you know it was not altogether nonsense that I talked then. I might well, and ought to, feel afraid. I am taking so much from you, and I can give so little. You are a child still; you are a bud not yet fully out, which will blossom more fully later; you love for the first time; while I——'

'Yes, tell me truly,' I said, but all at once I felt frightened of his answer. 'No, I don't want you to,' I added.

'Whether I have been in love before, eh?' he said, at once guessing my thought; 'that I can tell you. No, I haven't. Never anything like this feeling.' But suddenly it seemed as though some bitter recollection had flashed into his mind. 'No, and now I ought to have your heart to have the right to love you,' he said mournfully. 'So hadn't I good reason to think twice before saying that I loved you? What do I give you? Love, it is true.'

'Is that so little?' I said, looking into his eyes.

'Little, my dear, little for you,' he went on. 'You have beauty and youth. Often now I can't sleep at night for happiness, and all the time I'm thinking of how we will live our life together. I have lived through a great deal, and it seems to me that I have found what one wants to be happy—a quiet, secluded life in our remote countryside, with the power of doing good to people, to whom it's so easy to do good, who are so little used to it; then work, work which seems to be bringing forth fruit; then leisure, nature, books, music, love for one's neighbours; that is my happiness, and I dreamed of none higher. And now to crown all that, such a friend as you, a family perhaps, and all that a man can desire.'

'Yes,' I said.

'For me, who have outlived my youth, yes, but not for you,' he went on. 'You have seen nothing of life; you may perhaps want to seek happiness in something else, and perhaps you may find it in something else. You fancy now that this is happiness because you love me.'

'No, I have always loved this quiet home life, and wished for nothing else,' I said. 'And you are only saying what I have thought.'

He smiled.

'That only seems so to you, my dear. But it's little for you. You have beauty and youth,' he repeated musingly.

But I was irritated at his not believing me, and as it were reproaching me with my beauty and my youth.

'Then what do you love me for?' I said angrily—'for my youth or for myself?'

'I don't know, but I love you,' he answered, looking at me with his intent gaze that fascinated me.

I made no answer, and involuntarily I looked into his eyes. All at once something strange happened to me. At first I ceased to see what was around me, then his face vanished before my eyes, only his eyes shone it seemed just opposite my eyes, then it seemed to me that his eyes were piercing into me, everything was a blur, I saw nothing, and had to shut my eyes to tear myself away from the sensation of delight and terror produced in me by that gaze.

On the eve of the day fixed for our wedding the weather cleared. It had been summer when the rains had begun, now after they had ceased came the first cold fine evening of autumn. Everything was wet and cold and bright, and in the garden one observed for the first time the openness, the bright tints, and bareness of autumn. The sky was clear and chill and pale. I went to bed happy in the thought that the next day, the day of my wedding, would be fine. On the day I waked with the sun, and the thought that it was today . . . as it were, scared and amazed me. I went out into the garden. The sun had only just risen, and its light filtered in patches through the lime-trees of the avenue, which were losing their yellow leaves. The path was strewn with rustling leaves. The wrinkled bright red bunches of berries on the mountain ash gleamed on the branches among the few frost-bitten, curling leaves. The dahlias were withered and blackened. Frost lay for the first time like silver on the pale green of the grass and the trampled burdocks round the house. In the clear cold sky there was not, and could not be, a single cloud. 'Can it really be today?' I asked myself, not believing in my own happiness. 'Shall I really tomorrow wake up not here, but in the unfamiliar Nikolskoe house with colonnades? Shall I never any more meet him in the evenings and talk of him at night with Katya? Shall I never sit with him at the piano in the Pokrovskoe drawing-room, nor see him off and tremble for his safety in the dark night?' But I remembered that he had said yesterday that he should come for the last time, and Katya had made me try on my wedding dress, and had said, 'For tomorrow'; and for an instant I believed in it, and then doubted again. 'Can I truly be going from today to live there with my mother-in-law, without Nadyozha, without old Grigory, without Katya? Shall I go to bed without kissing my old nurse and hearing her say in her old way as she crosses me, "Good night, miss"? Shall I give Sonya no more lessons, nor play with her, nor knock through the wall to her in the morning, and hear her ringing laugh? Can it be that today I shall become someone that I don't know myself, and a new life, the realisation of my hopes and wishes, is opening before me? Will that new life be for always?'

Impatiently I awaited his arrival. I was unhappy alone with these thoughts. He came early, and it was only with him that I fully believed that I should be his wife today, and that thought lost its terrors for me.

Before dinner we walked to our church to attend a memorial service for my father.

'If only he could have been living now!' I thought, as we returned home, and without speaking I clung to the arm of the man who had been his dearest friend. During the prayers, kneeling with my head bowed down to the cold stone of the chapel floor, I so thoroughly believed that his soul was understanding me and blessing my choice, that even now it seemed to me that his spirit was hovering about us, and that I felt his blessing upon me. And memories and hopes and happiness and sorrow all melted together into one sweet and solemn feeling in harmony with the still keen air, the quietness, the bareness of the fields, and the pale sky, shedding on everything a bright but feeble sunshine that tried in vain to burn my cheek. I fancied that the man at my side understood and shared my feeling. He was walking slowly and in silence, and in his face, into which I peeped from time to time, showed the same grave emotion between sorrow and joy that was to be seen in nature, and was in my heart. All at once he turned to me. I saw he was going to say something. 'What if he speaks of something else, not what I am thinking of?' flashed into my mind. But he began speaking of my father without even mentioning his name.

'Once he said to me jokingly: "You had better marry my Masha!"' he said.

'How happy he would have been now!' I said, squeezing the arm on which mine was lying.

'Yes, you were a child then,' he went on, looking into my eyes. 'I used to kiss those eyes then, and loved them only because they were like his, and never dreamed they would be so dear to me on their own account. I used to call you Masha then.'

'Call me "thee,"' I said.

'I was just meaning to call thee so,' he said; 'it's only now that I feel thee quite mine.'[3] And a serene and happy gaze that drew my eyes to him rested upon me.

And we went on walking slowly along the indistinct field-path through the trampled, broken stubble, and our steps and our voices were all that we could hear. On one side across the ravine as far as the distant, bare-looking copse stretched the brownish stubble, on which on the side away from us a peasant was noiselessly at work with a wooden plough making wider and wider the black strip of earth. A drove of horses scattered over the hillside below seemed quite close. On the other side, and in front right up to the garden and our house, which could be seen beyond it, stretched the dark thawing field, with here and there strips of green winter-corn. The sun was shining on it all, bright but not hot, and on everything lay the long threads of spider webs. They were floating in the air about us, lying on the stubble where the frost had dried, falling into our eyes, on to our hair and our clothes. When we talked our voices resounded and seemed to hang in the still air above us, as though we were the only creatures in the midst of the whole world, and were alone under that blue dome, in which the mild sunshine played flashing and quivering.

I too longed to call him 'thee,' but I was ashamed to.

'Why art thou walking so fast?' I said hurriedly, almost in a whisper, and I could not help blushing. He walked more slowly and looked still more fondly, still more gladly and happily at me.

When we got home his mother was already there with the guests, whom we had not been able to avoid having, and up to the moment when we came out of church and got into the carriage to drive to Nikolskoe I was not alone with him.

The church was almost empty; at a glance I saw only his mother, standing on a rug in the choir, Katya in a cap with lilac ribbons, and two or three of our servants looking inquisitively at me. At him I did not look, but I felt his presence beside me. I listened intently to the words of the service and repeated them, but there was no response to them in my soul. I could not pray, and gazed blankly at the icons, at the lights, at the embroidered cross on the back of the priest's stole, at the picture-stand, at the church window, and understood nothing. I only felt that something extraordinary was being performed on me. When the priest turned to me with the cross, congratulated me, and said that he had christened, and now, by God's blessing, he had married me, and Katya and his mother kissed us, and I heard Grigory's voice calling the carriage, I wondered and was dismayed that everything was over, with no extraordinary feeling in my soul to correspond with the mysterious ceremony I had passed through. We kissed each other, and that kiss was so strange and remote from my feeling. 'And is that all?' I thought. We came out into the porch; the rumbling of the wheels resounded with a deeper note under the church roof; the fresh air blew into our faces; he put on his hat and gave me his arm to the carriage. From the carriage window I had a glimpse of a frosty moon with a ring round it. He sat down beside me and closed the door after him. Something seemed to stab me to the heart. It was as though I felt insulted by the assurance with which he did this. Katya's voice called for me to cover my head, the wheels rattled over the pavement, and then along the soft road, and we had driven off. Huddled up in a corner, I looked out of the window at the far-away moonlit fields, and at the road flying by in the chill light of the moon. And without looking at him, I felt him here beside me. 'Why, is this all from this minute of which I expected so much?' I thought, and it still seemed somehow degrading and humiliating to be sitting alone so close to him. I turned to him with the intention of saying something. But the words would not be uttered; it seemed as though there were no trace of my former feeling of tenderness in me, but a feeling of humiliation and dread had taken its place.

'Till this minute I could not believe that it was possible,' he said softly in response to my glance.

'Yes, but I'm somehow afraid,' I said.

'Afraid of me, my darling?' he said, taking my hand and letting his hand drop into it.

My hand lay lifeless in his hand, and my heart ached with cold.

'Yes,' I whispered.

But at that moment my heart suddenly began to beat more violently, my hand trembled and squeezed his hand; I felt warm, my eyes sought his in the dusk, and I suddenly felt that I was not afraid of him, that that dread was love, a new and still more tender and passionate love than before. I felt that I was altogether his, and that I was happy in his power over me.

PART II

VI

Days, weeks, two months of solitary country life had slipped by, imperceptibly it seemed at the time; but meanwhile there had been feeling, emotion, and happiness for a whole lifetime in those two months. My dreams and his of the ordering of our lives together in the country were fulfilled not at all as we had expected. But our life did not fall short of our dreams. There was none of that hard work, doing one's duty and sacrificing one's life for one's neighbour, that I had pictured to myself when I was engaged. There was, on the contrary, simply the egoistic feeling of love for each other, the desire to be loved, and a causeless, continual gaiety and forgetfulness of all else in the world. He did, it is true, go off at times to his study to do some sort of work; at times he did drive to the town on business, and superintend the management of the land. But I saw what an effort it was to him to tear himself away from me. And he would acknowledge himself, later, that everything in the world in which I had no share seemed to him so absurd that he could not understand how one could be interested in it. It was just the same with me. I used to read, and to interest myself with music, with his mother, and with the village school; but it was all simply because each of those pursuits was associated with him and won his approbation. But as soon as there was no idea of him associated with my pursuit, my hands dropped at my side, and it seemed to me quite amusing to think there was anything in the world besides him. Possibly this was a bad, selfish feeling, but this feeling gave me happiness, and lifted me high above the whole world. He was the only person existing on earth for me, and I regarded him as the best, the most faultless, man in the world. Consequently I could have no other object in life than him—than being in his eyes what he believed me to be. And he considered me the first and best woman in the world, endowed with every possible virtue; and I tried to be that woman in the eyes of the first and best man in the whole world.

One day he came into the room just as I was saying my prayers. I looked round at him and went on with my prayers. He sat down at the table so as not to disturb me, and opened a book. But I fancied he was watching me, and I looked round. He smiled, I laughed outright, and could not go on praying.

'Have you said your prayers already?' I asked.

'Yes; but you go on, I'll go away.'

'But you do say prayers, I hope?'

He would have gone out without answering; but I stopped him.

'My love, please, for my sake, read the prayers with me!'

He stood beside me, and letting his hands drop awkwardly, with a serious face he began hesitatingly to read. From time to time he turned to me and sought approval and encouragement in my face.

When he had finished, I laughed and hugged him.

'It's all you, all you! It's as though I were ten years old again,' he said, blushing and kissing my hands.

Our house was one of those old country houses in which several generations of a family have passed their lives, respecting and loving one another. Everything breathed of good, honourable, family memories which at once when I entered that house seemed to become my memories. The arrangement and the management of the house were all ordered by Tatyana Semyonovna in the old style. I cannot say that everything was elegant and beautiful; but from the servants, down to the furniture and the food, all was plentiful, all was neat, solid, and orderly, inspiring respect. In symmetrical arrangement the furniture stood in the drawing-room, and the portraits hung on the walls, and the home-made rugs and strips of matting were laid on the floors. In the divan-room there was an old harpsichord, two chiffoniers of different patterns, sofas, and little tables with lattice-work and raised ornaments. In my boudoir, decorated by Tatyana Semyonovna with special care, stood the best furniture of different ages and patterns, and among other things an old pier-glass, at which at first I could not look without feeling shy, though later on it became dear to me as an old friend. Tatyana Semyonovna's voice was never heard, but everything in the house went as though by clockwork. Though there were many superfluous servants, all those servants wearing soft boots without heels (Tatyana Semyonovna considered creaking shoes and clacking heels as the most disagreeable things in the world), all those servants seemed proud of their position, stood in awe of their old mistress, looked on my husband and me with patronising affection, and seemed to take a particular pleasure in doing their work.

Every Saturday regularly all the floors in the house were scrubbed and the carpets were beaten; on the first day of each month a service was held with sprinkling of holy water; always on Tatyana Semyonovna's name-day and her son's (mine, too, for the first time, that autumn) a banquet was given to the whole neighbourhood. And all this had been done without change for as long as Tatyana Semyonovna could remember. My husband took no part in the management of the house; he confined himself to looking after the land and the peasants, and a great deal of work that gave him. He used to get up even in the winter very early, so that when I waked up I did not find him. He usually came back to morning tea, which we drank alone together; and almost always at that time, after the exertions and worries of his work on the estate, he was in that particularly cheerful state of mind which we used to call *wild delight*.

Often I used to ask him to tell me what he had been doing in the morning, and he would tell me such nonsense that we went into fits of laughter. Sometimes I insisted on a serious account, and he would restrain a smile and tell me. I looked at his eyes, at his moving lips, and did not understand a word, but simply enjoyed seeing him and hearing his voice.

'Come, what did I say, repeat it?' he would ask. But I could never repeat anything, so ludicrous it seemed that he should talk to me, not of himself or me, but of something else, as though it mattered what happened outside us. Only much later I began to have some slight understanding of his cares and to be interested in them. Tatyana Semyonovna did not make her appearance till dinner-time; she drank her tea alone in the morning, and only sent greetings to us by messengers. In our private world of frantic happiness a voice from her staid, decorous nook, so different, sounded so strange that often I could not restrain myself, and simply giggled in response to the maid who, standing with folded hands, announced sedately that 'Tatyana Semyonovna desired me to inquire how you slept after yesterday's walk, and about herself desired me to inform you that all night long she had a pain in her side, and a stupid dog in the village barked so and prevented her sleeping. And I was desired to inquire also how you liked today's baking, and to beg you to observe that Taras did not do the baking today, but Nikolasha for the first time as an experiment, and very fairly well, she says, he has done, especially the dough-rings, but he has over-baked the tea-rusks.' Till dinner-time we were not much together. I played the piano and read alone, while he was writing and going his rounds on the land again. But at dinner-time, at four o'clock, we met together in the dining-room; mamma sailed out of her room; and the poor ladies, of whom there were always two or three staying in the house, appeared on the scene. Regularly every day my husband gave his arm in the old fashion to his mother to take her in to dinner. But she insisted on his offering me the other, and regularly every day we were squeezed and got in each other's way at the door. At dinner my mother-in-law presided, and a conversation was maintained decorously reasonable and rather solemn in tone. The simple phrases that passed between my husband and me made an agreeable break in the solemnity of these ceremonious dinners. Sometimes disputes would spring up between mother and son, and they mocked at each other. I particularly loved these disputes and their mockery of one another, because the tender and enduring love that bound them together was never more strongly expressed than on these occasions. After dinner mamma settled herself in a big armchair in the drawing-room, and powdered snuff, or cut the leaves of some newly-purchased book, while we read aloud, or went off to the divan-room to the harpsichord. We read a great deal together at that time, but music was our best and favourite pleasure, every time touching new chords in our hearts, and as it were revealing us to each other anew. When I played his favourite pieces, he sat on a sofa at some distance where I could scarcely see him, and from a sort of shame at his emotion tried to conceal the impression the music made on him. But often when he was not expecting it, I got up from the piano, ran to him, and tried to catch on his face traces of his emotion, an unnatural brightness and moisture in his eyes, which he tried in vain to conceal from me. Mamma often wanted to look at us in the divan-room, but no doubt she sometimes was afraid of being a constraint to us, and she would pass through the room with a serious and indifferent face, pretending not to look at us. But I knew she had no reason really for going so often to her room and returning again. Evening tea was poured out by me in the big drawing-room, and again all the family circle gathered round the table. This duty of solemnly presiding before the sacred shrine of the samovar and the array of glasses and cups was for a long while a source of confusion to me.[4] I always felt that I was not yet worthy of this honour; that I was too young and frivolous to turn the tap of such a big samovar, to set the glasses on the tray for Nikita, and to say as I did so, 'For Pyotr Ivanovich, for Marya Minichua'; to inquire, 'Is it sweet?' and to leave pieces of sugar for the old nurse and other deserving persons.

'Capital! capital!' my husband would often say, 'quite like a grown-up person'; and that only increased my confusion.

After tea mamma played patience or listened to Marya Minichua fortune-telling with the cards; then she kissed us both and made the sign of the cross on us, and we went to our own room. For the most part though, we used to sit up together till midnight, and this was our best and pleasantest time. He talked to me about his past; we made plans, philosophised sometimes, and tried to speak very softly all the time, so that we should not be heard upstairs and reported to

Tatyana Semyonovna, who expected us to go to bed early. Sometimes getting hungry, we would steal quietly to the sideboard, procure a cold supper through the good offices of Nikita, and eat it by the light of one candle in my boudoir. We lived like strangers in that big, old house in which the stern spirit of the old world and of Tatyana Semyonovna held sway over all. Not she only, but the house-serfs, the old maidservants, the furniture, the pictures, aroused in me respect, a sort of fear and a sense that he and I were a little out of our element, that we must live here very circumspectly and discreetly. Looking back now, I can see that many things, that fettering, unvarying routine, and that mass of idle, inquisitive people in our house, were inconvenient and burdensome, but at the time the very constraint added a zest to our love. He was as far as I was from showing any sign that anything was not to his liking. On the contrary, he positively shut his eyes as it were to what was amiss. Mamma's footman, Dmitry Sidorov, who was very fond of the pipe, used regularly, every day after dinner, when we were in the divan-room, to go into my husband's study and take his tobacco out of the drawer. And it was worth seeing the good-humoured consternation with which Sergei Mikhailych would come up to me on tiptoe, and holding up his finger and winking, point to Dmitry Sidorov, who had not the slightest suspicion that he was seen. And when Dmitry Sidorov had retreated without noticing us, my husband, delighted that everything had ended so satisfactorily, would declare, as at every other opportunity, that I was 'a darling,' and kiss me. Sometimes I did not like this easy-going readiness to forgive everything, this sort of disregard of everything, and without noticing that it was just the same with me, I considered it a weakness, 'Like a child who dare not show his will!' I thought.

'Ah, my dear,' he answered, when I said to him one day that I was surprised at his weakness, 'how can one be displeased at anything when one is as happy as I am? It's easier to give way oneself than to overrule others—of that I have long been convinced—and there is no position in which one cannot be happy. And we are so happy, I cannot be angry; for me now there is nothing wrong, it is all only pitiful or amusing. And above all—*le mieux est l'ennemi du bien*. Would you believe it, when I hear the bell ring, when I receive a letter, when I simply wake up, I'm in terror—terror at having to go on with life, at some change coming in it; for better than the present there can never be?'

I believed him, but I did not understand him; I was happy, but it seemed to me that this was always so and could not be otherwise, and was always so with every one, and that somewhere ahead there was another happiness, not greater, but different.

So passed two months. Winter had come with its frosts and its storms, and I had begun, in spite of his being with me, to feel lonely. I had begun to feel that life was a repetition of the same thing; that there was nothing new either in me or in him; and that, on the contrary, we kept going back as it were on what was old. He began to give himself up to his work apart from me more than before, and I began to feel again that he had in his soul a sort of private world of his own into which he did not wish to admit me. His everlasting serenity irritated me. I loved him no less than before, and was as happy as before in his love. But my love had come to a standstill, and was not growing greater, and besides my love a sort of new feeling of restlessness had begun to steal into my soul. Loving was not enough for me after the happiness I had known in learning to love him. I longed for activity, not for a peaceful evenly flowing life. I longed for excitement, danger, and sacrifice for my feeling. I had a surplus of energy that found no outlet in our quiet life. I had attacks of depression, which I tried to hide from him, as something wrong, and attacks of frenzied gaiety and passion that alarmed him. He was aware of my state of mind before I was, and suggested our going to town. But I begged him not to go, not to change our mode of life, not to break up our happiness. And I really was happy; but my torment was that this happiness cost me no sort of effort, no sort of sacrifice, while energy for effort, for sacrifice, was fretting me. I loved him, and saw that I was everything to him; but I longed for every one to see our love, for people to try and hinder my loving him, so that I could love him in spite of everything. My mind, and even my feelings, were occupied, but there was another feeling—the feeling of youth, the need of activity, which found no satisfaction in our quiet life. Why had he suggested that we might go to town when that was all I desired? If he had not said that, may be I should have seen that the feeling that made me miserable was harmful nonsense, was my fault; that the sacrifice I was looking for was here before me in the conquering of that feeling. The idea that I could escape from my depression simply by moving to town had involuntarily occurred to

me; and at the same time I should have been ashamed and sorry to
tear him away from all he loved for my sake. But time went by, the
snow drifted higher and higher against the walls of the house, and
we were still alone and alone, and were still the same to one another;
while far away somewhere, in bright light and noise, crowds of people were in movement, were suffering and rejoicing, without a
thought of us and our existence as it passed away. What was worst of
all to me was the feeling that every day the routine of our life was
nailing our life down into one definite shape; that our feeling was
becoming not spontaneous, but was affected by bondage to the
monotonous, passionless action of time. In the morning we were
cheerful, at dinner polite, in the evening tender. 'Good! . . .' I said to
myself, 'that's all very well, to do good and lead an upright life, as he
says, but we've plenty of time for that, and there is something else for
which I only have the energy now.' That was not what I needed, I
needed strife; I wanted feeling to guide us in life, and not life to be
the guide to feeling. I longed to go with him to the edge of a
precipice and to say, 'Another step, and I fling myself down! another
movement and I am lost!' and for him, pale at the edge of the abyss,
to snatch me up in his strong arms, hold me over it, so that my heart
would stand still, and bear me away whither he would.

My state of mind positively affected my health, and my nerves
began to suffer. One morning—I was worse than usual—he came
back from his counting-house out of humour, which was rare with
him. I noticed it at once, and asked him what was the matter; but he
would not tell me, saying it was of no consequence. As I found out
later, the captain of the district police had summoned our peasants,
and from ill-will to my husband had made illegal exactions from
them, and had used threats to them. My husband had not yet been
able to stomach all this so as to feel it all simply pitiful and absurd; he
was irritated, and so did not want to speak of it to me. But I fancied
that he did not care to tell me about it because he regarded me as a
child who could not understand what interested him. I turned away
from him, was silent, and then sent to Marya Minichua, who was
staying with us, to ask her to come to tea. After tea, which I finished
unusually quickly, I took Marya Minichua off to the divan-room and
began a loud conversation with her about some nonsense which was
utterly uninteresting to me. He walked about the room, glancing now

and then at us. Those glances for some reason or other had the effect on me of making me want to talk and even laugh more and more. Everything I said seemed funny to me, and everything Marya Minichua said. Without saying anything to me he went away into his study and closed the door after him. As soon as he was not there to hear, all my gaiety suddenly vanished, so that Marya Minichua wondered and asked me what was the matter. . . . I did not answer, but sat down on a sofa and felt inclined to cry. 'And what is he inventing to worry over?' I thought. 'Some nonsense which he thinks important; but if he will only tell me, I'll show him it's all rubbish. No; he must needs suppose I shouldn't understand, must needs humiliate me with his stately composure, and always be in the right with me. But I'm right too when I'm bored and dreary, when I want to live, to move about,' I thought, 'and not to stick in the same place and feel that time is passing over me. I want to go forward, and every day, every hour, I want novelty; while he wants to stop still and to keep me stopping still with him. And how easy it would be for him! There's no need for this to take me to town; all he needs to do is to be as I am, not to school himself away from his nature, not to hold himself in, but to live simply. That's the very thing he tells me to do, but he's not simple himself. So there!' I felt that tears were gathering, and that I was angry with him. I was dismayed at this anger, and went in to him. He was sitting in his study writing. Hearing my footsteps, he looked round for an instant, carelessly and calmly, and went on writing. That glance displeased me; instead of going up to him I stood at the table at which he was writing, and opening a book began looking at it. He broke off once more and looked at me.

'Masha, are you cross?' he said.

I responded by a cold glance, which said, 'You needn't ask—why this politeness?' He shook his head and smiled timidly and tenderly, but for the first time my smile did not respond to his smile.

'What happened today?' I asked. 'Why wouldn't you tell me?'

'Nothing of consequence, a trifling annoyance!' he answered. 'I can tell you now, though. Two peasants had gone to the town . . .'

But I did not let him finish his tale.

'Why was it you wouldn't tell me when I asked you at tea?'

'I should have said something stupid; I was angry then.'

'It was then I wanted you to.'

'What for?'

'Why do you imagine that I can never be any help to you in anything?'

'What do I imagine?' he said, flinging down his pen. 'I imagine that I can't live without you. In everything, everything you're not merely a help to me, but you do everything. So that's the discovery you've been making!' he laughed. 'I only live through you. It seems to me that all is well simply because you are here, because you . . .'

'Yes, I know all that; I'm a dear child who must be tranquillised!' I said, in such a tone that he looked at me in wonder, as though he was seeing me for the first time. 'I don't want tranquillity, there's enough of it in you, quite enough,' I added.

'Well, do you see this was what was the matter,' he began hurriedly, interrupting me, evidently afraid to let me give utterance to all I was feeling. 'What would you say about it?'

'I don't care to hear it now!' I answered. Though I did want to hear him, it was so agreeable to me to trouble his tranquillity of mind. 'I don't want to play at life, I want to live,' I said, 'just as you do.'

On his face, which always reflected every feeling so quickly and so vividly, there was a look of pain and of intense attention.

'I want to live with you on equal terms.' But I could not go on; such sadness, such profound sadness, was apparent in his face. He was silent for a little.

'But in what way are you not on equal terms with me?' he said. 'Is it because I, and not you, have to deal with the police captain and drunken peasants?'

'Oh, not only that,' I said.

'For God's sake, understand me, my dear,' he went on. 'I know that we are always hurt by shocks; I have lived and learned that. I love you, and consequently I can't help wanting to save you from shocks. That's my life, my love for you, so don't you hinder my living either.'

'You are always right!' I said, not looking at him.

It annoyed me that again in his soul all was clear and calm, while I was full of vexation and a feeling like remorse.

'Masha! what is the matter with you?' he said. 'The point is not whether I am right or you are right, but of something quite different.

What have you against me? Don't speak at once, think a little, and tell me all you are thinking about. You are vexed with me, and you're probably right, but do let me know what I've done wrong?'

But how could I tell him all that was in my heart? The fact that he understood me at once; that again I was a child before him; that I could do nothing that he would not understand and have foreseen, exasperated me more than ever.

'I have nothing against you,' I said; 'it's simply that I'm dull, and I don't want to be dull. But you say it must be so, and again you are right!'

I said this and glanced at him. I had attained my aim; his tranquillity had gone, alarm and pain were visible in his face.

'Masha,' he began in a gentle, troubled voice, 'this is no jesting matter what we are doing now. It is our fate that is being decided now. I beg you to make no answer, but to listen to me. Why do you want to make me suffer?'

But I interrupted him.

'I know you will be right. You'd better not speak—you are right!' I said coldly, as though not I, but some evil spirit in me were speaking.

'If you only knew what you are doing!' he said in a shaking voice.

I burst into tears, and I felt better. He sat down beside me and kept silence. I felt sorry for him and ashamed of myself, and vexed at what I had done. I did not look at him. It seemed to me that he must be looking at me either severely or in perplexity at that moment. I looked round; a soft tender glance was fixed upon me as though asking forgiveness. I took him by the hand and said—

'Forgive me—I don't know what I said myself.'

'No; but I know what you said, and you said what is true.'

'What?' I asked.

'That we must go to Petersburg,' he said; 'there's nothing for us to do here now.'

'As you wish,' I said.

He put his arms round me and kissed me.

'You forgive me,' he said; 'I have acted wrongly towards you.'

That evening I played to him a long while, and he walked about the room murmuring something. He had the habit of murmuring to himself, and I often used to ask him what he was whispering, and he would always after a moment's thought tell me exactly what he had been saying; generally, lines of verse, and sometimes fearful nonsense, but always of a kind which showed me his humour at the time.

'What are you whispering today?' I asked.

He stopped, thought a little, and with a smile quoted the two lines of Lermontov—

'And in his madness prays for storms,
As though in storms he might find peace.'*

'No, he's more than a man, he knows everything!' I thought. 'How can one help loving him?'

I got up, took him by the arm, and began walking with him, trying to keep step with him.

'Yes?' he asked smiling, and watching me.

'Yes,' I said in a whisper, and a sort of mood of mirth came upon us both, our eyes laughed, and we made our strides longer and longer, and rose more and more upon tiptoe. And with this stride, to the great horror of Grigory and the amazement of mamma, who was playing patience in the drawing-room, we pranced through all the rooms as far as the dining-room, and there stopped, looked at each other, and went off into a roar of laughter.

A fortnight later, before Christmas, we were in Petersburg.

VII

Our journey to Petersburg, the week in Moscow, my relations and his, settling into a new home, the road, the new places and persons—all this passed like a dream. It was all so varied, so new, so gay; it was all so warmly and brightly lighted up by his presence, his love, that our quiet country life seemed to me something long past and of no importance. To my great astonishment, instead of the worldly haughtiness and frigidity I had expected to find in people, every one met me with such unfeigned cordiality and pleasure (not only our kinsfolk, but strangers too), that it seemed as though they had been

---

*The concluding lines of "The Sail" (1832), by Russian Romantic Poet Mikhail Lermontov (1814–1841).

thinking of nothing but me, had only been waiting for me to be happy themselves. It was also something quite unexpected by me that in the circle of society, which seemed to me the very best, my husband had, as it appeared, many acquaintances of whom he had never talked to me. And often it seemed strange and unpleasant to me to hear from him severe criticisms of some of those people who seemed to me so nice. I could not understand why he was so reserved with them, and tried to avoid making many acquaintances which seemed to me flattering. It seemed to me that the more nice people one knew the better, and that all were nice.

'This is how we will manage, do you see,' he had said to me just before we left the country: 'here I am a little Croesus, but there we shall be people of very modest means, and so we must only stay in town till Easter, and not go into society, or else we shall get into difficulties; and besides, I shouldn't care to for your sake.'

'Why go into society?' I answered; 'we'll only see the theatres and our relations, hear the opera and some good music, and even before Easter will go back to the country.'

But as soon as we had arrived in Petersburg these plans were forgotten. I found myself all of a sudden in such a new happy world, so many delights encompassed me, such new interests opened out before me, that at once, though unconsciously, I renounced all my past and all the plans of that past. 'That was after all mere trifling; it hadn't begun, but this is the thing! And what will come next?' I thought. The restlessness and the fits of depression that had worried me in the country had all at once, as though by magic, completely vanished. My love for my husband had become calmer, and it never occurred to me here to wonder whether he loved me less. And indeed I could not doubt his love; every thought I had was instantly understood, every feeling was shared, every desire fulfilled. His tranquillity disappeared here or no longer irritated me. Besides I felt that here, besides his former love for me, he was admiring me too. Often after paying a call, on being introduced to some new acquaintance, or entertaining a party of friends in the evening, when I had performed the duties of hostess, trembling inwardly in fear of making some blunder, he would say: 'Ah! bravo, little girl, capital, don't be frightened! That's capital, really!' And I was highly delighted. Soon after our arrival he wrote a letter to his mother; and when he called me to add a word from myself, he would not let me read what he had written, which led me of course to insist, and I read: 'You would not know Masha,' he wrote; 'indeed, I hardly know her myself. Where can she have picked up this charming, gracious composure, affability, social tact, and high breeding, in fact. And it's all so simple, charming, sweet. Every one's in ecstasies over her, and I myself am never tired of admiring her, and, if it were possible, I should love her more than before.'

'Oh! so that's what I am like!' I thought. And I was so gay and happy, I even fancied that I loved him more than ever. My success with all our acquaintances was a complete surprise to me. I was continually being told on all hands that there I had made a particularly good impression on an uncle; that here an aunt had been quite bewitched by me; here a man declared that there were no women like me in Petersburg; and there a lady assures me that I have but to wish it in order to become the woman most sought after in society. A cousin of my husband's, in particular, a Princess D., a society woman no longer young, who had impetuously fallen in love with me, used more than any one to say flattering things to me that turned my head. When this cousin invited me for the first time to go to a ball, and asked my husband about it, he turned to me, and with a scarcely perceptible sly smile, asked, 'Did I want to go?' I bent my head in token of assent, and felt that I blushed.

'She's like a criminal confessing what she wants,' he said, laughing good-humouredly.

'But, you know, you said that we couldn't go into society, and besides, you don't like it,' I answered, smiling, and looking with imploring eyes at him.

'If you want to very much, we'll go,' he said.

'We had better not, really.'

'Do you want to . . . very much?' he asked again.

I did not answer.

'Society is no great calamity so far,' he went on; 'but an unsatisfied craving for society, that's bad, and ugly too. We certainly must go, and we will go,' he wound up resolutely.

'To tell you the truth,' I said, 'I never longed for anything in the world so much as this ball.'

We went to the ball, and my enjoyment of it surpassed all my expectations. At the ball, even more than before, it seemed to me that I was the centre round which everything was moving; that it was only for me that the great hall was lighted up, the music was playing, and that crowd of people, ecstatically admiring me, had come together. Every one, from the hairdresser and the ladiesmaid, to my partners and the old gentlemen walking about the hall, told me, or gave me to understand, that they loved me. The general criticism passed upon me at that ball, and reported to me afterwards by our cousin, was that I was utterly unlike other women, that there was something individual in me, the charm of the country, simple and exquisite. This success so flattered me that I frankly told my husband how I should like that year to go to two or three more balls, 'so as to have had quite enough of them,' I added hypocritically.

My husband readily agreed, and at first accompanied me with evident pleasure, enjoying my triumph, and apparently quite forgetting or giving up the decision he had expressed before.

Later on he became obviously bored and weary of the life we were leading. But I had no thoughts for that; if I did sometimes notice his intent, serious gaze, fixed inquiringly upon me, I refused to understand its significance. I was so blinded by that devotion to me I seemed to see suddenly aroused in all outsiders, that atmosphere of luxury, pleasure, and novelty, which I was breathing here for the first time, his moral influence that had repressed me had so quickly vanished here. It was so pleasant for me in this world to feel not merely on a level with him, but superior to him, and for that to love him even more and more independently than before, that I could not imagine what drawbacks he could see for me in fashionable life. I had a feeling of pride and self-satisfaction quite new to me when, as we entered a ballroom, all eyes were turned upon me; while he, as though ashamed to claim his ownership of me before the crowd, made haste to leave me and obliterate himself in the throng of black coats.

'Wait a little!' I often thought while my eyes sought him, an inconspicuous, often weary-looking figure at the further end of the hall. 'Wait a little!' I thought: 'we shall go home, and you will see and understand for whose sake I tried to be beautiful and brilliant, and what it is I love out of all that surrounds me this evening.' I quite sincerely fancied, indeed, that my triumphs only delighted me by enabling me to sacrifice them to him. The only way in which fashionable life might be harmful to me was, I thought, the possibility of being attracted by one of the men I met in society, of arousing my husband's jealousy. But he had such trust in me, he seemed so tranquil and indifferent, and all the young men I met seemed so unimportant in comparison with him, that the sole danger of society, as I considered it, did not frighten me. But, all the same, the attentions of many men in society afforded me gratification, flattered my vanity, led me to imagine that there was a sort of merit in my love for my husband, and made my behaviour with him more self-confident and, as it were, more casual.

'Oh, I saw how eagerly you were talking with N. N.,' I said one evening on the way home from a ball, shaking my finger at him, and mentioning a well-known Petersburg lady with whom he had been talking that evening. I said this to rouse him—he was particularly silent and bored.

'Oh, why talk like that? And you it is talking like that, Masha!' he murmured through his teeth, knitting his brow as though in physical pain. 'How unsuitable it is with you and me! Leave that to others; these false relations may spoil our real ones, and I still hope the real will come back.'

I felt ashamed, and I did not speak.

'Will they come back, Masha? What do you think?' he asked.

'They have never been spoilt, and will not be spoilt,' I said. And at the time I really thought so.

'God grant it may be so,' he commented, 'or else it would be high time for us to be back in the country.'

But it was only once that he spoke like this, the rest of the time it seemed to me that he was as well content as I was, and I was so delighted and happy. If he really were dull sometimes, I comforted myself by reflecting I too had been dull for his sake in the country. If our relations really had altered somewhat, it would all come back again as soon as we were by ourselves again in the summer with Tatyana Semyonovna in our house at Nikolskoe.

So the winter slipped away without my noticing it, and, regardless of our plans, we spent Holy Week too in Petersburg. On Low Sunday, when we were making preparations for our departure, everything had been packed, and my husband, who had already made purchases of presents, flowers, and various things for our country life, was in a particularly warm and cheerful state of mind, his cousin arrived unexpectedly, and began begging me to stay till Saturday so as to go to a *soirée* at Countess R.'s. She said that Countess R. was most pressing in her invitation; that a certain foreign Prince M. had been eager to make my acquaintance ever since the last ball; that it was simply with that object that he was coming to the *soirée*, and that he said that I was the prettiest woman in Russia. All Petersburg was to be there, and in fact it would be simply monstrous if I were not to go.

My husband was at the other end of the drawing-room talking to someone.

'Well, so you'll come, Marie, eh?' said his cousin.

'We meant to go into the country the day after tomorrow,' I answered irresolutely, glancing at my husband. Our eyes met; he hurriedly turned away.

'I will persuade him to stay,' said his cousin, 'and we'll go on Saturday to break hearts, eh?'

'That would upset our plans, and we've packed,' I answered, beginning to yield.

'Why, she'd better drive round this evening and pay her respects to the prince,' my husband said from the other end of the room, in a tone of repressed anger, such as I had never heard from him.

'Oh, he's jealous; why, it's the first time I've seen it!' laughed his cousin. 'Why, it's not for the prince's sake, Sergei Mikhailych, but for all of us, I'm trying to persuade her. How Countess R. did entreat her to come!'

'It rests with her,' my husband commented frigidly, and he went out of the room.

I saw that he was moved beyond his wont. This distressed me, and I made no promise to his cousin. As soon as she had gone, I went in to my husband. He was walking up and down absorbed in thought, and neither saw nor heard me come into the room on tiptoe.

'He's picturing his dear Nikolskoe,' I thought, looking at him, 'and his morning coffee in the light drawing-room, and his fields and the peasants, and the evenings in the divan-room, and our secret suppers in the night. . . . No,' I decided inwardly, 'I'd give up all the balls in the world, and the flattery of all the princes in the world, for his glad confusion, his gentle caress.' I was going to tell him that I wouldn't go to the *soirée*, and didn't want to go, when he suddenly looked round, and seeing me, frowned, and the gently dreamy expression of his face changed. Again penetration, sagacity, and patronising composure were expressed in his eyes. He did not care for me to see him as a plain man; he wanted always to be a demigod standing on a pedestal before me.

'What is it, my dear?' he asked, turning carelessly and calmly to me.

I did not answer. It annoyed me that he was reserved with me, would not remain as I loved him.

'You want to go on Saturday to the *soirée*?' he queried.

'I did want to,' I answered, 'but you dislike it. Besides, everything's packed,' I added.

Never had he looked at me so coldly, never had he spoken so coldly to me.

'I won't go till Tuesday, and will order the things to be unpacked,' he said, 'so that you can go if you are disposed. As a favour to me, do go. I'm not going away.'

He began, as he always did when he was troubled, to walk jerkily up and down the room, without looking at me.

'I positively don't understand you,' I said, standing still and following him with my eyes: 'you say you are always so calm?' He never had said so. 'Why do you talk to me so strangely? I am ready to sacrifice this pleasure for your sake, and in a sort of ironical way in which you've never spoken to me before you insist on my going.'

'Well! you make *sacrifices* (he laid special stress on this word), and I make sacrifices—what can be better? It's a conflict of generosity. Isn't that what you call family happiness?'

It was the first time I had heard from him such bitterly sneering words. And the sneer did not put me to shame, but offended me; and the bitterness did not alarm me, but infected me. Did he say this, he who had always shunned equivocation in our relations, he always genuine and direct? And in return for what? For my really having wanted to sacrifice for him a pleasure in which I could see nothing wrong, and for my having so well understood and loved him a minute before. Our parts were changed; he avoided direct and simple statements, while I sought them.

'You are very much changed,' I said, sighing; 'in what way have I been in fault? It's not the *soirée*, but something before that that you have in your heart against me. Why this want of straightforwardness?

Didn't you feel such dread of it yourself once? Tell me straight out what you have against me?' 'What can he say?' I wondered, reflecting complacently that there had been nothing he could reproach me with all that winter.

I came forward into the middle of the room, so that he was obliged to pass close by me, and looked at him. He would come up, embrace me, and all would be over, was the thought that occurred to me, and I felt positively sorry I should not have the chance of showing him how wrong he was. But he stopped at the end of the room and stared at me.

'Do you still not understand?' he said.

'No.'

'Well, then, I will tell you. It's loathsome to me, for the first time what I feel and cannot help feeling is loathsome to me . . .' He stopped, evidently shocked at the harsh sound of his own voice.

'But what is it?' I asked, with tears of indignation in my eyes.

'It's loathsome that the prince thought you pretty, and that consequently you are rushing to meet him, forgetting your husband and yourself and womanly dignity, and refuse to understand what your husband must feel about you, if you've no feeling of dignity in yourself. On the contrary, you come to tell your husband that you will *sacrifice* it, that is, "to exhibit myself to His Highness, would have been a great happiness, but I *sacrifice* it."'

The longer he spoke, the more furious he grew with the sound of his own voice, and that voice had a cruel, malignant, coarse note in it. I had never seen, had never expected to see him like this. The blood rushed to my heart, I was frightened, but a feeling of undeserved shame and wounded vanity excited me, and I longed to revenge myself on him.

'I have long been expecting this,' I said; 'say it, say it!'

'I don't know what you've been expecting,' he went on. 'I might well have expected the worst, seeing you every day in the uncleanness and idleness and luxury of this silly society, and I've got it too. I've come to feeling ashamed and sick today, as I have never felt for myself. When your friend with her unclean hands pryed into my heart and began talking of jealousy, my jealousy—of whom?—a man whom neither I nor you know. And you, on purpose it seems—refuse to understand me and want to sacrifice to me—what? . . . I'm ashamed of you, ashamed of your degradation! . . . Sacrifice!' he repeated.

'Ah, here we have it, the power of the husband,' I thought, 'to insult and humiliate his wife, who is in no way to blame. These are a husband's rights, but I won't submit to it.'

'No, I won't sacrifice anything to you,' I declared, feeling my nostrils dilating unnaturally and the blood deserting my face. 'I'm going to the soirée on Saturday; I shall certainly go!'

'And God grant you may enjoy it, only everything's over between us!' he shouted in a fit of ungovernable fury. 'But you will never torture me any more. I was a fool to . . .' he began again, but his lips quivered, and with a visible effort he refrained from finishing what he was saying.

I feared and hated him at that moment. I wanted to say a great deal to him and to revenge all his insults. But if I had opened my mouth, I should have cried and lowered myself before him. I walked out of the room without a word. But as soon as I ceased to hear his steps, I was at once aghast at what we had done. I was in terror that the tie which made up my whole happiness would be severed for ever, and I wanted to go back. 'But has he sufficiently recovered his composure to understand me when I mutely hold out my hand to him and look at him?' I wondered. 'Will he understand my generosity? What if he calls my sorrow hypocrisy? Or with a sense of his rectitude and haughty composure, accepts my repentance and forgives me? And why, why has he, whom I loved so much, so cruelly insulted me?'

I went not to him, but to my own room, where I sat a long while alone, and wept with terror, going over every word of the conversation between us, substituting for those words others, adding other kind words, and again with horror and a feeling of humiliation remembering what had happened. When I went in to tea in the evening, and in the presence of S., who had called, met my husband, I felt that from that day a gulf had opened between us. S. asked me when we were going? Before I had time to answer, my husband replied, 'On Tuesday; we're going to the soirée at Countess R.'s? You're going, of course?' he said, turning to me.

I was frightened at the sound of this direct speech, and looked timidly at my husband. His eyes were looking straight at me, their expression was vindictive and sneering, his voice was cold and steady.

'Yes,' I answered.

In the evening when we were alone, he came up to me and held out his hand.

'Please forget what I said to you!' he said. I took his hand, a faltering smile was on my face, and tears were ready to gush from my eyes, but he drew back his hand; and as though dreading a sentimental scene, sat down in a low chair at some distance from me. 'Can he possibly still consider himself in the right?' I wondered, and the words of reconciliation and the entreaty not to go to the soirée that were on the tip of my tongue were never uttered.

'We must write to mother that we've put off leaving,' he said, 'or else she'll be uneasy.'

'But when are you thinking of going?' I asked.

'On Tuesday, after the soirée,' he answered.

'I hope that's not on my account?' I said, looking into his eyes. But his eyes looked blankly at me and told me nothing, as though they were hidden by a cloud from me. His face struck me suddenly as old and disagreeable.

We went to the soirée, and good, friendly relations seemed re-established between us; but these relations were quite different from what had been once.

At the soirée I was sitting among some ladies when the prince came up to me in such a way that I had to get up to talk to him. As I got up, I could not help looking for my husband, and I saw him look at me from the other end of the room and turn away. I felt suddenly so ashamed and sick that I was miserably confused, and blushed all over my face and neck under the prince's eyes. But I was obliged to stand up and listen to what he said to me, as he scanned me, looking down at me. Our conversation did not last long—there was nowhere for him to sit down beside me, and he probably felt that I was very uncomfortable with him. We talked of the last ball, of where I was to spend the summer, and so on. On leaving me, he expressed a desire to be introduced to my husband, and I saw them brought together and talking at the other end of the room. The prince probably said something about me, for in the middle of the conversation he looked with a smile in my direction.

My husband all at once flushed hotly, made a low bow, and walked away from the prince. I blushed too; I was ashamed to think what an impression the prince must have received of me, and still more of my husband. It seemed to me that every one noticed my awkward embarrassment while I was talking to the prince and my husband's strange behaviour in leaving his side. There was no knowing what interpretation they would put on it. Didn't they know by now of my talk with my husband about the prince? His cousin took me home, and on the way I talked to her about my husband. I could not restrain myself, and told her all that had passed between us in regard to this luckless *soirée*. She comforted me, assuring me that it was just an ordinary tiff, of no importance, and leaving no traces. She explained to me my husband's character from her point of view, saying that he had grown very haughty and unsociable. I agreed with her, and it seemed to me that I myself understood him better and more sensibly now.

But afterwards, when I was alone with my husband, this criticism of him lay on my conscience like a crime, and I felt that the gulf that separated us had grown wider.

VIII

From that day our life and our relations were completely changed. We were not so happy by ourselves as before. There were questions we avoided touching upon, and conversation came easier to us before a third person than face to face. Whenever the conversation turned on life in the country or touched on the ball, we were both as it were a little dizzy, and had an awkwardness in looking at one another. It was as though we were both aware where the gulf lay that parted us, and dreaded going near it. I was persuaded that he was proud and hot-tempered, and that I must be on my guard not to irritate him on his weak points. He was convinced that I could not live without society, that the country was distasteful to me, and that he must submit to this unfortunate taste; and we both avoided plain speech about these subjects, and both judged each other falsely. We had long ceased to be the most perfect creatures in the world in each other's eyes; now we made comparisons with others, and secretly judged each other. I fell ill just before we were to leave town; and instead of going back to the country, we moved to a summer villa in the outskirts, and from there my husband went home alone to see his mother. When he left me, I had recovered sufficiently to have gone with him, but he persuaded me to stay where I was, on the pretext of anxiety about my health. I felt that he was not afraid for my health, but of our not getting on well in the country; I did not insist very warmly, and was left behind. Without him I felt dull and solitary; but when he came back, I saw that he did not add to my life what he had added once. Our old relations—when any thought, any impression, not shared with him, weighed on me like a crime, when every act, every word of his, seemed to me the pattern of perfection, when we wanted to laugh for glee, looking at each other,— these relations had so imperceptibly passed into others that we had not discovered that they were no more. Each of us had found our separate interests, which we did not now attempt to share. It had even ceased to trouble us that each had a separate private world, shut off from the other. We had grown used to that idea, and a year later we no longer felt awkward when we looked at each other. Utterly vanished were his moods of wild gaiety with me, his boyishness, his readiness to forgive everything, and carelessness of everything, which had once worried me; there was no more that deep gaze that had once troubled and rejoiced me, no more prayers and ecstasies together. We did not often see each other even. He was continually absent on journeys, and did not dread, did not regret leaving me, while I was continually in society where I had no need of him.

There were no more scenes and quarrels between us; I tried to satisfy him; he did everything I wished, and we loved one another in a way.

When we were left alone, which rarely happened, I felt no joy, no emotion, no confusion, in being with him; it was as though I were by myself. I knew very well that this was my husband—not any new, unknown person, but a good man—my husband, whom I knew as I knew myself. I was certain that I knew everything he would do, what he would say, and how he would look; and if he acted or looked not as I had expected, it seemed to me indeed that it was by mistake. I expected nothing from him. In fact, he was my husband and nothing more. It seemed to me that this was as it should be indeed, and that any other relations do not generally exist, and, indeed, between us never had existed. When he was away, particularly at first, I had felt lonely, nervous; in his absence, I recognised more keenly the value of his support to me. When he returned, I flung myself on his neck in delight, though two hours later I had completetly forgotten this delight, and I had nothing to say to him. Only in the moments of quiet, sober tenderness, which did occur between us, it seemed to me that something was wrong, that I had an ache at my heart, and in his eyes it seemed to me I read the same thing. I was conscious of that limit of feeling beyond which he, it seemed, would not and I could not step. Sometimes this was a grief to me, but I had no time for brooding over anything, and I tried to forget this grief at the vaguely felt change in diversions which were always in readiness for me. Society life, which at first had dazzled me by its brilliance and the flattery of my vanity, soon had a complete hold on my inclinations, became a habit, laid its shackles upon me, and occupied in my heart all the space there was for feeling. I never remained alone, and dreaded brooding over my position. All my time, from late in the morning to late at night, was occupied and did not belong to me, even if I did not go out anywhere. This was now neither pleasing nor boring to me, but it seemed that so and not otherwise it must always have been.

So passed three years, during which our relations remained the same, came as it were to a full stop, crystallised, and could become neither worse nor better. In these three years two events of importance occurred in our family life, but neither of them affected my life. They were the birth of my first baby and the death of Tatyana Semyonovna. At first the feeling of motherhood came upon me with such force, and produced such unexpected ecstasy in me, that I thought a new life was beginning for me; but two months later, when I began to go out into society again, this feeling, growing less and less, passed into habit and coldly doing my duty. My husband, on the contrary, from the time of the birth of our first child, became the gentle, tranquil man he had been in the past, always in his own home, and the same tenderness and gaiety he had shown in the past was now devoted to the child. Often when I went into the nursery in a ball dress to sign my child with the cross for the night, and found my husband in the nursery, I caught his eyes fixed on me, as it were reproachfully and sternly scrutinising, and I felt ashamed. I was suddenly horrified at my indifference to my child, and asked myself, 'Can I be worse than other women? But what can I do?' I thought. 'I love my son, but I can't sit for days at a time with him; it bores me, and I'm not going to sham feeling for anything.' His mother's death was a great grief to him. It was painful to him, as he said, to be at Nikolskoe after her loss; but for me, though I was sorry for her and sympathised with my husband's grief, it was pleasanter and more comfortable now in the country. The

greater part of all these three years we spent in town. I was only once
for two months in the country, and in the third year we went abroad.

We spent the summer at a watering-place. I was then twenty-one.
Our circumstances were, I supposed, in a flourishing condition; from
my home life I demanded nothing more than it gave. Every one I
knew, it seemed to me, loved me; my health was good, my dresses
were the smartest at the springs; I knew that I was handsome. The
weather was magnificent; a peculiar atmosphere of beauty and elegance surrounded me, and I was very happy. I was not happy as I used
to be at Nikolskoe, when I felt that I was happy in myself, that I
deserved that happiness, that my happiness was great, but that it must
be even greater because one longed for more and more happiness.
Then it was different, but this summer, too, I was well content. I
wanted nothing; I hoped for nothing; I feared nothing. My life, it
seemed to me, was full, and my conscience, it seemed, was at rest. Of
all the young men I met that season, there was not one whom I distinguished in any way from the rest, or even from old Prince K., our
ambassador, who was very attentive to me. One was young, another
was old; one was a light-haired Englishman, another a Frenchman
with a beard; all were alike to me, but all were indispensable. It was
all these equally indistinguishable persons that made up the joyous
atmosphere of life about me. Only one of them, an Italian, Marchese
D——, drew my attention more than the rest by the boldness with
which he expressed his adoration to me. He never let slip a chance of
being with me, of dancing, riding, being at the casino and so on with
me, and of telling me that I was beautiful. Sometimes I saw him out
of window near our house, and often the unpleasant intent stare of
his brilliant eyes made me blush and look round. He was young,
handsome, elegant, and, above all, in his smile and the expression
of his brow he resembled my husband, though he was far better
looking. This likeness struck me in him, although in general, in his
lips, in his eyes, in his long chin, instead of the exquisite expression of
kindliness and idealistic serenity of my husband, there was something
coarse and animal. I imagined at the time that he loved me passionately,
and sometimes thought of him with proud commiseration. I sometimes tried to pacify him, to lead him into a tone of gentle, half-
affectionate confidence, but he abruptly repelled those attempts and
continued to disturb me disagreeably by his unexpressed passion,

that threatened every moment to find expression. Though I did not own it to myself, I was afraid of this man, and against my will I often thought of him. My husband was acquainted with him, and he behaved even more coldly and superciliously with him than with our other acquaintances, to whom he existed only as the husband of his wife. Towards the end of the season I was ill, and did not leave the house for a fortnight. When, for the first time after my illness, I went out in the evening to listen to the music, I found out that a certain Lady S., a famous beauty, who had long been expected, had arrived during this interval. A circle gathered round me, people met me with delight; but an even better circle had gathered around the celebrated beauty. Every one about me was talking of nothing but her and her beauty. She was pointed out to me, and she certainly was charming; but what struck me disagreeably was the conceited expression of her face, and I said so. That day everything seemed to me dull that had before seemed so agreeable. Next day Lady S. got up a party to visit the castle, which I declined to join. Scarcely any one remained with me, and everything was utterly transformed in my eyes. Everything and every one seemed to me stupid and dull; I wanted to cry, to make haste and finish our cure, and to return to Russia. In my soul there was a sort of evil feeling, but I had not yet acknowledged it to myself. I declared myself still not strong, and gave up showing myself in society, merely going out now and then in the morning alone to drink the waters, or taking drives into the neighbouring country with L. M., a Russian lady of my acquaintance. My husband was not there at that time; he had gone away for a few days to Heidelberg, while waiting for the end of my cure to return to Russia, and he only came over to see me from time to time.

One day Lady S. carried off all the fashionable society of the place to a hunt, and L. M. and I drove after dinner to the castle. While we were driving slowly in our carriage up the winding road under the venerable chestnut trees through which the pretty, elegant environs of Baden lay before us in the distance lighted up by the setting sun, we talked seriously, as we had not talked before. L. M., whom I had known for a long while, struck me now for the first time as a good intelligent woman, to whom one could say anything, and with whom it was pleasant to be friends. We talked of home and children, and the emptiness of the life here; we longed to be in Russia, in the country, and felt a sort of pleasant melancholy. Under the influence of this serious feeling we went into the castle. Within the walls it was cool and shady, overhead the sun played about the ruins, steps and voices were audible. Framed as it were by the doorway, we saw that view of Baden, exquisite, though frigid to our Russian eyes. We sat down to rest, and gazed in silence at the setting sun. The voices reached us more distinctly, and it seemed to me that my surname was mentioned. I began listening, and unconsciously we heard every word. The voices I knew; it was Marchese D. and the Frenchman, a friend of his, whom I knew too. They were talking about me and Lady S. The Frenchman compared her with me, and analysed the beauty of each. He said nothing insulting, but the blood rushed to my heart when I heard his words. He enumerated minutely the good points in me and in Lady S. I had already had a child, while Lady S. was only nineteen. My hair was better, but Lady S. had a more graceful figure; Lady S. was a grand lady; 'while yours,' said he, 'is only middling, one of those little Russian princesses who so often turn up here nowadays.' He wound up by saying that I did well not to fight it out with Lady S., and that I was as good as buried in Baden.

'I'm sorry for her.'

'If only she doesn't want to console herself with you . . .' he added with a cruel laugh of amusement.

'If she goes away, I go after her!' a voice declared coarsely in an Italian accent.

'Happy mortal, he can still love!' laughed the Frenchman.

'Love!' said the voice, and paused. 'I can't not love—there's no life without it. To make a romance of life is the one thing worth while. And my romance never stops in the middle, and this I will carry through to the end.'

'*Bonne chance, mon ami,*' said the Frenchman.

We heard no further, for they had gone round the corner, and we heard their steps on the other side. They came down the stairs, and a few minutes later came out of a side door, and were much surprised to see us. I blushed when Marchese D. approached me, and felt frightened when, on leaving the castle, he gave me his arm. I could not refuse, and we walked together to our carriage behind L. M., who was walking with his friend. I was mortified by what the Frenchman had said about me, though I secretly owned that he only put into words what

I had myself been feeling. But the Marchese's words had astounded
and shocked me by their coarseness. I was miserable at the thought
that I had heard his words, and in spite of that he was not afraid of
me. I was disgusted at feeling him so close to me; and without looking
at him, without answering him, I tried to hold my arm so as not
to hear what he said while I walked hurriedly after L. M. and the
Frenchman. The Marchese said something about the fine view, about
the unexpected happiness of meeting me, and something more, but I
did not hear him. I was thinking just then of my husband, my child,
Russia; I felt ashamed of something, regretted something, longed for
something; and I was in a hurry to get home to my solitary room in
the Hôtel de Bade so as to ponder at my leisure over all that had only
just begun to stir in my heart. But L. M. walked slowly; it was still
some distance to the carriage; my escort, as I fancied, obstinately
slackened his pace, as though trying to keep me. 'Impossible!' I
thought, and resolutely walked faster. But he positively detained me,
and even squeezed my arm. L. M. turned the corner of the road, and
we were completely alone. I felt frightened. 'Excuse me!' I said coldly,
and tried to get my hand free, but the lace of my sleeve caught in his
button. Bending down with his chest towards me, he began to disentangle it, and his ungloved fingers touched my hand. A feeling new
to me—half terror, half pleasure—ran like a shiver down my back. I
glanced at him to show by a cold look all the contempt I felt for him.
But my glance expressed not that—it expressed alarm and excitement. His glowing, moist eyes, close up to my very face, stared passionately at me, at my neck, at my bosom, both his hands fingered my
arm above the wrist, his open lips said something—said that he loved
me, that I was everything to him—and those lips were approaching
me, and those hands squeezed mine more tightly, and seemed to
burn me. A flame ran through my veins, a mist was before my eyes, I
shuddered, and the words with which I tried to stop him died away
in my throat. Suddenly I felt a kiss on my cheek, and all chill and
shivering I stopped and looked at him. Incapable of either speaking
or moving, I stood in terror, expecting and desiring something. It all
lasted for one moment. But that moment was awful! I saw the whole
of him so completely at that moment. I understood his face so thoroughly; under the straw hat, that steep, low brow, so like my husband's, that handsome straight nose with dilated nostrils, those long

moustaches and little beard waxed into points, those smooth shaven cheeks and sunburnt neck. I hated, I feared him—he belonged to a different world. But at that moment something in me responded so intensely to the excitement and passion of that hated alien man. Such an insuperable longing was in me to abandon myself to the kisses of that coarse and handsome mouth, to the embraces of those white hands with delicate veins and rings on their fingers. Such a craving possessed me to fling myself headlong into the inviting abyss of forbidden pleasures that had suddenly opened at my feet.

'I'm so miserable,' I thought; 'let more and more misery gather about me.'

He put one arm about me, and bent down to my face.

'Let more and more shame and sin be heaped up on my head.'

'Je vous aime,' he whispered, in the voice which was so like my husband's voice. It brought back to me my husband and child, beings so long precious to me, with whom now all was over. But suddenly at that moment L. M., out of sight round the turn in the road, called to me. I came to myself, tore my hand away, and not looking at him almost ran after L. M. We got into the carriage, and only then I glanced at him. He took off his hat and asked me something, smiling. He had no notion of the unutterable loathing I was feeling for him at that instant.

My life seemed to me so miserable, the future so hopeless, the past so black. L. M. talked to me, but I did not take in what she said. It seemed to me that she was talking to me simply from pity, to conceal the contempt I aroused in her. In every word, in every look, I seemed to detect that contempt and insulting pity. The kiss burnt my cheek with shame, and the thought of my husband and child was more than I could bear. I had hoped to think over my position when I was alone in my room, but I was afraid to be alone. I did not drink the tea they brought me; and, not knowing why I did so, began at once with feverish haste to get ready for the evening train to go to Heidelberg to my husband. When I was sitting with my maid in an empty carriage, when the engine had started and the fresh air blew on me from the window, I began to recover my self-possession, and to picture my past and my future more clearly. All my married life from the day when we moved to Petersburg suddenly presented itself to me in a new light, and lay like a reproach on my conscience. For the first time I vividly recalled our early days together in the country, our plans; for the first time it occurred to me to ask, 'What had been his joys all this time?' And I felt that I had wronged him. 'But why didn't he stop me? Why was he hypocritical with me? Why did he avoid frank discussion? Why did he humiliate me ?' I asked myself. 'Why did he not use all the power love gave him over me? Or did he not love me?' But however he might be to blame, a stranger's kiss lay on my cheek, and I felt it. The nearer I got to Heidelberg, the more definitely I imagined my husband, and the more terrible did the approaching interview with him seem to me. 'I will tell him all, all; I will wipe out all with tears of repentance,' I thought, 'and he will forgive me.' But I could not have said what was the 'all' I would tell him, and I did not believe myself that he would forgive me.

But as soon as I went into the room to my husband, and saw his tranquil, though surprised, face, I felt that I had nothing to tell him, nothing to confess, and nothing to ask his forgiveness for. My grief and remorse must remain locked up within me.

'What fancy is this?' he said. 'Why, I meant to come to you tomorrow.' But looking more closely into my face, he seemed alarmed. 'What is it? what's the matter?' he said.

'Nothing,' I answered, hardly able to restrain my tears. 'I've come for good. Let's start tomorrow for Russia.'

He bent a rather long, silent, and intent look upon me.

'But tell me what has happened to you?' he said.

I could not help blushing and dropping my eyes. In his eyes there was a gleam of mortification and anger. I was dismayed at the ideas that might occur to him; and with a ready hypocrisy I had never expected of myself, I said—

'Nothing has happened, simply I felt dull and depressed alone, and I have been thinking a great deal of our life and of you. For such a long time I have been to blame towards you! Why should you come out here with me, where you've no wish to be? I've long been to blame in my behaviour to you,' I repeated, and again tears came into my eyes. 'Let us go back to the country and stay there for ever.'

'Oh, my dear, spare me sentimental scenes,' he said coldly. 'So far as wanting to go back to the country goes, it's a good thing indeed, for our money's running short; but your "for ever's" a dream. I know you won't stay long. Now drink some tea, and you'll feel better,' he concluded, getting up to ring for the waiter.

I imagined all he might be thinking of me, and I was humiliated at the fearful thought I ascribed to him, as I met his incredulous, and, as it were, shame-stricken eyes fixed upon me. No, he cannot and will not understand me! I said I would go and have a look at the baby, and went out of the room. I longed to be alone and to weep and weep and weep.

IX

The Nikolskoe house, so long empty and unwarmed, was full of life again, but not so those who lived in it. My mother-in-law was no more, and we were alone face to face with each other. But now we were far from wanting solitude; it was a constraint to us indeed. The winter was all the worse for me from my being unwell; and I only recovered my health, indeed, after the birth of my second son. My relations with my husband continued to be the same cold, friendly relations as during our life in town. But in the country every board, every wall, every sofa recalled to me what he had been to me, and what I had lost. It was as if an unforgiven injury lay between us, as though he were punishing me for something, and affecting to be himself unaware of it. There was nothing to beg forgiveness for, nothing to ask for mercy from; he punished me simply by not giving me up all himself, all his soul as before. But to no one, to nothing did he give it, as though he had it not. Sometimes it occurred to me that he was only pretending to be like this to torment me; that the old feeling was still living in him, and I tried to evoke it. But every time he seemed to shun frankness, as though he suspected me of affectation and dreaded all sentiment as ludicrous. His look and tone said: 'I know it all; I know it all—no need to talk about it; and all you want to say I know too. And I know, too, that you say one thing and do another.' At first I was offended by this avoidance of openness, but afterward I got used to think that it was not the fear of openness, but the absence of the desire for openness. I could not easily bring my tongue now to tell him that I loved him, or to ask him to read the prayers with me, or to invite him to listen while I played. One could feel the existence of certain settled stipulations of propriety between us now. We lived each our separate life; he with his pursuits, in which I had no need and no desire now to share; I with my idleness, which did not vex or grieve him now as before. The children were too little, and could not as yet be a bond between us.

But spring came. Katya and Sonya had come for the summer to the country, alterations were to be made in the house at Nikolskoe, and we removed to Pokrovskoe. The old house was just the same, with its verandah, its folding table and piano in the bright hall, and my old room, with its white curtains and dreams of girlhood, that seemed left forgotten in that house. In that room there were two beds—one, in old days mine, in which my fat little Kokosha lay when I made the sign of the cross over him in the evenings, while in the other, a little one, Vanya's little face peeped out of his nightclothes. After signing them with the cross, I often used to stand still in the middle of the quiet room; and all at once, from every corner, from the walls, from the curtains, there rose up the old forgotten visions of youth. The old voices of the songs of girlhood began singing again. And where were those visions? What had become of those sweet, tender songs? All had come to pass that I had scarcely dared to hope for. The vague dreams melting into one another had become reality, and the reality had become a dreary, difficult, and joyless life. And everything was the same; the same garden one could see from the window, the same path, the same seat out there above the ravine, the same nightingale's songs floating in from near the pond, the same lilac in full flower, and the same moon over our house—and yet all so terribly, so incredibly changed! Everything so cold that might be so precious and so near one's heart! Just as in old days, sitting in the drawing-room, Katya and I, we talk softly together, and we talk of him. But Katya is yellow and wrinkled, her eyes do not sparkle with joy and hope, but express sympathetic distress and commiseration. We do not sing his praises as we did of old, we criticise him; we don't wonder what we have done to be so happy; nor long, as of old, to tell all the world what we think. Like conspirators, we whisper to one another, and ask each other for the hundredth time, Why has it all changed so sadly? And he is still the same, except that the line is deeper between his brows, and there is more grey hair about his temples; but the profound, intense look in his eyes is clouded over for ever from me. I, too, am still the same, but I have no love nor the desire of love, no longing for work, nor content with myself. And so remote and impossible seemed to me now my old religious ecstasies, my old love for him, and my old intense life, I could not have understood now what had once seemed so dear and right to me—the happiness of living for others. Why for others, when one did not care even to live for oneself?

I had completely given up music ever since we moved to Petersburg; but now the old piano, the old music-books were a refuge for me again.

One day I was not well, I stopped at home alone; Katya and Sonya had driven with him to Nikolskoe to look at the new building there. The table was set for tea, I went down, and while waiting for them sat down to the piano. I opened the sonata *quasi una fantasia*, and began playing it. No one was within sight or hearing, the windows were open into the garden, and the familiar, majestically melancholy music resounded in the room. I finished the first part, and quite unconsciously, from old habit, looked round to the corner in which he used once to sit listening to me. But he was not there. The chair, long unmoved, stood in the corner; and past the open window I could see the lilac in the bright sunset, and the evening freshness flowed into the room. I leaned my elbows on the piano, hid my face in both hands, and pondered. I sat a long while so, with a heartache recalling all the past that could not come back, and timidly considering what was to come. But before me it seemed that there was nothing; it seemed that I desired nothing and hoped for nothing. 'Can I have lived out my life?' I thought with horror; and lifting my head, I tried to forget myself, to escape thinking by playing again, and began again the same andante. 'My God!' I thought, 'forgive me, if I am in fault, or restore me what was once so good in my soul, and teach me what to do, how to live now!' The sound of wheels over the grass and at the entrance reached me, and familiar steps could be heard stepping cautiously in the verandah and ceasing. But the old feeling did not stir in response to those familiar footsteps. When I had finished, I heard the steps behind me, and a hand was laid on my shoulder.

'What a clever girl you are to play that sonata!' he said.

I did not speak.

'Have you had tea?'

I shook my head, and did not look round at him for fear of betraying the traces of emotion left on my face.

'They'll be here directly; the horse was too fresh, and they've come on foot from the highroad,' he said.

'Let's wait for them,' I said, and went out into the verandah, hoping he would come after me; but he asked after the children and went up to them. Again his presence, his simple, kindly voice made me doubt whether anything had been lost by me. 'What more could I desire? He's kind and gentle, he's a good father, and I don't know myself what more I want.' I went out on the balcony and sat under the verandah awning on the very seat on which I had sat on the day of our avowal of love to one another. The sun had set now; it was beginning to get dusk; and one of the dark rainclouds of springtime was hanging over the house and garden. Only through the trees could be seen the clear rim of the sky with the fading glow and the evening star beginning to shine. Over all hung the shadow of a transparent cloud, and everything seemed waiting for a gentle spring shower. The wind had dropped; not one leaf, not one blade of grass was stirring; the scent of the lilac and the wild cherry, strong as though all the air were in flower, hovered over the garden and verandah suddenly in gusts growing fainter, and intenser, so that one wanted to close one's eyes and see nothing, hear nothing, shutting out everything but this sweet fragrance. The dahlias and the rosebushes, not yet in flower, stood immovably erect on their well-dug black bed as though they were slowly growing upwards on their white-shaved sticks. In piercing chorus the frogs croaked with all their might from the ravine, as though for the last time before the rain which would drive them to the water. The single continuous sound of water rose above their harsh croak. The nightingales called at intervals, and one could hear them flitting in alarm from spot to spot. Again this spring a nightingale was building in a bush under the window; and when I came out, I heard him fly away to the avenue, and there utter one note; then he ceased, waiting too.

In vain I tried to be calm, and waited and grieved for something. He came back from upstairs and sat down beside me.

'I think they'll get wet,' he said.

'Yes,' I assented, and we were both for a long while silent.

The cloud sank lower and lower in the windless sky; everything became more hushed, more fragrant, and more still; and all at once a drop fell and, as it were, leaped up again on the sailcloth awning of the verandah, another splashed on the gravel of the path, there was a patter on the burdocks, and the fresh rain began falling more heavily in big drops. The nightingales and the frogs were quite silent, only the thin sound of water, though it seemed further off through the rain, still persisted; and some bird hidden in the dry leaves, probably near the verandah, repeated regularly its monotonous two notes. He got up, and was about to go away.

'Where are you going?' I asked, detaining him. 'It's so nice here.'

'I meant to send them an umbrella and goloshes,' he said.

'There's no need; it will soon be over.' He agreed with me, and we remained together by the verandah balustrade. I rested my arm on the slippery, wet rail and put my head out. The fresh rain pattered unevenly on my hair and neck. The cloud, getting lighter and thinner, was passing over us; the even patter of the rain changed into drops, dripping irregularly from above and from the leaves. Again the frogs began croaking below, again the nightingales began to stir, and from the wet bushes called to one another from one side and then from the other. All the sky was clear again in front of us.

'How nice it is!' he said, sitting near me on the balustrade, and passing his hand over my wet hair.

This simple caress affected me like a reproach. I wanted to cry.

'And what more can a man want?' he said. 'I am so contented now that I want nothing; perfectly happy!'

'That was not how you used once to speak of your happiness!' I thought. 'However great it was, you used to say that you always wanted more and more. But now you are satisfied and content, while my heart is full as it were of unuttered repentance and unshed tears.'

'And I feel it's nice,' I said; 'but I'm sad just from it's all being so nice before my eyes. It's all so disconnected, so incomplete in me, there's a continual longing for something, though it's so peaceful and happy here. Surely you too have a sort of melancholy mingling in your enjoyment of nature, as though you longed for some thing of the past?'

He took his hand from my head and was silent for a while.

'Yes, it used to be so with me, particularly in the spring,' he said, as though recalling it. 'And I used to sit up the whole night too, long-ing and hoping, and happy nights they were! . . . But then everything was in the future, and now it's all behind; now what is, is enough for me, and I find it splendid,' he concluded, with such convincing carelessness, that painful as it was to hear it, the belief forced itself on me that he was speaking the truth.

'And is there nothing you wish for?' I asked.

'Nothing impossible,' he answered, guessing my feeling. 'See, you're getting your head wet,' he added, once more passing his hand over my hair as though caressing a child; 'you envy the leaves and the grass for the rain wetting them; you would like to be the grass and the leaves and the rain; while I merely rejoice in them, as I do in everything in the world that is good and young and happy.'

'And do you regret nothing of the past?' I went on questioning, feeling that my heart was growing heavier and heavier.

He pondered and was silent again. I saw that he wanted to answer quite sincerely.

'No!' he answered briefly.

'Not true, not true!' I said, turning to him and looking into his eyes. 'You don't regret the past?'

'No,' he repeated once more. 'I am thankful for it, but I don't regret the past.'

'Do you mean to say you would not desire to have it back?' I said.

He turned and began looking into the garden.

'I don't desire it, as I don't desire to have wings,' he said. 'It's impossible!'

'And would you not correct the past; don't you reproach yourself or me?'

'Never! All has been for the best.'

'Listen!' I said, touching his arm to make him look round at me. 'Listen: why did you never tell me that you wanted me to live just as you did want me to? Why did you give me a freedom I did not know how to use? Why did you give up teaching me? If you had cared, if you had managed me differently, nothing, nothing would have happened!' I said in a voice more and more intensely expressive of cold anger and reproach, and not the love of old days.

'What wouldn't have happened?' he said in surprise, turning to me; 'why nothing did, as it is. All's well. Very well!' he added, smiling.

'Can it be he does not understand, or, worse still, doesn't want to understand?' I thought, and tears came into my eyes.

'It wouldn't have happened that though I have done you no

wrong, I am punished by your indifference, your contempt even!' I burst out suddenly. 'It wouldn't have happened that for no fault of mine you took away from me all that was precious to me.'

'What do you mean, my dear?' he said, as though not understanding what I was saying.

'No, let me speak. . . . You took away from me your confidence, your love, your respect even, because I don't believe that you love me now after what it was in old days. No; I want to have out once for all what has been making me miserable a long while,' I said, preventing his speaking again. 'Was it my fault that I knew nothing of life, and you left me to find it out alone? . . . Is it my fault that now when of myself I have come to see what is essential, when for nearly a year I've been struggling to get back to you—you repel me as though not understanding what I want, and all in such a way that it's impossible to reproach you while I'm either to blame or unhappy? Yes, you want to fling me back into that life, which might well make the misery of us both.'

'But in what way have I shown you that?' he asked, in genuine dismay and surprise.

'Didn't you only yesterday say, and you're for ever saying that I can't stand being here, and that we shall have to go back for the winter to Petersburg, which is hateful to me?' I went on. 'Instead of being a support to me, you avoid all frank speech, any sincere tender word with me. And then when I fall utterly, you will reproach me and rejoice at my fall.'

'Stop, stop!' he said sternly and coldly; 'that's wrong what you're saying now. That only proves that you feel ill will against me, that you do not——'

'That I don't love you? . . . Say it, say it!' I completed his sentence, and tears streamed from my eyes. I sat down on the seat and hid my face in my handkerchief.

'This is how he understands me!' I thought, trying to restrain the sobs that choked me. 'Our old love is over, over!' a voice said in my heart. He did not come to me, did not comfort me. He was offended by what I had said. His voice was dry and composed.

'I don't know what it is you reproach me with,' he began; 'if it is that I don't love you as once I did' . . .

'Did love!' I exclaimed in the handkerchief, and the bitter tears streamed more violently into it.

'Time is to blame for that and we ourselves. Each stage has its love.' He paused. 'And shall I tell you the whole truth if you desire frank speech? . . . Just as that year when I got to know you I spent sleepless nights thinking of you and created my love for myself, and that love grew and grew in my heart, in the same way in Petersburg and abroad I spent awful nights without sleep, and crushed, tore to shreds, that love that was my torture. I did not crush it, but only what tortured me. I found peace, and still I love you, but with a different love.'

'Yes, you call it love, but it's a torture!' I said. 'Why did you let me go into society if you thought it so harmful that you lost your love for me on account of it?'

'It was not society, my dear!' he said.

'Why didn't you use your authority?' I went on. 'Why didn't you tie me up, kill me? It would have been better for me now than to be deprived of all that made my happiness. I should be happy, I shouldn't be ashamed.'

I sobbed again, and hid my face.

At that moment Katya and Sonya, wet and good-humoured, came into the verandah, loudly chattering and laughing; but seeing us, they were quiet, and at once went in.

We sat a long while silent when they had gone; I wept away my tears, and felt better. I glanced at him. He was sitting with his head propped in his hands, and he wanted to say something in response to my look, but he only sighed heavily, and again leaned on his elbow. I went up to him and took away his hand. His eyes rested dreamily upon me.

'Yes,' he began, as though going on with his thoughts. 'All of us, especially you women, have to go for themselves through all the non-sense of life to come back to life itself; they can't believe any one else. You were far then from having got through all that sweet charming nonsense, which I used to admire as I watched you, and I left you to get through it, and felt that I had no right to hinder you, though for me that time had long gone by.'

'Why did you live through it with me and let me live through that nonsense if you loved me?' I said.

'Because you would have tried, but would not have been able, to believe me; you had to find out for yourself . . . and you have found it out.'

'You reasoned, you reasoned much,' said I. 'You loved little.'

Again we were silent.

'That's cruel what you said just now, but it's the truth!' he said suddenly, getting up and walking about the verandah. 'Yes, it's the truth. I was to blame,' he added, stopping opposite me. 'Either I ought not to have let myself love you at all, or I ought to have loved you more simply, yes!'

'Let us forget it all . . .' I said timidly.

'No, what's past will not come back, one can never bring it back!' and his voice softened as he said this.

'Everything has returned now . . .' I said, laying my hand on his shoulder.

He took my hand away and pressed it.

'No; it was not true when I said I did not regret the past. No, I do regret it, I weep for our past love—love which is no more, and can never come again. Who is to blame for it, I don't know. Love is left, but not the same; its place is left, but it is all wasted away; there is no strength and substance in it, there are left memories and gratitude, but——'

'Don't say so!' I interrupted. 'Let it all be again as it was before. . . . It can be, can't it?' I asked, looking into his eyes. But his eyes were clear and untroubled, and they did not look deeply into mine. At the moment I was saying it, I felt that what I desired and asked him about was impossible. He smiled a quiet, gentle, as it seemed to me, elderly smile.

'How young you are still, and I am so old!' he said. 'There is not in me what you are looking for. . . . Why deceive ourselves?' he added, still with the same smile.

I stood mutely beside him, and there was greater peace in my heart.

'Don't let us try to repeat life,' he went on; 'we won't lie to ourselves. And that we are rid of the heartaches and emotions of old days, thank God indeed! We have no need to seek and be troubled. We have found what we sought, and happiness enough has fallen to our lot. It's time now for us to stand aside and make way, see, for this person!' he said, pointing to Vanya, in the arms of the nurse, who was standing at the verandah doors. 'That's so, dear one,' he ended, drawing my head to him and kissing it. It was not a lover, but an old friend kissing me. And from the garden the fragrant freshness of the night rose sweeter and stronger, the night sounds and stillness grew more and more solemn, and the stars thronged more thickly in the sky. I looked at him, and there was a sudden sense of ease in my soul, as though that sick moral nerve which made me suffer had been removed. All at once I felt clearly and calmly that the feeling of that time had gone never to return, like the time itself, and that to bring it back now would be not only impossible, but painful and forced. And indeed was that time so good which seemed to me so happy? And it was all so long, so long ago!

'It's time for tea though!' he said, and we went together into the drawing-room. At the door we met again the nurse and Vanya. I took the baby into my arms, covered his bare red little toes, hugged him to me and kissed him, just touching him with my lips. He moved his little hand with outspread wrinkled fingers, as though in his sleep, and opened vague eyes, as though seeking or recalling something. Suddenly those little eyes rested on me, a spark of intelligence flashed in them, the full pouting lips began to work, and parted in a smile. 'Mine, mine, mine!' I thought, with a blissful tension in all my limbs, pressing him to my bosom, and with an effort restraining myself from hurting him.

And I began kissing his little cold feet, his little stomach, his hand and his little head, scarcely covered with soft hair. My husband came up to me; I quickly covered the child's face and uncovered it again.

'Ivan Sergeich!' said my husband, chucking him under the chin. But quickly I hid Ivan Sergeich again. No one but I was to look at him for long. I glanced at my husband, his eyes laughed as he watched me, and for the first time for a long while it was easy and sweet to me to look into them.

With that day ended my love-story with my husband, the old feeling became a precious memory never to return; but the new feeling of love for my children and the father of my children laid the foundation of another life, happy in quite a different way, which I am still living up to the present moment.

1859.

THE DEATH
OF IVAN ILYCH

I

Inside the great building of the Law Courts, during the interval in the hearing of the Melvinsky case, the members of the judicial council and the public prosecutor were gathered together in the private room of Ivan Yegorovich Shebek, and the conversation turned upon the celebrated Krasovsky case. Fyodor Vasilievich hotly maintained that the case was not in the jurisdiction of the court. Yegor Ivanovich stood up for his own view; but from the first Pyotr Ivanovich, who had not entered into the discussion, took no interest in it, but was looking through the newspapers which had just been brought in.

'Gentlemen!' he said, 'Ivan Ilych is dead!'

'You don't say so!'

'Here, read it,' he said to Fyodor Vasilievich, handing him the fresh still damp-smelling paper.

Within a black margin was printed: 'Praskovya Fyodorovna Golovin with heartfelt affliction informs friends and relatives of the decease of her beloved husband, member of the Court of Justice, Ivan Ilych Golovin, who passed away on the 4th of February. The funeral will take place on Thursday at one o'clock.'

Ivan Ilych was a colleague of the gentlemen present, and all liked him. It was some weeks now since he had been taken ill; his illness had been said to be incurable. His post had been kept open for him, but it had been thought that in case of his death Alexyeev might receive his appointment, and either Vinnikov or Shtabel would succeed to Alexyeev's. So that on hearing of Ivan Ilych's death, the first thought of each of the gentlemen in the room was of the effect this death might have on the transfer or promotion of themselves or their friends.

'Now I am sure of getting Shtabel's place or Vinnikov's,' thought Fyodor Vasilievich. 'It was promised me long ago, and the promotion means eight hundred roubles additional income, besides the grants for office expenses.'

'Now I shall have to petition for my brother-in-law to be transferred from Kaluga,' thought Pyotr Ivanovich. 'My wife will be very glad. She won't be able to say now that I've never done anything for her family.'

'I thought somehow that he'd never get up from his bed again,' Pyotr Ivanovich said aloud. 'I'm sorry!'

'But what was it exactly that was wrong with him?'

'The doctors could not decide. That's to say, they did decide, but differently. When I saw him last, I thought he would get over it.'

'Well, I positively haven't called there ever since the holidays. I've kept meaning to go.'

'Had he any property?'

'I think there's something, very small, of his wife's. But something quite trifling.'

'Yes, one will have to go and call. They live such a terribly long way off.'

'A long way from you, you mean. Everything's a long way from your place.'

'There, he can never forgive me for living the other side of the river,' said Pyotr Ivanovich, smiling at Shebek. And they began to talk of the great distances between different parts of the town, and went back into the court.

Besides the reflections upon the changes and promotions in the service likely to ensue from this death, the very fact of the death of an intimate acquaintance excited in every one who heard of it, as such a fact always does, a feeling of relief that 'it is he that is dead, and not I.'

'Only think! he is dead, but here am I all right,' each one thought or felt. The more intimate acquaintances, the so-called friends of Ivan Ilych, could not help thinking too that now they had the exceedingly tiresome social duties to perform of going to the funeral service and paying the widow a visit of condolence.

The most intimately acquainted with their late colleague were Fyodor Vasilievich and Pyotr Ivanovich.

Pyotr Ivanovich had been a comrade of his at the school of jurisprudence, and considered himself under obligations to Ivan Ilych.

Telling his wife at dinner of the news of Ivan Ilych's death and his reflections as to the possibility of getting her brother transferred into their circuit, Pyotr Ivanovich, without lying down for his usual nap, put on his frockcoat and drove to Ivan Ilych's.

At the entrance before Ivan Ilych's flat stood a carriage and two hired flies. Downstairs in the entry near the hat-stand there was leaning against the wall a coffin-lid with tassels and braiding freshly rubbed up with pipeclay. Two ladies were taking off their cloaks. One of them he knew, the sister of Ivan Ilych; the other was a lady he did not know. Pyotr Ivanovich's colleague, Shvarts, was coming down; and from the top stair, seeing who it was coming in, he stopped and winked at him, as though to say: 'Ivan Ilych has made a mess of it; it's a very different matter with you and me.'

Shvarts's face, with his English whiskers and all his thin figure in his frockcoat, had, as it always had, an air of elegant solemnity; and this solemnity, always such a contrast to Shvarts's playful character, had a special piquancy here. So thought Pyotr Ivanovich.

Pyotr Ivanovich let the ladies pass on in front of him, and walked slowly up the stairs after them. Shvarts had not come down, but was waiting at the top. Pyotr Ivanovich knew what for; he wanted obviously to settle with him where their game of 'bridge' was to be that evening.[1] The ladies went up to the widow's room; while Shvarts, with his lips tightly and gravely shut, and amusement in his eyes, with a twitch of his eyebrows motioned Pyotr Ivanovich to the right, to the room where the dead man was.

Pyotr Ivanovich went in, as people always do on such occasions, in uncertainty as to what he would have to do there. One thing he felt sure of—that crossing oneself never comes amiss on such occasions. As to whether it was necessary to bow down while doing so, he did not feel quite sure, and so chose a middle course. On entering the room he began crossing himself, and made a slight sort of bow. So far as the movements of his hands and head permitted him, he glanced while doing so about the room. Two young men, one a high school boy, nephews probably, were going out of the room, crossing themselves. An old lady was standing motionless; and a lady, with her eyebrows queerly lifted, was saying something to her in a whisper. A deacon in a frockcoat, resolute and hearty, was reading something aloud with an expression that precluded all possibility of contradiction. A young peasant who used to wait at table, Gerasim, walking with light footsteps in front of Pyotr Ivanovich, was sprinkling something on the floor. Seeing this, Pyotr Ivanovich was at once aware of the faint odour of the decomposing corpse. On his last visit to Ivan Ilych Pyotr Ivanovich had seen this peasant in his room; he was performing the duties of a sicknurse, and Ivan Ilych liked him particularly. Pyotr Ivanovich continued crossing himself and bowing in a direction intermediate between the coffin, the deacon, and the holy pictures on the table in the corner. Then when this action of making the sign of the cross with his hand seemed to him to have been unduly prolonged, he stood still and began to scrutinise the dead man.

The dead man lay, as dead men always do lie, in a peculiarly heavy dead way, his stiffened limbs sunk in the cushions of the coffin, and his head bent back for ever on the pillow, and thrust up, as dead men always do, his yellow waxen forehead with bald spots on the sunken temples, and his nose that stood out sharply and as it were squeezed on the upper lip. He was much changed, even thinner since Pyotr Ivanovich had seen him, but his face—as always with the dead—was more handsome, and, above all, more impressive than it had been when he was alive. On the face was an expression of what had to be done having been done, and rightly done. Besides this, there was too in that expression a reproach or a reminder for the living. This reminder seemed to Pyotr Ivanovich, uncalled for, or, at least, to have nothing to do with him. He felt something unpleasant; and so Pyotr Ivanovich once more crossed himself hurriedly, and, as it struck him, too hurriedly, not quite in accordance with the proprieties, turned and went to the door. Shvarts was waiting for him in the adjoining room, standing with his legs apart and both hands behind his back playing with his top hat. A single glance at the playful, sleek, and elegant figure of Shvarts revived Pyotr Ivanovich. He felt that he, Shvarts, was above it, and would not give way to depressing impressions. The mere sight of him said plainly: the incident of the service over the body of Ivan Ilych cannot possibly constitute a sufficient ground for recognising the business of the session suspended,—in other words, in no way can it hinder us from shuffling and cutting a pack of cards this evening, while the footman sets four unsanctified candles on the table for us; in fact, there is no ground for supposing that this incident could prevent us from spending the evening agreeably. He said as much indeed to Pyotr Ivanovich as he came out, proposing that the party should meet at Fyodor Vasilievich's. But apparently it was Pyotr Ivanovich's destiny not to play 'bridge' that evening. Praskovya Fyodorovna, a short, fat woman who, in spite of all efforts in a contrary direction, was steadily broader from her shoulders downwards, all in black, with lace on her head and her eyebrows as queerly arched as the lady standing beside the coffin, came out of her own apartments with some other ladies, and conducting them to the dead man's room, said: 'The service will take place immediately; come in.'

Shvarts, making an indefinite bow, stood still, obviously neither accepting nor declining this invitation. Praskovya Fyodorovna, recognising Pyotr Ivanovich, sighed, went right up to him, took his hand, and said, 'I know that you were a true friend of Ivan Ilych's . . .' and looked at him, expecting from him the suitable action in response to these words. Pyotr Ivanovich knew that, just as before he had to cross himself, now what he had to do was to press her hand, to sigh and to say, 'Ah, I was indeed!' And he did so. And as he did so, he felt that the desired result had been attained; that he was touched, and she was touched.

'Come, since it's not begun yet, I have something I want to say to you,' said the widow. 'Give me your arm.'

Pyotr Ivanovich gave her his arm, and they moved towards the inner rooms, passing Shvarts, who winked gloomily at Pyotr Ivanovich.

'So much for our "bridge"! Don't complain if we find another partner. You can make a fifth when you do get away,' said his humorous glance.

Pyotr Ivanovich sighed still more deeply and despondently, and Praskovya Fyodorovna pressed his hand gratefully. Going into her drawing-room, that was upholstered with pink cretonne and lighted by a dismal-looking lamp, they sat down at the table, she on a sofa and Pyotr Ivanovich on a low ottoman with deranged springs which yielded spasmodically under his weight. Praskovya Fyodorovna was about to warn him to sit on another seat, but felt such a recommendation out of keeping with her position, and changed her mind. Sitting down on the ottoman, Pyotr Ivanovich remembered how Ivan Ilych had arranged this drawing-room, and had consulted him about this very pink cretonne with green leaves. Seating herself on the sofa, and pushing by the table (the whole drawing-room was crowded with furniture and things), the widow caught the lace of her black fichu in the carving of the table. Pyotr Ivanovich got up to disentangle it for her; and the ottoman, freed from his weight, began bobbing up spasmodically under him. The widow began unhooking her lace herself, and Pyotr Ivanovich again sat down, suppressing the mutinous ottoman springs under him. But the widow could not quite free herself, and Pyotr Ivanovich rose again, and again the ottoman became mutinous and popped up with a positive snap. When this was all over, she took out a clean cambric handkerchief and began weeping. Pyotr Ivanovich had been chilled off by the incident with the lace and the struggle with the ottoman springs, and he sat looking sullen. This awkward position was cut short by the entrance of Sokolov, Ivan Ilych's butler, who came in to announce that the place in the cemetery fixed on by Praskovya Fyodorovna would cost two hundred roubles. She left off weeping, and with the air of a victim glancing at Pyotr Ivanovich, said in French that it was very terrible for her. Pyotr Ivanovich made a silent gesture signifying his unhesitating conviction that it must indeed be so.

'Please, smoke,' she said in a magnanimous, and at the same time, crushed voice, and she began discussing with Sokolov the question of the price of the site for the grave.

Pyotr Ivanovich, lighting a cigarette, listened to her very circumstantial inquiries as to the various prices of sites and her decision as to the one to be selected. Having settled on the site for the grave, she made arrangements also about the choristers. Sokolov went away.

'I see to everything myself,' she said to Pyotr Ivanovich, moving on one side the albums that lay on the table; and noticing that the table was in danger from the cigarette-ash, she promptly passed an ashtray to Pyotr Ivanovich, and said: 'I consider it affectation to pretend that my grief prevents me from looking after practical matters. On the contrary, if anything could—not console me . . . but distract me, it is seeing after everything for him.' She took out her handkerchief again, as though preparing to weep again; and suddenly, as though struggling with herself, she shook herself, and began speaking calmly: 'But I've business to talk about with you.'

Pyotr Ivanovich bowed, carefully keeping in check the springs of the ottoman, which had at once begun quivering under him.

'The last few days his sufferings were awful.'

'Did he suffer very much?' asked Pyotr Ivanovich.

'Oh, awfully! For the last moments, hours indeed, he never left off screaming. For three days and nights in succession he screamed incessantly. It was insufferable. I can't understand how I bore it; one could hear it through three closed doors. Ah, what I suffered!'

'And was he really conscious?' asked Pyotr Ivanovich.

'Yes,' she whispered, 'up to the last minute. He said good-bye to us a quarter of an hour before his death, and asked Volodya to be taken away too.'

The thought of the sufferings of a man he had known so intimately, at first as a light-hearted boy, a schoolboy, then grown up as a partner at whist, in spite of the unpleasant consciousness of his own and this woman's hypocrisy, suddenly horrified Pyotr Ivanovich. He saw again that forehead, the nose that seemed squeezing the lip, and he felt frightened for himself. 'Three days and nights of awful suffering and death. Why, that may at once, any minute, come upon me too,' he thought, and he felt for an instant terrified. But immediately, he could not himself have said how, there came to his support the customary reflection that this had happened to Ivan Ilych and not to him, and that to him this must not and could not happen; that in thinking thus he was giving way to depression, which was not the right thing to do, as was evident from Shvarts's expression of face. And making these reflections, Pyotr Ivanovich felt reassured, and began with interest inquiring details about Ivan Ilych's end, as though death were a mischance peculiar to Ivan Ilych, but not at all incidental to himself.

After various observations about the details of the truly awful physical sufferings endured by Ivan Ilych (these details Pyotr Ivanovich learned only through the effect Ivan Ilych's agonies had had on the nerves of Praskovya Fyodorovna), the widow apparently thought it time to get to business.

'Ah, Pyotr Ivanovich, how hard it is, how awfully, awfully hard!' and she began to cry again.

Pyotr Ivanovich sighed, and waited for her to blow her nose. When she had done so, he said, 'Indeed it is,' and again she began to talk, and brought out what was evidently the business she wished to discuss with him; that business consisted in the inquiry as to how on the occasion of her husband's death she was to obtain a grant from the government. She made a show of asking Pyotr Ivanovich's advice about a pension. But he perceived that she knew already to the minutest details, what he did not know himself indeed, everything that could be got out of the government on the ground of this death; but that what she wanted to find out was, whether there were not any means of obtaining a little more? Pyotr Ivanovich tried to imagine such means; but after pondering a little, and out of politeness abusing the government for its stinginess, he said that he believed that it was impossible to obtain more. Then she sighed and began unmistakably looking about for an excuse for getting rid of her visitor. He perceived this, put out his cigarette, got up, pressed her hand, and went out into the passage.

In the dining-room, where was the bric-à-brac clock that Ivan Ilych had been so delighted at buying, Pyotr Ivanovich met the priest and several people he knew who had come to the service for the dead, and saw too Ivan Ilych's daughter, a handsome young lady. She was all in black. Her very slender figure looked even slenderer than usual. She had a gloomy, determined, almost wrathful expression. She bowed to Pyotr Ivanovich as though he were to blame in some way. Behind the daughter, with the same offended air on his face, stood a rich young man, whom Pyotr Ivanovich knew too, an examining magistrate, the young lady's fiancé, as he had heard. He bowed dejectedly to him, and would have gone on into the dead man's room, when from the staircase there appeared the figure of the son, the high school boy, extraordinarily like Ivan Ilych. He was the little Ivan Ilych over again as Pyotr Ivanovich remembered him at school. His eyes were red with crying, and had that look often seen in unclean boys of thirteen or fourteen. The boy, seeing Pyotr Ivanovich, scowled morosely and bashfully. Pyotr Ivanovich nodded to him and went into the dead man's room. The service for the dead began—candles, groans, incense, tears, sobs. Pyotr Ivanovich stood frowning, staring at his feet in front of him. He did not once glance at the dead man, and right through to the end did not once give way to depressing influences, and was one of the first to walk out. In the hall there was no one. Gerasim, the young peasant, darted out of the dead man's room, tossed over with his strong hand all the fur cloaks to find Pyotr Ivanovich's, and gave it him.

'Well, Gerasim, my boy?' said Pyotr Ivanovich, so as to say something. 'A sad business, isn't it?'

'It's God's will. We shall come to the same,' said Gerasim, showing his white, even, peasant teeth in a smile, and, like a man in a rush of extra work, he briskly opened the door, called up the coachman, saw Pyotr Ivanovich into the carriage, and darted back to the steps as though bethinking himself of what he had to do next.

Pyotr Ivanovich had a special pleasure in the fresh air after the smell of incense, of the corpse, and of carbolic acid.

'Where to?' asked the coachman.

'It's not too late. I'll still go round to Fyodor Vasilievich's.'

And Pyotr Ivanovich drove there. And he did, in fact, find them just finishing the first rubber, so that he came just at the right time to take a hand.

II

The previous history of Ivan Ilych was the simplest, the most ordinary, and the most awful.

Ivan Ilych died at the age of forty-five, a member of the Judicial Council. He was the son of an official, whose career in Petersburg through various ministries and departments had been such as leads people into that position in which, though it is distinctly obvious that they are unfit to perform any kind of real duty, they yet cannot, owing to their long past service and their official rank, be dismissed;[2] and they therefore receive a specially created fictitious post, and by no means fictitious thousands—from six to ten—on which they go on living till extreme old age.

Such was the privy councillor, the superfluous member of various superfluous institutions, Ilya Efimovich Golovin.

He had three sons. Ivan Ilych was the second son. The eldest son's career was exactly like his father's, only in a different department, and he was by now close upon that stage in the service in which the same sinecure would be reached. The third son was the unsuccessful one. He had in various positions always made a mess of things, and was now employed in the railway department. And his father and his brothers, and still more their wives, did not merely dislike meeting

him, but avoided, except in extreme necessity, recollecting his existence. His sister had married Baron Greff, a Petersburg official of the
same stamp as his father-in-law. Ivan Ilych was le phénix de la famille,* as
people said. He was not so frigid and precise as the eldest son, nor so
wild as the youngest. He was the happy mean between them—a
shrewd, lively, pleasant, and well-bred man. He had been educated
with his younger brother at the school of jurisprudence. The younger
brother had not finished the school course, but was expelled when in
the fifth class. Ivan Ilych completed the course successfully. At school
he was just the same as he was later on all his life—an intelligent fellow, highly good-humoured and sociable, but strict in doing what he
considered to be his duty. His duty he considered whatever was so
considered by those persons who were set in authority over him. He
was not a toady as a boy, nor later on as a grown-up person; but from
his earliest years he was attracted, as a fly to the light, to persons of
good standing in the world, assimilated their manners and their
views of life, and established friendly relations with them. All the
enthusiasms of childhood and youth passed, leaving no great traces
in him; he gave way to sensuality and to vanity, and latterly when in
the higher classes at school to liberalism, but always keeping within
certain limits which were unfailingly marked out for him by his
instincts.

At school he had committed actions which had struck him beforehand as great vileness, and gave him a feeling of loathing for himself
at the very time he was committing them. But later on, perceiving
that such actions were committed also by men of good position, and
were not regarded by them as base, he was able, not to regard them
as good, but to forget about them completely, and was never mortified by recollections of them.

Leaving the school of jurisprudence in the tenth class, and receiving
from his father a sum of money for his outfit, Ivan Ilych ordered his
clothes at Sharmer's,† hung on his watch-chain a medallion inscribed
respice finem,‡ said good-bye to the prince who was the principal of his

---

*The phoenix of the family (French).
†A fashionable tailoring establishment in St. Petersburg.
‡Look toward the end (Latin).

school, had a farewell dinner with his comrades at Donon's,* and with all his new fashionable belongings—travelling trunk, linen, suits of clothes, shaving and toilet appurtenances, and travelling rug, all ordered and purchased at the very best shops—set off to take the post of secretary on special commissions for the governor of a province, a post which had been obtained for him by his father.

In the province Ivan Ilych without loss of time made himself a position as easy and agreeable as his position had been in the school of jurisprudence. He did his work, made his career, and at the same time led a life of well-bred social gaiety. Occasionally he visited various districts on official duty, behaved with dignity both with his superiors and his inferiors; and with exactitude and an incorruptible honesty of which he could not help feeling proud, performed the duties with which he was intrusted, principally having to do with the dissenters. When engaged in official work he was, in spite of his youth and taste for frivolous amusements, exceedingly reserved, official, and even severe. But in social life he was often amusing and witty, and always good-natured, well bred, and *bon enfant*,† as was said of him by his chief and his chief's wife, with whom he was like one of the family.

In the province there was, too, a connection with one of the ladies who obtruded their charms on the stylish young lawyer. There was a dressmaker, too, and there were drinking bouts with smart officers visiting the neighbourhood, and visits to a certain outlying street after supper; there was a rather cringing obsequiousness in his behaviour, too, with his chief, and even his chief's wife. But all this was accompanied with such a tone of the highest breeding, that it could not be called by harsh names; it all came under the rubric of the French saying, *Il faut que la jeunesse se passe*.‡ Everything was done with clean hands, in clean shirts, with French phrases, and, what was of most importance, in the highest society, and consequently with the approval of people of rank.

Such was Ivan Ilych's career for five years, and then came a change

---

*A fancy restaurant in St. Petersburg.
†A good fellow (French).
‡Youth must have its day (French).

in his official life. New methods of judicial procedure were established; new men were wanted to carry them out. And Ivan Ilych became such a new man. Ivan Ilych was offered the post of examining magistrate, and he accepted it in spite of the fact that this post was in another province, and he would have to break off all the ties he had formed and form new ones. Ivan Ilych's friends met together to see him off, had their photographs taken in a group, presented him with a silver cigarette-case, and he set off to his new post.

As an examining magistrate, Ivan Ilych was as *comme il faut*,* as well bred, as adroit in keeping official duties apart from private life, and as successful in gaining universal respect, as he had been as secretary of private commissions. The duties of his new office were in themselves of far greater interest and attractiveness for Ivan Ilych. In his former post it had been pleasant to pass in his smart uniform from Sharmer's through the crowd of petitioners and officials waiting timorously and envying him, and to march with his easy swagger straight into the governor's private room, there to sit down with him to tea and cigarettes. But the persons directly subject to his authority were few. The only such persons were the district police superintendents and the dissenters, when he was serving on special commissions. And he liked treating such persons affably, almost like comrades; liked to make them feel that he, able to annihilate them, was behaving in this simple, friendly way with them. But such people were then few in number. Now as an examining magistrate Ivan Ilych felt that every one—every one without exception—the most dignified, the most self-satisfied people, all were in his hands, and that he had but to write certain words on a sheet of paper with a printed heading, and this dignified self-satisfied person would be brought before him in the capacity of a defendant or a witness; and if he did not care to make him sit down, he would have to stand up before him and answer his questions. Ivan Ilych never abused this authority of his; on the contrary, he tried to soften the expression of it. But the consciousness of this power and the possibility of softening its effect constituted for him the chief interest and attractiveness of his new position. In the work itself, in the preliminary inquiries, that is, Ivan

---

*Proper (French).

Ilych very rapidly acquired the art of setting aside every consideration irrelevant to the official aspect of the case, and of reducing every case, however complex, to that form in which it could in a purely external fashion be put on paper completely excluding his personal view of the matter, and what was of paramount importance, observing all the necessary formalities. All this work was new. And he was one of the first men who put into practical working the reforms in judicial procedure enacted in 1864.

On settling in a new town in his position as examining magistrate, Ivan Ilych made new acquaintances, formed new ties, took up a new line, and adopted a rather different attitude. He took up an attitude of somewhat dignified aloofness towards the provincial authorities, while he picked out the best circle among the legal gentlemen and wealthy gentry living in the town, and adopted a tone of slight dissatisfaction with the government, moderate liberalism, and lofty civic virtue. With this, while making no change in the elegance of his get-up, Ivan Ilych in his new office gave up shaving, and left his beard free to grow as it liked. Ivan Ilych's existence in the new town proved to be very agreeable; the society which took the line of opposition to the governor was friendly and good; his income was larger, and he found a source of increased enjoyment in whist, at which he began to play at this time; and having a faculty for playing cards good-humouredly, and being rapid and exact in his calculations, he was as a rule on the winning side.

After living two years in the new town, Ivan Ilych met his future wife. Praskovya Fyodorovna Mihel was the most attractive, clever, and brilliant girl in the set in which Ivan Ilych moved. Among other amusements and recreations after his labours as a magistrate, Ivan Ilych started a light, playful flirtation with Praskovya Fyodorovna.

Ivan Ilych when he was an assistant secretary had danced as a rule; as an examining magistrate he danced only as an exception. He danced now as it were under protest, as though to show 'that though I am serving on the new reformed legal code, and am of the fifth class in official rank, still if it comes to a question of dancing, in that line too I can do better than others.' In this spirit he danced now and then towards the end of the evening with Praskovya Fyodorovna, and it was principally during these dances that he won the heart of Praskovya Fyodorovna. She fell in love with him. Ivan Ilych had no

clearly defined intention of marrying; but when the girl fell in love
with him, he put the question to himself: 'After all, why not get married?' he said to himself.

The young lady, Praskovya Fyodorovna, was of good family, nice-
looking. There was a little bit of property. Ivan Ilych might have reckoned on a more brilliant match, but this was a good match. Ivan Ilych
had his salary; she, he hoped, would have as much of her own. It was
a good family; she was a sweet, pretty, and perfectly comme il faut
young woman. To say that Ivan Ilych got married because he fell in
love with his wife and found in her sympathy with his views of life,
would be as untrue as to say that he got married because the people
of his world approved of the match. Ivan Ilych was influenced by
both considerations; he was doing what was agreeable to himself in
securing such a wife, and at the same time doing what persons of
higher standing looked upon as the correct thing.

And Ivan Ilych got married.

The process itself of getting married and the early period of married life, with the conjugal caresses, the new furniture, the new
crockery, the new house linen, all up to the time of his wife's pregnancy, went off very well; so that Ivan Ilych had already begun to
think that so far from marriage breaking up that kind of frivolous,
agreeable, light-hearted life, always decorous and always approved by
society, which he regarded as the normal life, it would even increase
its agreeableness. But at that point, in the early months of his wife's
pregnancy, there came in a new element, unexpected, unpleasant,
tiresome and unseemly, which could never have been anticipated,
and from which there was no escape.

His wife, without any kind of reason, it seemed to Ivan Ilych, de
gaité de cœur,* as he expressed it, began to disturb the agreeableness
and decorum of their life. She began without any sort of justification
to be jealous, exacting in her demands on his attention, squabbled
over everything, and treated him to the coarsest and most unpleasant
scenes.

At first Ivan Ilych hoped to escape from the unpleasantness of this
position by taking up the same frivolous and well-bred line that had

---

*For the sake of amusement (French).

served him well on other occasions of difficulty. He endeavoured to ignore his wife's ill-humour, went on living light-heartedly and agreeably as before, invited friends to play cards, tried to get away himself to the club or to his friends. But his wife began on one occasion with such energy, abusing him in such coarse language, and so obstinately persisted in her abuse of him every time he failed in carrying out her demands, obviously having made up her mind firmly to persist till he gave way, that is, stayed at home and was as dull as she was, that Ivan Ilych took alarm. He perceived that matrimony, at least with his wife, was not invariably conducive to the pleasures and proprieties of life; but, on the contrary, often destructive of them, and that it was therefore essential to erect some barrier to protect himself from these disturbances. And Ivan Ilych began to look about for such means of protecting himself. His official duties were the only thing that impressed Praskovya Fyodorovna, and Ivan Ilych began to use his official position and the duties arising from it in his struggle with his wife to fence off his own independent world apart.

With the birth of the baby, the attempts at nursing it, and the various unsuccessful experiments with foods, with the illnesses, real and imaginary, of the infant and its mother, in which Ivan Ilych was expected to sympathise, though he never had the slightest idea about them, the need for him to fence off a world apart for himself outside his family life became still more imperative. As his wife grew more irritable and exacting, so did Ivan Ilych more and more transfer the centre of gravity of his life to his official work. He became fonder and fonder of official life, and more ambitious than he had been.

Very quickly, not more than a year after his wedding, Ivan Ilych had become aware that conjugal life, though providing certain comforts, was in reality a very intricate and difficult business towards which one must, if one is to do one's duty, that is, lead the decorous life approved by society, work out for oneself a definite line, just as in the government service.

And such a line Ivan Ilych did work out for himself in his married life. He expected from his home life only those comforts—of dinner at home, of housekeeper and bed which it could give him, and, above all, that perfect propriety in external observances required by public opinion. For the rest, he looked for good-humoured pleasantness, and if he found it he was very thankful. If he met with antagonism and querulousness, he promptly retreated into the separate world he had shut off for himself in his official life, and there he found solace.

Ivan Ilych was prized as a good official, and three years later he was made assistant public prosecutor. The new duties of this position, their dignity, the possibility of bringing any one to trial and putting any one in prison, the publicity of the speeches and the success Ivan Ilych had in that part of his work,—all this made his official work still more attractive to him.

Children were born to him. His wife became steadily more querulous and ill-tempered, but the line Ivan Ilych had taken up for himself in home life put him almost out of reach of her grumbling.

After seven years of service in the same town, Ivan Ilych was transferred to another province with the post of public prosecutor. They moved, money was short, and his wife did not like the place they had moved to. The salary was indeed a little higher than before, but their expenses were larger. Besides, a couple of children died, and home life consequently became even less agreeable for Ivan Ilych.

For every mischance that occurred in their new place of residence, Praskovya Fyodorovna blamed her husband. The greater number of subjects of conversation between husband and wife, especially the education of the children, led to questions which were associated with previous quarrels, and quarrels were ready to break out at every instant. There remained only those rare periods of being in love which did indeed come upon them, but never lasted long. These were the islands at which they put in for a time, but they soon set off again upon the ocean of concealed hostility, that was made manifest in their aloofness from one another. This aloofness might have distressed Ivan Ilych if he had believed that this ought not to be so, but by now he regarded this position as perfectly normal, and it was indeed the goal towards which he worked in his home life. His aim was to make himself more and more free from the unpleasant aspects of domestic life and to render them harmless and decorous. And he attained this aim by spending less and less time with his family; and when he was forced to be at home, he endeavoured to secure his tranquillity by the presence of outsiders. The great thing for Ivan Ilych was having his office. In the official world all the interest of life was concentrated for him. And this interest absorbed him. The sense of his own power, the consciousness of being able to ruin any one he wanted to ruin, even the external dignity of his office, when he made his entry into the court or met subordinate officials, his success in the eyes of his superiors and his subordinates, and, above all, his masterly handling of cases, of which he was conscious,—all this delighted him and, together with chat with his colleagues, dining out, and whist, filled his life. So that, on the whole, Ivan Ilych's life still went on in the way he thought it should go—agreeably and decorously.

So he lived for another seven years. His eldest daughter was already sixteen, another child had died, and there was left only one other, a boy at the high school, a subject of dissension. Ivan Ilych wanted to send him to the school of jurisprudence, while Praskovya Fyodorovna to spite him sent him to the high school. The daughter had been educated at home, and had turned out well; the boy too did fairly well at his lessons.

III

Such was Ivan Ilych's life for seventeen years after his marriage. He had been by now a long while prosecutor, and had refused several appointments offered him, looking out for a more desirable post, when there occurred an unexpected incident which utterly destroyed his peace of mind. Ivan Ilych had been expecting to be appointed presiding judge in a university town, but a certain Goppe somehow stole a march on him and secured the appointment. Ivan Ilych took offence, began upbraiding him, and quarrelled with him and with his own superiors. A coolness was felt towards him, and on the next appointment that was made he was again passed over.

This was in the year 1880. That year was the most painful one in Ivan Ilych's life. During that year it became evident on the one hand that his pay was insufficient for his expenses; on the other hand, that he had been forgotten by every one, and that what seemed to him the most monstrous, the cruelest injustice, appeared to other people as a quite commonplace fact. Even his father felt no obligation to assist him. He felt that every one had deserted him, and that every one regarded his position with an income of three thousand five hundred roubles as a quite normal and even fortunate one. He alone, with a sense of the injustice done him, and the everlasting nagging of his wife and the debts he had begun to accumulate, living beyond his means, knew that his position was far from being normal.

The summer of that year, to cut down his expenses, he took a holiday and went with his wife to spend the summer in the country at her brother's.

In the country, with no official duties to occupy him, Ivan Ilych was for the first time a prey not to simple boredom, but to intolerable depression; and he made up his mind that things could not go on like that, and that it was absolutely necessary to take some decisive steps.

After a sleepless night spent by Ivan Ilych walking up and down the terrace, he determined to go to Petersburg to take active steps and to get transferred to some other department, so as to revenge himself on them, the people, that is, who had not known how to appreciate him.

Next day, in spite of all the efforts of his wife and his mother-in-law to dissuade him, he set off to Petersburg.

He went with a single object before him—to obtain a post with an income of five thousand. He was ready now to be satisfied with a post in any department, of any tendency, with any kind of work. He must only have a post—a post with five thousand, in the executive department, the banks, the railways, the Empress Marya's institutions, even in the customs duties—what was essential was five thousand, and essential it was, too, to get out of the department in which they had failed to appreciate his value.

And, behold, this quest of Ivan Ilych's was crowned with wonderful, unexpected success. At Kursk there got into the same first-class carriage F. S. Ilyin, an acquaintance, who told him of a telegram just received by the governor of Kursk, announcing a change about to take place in the ministry—Pyotr Ivanovich was to be superseded by Ivan Semyonovich.

The proposed change, apart from its significance for Russia, had special significance for Ivan Ilych from the fact that by bringing to the front a new person, Pyotr Petrovich, and obviously, therefore, his friend Zahar Ivanovich, it was in the highest degree propitious to

Ivan Ilych's own plans. Zahar Ivanovich was a friend and schoolfellow of Ivan Ilych's.

At Moscow the news was confirmed. On arriving at Petersburg, Ivan Ilych looked up Zahar Ivanovich, and received a positive promise of an appointment in his former department—that of justice.

A week later he telegraphed to his wife: '*Zahar Miller's place. At first report I receive appointment.*'

Thanks to these changes, Ivan Ilych unexpectedly obtained, in the same department as before, an appointment which placed him two stages higher than his former colleagues, and gave him an income of five thousand, together with the official allowance of three thousand five hundred for travelling expenses. All his ill-humour with his former enemies and the whole department was forgotten, and Ivan Ilych was completely happy.

Ivan Ilych went back to the country more light-hearted and good-tempered than he had been for a very long while. Praskovya Fyodorovna was in better spirits, too, and peace was patched up between them. Ivan Ilych described what respect every one had shown him in Petersburg; how all those who had been his enemies had been put to shame, and were cringing now before him; how envious they were of his appointment, and still more of the high favour in which he stood at Petersburg.

Praskovya Fyodorovna listened to this, and pretended to believe it, and did not contradict him in anything, but confined herself to making plans for her new arrangements in the town to which they would be moving. And Ivan Ilych saw with delight that these plans were his plans; that they were agreed; and that his life after this disturbing hitch in its progress was about to regain its true, normal character of light-hearted agreeableness and propriety.

Ivan Ilych had come back to the country for a short stay only. He had to enter upon the duties of his new office on the 10th of September; and besides, he needed some time to settle in a new place, to move all his belongings from the other province, to purchase and order many things in addition; in short, to arrange things as settled in his own mind, and almost exactly as settled in the heart too of Praskovya Fyodorovna.

And now when everything was so successfully arranged, and when he and his wife were agreed in their aim, and were, besides, so little together, they got on with one another as they had not got on together since the early years of their married life. Ivan Ilych had thought of taking his family away with him at once; but his sister and his brother-in-law, who had suddenly become extremely cordial and intimate with him and his family, were so pressing in urging them to stay that he set off alone.

Ivan Ilych started off; and the light-hearted temper produced by his success, and his good understanding with his wife, one thing backing up another, did not desert him all the time. He found a charming set of apartments, the very thing both husband and wife had dreamed of. Spacious, lofty reception-rooms in the old style, a comfortable, dignified-looking study for him, rooms for his wife and daughter, a school-room for his son, everything as though planned on purpose for them. Ivan Ilych himself looked after the furnishing of them, chose the wall-papers, bought furniture, by preference antique furniture, which had a peculiar comme-il-faut style to his mind, and it all grew up and grew up, and really attained the ideal he had set before himself. When he had half finished arranging the house, his arrangement surpassed his own expectations. He saw the comme-il-faut character, elegant and free from vulgarity, that the whole would have when it was all ready. As he fell asleep he pictured to himself the reception-room as it would be. Looking at the drawing-room, not yet finished, he could see the hearth, the screen, the étagère, and the little chairs dotted here and there, the plates and dishes on the wall, and the bronzes as they would be when they were all put in their places. He was delighted with the thought of how he would impress Praskovya and Lizanka, who had taste too in this line. They would never expect anything like it. He was particularly successful in coming across and buying cheap old pieces of furniture, which gave a peculiarly aristocratic air to the whole. In his letters he purposely disparaged everything so as to surprise them. All this so absorbed him that the duties of his new office, though he was so fond of his official work, interested him less than he had expected. During sittings of the court he had moments of inattention; he pondered the question which sort of cornices to have on the window-blinds, straight or fluted. He was so interested in this business that he often set to work with his own hands, moved a piece of furniture, or hung up curtains himself. One day he went up a ladder to show a workman, who did not understand, how he wanted some hangings draped, made a false step and slipped; but, like a strong and nimble person, he clung on, and only knocked his side against the corner of a frame. The bruised place ached, but it soon passed off. Ivan Ilych felt all this time particularly good-humoured and well. He wrote: 'I feel fifteen years younger.' He thought his house-furnishing would be finished in September, but it dragged on to the middle of October. But then the effect was charming; not he only said so, but every one who saw it told him so too.

In reality, it was all just what is commonly seen in the houses of people who are not exactly wealthy but want to look like wealthy people, and so succeed only in being like one another—hangings, dark wood, flowers, rugs and bronzes, everything dark and highly polished, everything that all people of a certain class have so as to be like all people of a certain class. And in his case it was all so like that it made no impression at all; but it all seemed to him somehow special. When he met his family at the railway station and brought them to his newly furnished rooms, all lighted up in readiness, and a footman in a white tie opened the door into an entry decorated with flowers, and then they walked into the drawing-room and the study, uttering cries of delight, he was very happy, conducted them everywhere, eagerly drinking in their praises, and beaming with satisfaction. The same evening, while they talked about various things at tea, Praskovya Fyodorovna inquired about his fall, and he laughed and showed them how he had gone flying, and how he had frightened the upholsterer.

'It's as well I'm something of an athlete. Another man might have been killed, and I got nothing worse than a blow here; when it's touched it hurts, but it's going off already; nothing but a bruise.'

And they began to live in their new abode, which, as is always the case, when they had got thoroughly settled in they found to be short of just one room, and with their new income, which, as always, was only a little—some five hundred roubles—too little, and everything went very well. Things went particularly well at first, before everything was quite finally arranged, and there was still something to do to the place—something to buy, something to order, something to move, something to make to fit. Though there were indeed several disputes between husband and wife, both were so well satisfied, and there was so much to do, that it all went off without serious quarrels. When there was nothing left to arrange, it became a little dull, and something seemed to be lacking, but by then they were making acquaintances and forming habits, and life was filled up again.

Ivan Ilych, after spending the morning in the court, returned home to dinner, and at first he was generally in a good humour, although this was apt to be upset a little, and precisely on account of the new abode. Every spot on the tablecloth, on the hangings, the string of a window blind broken, irritated him. He had devoted so much trouble to the arrangement of the rooms that any disturbance of their order distressed him. But, on the whole, the life of Ivan Ilych ran its course as, according to his conviction, life ought to do—easily, agreeably, and decorously. He got up at nine, drank his coffee, read the newspaper, then put on his official uniform, and went to the court. There the routine of the daily work was ready mapped out for him, and he stepped into it at once. People with petitions, inquiries in the office, the office itself, the sittings—public and preliminary. In all this the great thing necessary was to exclude everything with the sap of life in it, which always disturbs the regular course of official business, not to admit any sort of relations with people except the official relations; the motive of all intercourse had to be simply the official motive, and the intercourse itself to be only official. A man would come, for instance, anxious for certain information. Ivan Ilych, not being the functionary on duty, would have nothing whatever to do with such a man. But if this man's relation to him as a member of the court is such as can be formulated on official stamped paper—within the limits of such a relation Ivan Ilych would do everything, positively everything he could, and in doing so would observe the semblance of human friendly relations, that is, the courtesies of social life. But where the official relation ended, there everything else stopped too. This art of keeping the official aspect of things apart from his real life, Ivan Ilych possessed in the highest degree; and through long practice and natural aptitude, he had brought it to such a pitch of perfection that he even permitted himself at times, like a skilled specialist as it were in jest, to let the human and official relations mingle. He allowed himself this liberty just because he felt he had the power at any moment if he wished it to take up the purely official line again and to drop the human relation. This thing was not simply easy, agreeable, and decorous; in Ivan Ilych's hands it attained a positively artistic character. In the intervals of business he smoked, drank tea, chatted a little about politics, a little about public affairs, a little about cards, but most of all about appointments in the service. And tired, but feeling like some artist who has skilfully played his part in the performance, one of the first violins in the orchestra, he returned home. At home his daughter and her mother had been paying calls somewhere, or else someone had been calling on them; the son had been at school, had been preparing his lessons with his teachers, and duly learning correctly what was taught at the high school. Everything was as it should be. After dinner, if there were no visitors, Ivan Ilych sometimes read some book of which people were talking, and in the evening sat down to work, that is, read official papers, compared them with the laws, sorted depositions, and put them under the laws. This he found neither tiresome nor entertaining. It was tiresome when he might have been playing 'bridge'; but if there were no 'bridge' going on, it was anyway better than sitting alone or with his wife. Ivan Ilych's pleasures were little dinners, to which he invited ladies and gentlemen of good social position, and such methods of passing the time with them as were usual with such persons, so that his drawing-room might be like all other drawing-rooms.

Once they even gave a party—a dance. And Ivan Ilych enjoyed it, and everything was very successful, except that it led to a violent quarrel with his wife over the tarts and sweetmeats. Praskovya Fyodorovna had her own plan; while Ivan Ilych insisted on getting everything from an expensive pastry-cook, and ordered a great many tarts, and the quarrel was because these tarts were left over and the pastry-cook's bill came to forty-five roubles. The quarrel was a violent and unpleasant one, so much so that Praskovya Fyodorovna called him, 'Fool, imbecile.' And he clutched at his head, and in his anger made some allusion to a divorce. But the party itself was enjoyable. There were all the best people, and Ivan Ilych danced with Princess Trufonov, the sister of the one so well known in connection with the charitable association called, 'Bear my Burden.' His official pleasures lay in the gratification of his pride; his social pleasures lay in the gratification of his vanity. But Ivan Ilych's most real pleasure was the pleasure of playing 'bridge.' He admitted to himself that after all, after whatever unpleasant incidents there had been in his life, the pleasure which burned like a candle before all others was sitting with good players, and not noisy partners, at bridge; and, of course, a four-hand game (playing with five was never a success, though one pretends to like it particularly), and with good cards, to play a shrewd, serious game, then supper and a glass of wine. And after bridge, especially after winning some small stakes (winning large sums was unpleasant), Ivan Ilych went to bed in a particularly happy frame of mind.

So they lived. They moved in the very best circle, and were visited by people of consequence and young people.

In their views of their circle of acquaintances, the husband, the wife, and the daughter were in complete accord; and without any expressed agreement on the subject, they all acted alike in dropping and shaking off various friends and relations, shabby persons who swooped down upon them in their drawing-room with Japanese plates on the walls, and pressed their civilities on them. Soon these shabby persons ceased fluttering about them, and none but the very best society was seen at the Golovins. Young men began to pay attention to Lizanka; and Petrishchev, the son of Dmitry Ivanovich Petrishchev, and the sole heir of his fortune, an examining magistrate, began to be so attentive to Lizanka, that Ivan Ilych had raised the question with his wife whether it would not be as well to arrange a sledge drive for them, or to get up some theatricals. So they lived. And everything went on in this way without change, and everything was very nice.

IV

All were in good health. One could not use the word ill-health in connection with the symptoms Ivan Ilych sometimes complained of, namely, a queer taste in his mouth and a sort of uncomfortable feeling on the left side of the stomach.

But it came to pass that this uncomfortable feeling kept increasing, and became not exactly a pain, but a continual sense of weight in his side and irritable temper. This irritable temper continually growing and growing, began at last to mar the agreeable easiness and decorum that had reigned in the Golovin household. Quarrels between the husband and wife became more and more frequent, and soon all the easiness and amenity of life had fallen away, and mere propriety was maintained with difficulty. Scenes became again more frequent. Again there were only islands in the sea of contention—and but few of these—at which the husband and wife could meet without an outbreak. And Praskovya Fyodorovna said now, not without grounds, that her husband had a trying temper. With her characteristic exaggeration, she said he had always had this awful temper, and she had needed all her sweetness to put up with it for twenty years. It was true that it was he now who began the quarrels. His gusts of temper always broke out just before dinner, and often just as he was beginning to eat, at the soup. He would notice that some piece of the crockery had been chipped, or that the food was not nice, or that his son put his elbow on the table, or his daughter's hair was not arranged as he liked it. And whatever it was, he laid the blame of it on Praskovya Fyodorovna. Praskovya Fyodorovna had at first retorted in the same strain, and said all sorts of horrid things to him; but on two occasions, just at the beginning of dinner, he had flown into such a frenzy that she perceived that it was due to physical derangement, and was brought on by taking food, and she controlled herself; she did not reply, but simply made haste to get dinner over. Praskovya Fyodorovna took great credit to herself for this exercise of self-control. Making up her mind that her husband had a fearful temper, and made her life miserable, she began to feel sorry for herself. And the more she felt for herself, the more she hated her husband. She began to wish he were dead; yet could not wish it, because then there would be no income. And this exasperated her against him even more. She considered herself dreadfully unfortunate, precisely because even his death could not save her, and she felt irritated and concealed it, and this hidden irritation on her side increased his irritability.

After one violent scene, in which Ivan Ilych had been particularly unjust, and after which he had said in explanation that he certainly was irritable, but that it was due to illness, she said that if he were ill he ought to take steps, and insisted on his going to see a celebrated doctor.

He went. Everything was as he had expected; everything was as it always is. The waiting and the assumption of dignity, that professional dignity he knew so well, exactly as he assumed it himself in court, and the sounding and listening and questions that called for answers that were foregone conclusions and obviously superfluous, and the significant air that seemed to insinuate—you only leave it all to us, and we will arrange everything, for us it is certain and incontestable how to arrange everything, everything in one way for every man of every sort. It was all exactly as in his court of justice. Exactly the same air as he put on in dealing with a man brought up for judgment, the doctor put on for him.

The doctor said: This and that proves that you have such-and-such a thing wrong inside you; but if that is not confirmed by analysis of this and that, then we must assume this and that. If we assume this and that, then—and so on. To Ivan Ilych there was only one question of consequence, Was his condition dangerous or not? But the doctor ignored that irrelevant inquiry. From the doctor's point of view this was a side issue, not the subject under consideration; the only real question was the balance of probabilities between a loose kidney, chronic catarrh, and appendicitis. It was not a question of the life of Ivan Ilych, but the question between the loose kidney and the intestinal appendix. And this question, as it seemed to Ivan Ilych, the doctor solved in a brilliant manner in favour of the appendix, with the reservation that analysis of the water might give a fresh clue, and that then the aspect of the case would be altered. All this was point for point identical with what Ivan Ilych had himself done in brilliant fashion a thousand times over in dealing with some man on his trial. Just as brilliantly the doctor made his summing-up, and triumphantly, gaily even, glanced over his spectacles at the prisoner in the dock. From the doctor's summing-up Ivan Ilych deduced the conclusion—that things looked bad, and that he, the doctor, and most likely every one else, did not care, but that things looked bad for him. And this conclusion impressed Ivan Ilych morbidly, arousing in him a great feeling of pity for himself, of great anger against this doctor who could be unconcerned about a matter of such importance.

But he said nothing of that. He got up, and, laying the fee on the table, he said, with a sigh, 'We sick people probably often ask inconvenient questions. Tell me, is this generally a dangerous illness or not?'

The doctor glanced severely at him with one eye through his spectacles, as though to say: 'Prisoner at the bar, if you will not keep within the limits of the questions allowed you, I shall be compelled to take measures for your removal from the precincts of the court.' 'I have told you what I thought necessary and suitable already,' said the doctor; 'the analysis will show anything further.' And the doctor bowed him out.

Ivan Ilych went out slowly and dejectedly, got into his sledge, and drove home. All the way home he was incessantly going over all the doctor had said, trying to translate all these complicated, obscure, scientific phrases into simple language, and to read in them an answer to the question, It's bad—is it very bad, or nothing much as yet? And it seemed to him that the upshot of all the doctor had said was that it was very bad. Everything seemed dismal to Ivan Ilych in the streets. The sledge-drivers were dismal, the houses were dismal, the people passing, and the shops were dismal. This ache, this dull gnawing ache, that never ceased for a second, seemed, when connected with the doctor's obscure utterances, to have gained a new, more serious significance. With a new sense of misery Ivan Ilych kept watch on it now.

He reached home and began to tell his wife about it. His wife listened; but in the middle of his account his daughter came in with her hat on, ready to go out with her mother. Reluctantly she half sat down to listen to these tedious details, but she could not stand it for long, and her mother did not hear his story to the end.

'Well, I'm very glad,' said his wife; 'now you must be sure and take the medicine regularly. Give me the prescription; I'll send Gerasim to the chemist's!' And she went to get ready to go out.

He had not taken breath while she was in the room, and he heaved a deep sigh when she was gone.

'Well,' he said, 'may be it really is nothing as yet.'

He began to take the medicine, to carry out the doctor's directions, which were changed after the analysis of the water. But it was just at this point that some confusion arose, either in the analysis or in what ought to have followed from it. The doctor himself, of course, could not be blamed for it, but it turned out that things had not gone as the doctor had told him. Either he had forgotten or told a lie, or was hiding something from him.

But Ivan Ilych still went on just as exactly carrying out the doctor's direction, and in doing so he found comfort at first.

From the time of his visit to the doctor Ivan Ilych's principal occupation became the exact observance of the doctor's prescriptions as regards hygiene and medicine and the careful observation of his ailment in all the functions of his organism. Ivan Ilych's principal interest came to be people's ailments and people's health. When anything was said in his presence about sick people, about deaths and recoveries, especially in the case of an illness resembling his own, he listened, trying to conceal his excitement, asked questions, and applied what he heard to his own trouble.

The ache did not grow less; but Ivan Ilych made great efforts to force himself to believe that he was better. And he succeeded in deceiving himself so long as nothing happened to disturb him. But as soon as he had a mischance, some unpleasant words with his wife, a failure in his official work, an unlucky hand at 'bridge,' he was at once acutely sensible of his illness. In former days he had borne with such mishaps, hoping soon to retrieve the mistake, to make a struggle, to reach success later, to have a lucky hand. But now he was cast down by every mischance and reduced to despair. He would say to himself: 'Here I'm only just beginning to get better, and the medicine has begun to take effect, and now this mischance or disappointment.' And he was furious against the mischance or the people who were causing him the disappointment and killing him, and he felt that this fury was killing him, but could not check it. One would have thought that it should have been clear to him that this exasperation against circumstances and people was aggravating his disease, and that therefore he ought not to pay attention to the unpleasant incidents. But his reasoning took quite the opposite direction. He said that he needed peace, and was on the watch for everything that disturbed his peace, and at the slightest disturbance of it he flew into a rage. What made his position worse was that he read medical books and consulted doctors. He got worse so gradually that he might have deceived himself, comparing one day with another, the difference was so slight. But when he consulted the doctors, then it seemed to him that he was getting worse, and very rapidly so indeed. And in spite of this, he was continually consulting the doctors.

That month he called on another celebrated doctor. The second celebrity said almost the same as the first, but put his questions differently; and the interview with this celebrity only redoubled the doubts and terrors of Ivan Ilych. A friend of a friend of his, a very good doctor, diagnosed the disease quite differently; and in spite of the fact that he guaranteed recovery, by his questions and his suppositions he confused Ivan Ilych even more and strengthened his suspicions. A homœopath gave yet another diagnosis of the complaint, and prescribed medicine, which Ivan Ilych took secretly for a week; but after a week of the homœopathic medicine he felt no relief, and losing faith both in the other doctor's treatment and in this, he fell into even deeper depression. One day a lady of his acquaintance talked to him of the healing wrought by icons. Ivan Ilych caught himself listening attentively and believing in the reality of the facts alleged. This incident alarmed him. 'Can I have degenerated to such a point of intellectual feebleness?' he said to himself. 'Nonsense! it's all rubbish. I must not give way to nervous fears, but fixing on one doctor, adhere strictly to his treatment. That's what I will do. Now it's settled. I won't think about it, but till next summer I will stick to the treatment, and then I shall see. Now I'll put a stop to this wavering!' It was easy to say this, but impossible to carry it out. The pain in his side was always dragging at him, seeming to grow more acute and ever more incessant; it seemed to him that the taste in his mouth was queerer, and there was a loathsome smell even from his breath, and his appetite and strength kept dwindling. There was no deceiving himself; something terrible, new, and so important that nothing more important had ever been in Ivan Ilych's life, was taking place in him, and he alone knew of it. All about him did not or would not understand, and believed that everything in the world was going on as before. This was what tortured Ivan Ilych more than anything. Those of his own household, most of all his wife and daughter, who were absorbed in a perfect whirl of visits, did not, he saw, comprehend it at all, and were annoyed that he was so depressed and exacting, as though he were to blame for it. Though they tried indeed to disguise it, he saw he was a nuisance to them; but that his wife had taken up a definite line of her own in regard to his illness, and stuck to it regardless of what he might say and do. This line was expressed thus: 'You know,' she would say to acquaintances, 'Ivan Ilych cannot, like all other simple-hearted folks, keep to the treatment prescribed him. One day he'll take his drops and eat what he's ordered, and go to bed in good time; the next day, if I don't see to it, he'll suddenly forget to take his medicine, eat sturgeon (which is forbidden by the doctors), yes, and sit up at "bridge," till past midnight.'

'Why, when did I do that?' Ivan Ilych asked in vexation one day at Pyotr Ivanovich's.

'Why, yesterday, with Shebek.'

'It makes no difference. I couldn't sleep for pain.'

'Well, it doesn't matter what you do it for, only you'll never get well like that, and you make us wretched.'

Praskovya Fyodorovna's external attitude to her husband's illness, openly expressed to others and to himself, was that Ivan Ilych was to blame in the matter of his illness, and that the whole illness was another injury he was doing to his wife. Ivan Ilych felt that the expression of this dropped from her unconsciously, but that made it no easier for him.

In his official life, too, Ivan Ilych noticed, or fancied he noticed, a strange attitude to him. At one time it seemed to him that people were looking inquisitively at him, as a man who would shortly have to vacate his position; at another time his friends would suddenly begin chaffing him in a friendly way over his nervous fears, as though that awful and horrible, unheard-of thing that was going on within him, incessantly gnawing at him, and irresistibly dragging him away somewhere, were the most agreeable subject for joking. Shvarts especially, with his jocoseness, his liveliness, and his comme-il-faut tone, exasperated Ivan Ilych by reminding him of himself ten years ago.

Friends came sometimes to play cards. They sat down to the card-table; they shuffled and dealt the new cards. Diamonds were led and followed by diamonds, the seven. His partner said, 'Can't trump,' and played the two of diamonds. What then? Why, delightful, capital, it should have been—he had a trump hand. And suddenly Ivan Ilych feels that gnawing ache, that taste in his mouth, and it strikes him as something grotesque that with that he could be glad of a trump hand.

He looks at Mikhail Mikhailovich, his partner, how he taps on the table with his red hand, and affably and indulgently abstains from snatching up the trick, and pushes the cards towards Ivan Ilych so as to give him the pleasure of taking them up, without any trouble, without even stretching out his hand. 'What, does he suppose that

I'm so weak that I can't stretch out my hand?' thinks Ivan Ilych, and he forgets the trumps, and trumps his partner's cards, and plays his trump hand without making three tricks; and what's the most awful thing of all is that he sees how upset Mikhail Mikhailovich is about it, while he doesn't care a bit, and it's awful for him to think why he doesn't care.

They all see that he's in pain, and say to him, 'We can stop if you're tired. You go and lie down.' Lie down? No, he's not in the least tired; they will play the rubber. All are gloomy and silent. Ivan Ilych feels that it is he who has brought this gloom upon them, and he cannot disperse it. They have supper, and the party breaks up, and Ivan Ilych is left alone with the consciousness that his life is poisoned for him and poisons the life of others, and that this poison is not losing its force, but is continually penetrating more and more deeply into his whole existence.

And with the consciousness of this, and with the physical pain in addition, and the terror in addition to that, he must lie in his bed, often not able to sleep for pain the greater part of the night; and in the morning he must get up again, dress, go to the law-court, speak, write, or, if he does not go out, stay at home for all the four-and-twenty hours of the day and night, of which each one is a torture. And he had to live thus on the edge of the precipice alone, without one man who would understand and feel for him.

V

In this way one month, then a second, passed by. Just before the New Year his brother-in-law arrived in the town on a visit to them. Ivan Ilych was at the court when he arrived. Praskovya Fyodorovna had gone out shopping. Coming home and going into his study, he found there his brother-in-law, a healthy, ruddy man, engaged in unpacking his trunk. He raised his head, hearing Ivan Ilych's step, and for a second stared at him without a word. That stare told Ivan Ilych everything. His brother-in-law opened his mouth to utter an 'Oh!' of surprise, but checked himself. That confirmed it all.

'What! have I changed?'

'Yes, there is a change.'

And all Ivan Ilych's efforts to draw him into talking of his appearance his brother-in-law met with obstinate silence. Praskovya Fyodorovna came in; the brother-in-law went to see her. Ivan Ilych locked his door, and began gazing at himself in the looking-glass, first full face, then in profile. He took up his photograph, taken with his wife, and compared the portrait with what he saw in the looking-glass. The change was immense. Then he bared his arm to the elbow, looked at it, pulled the sleeve down again, sat down on an ottoman, and felt blacker than night.

'I mustn't, I mustn't,' he said to himself, jumped up, went to the table, opened some official paper, tried to read it, but could not. He opened the door, went into the drawing-room. The door into the drawing-room was closed. He went up to it on tiptoe and listened.

'No,, you're exaggerating,' Praskovya Fyodorovna was saying.

'Exaggerating? You can't see it. Why, he's a dead man. Look at his eyes—there's no light in them. But what's wrong with him?'

'No one can tell. Nikolaev' (that was another doctor) 'said something, but I don't know. Leshchetitsky' (this was the celebrated doctor) 'said the opposite.'

Ivan Ilych walked away, went to his own room, lay down, and fell to musing. 'A kidney—a loose kidney.' He remembered all the doctors had told him, how it had been detached, and how it was loose; and by an effort of imagination he tried to catch that kidney and to stop it, to strengthen it. So little was needed, he fancied. 'No, I'll go again to Pyotr Ivanovich' (this was the friend who had a friend a doctor). He rang, ordered the horse to be put in, and got ready to go out.

'Where are you off to, Jean?'* asked his wife with a peculiarly melancholy and exceptionally kind expression.

This exceptionally kind expression exasperated him. He looked darkly at her.

'I want to see Pyotr Ivanovich.'

He went to the friend who had a friend a doctor. And with him to the doctor's. He found him in, and had a long conversation with him.

---

*French form of Ivan.

Reviewing the anatomical and physiological details of what, according to the doctor's view, was taking place within him, he understood it all. It was just one thing—a little thing wrong with the appendix. It might all come right. Only strengthen one sluggish organ, and decrease the undue activity of another, and absorption would take place, and all would be set right. He was a little late for dinner. He ate his dinner, talked cheerfully, but it was a long while before he could go to his own room to work. At last he went to his study, and at once sat down to work. He read his legal documents and did his work, but the consciousness never left him of having a matter of importance very near to his heart which he had put off, but would look into later. When he had finished his work, he remembered that the matter near his heart was thinking about the appendix. But he did not give himself up to it; he went into the drawing-room to tea. There were visitors; and there was talking, playing on the piano, and singing; there was the young examining magistrate, the desirable match for the daughter. Ivan Ilych spent the evening, as Praskovya Fyodorovna observed, in better spirits than any of them; but he never forgot for an instant that he had the important matter of the appendix put off for consideration later. At eleven o'clock he said good night and went to his own room. He had slept alone since his illness in a little room adjoining his study. He went in, undressed, and took up a novel of Zola, but did not read it; he fell to thinking. And in his imagination the desired recovery of the appendix had taken place. There had been absorption, rejection, re-establishment of the regular action.

'Why, it's all simply that,' he said to himself. 'One only wants to assist nature.' He remembered the medicine, got up, took it, lay down on his back, watching for the medicine to act beneficially and overcome the pain. 'It's only to take it regularly and avoid injurious influences; why, already I feel rather better, much better.' He began to feel his side; it was not painful to the touch. 'Yes, I don't feel it—really, much better already.' He put out the candle and lay on his side. 'The appendix is getting better, absorption.' Suddenly he felt the familiar, old, dull, gnawing ache, persistent, quiet, in earnest. In his mouth the same familiar loathsome taste. His heart sank, his brain felt dim, misty. 'My God, my God!' he said, 'again, again, and it will never cease.' And suddenly the whole thing rose before him in quite a different aspect.

'Appendix! kidney!' he said to himself. 'It's not a question of the appendix, not a question of the kidney, but of life and . . . death. Yes, life has been and now it's going, going away, and I cannot stop it. Yes. Why deceive myself? Isn't it obvious to every one, except me, that I'm dying, and it's only a question of weeks, of days—at once perhaps. There was light, and now there is darkness. I was here, and now I am going! Where?' A cold chill ran over him, his breath stopped. He heard nothing but the throbbing of his heart.

'I shall be no more, then what will there be? There'll be nothing. Where then shall I be when I'm no more? Can this be dying? No; I don't want to!' He jumped up, tried to light the candle; and fumbling with trembling hands, he dropped the candle and the candlestick on the floor and fell back again on the pillow. 'Why trouble? it doesn't matter,' he said to himself, staring with open eyes into the darkness. 'Death. Yes, death. And they—all of them—don't understand, and don't want to understand, and feel no pity. They are playing. (He caught through the closed doors the faraway cadence of a voice and the accompaniment.) They don't care, but they will die too. Fools! Me sooner and them later; but it will be the same for them. And they are merry. The beasts!' Anger stifled him. And he was agonisingly, insufferably miserable. 'It cannot be that all men always have been doomed to this awful horror!' He raised himself.

'There is something wrong in it; I must be calm, I must think it all over from the beginning.' And then he began to consider. 'Yes, the beginning of my illness. I knocked my side, and I was just the same, that day and the days after; it ached a little, then more, then doctors, then depression, misery, and again doctors; and I've gone on getting closer and closer to the abyss. Strength growing less. Nearer and nearer. And here I am, wasting away, no light in my eyes. I think of how to cure the appendix, but this is death. Can it be death?' Again a horror came over him; gasping for breath, he bent over, began feeling for the matches, and knocked his elbow against the bedside table. It was in his way and hurt him; he felt furious with it, in his anger knocked against it more violently, and upset it. And in despair, breathless, he fell back on his spine waiting for death to come that instant.

The visitors were leaving at that time. Praskovya Fyodorovna was seeing them out. She heard something fall, and came in.

'What is it?'

'Nothing. I dropped something by accident.'

She went out, brought a candle. He was lying, breathing hard and fast, like a man who has run a mile, and staring with fixed eyes at her.

'What is it, Jean?'

'No—othing, I say. I dropped something.'—'Why speak? She won't understand,' he thought.

She certainly did not understand. She picked up the candle, lighted it for him, and went out hastily. She had to say good-bye to a departing guest. When she came back, he was lying in the same position on his back, looking upwards.

'How are you—worse?'

'Yes.'

She shook her head, sat down.

'Do you know what, Jean? I wonder if we hadn't better send for Leshchetitsky to see you here?'

This meant calling in the celebrated doctor, regardless of expense. He smiled malignantly, and said no. She sat a moment longer, went up to him, and kissed him on the forehead.

He hated her with all the force of his soul when she was kissing him, and had to make an effort not to push her away.

'Good night. Please God, you'll sleep.'

'Yes.'

VI

Ivan Ilych saw that he was dying, and was in continual despair.

At the bottom of his heart Ivan Ilych knew that he was dying; but so far from growing used to this idea, he simply did not grasp it—he was utterly unable to grasp it.

The example of the syllogism that he had learned in Kiseveter's logic—Caius is a man, men are mortal, therefore Caius is mortal—had seemed to him all his life correct only as regards Caius, but not at all as regards himself. In that case it was a question of Caius, a man, an abstract man, and it was perfectly true, but he was not Caius, and was not an abstract man; he had always been a creature quite, quite different from all others; he had been little Vanya with a mamma and papa, and Mitya and Volodya, with playthings and a coachman and a nurse; afterwards with Katenka, with all the joys and griefs and ecstasies of childhood, boyhood, and youth. What did Caius know of the smell of the leathern ball Vanya had been so fond of? Had Caius kissed his mother's hand like that? Caius had not heard the silk rustle of his mother's skirts. He had not made a riot at school over the pudding. Had Caius been in love like that? Could Caius preside over the sittings of the court?

And Caius certainly was mortal, and it was right for him to die; but for me, little Vanya, Ivan Ilych, with all my feelings and ideas—for me it's a different matter. And it cannot be that I ought to die. That would be too awful.

That was his feeling.

'If I had to die like Caius, I should have known it was so, some inner voice would have told me so. But there was nothing of the sort in me. And I and all my friends, we felt that it was not at all the same as with Caius. And now here it is!' he said to himself. 'It can't be! It can't be, but it is! How is it? How's one to understand it?' And he could not conceive it, and tried to drive away this idea as false, incorrect, and morbid, and to supplant it by other, correct, healthy ideas. But this idea, not as an idea merely, but as it were an actual fact, came back again and stood confronting him.

And to replace this thought he called up other thoughts, one after another, in the hope of finding support in them. He tried to get back into former trains of thought, which in old days had screened off the thought of death. But, strange to say, all that had in old days covered up, obliterated the sense of death, could not now produce the same effect. Latterly, Ivan Ilych spent the greater part of his time in these efforts to restore his old trains of thought which had shut off death. At one time he would say to himself, 'I'll put myself into my official work; why, I used to live in it.' And he would go to the law-courts, banishing every doubt. He would enter into conversation with his colleagues, and would sit carelessly, as his old habit was, scanning the crowd below dreamily, and with both his wasted hands he would lean on the arms of the oak arm-chair just as he always did; and bending over to a colleague, pass the papers to him and whisper to him, then suddenly dropping his eyes and sitting up straight, he would pronounce the familiar words that opened the proceedings. But suddenly in the middle, the pain in his side, utterly regardless of the stage he had reached in his conduct of the case, began its work. It riveted Ivan Ilych's attention. He drove away the thought of it, but it still did its work, and then It came and stood confronting him and looked at him, and he felt turned to stone, and the light died away in his eyes, and he began to ask himself again, 'Can it be that It is the only truth?' And his colleagues and his subordinates saw with surprise and distress that he, the brilliant, subtle judge, was losing the thread of his speech, was making blunders. He shook himself, tried to regain his self-control, and got somehow to the end of the sitting, and went home with the painful sense that his judicial labours could not as of old hide from him what he wanted to hide; that he could not by means of his official work escape from It. And the worst of it was that It drew him to itself not for him to do anything in particular, but simply for him to look at It straight in the face, to look at It and, doing nothing, suffer unspeakably.

And to save himself from this, Ivan Ilych sought amusements, other screens, and these screens he found, and for a little while they did seem to save him; but soon again they were not so much broken down as let the light through, as though It pierced through everything, and there was nothing that could shut It off.

Sometimes during those days he would go into the drawing-room he had furnished, that drawing-room where he had fallen, for which—how bitterly ludicrous it was for him to think of it!—for the decoration of which he had sacrificed his life, for he knew that it was that bruise that had started his illness. He went in and saw that the polished table had been scratched by something. He looked for the cause, and found it in the bronze clasps of the album, which had been twisted on one side. He took up the album, a costly one, which he had himself arranged with loving care, and was vexed at the carelessness of his daughter and her friends. Here a page was torn, here the photographs had been shifted out of their places. He carefully put it to rights again and bent the clasp back.

Then the idea occurred to him to move all this établissement of the albums to another corner where the flowers stood. He called the footman; or his daughter or his wife came to help him. They did not agree with him, contradicted him; he argued, got angry. But all that was very well, since he did not think of It; It was not in sight.

But then his wife would say, as he moved something himself, 'Do let the servants do it, you'll hurt yourself again,' and all at once It peeped through the screen; he caught a glimpse of It. He caught a glimpse of It, but still he hoped It would hide itself. Involuntarily though, he kept watch on his side; there it is just the same still, aching still, and now he cannot forget it, and It is staring openly at him from behind the flowers. What's the use of it all?

'And it's the fact that here, at that curtain, as if it had been storming a fort, I lost my life. Is it possible? How awful and how silly! It cannot be! It cannot be, and it is.'

He went into his own room, lay down, and was again alone with It. Face to face with It, and nothing to be done with It. Nothing but to look at It and shiver.

VII

How it came to pass during the third month of Ivan Ilych's illness, it would be impossible to say, for it happened little by little, imperceptibly, but it had come to pass that his wife and his daughter and his son and their servants and their acquaintances, and the doctors, and, most of all, he himself—all were aware that all interest in him for other people consisted now in the question how soon he would leave his place empty, free the living from the constraint of his presence, and be set free himself from his sufferings.

He slept less and less; they gave him opium, and began to inject morphine. But this did not relieve him. The dull pain he experienced in the half-asleep condition at first only relieved him as a change, but then it became as bad, or even more agonising, than the open pain. He had special things to eat prepared for him according to the doctors' prescriptions; but these dishes became more and more distasteful, more and more revolting to him.

Special arrangements, too, had to be made for his other physical needs, and this was a continual misery to him. Misery from the uncleanliness, the unseemliness, and the stench, from the feeling of another person having to assist in it.

But just from this most unpleasant side of his illness there came comfort to Ivan Ilych. There always came into his room on these occasions to clear up for him the peasant who waited at table, Gerasim.

Gerasim was a clean, fresh, young peasant, who had grown stout and hearty on the good fare in town. Always cheerful and bright. At first the sight of this lad, always cleanly dressed in the Russian style, engaged in this revolting task, embarrassed Ivan Ilych.

One day, getting up from the night-stool, too weak to replace his clothes, he dropped on to a soft low chair and looked with horror at his bare, powerless thighs, with the muscles so sharply standing out on them.

Then there came in with light, strong steps Gerasim, in his thick boots, diffusing a pleasant smell of tar from his boots, and bringing in the freshness of the winter air. Wearing a clean hempen apron, and a clean cotton shirt, with his sleeves tucked up on his strong, bare young arms, without looking at Ivan Ilych, obviously trying to check the radiant happiness in his face so as not to hurt the sick man, he went up to the night-stool.

'Gerasim,' said Ivan Ilych faintly.

Gerasim started, clearly afraid that he had done something amiss, and with a rapid movement turned towards the sick man his fresh, good-natured, simple young face, just beginning to be downy with the first growth of beard.

'Yes, your honour.'

'I'm afraid this is very disagreeable for you. You must excuse me. I can't help it.'

'Why, upon my word, sir!' And Gerasim's eyes beamed, and he showed his white young teeth in a smile. 'What's a little trouble? It's a case of illness with you, sir.'

And with his deft, strong arms he performed his habitual task, and went out, stepping lightly. And five minutes later, treading just as lightly, he came back.

Ivan Ilych was still sitting in the same way in the arm-chair.

'Gerasim,' he said, when the latter had replaced the night-stool all sweet and clean, 'please help me; come here.' Gerasim went up to him. 'Lift me up. It's difficult for me alone, and I've sent Dmitry away.'

Gerasim went up to him; as lightly as he stepped he put his strong arms round him, deftly and gently lifted and supported him, with the other hand pulled up his trousers, and would have set him down again. But Ivan Ilych asked him to carry him to the sofa. Gerasim, without effort, carefully not squeezing him, led him, almost carrying him, to the sofa, and settled him there.

'Thank you; how neatly and well . . . you do everything.'

Gerasim smiled again, and would have gone away. But Ivan Ilych felt his presence such a comfort that he was reluctant to let him go.

'Oh, move that chair near me, please. No, that one, under my legs. I feel easier when my legs are higher.'

Gerasim picked up the chair, and without letting it knock, set it gently down on the ground just at the right place, and lifted Ivan Ilych's legs on to it. It seemed to Ivan Ilych that he was easier just at the moment when Gerasim lifted his legs higher.

'I'm better when my legs are higher,' said Ivan Ilych. 'Put that cushion under me.'

Gerasim did so. Again he lifted his legs to put the cushion under them. Again it seemed to Ivan Ilych that he was easier at that moment when Gerasim held his legs raised. When he laid them down again, he felt worse.

'Gerasim,' he said to him, 'are you busy just now?'

'Not at all, sir,' said Gerasim, who had learned among the town-bred servants how to speak to gentlefolks.

'What have you left to do?'

'Why, what have I to do? I've done everything, there's only the wood to chop for tomorrow.'

'Then hold my legs up like that—can you?'

'To be sure, I can.' Gerasim lifted the legs up. And it seemed to Ivan Ilych that in that position he did not feel the pain at all.

'But how about the wood?'

'Don't you trouble about that, sir. We shall have time enough.'

Ivan Ilych made Gerasim sit and hold his legs, and began to talk to him. And, strange to say, he fancied he felt better while Gerasim had hold of his legs.

From that time forward Ivan Ilych would sometimes call Gerasim, and get him to hold his legs on his shoulders, and he liked talking with him. Gerasim did this easily, readily, simply, and with a good-nature that touched Ivan Ilych. Health, strength, and heartiness in all other people were offensive to Ivan Ilych; but the strength and heartiness of Gerasim did not mortify him, but soothed him.

Ivan Ilych's great misery was due to the deception that for some reason or other every one kept up with him—that he was simply ill, and not dying, and that he need only keep quiet and follow the doctor's orders, and then some great change for the better would be the result. He knew that whatever they might do, there would be no result except more agonising sufferings and death. And he was made miserable by this lie, made miserable at their refusing to acknowledge what they all knew and he knew, by their persisting in lying over him about his awful position, and in forcing him too to take part in this lie. Lying, lying, this lying carried on over him on the eve of his death, and destined to bring that terrible, solemn act of his death down to the level of all their visits, curtains, sturgeons for dinner . . . was a horrible agony for Ivan Ilych. And, strange to say, many times when they had been going through the regular performance over him, he had been within a hair's-breadth of screaming at them: 'Cease your lying! You know, and I know, that I'm dying; so do, at least, give over lying!' But he had never had the spirit to do this. The terrible, awful act of his dying was, he saw, by all those about him, brought down to the level of a casual, unpleasant, and to some extent indecorous, incident (somewhat as they would behave with a person who should enter a drawing-room smelling unpleasant). It was brought down to this level by that very decorum to which he had been enslaved all his life. He saw that no one felt for him, because no one would even grasp his position. Gerasim was the only person who recognised the position, and felt sorry for him. And that was why Ivan Ilych was only at ease with Gerasim. He felt comforted when Gerasim sometimes supported his legs for whole nights at a stretch, and would not go away to bed, saying, 'Don't you worry yourself, Ivan Ilych, I'll get sleep enough yet,' or when suddenly dropping into the familiar peasant forms of speech, he added: 'If thou weren't sick, but as 'tis, 'twould be strange if I didn't wait on thee.' Gerasim alone did not lie; everything showed clearly that he alone understood what it meant, and saw no necessity to disguise it, and simply felt sorry for his sick, wasting master. He even said this once straight out, when Ivan Ilych was sending him away.

'We shall all die. So what's a little trouble?' he said, meaning by this to express that he did not complain of the trouble just because he was taking this trouble for a dying man, and he hoped that for him too someone would be willing to take the same trouble when his time came.

Apart from this deception, or in consequence of it, what made the greatest misery for Ivan Ilych was that no one felt for him as he would have liked them to feel for him. At certain moments, after prolonged suffering, Ivan Ilych, ashamed as he would have been to own it, longed more than anything for someone to feel sorry for him, as for a sick child. He longed to be petted, kissed, and wept over, as children are petted and comforted. He knew that he was an important member of the law-courts, that he had a beard turning grey, and that therefore it was impossible. But still he longed for it. And in his relations with Gerasim there was something approaching to that. And that was why being with Gerasim was a comfort to him. Ivan Ilych longs to weep, longs to be petted and wept over, and then there comes in a colleague, Shebek; and instead of weeping and being petted, Ivan Ilych puts on his serious, severe, earnest face, and from mere inertia gives his views on the effect of the last decision in the Court of Appeal, and obstinately insists upon them. This falsity around him and within him did more than anything to poison Ivan Ilych's last days.

VIII

It was morning. All that made it morning for Ivan Ilych was that Gerasim had gone away, and Pyotr the footman had come in; he had put out the candles, opened one of the curtains, and begun surreptitiously setting the room to rights. Whether it were morning or evening, Friday or Sunday, it all made no difference; it was always just the same thing. Gnawing, agonising pain never ceasing for an instant; the hopeless sense of life always ebbing away, but still not yet gone; always swooping down on him that fearful, hated death, which was the only reality, and always the same falsity. What were days, or weeks, or hours of the day to him?

'Will you have tea, sir?'

'He wants things done in their regular order. In the morning the family should have tea,' he thought, and only said—

'No.'

'Would you care to move on to the sofa?'

'He wants to make the room tidy, and I'm in his way. I'm uncleanness, disorder,' he thought, and only said—

'No, leave me alone.'

The servant still moved busily about his work. Ivan Ilych stretched out his hand. Pyotr went up to offer his services.

'What can I get you?'

'My watch.'

Pyotr got out the watch, which lay just under his hand, and gave it him.

'Half-past eight. Are they up?'

'Not yet, sir. Vladimir Ivanovich' (that was his son) 'has gone to the high school, and Praskovya Fyodorovna gave orders that she was to be waked if you asked for her. Shall I send word?'

'No, no need. Should I try some tea?' he thought.

'Yes, tea . . . bring it.'

Pyotr was on his way out. Ivan Ilych felt frightened of being left alone. 'How keep him? Oh, the medicine. Pyotr, give me my medicine. Oh well, may be, medicine may still be some good.' He took the spoon, drank it. 'No, it does no good. It's all rubbish, deception,' he decided, as soon as he tasted the familiar, mawkish, hopeless taste. 'No, I can't believe it now. But the pain, why this pain; if it would only cease for a minute.' And he groaned. Pyotr turned round. 'No, go on. Bring the tea.'

Pyotr went away. Ivan Ilych, left alone, moaned, not so much from the pain, awful as it was, as from misery. Always the same thing again and again, all these endless days and nights. If it would only be quicker. Quicker to what? Death, darkness. No, no. Anything better than death!'

When Pyotr came in with the tea on a tray, Ivan Ilych stared for some time absent-mindedly at him, not grasping who he was and what he wanted. Pyotr was disconcerted by this stare. And when he showed he was disconcerted, Ivan Ilych came to himself.

'Oh yes,' he said, 'tea, good, set it down. Only help me to wash and put on a clean shirt.'

And Ivan Ilych began his washing. He washed his hands slowly, and then his face, cleaned his teeth, combed his hair, and looked in the looking-glass. He felt frightened at what he saw, especially at the way his hair clung limply to his pale forehead. When his shirt was being changed, he knew he would be still more terrified if he glanced at his body, and he avoided looking at himself. But at last it was all over. He put on his dressing-gown, covered himself with a rug, and sat in the armchair to drink his tea. For one moment he felt refreshed; but as soon as he began to drink the tea, again there was the same taste, the same pain. He forced himself to finish it, and lay down, stretching out his legs. He lay down and dismissed Pyotr.

Always the same. A gleam of hope flashes for a moment, then again the sea of despair roars about him again, and always pain, always pain, always heartache, and always the same thing. Alone it is awfully dreary; he longs to call someone, but he knows beforehand that with others present it will be worse. 'Morphine again—only to forget again. I'll tell him, the doctor, that he must think of something else. It can't go on; it can't go on like this.'

One hour, two hours pass like this. Then there is a ring at the front door. The doctor, perhaps. Yes, it is the doctor, fresh, hearty, fat, and cheerful, wearing that expression that seems to say, 'You there are in a panic about something, but we'll soon set things right for you.' The doctor is aware that this expression is hardly fitting here, but he has put it on once and for all, and can't take it off; like a man who has put on a frockcoat to pay a round of calls.

In a hearty, reassuring manner the doctor rubs his hands.

'I'm cold. It's a sharp frost. Just let me warm myself,' he says with an expression, as though it's only a matter of waiting a little till he's warm, and as soon as he's warm he'll set everything to rights.

'Well, now, how are you?'

Ivan Ilych feels that the doctor would like to say, 'How's the little trouble?' but that he feels that he can't talk like that, and says, 'How did you pass the night?'

Ivan Ilych looks at the doctor with an expression that asks—

'Is it possible you're never ashamed of lying?'

But the doctor does not care to understand this look.

And Ivan Ilych says—

'It's always just as awful. The pain never leaves me, never ceases. If only there were something!'

'Ah, you're all like that, all sick people say that. Come, now I do believe I'm thawed; even Praskovya Fyodorovna, who's so particular, could find no fault with my temperature. Well, now I can say good morning.' And the doctor shakes hands.

And dropping his former levity, the doctor, with a serious face, proceeds to examine the patient, feeling his pulse, to take his temperature, and then the tappings and soundings begin.

Ivan Ilych knows positively and indubitably that it's all nonsense and empty deception; but when the doctor, kneeling down, stretches over him, putting his ear first higher, then lower, and goes through various gymnastic evolutions over him with a serious face, Ivan Ilych is affected by this, as he used sometimes to be affected by the speeches of the lawyers in court, though he was perfectly well aware that they were telling lies all the while and why they were telling lies.

The doctor, kneeling on the sofa, was still sounding him, when there was the rustle of Praskovya Fyodorovna's silk dress in the doorway, and she was heard scolding Pyotr for not having let her know that the doctor had come.

She comes in, kisses her husband, and at once begins to explain that she has been up a long while, and that it was only through a misunderstanding that she was not there when the doctor came.

Ivan Ilych looks at her, scans her all over, and sets down against her her whiteness and plumpness, and the cleanness of her hands and neck, and the glossiness of her hair, and the gleam full of life in her eyes. With all the force of his soul he hates her. And when she touches him it makes him suffer from the thrill of hatred he feels for her.

Her attitude to him and his illness is still the same. Just as the doctor had taken up a certain line with the patient which he was not now able to drop, so she too had taken up a line with him—that he was not doing something he ought to do, and was himself to blame, and she was lovingly reproaching him for his neglect, and she could not now get out of this attitude.

'Why, you know, he won't listen to me; he doesn't take his medicine at the right times. And what's worse still, he insists on lying in a position that surely must be bad for him—with his legs in the air.'

She described how he made Gerasim hold his legs up.

The doctor smiled with kindly condescension that said, 'Oh well, it can't be helped, these sick people do take up such foolish fancies; but we must forgive them.'

When the examination was over, the doctor looked at his watch, and then Praskovya Fyodorovna informed Ivan Ilych that it must of course be as he liked, but she had sent today for a celebrated doctor, and that he would examine him, and have a consultation with Mikhail Danilovich (that was the name of their regular doctor).

'Don't oppose it now, please. This I'm doing entirely for my own sake,' she said ironically, meaning it to be understood that she was doing it all for his sake, and was only saying this to give him no right to refuse her request. He lay silent, knitting his brows. He felt that he was hemmed in by such a tangle of falsity that it was hard to disentangle anything from it.

Everything she did for him was entirely for her own sake, and she told him she was doing for her own sake what she actually was doing for her own sake as something so incredible that he would take it as meaning the opposite.

At half-past eleven the celebrated doctor came. Again came the sounding, and then grave conversation in his presence and in the other room about the kidney and the appendix, and questions and answers, with such an air of significance, that again, instead of the real question of life and death, which was now the only one that confronted him, the question that came uppermost was of the kidney and the appendix, which were doing something not as they ought to do, and were for that reason being attacked by Mikhail Danilovich and the celebrated doctor, and forced to mend their ways.

The celebrated doctor took leave of him with a serious, but not a hopeless face. And to the timid question that Ivan Ilych addressed to him while he lifted his eyes, shining with terror and hope, up towards him, Was there a chance of recovery? he answered that he could not answer for it, but that there was a chance. The look of hope with which Ivan Ilych watched the doctor out was so piteous that, seeing it, Praskovya Fyodorovna positively burst into tears, as she went out of the door to hand the celebrated doctor his fee in the next room.

The gleam of hope kindled by the doctor's assurance did not last long. Again the same room, the same pictures, the curtains, the wallpaper, the medicine-bottles, and ever the same, his aching suffering body. And Ivan Ilych began to moan; they gave him injections, and he sank into oblivion. When he waked up it was getting dark; they brought him his dinner. He forced himself to eat some broth; and again everything the same, and again the coming night.

After dinner at seven o'clock, Praskovya Fyodorovna came into his room, dressed as though to go to a *soirée*, with her full bosom laced in tight, and traces of powder on her face. She had in the morning mentioned to him that they were going to the theatre. Sarah Bernhardt* was visiting the town, and they had a box, which he had insisted on their taking. By now he had forgotten about it, and her smart attire was an offence to him. But he concealed this feeling when he recollected that he had himself insisted on their taking a box and going, because it was an æsthetic pleasure, beneficial and instructive for the children.

Praskovya Fyodorovna came in satisfied with herself, but yet with something of a guilty air. She sat down, asked how he was, as he saw, simply for the sake of asking, and not for the sake of learning anything, knowing indeed that there was nothing to learn, and began telling him how absolutely necessary it was; how she would not have gone for anything, but the box had been taken, and Ellen and their daughter, and Petrishchev (the examining lawyer, the daughter's suitor) were going, and that it was out of the question to let them go alone. But that she would have liked much better to stay with him. If only he would be sure to follow the doctor's prescription while she was away.

'Oh, and Fyodor Dmitryevich' (the suitor) 'would like to come in. May he? And Liza?'

'Yes, let them come in.'

The daughter came in, in full dress, her fresh young body bare, while his body made him suffer so. But she made a show of it; she was strong, healthy, obviously in love, and impatient of the illness, suffering, and death that hindered her happiness.

Fyodor Dmitryevich came in too in evening dress, his hair curled à la *Capoul*,† with his long sinewy neck tightly fenced round by a white collar, with his vast expanse of white chest and strong thighs

---

*The great French actress toured Russia in the winter of 1881–1882.

†In a style set by Joseph Capoul, a popular French tenor of the day.

displayed in narrow black trousers, with one white glove in his hand and a crush opera hat.

Behind him crept in unnoticed the little high school boy in his new uniform, poor fellow, in gloves, and with that awful blue ring under his eyes that Ivan Ilych knew the meaning of.

He always felt sorry for his son. And pitiable indeed was his scared face of sympathetic suffering. Except Gerasim, Ivan Ilych fancied that Volodya was the only one that understood and was sorry.

They all sat down; again they asked how he was. A silence followed. Liza asked her mother about the opera-glass. An altercation ensued between the mother and daughter as to who had taken it, and where it had been put. It turned into an unpleasant squabble.

Fyodor Dmitryevich asked Ivan Ilych whether he had seen Sarah Bernhardt? Ivan Ilych could not at first catch the question that was asked him, but then he said, 'No, have you seen her before?'

'Yes, in *Adrienne Lecouvreur*.'

Praskovya Fyodorovna observed that she was particularly good in that part. The daughter made some reply. A conversation sprang up about the art and naturalness of her acting, that conversation that is continually repeated and always the same.

In the middle of the conversation Fyodor Dmitryevich glanced at Ivan Ilych and relapsed into silence. The others looked at him and became mute too. Ivan Ilych was staring with glittering eyes straight before him, obviously furious with them. This had to be set right, but it could not anyhow be set right. This silence had somehow to be broken. No one would venture on breaking it, and all began to feel alarmed that the decorous deception was somehow breaking down, and the facts would be exposed to all. Liza was the first to pluck up courage. She broke the silence. She tried to cover up what they were all feeling, but inadvertently she gave it utterance.

'If *we are going*, though, it's time to start,' she said, glancing at her watch, a gift from her father; and with a scarcely perceptible meaning smile to the young man, referring to something only known to themselves, she got up with a rustle of her skirts.

They all got up, said good-bye, and went away. When they were gone, Ivan Ilych fancied he was easier; there was no falsity—that had gone away with them, but the pain remained. That continual pain, that continual terror, made nothing harder, nothing easier. It was always worse.

Again came minute after minute, hour after hour, still the same and still no end, and ever more terrible the inevitable end.

'Yes, send Gerasim,' he said in answer to Pyotr's question.

IX

Late at night his wife came back. She came in on tiptoe, but he heard her, opened his eyes, and made haste to close them again. She wanted to send away Gerasim and sit up with him herself instead. He opened his eyes and said, 'No, go away.'

'Are you in great pain?'

'Always the same.'

'Take some opium.'

He agreed, and drank it. She went away.

Till three o'clock he slept a miserable sleep. It seemed to him that he and his pain were being thrust somewhere into a narrow, deep, black sack, and they kept pushing him further and further in, and still could not thrust him to the bottom. And this operation was awful to him, and was accompanied with agony. And he was afraid, and yet wanted to fall into it, and struggled and yet tried to get into it. And all of a sudden he slipped and fell and woke up. Gerasim, still the same, is sitting at the foot of the bed half-dozing peacefully, patient. And he is lying with his wasted legs clad in stockings, raised on Gerasim's shoulders, the same candle burning in the alcove, and the same interminable pain.

'Go away, Gerasim,' he whispered.

'It's all right, sir. I'll stay a bit longer.'

'No, go away.'

He took his legs down, lay sideways on his arm, and he felt very sorry for himself. He only waited till Gerasim had gone away into the next room; he could restrain himself no longer, and cried like a child. He cried at his own helplessness, at his awful loneliness, at the cruelty of people, at the cruelty of God, at the absence of God.

'Why hast Thou done all this? What brought me to this? Why, why torture me so horribly?'

He did not expect an answer, and wept indeed that there was and could be no answer. The pain grew more acute again, but he did not stir, did not call.

He said to himself, 'Come, more then; come, strike me! But what for? What have I done to Thee? what for?'

Then he was still, ceased weeping, held his breath, and was all attention; he listened, as it were, not to a voice uttering sounds, but to the voice of his soul, to the current of thoughts that rose up within him.

'What is it you want?' was the first clear idea able to be put into words that he grasped.

'What? Not to suffer, to live,' he answered.

And again he was utterly plunged into attention so intense that even the pain did not distract him.

'To live? Live how?' the voice of his soul was asking.

'Why, live as I used to live before—happily and pleasantly.'

'As you used to live before—happily and pleasantly?' queried the voice. And he began going over in his imagination the best moments of his pleasant life. But, strange to say, all these best moments of his pleasant life seemed now not at all what they had seemed then. All—except the first memories of childhood—there, in his childhood there had been something really pleasant in which one could have lived if it had come back. But the creature who had this pleasant experience was no more; it was like a memory of someone else.

As soon as he reached the beginning of what had resulted in him as he was now, Ivan Ilych, all that had seemed joys to him then now melted away before his eyes and were transformed into something trivial, and often disgusting.

And the further he went from childhood, the nearer to the actual present, the more worthless and uncertain were the joys. It began with life at the school of jurisprudence. Then there had still been something genuinely good; then there had been gaiety; then there had been friendship; then there had been hopes. But in the higher classes these good moments were already becoming rarer. Later on, during the first period of his official life, at the governor's, good moments appeared; but it was all mixed, and less and less of it was good. And further on even less was good, and the further he went the less good there was.

His marriage . . . as gratuitous as the disillusion of it and the smell of his wife's breath and the sensuality, the hypocrisy! And that deadly official life, and anxiety about money, and so for one year, and two, and ten, and twenty, and always the same thing. And the further he went, the more deadly it became. 'As though I had been going steadily downhill, imagining that I was going uphill. So it was in fact. In public opinion I was going uphill, and steadily as I got up it life was ebbing away from me. . . . And now the work's done, there's only to die.'

'But what is this? What for? It cannot be! It cannot be that life has been so senseless, so loathsome? And if it really was so loathsome and senseless, then why die, and die in agony? There's something wrong.'

'Can it be I have not lived as one ought?' suddenly came into his head. 'But how not so, when I've done everything as it should be done?' he said, and at once dismissed this only solution of all the enigma of life and death as something utterly out of the question.

'What do you want now? To live? Live how? Live as you live at the courts when the usher booms out; "The judge is coming!" . . . The judge is coming, the judge is coming,' he repeated to himself. 'Here he is, the judge! But I'm not to blame!' he shrieked in fury. 'What's it for?' And he left off crying, and turning with his face to the wall, fell to pondering always on the same question, 'What for, why all this horror?'

But however much he pondered, he could not find an answer. And whenever the idea struck him, as it often did, that it all came of his never having lived as he ought, he thought of all the correctness of his life and dismissed this strange idea.

X

Another fortnight had passed. Ivan Ilych could not now get up from the sofa. He did not like lying in bed, and lay on the sofa. And lying almost all the time facing the wall, in loneliness he suffered all the inexplicable agonies, and in loneliness pondered always that inexplicable question, 'What is it? Can it be true that it's

death?' And an inner voice answered, 'Yes, it is true.' 'Why these agonies?' and a voice answered, 'For no reason.' Beyond and besides this
there was nothing.

From the very beginning of his illness, ever since Ivan Ilych first
went to the doctor's, his life had been split up into two contradictory
moods, which were continually alternating—one was despair and
the anticipation of an uncomprehended and awful death; the other
was hope and an absorbed watching over the actual condition of his
body. First there was nothing confronting him but a kidney or intes-
tine which had temporarily declined to perform their duties, then
there was nothing but unknown awful death, which there was no
escaping.

These two moods had alternated from the very beginning of the
illness; but the further the illness progressed, the more doubtful and
fantastic became the conception of the kidney, and the more real the
sense of approaching death.

He had but to reflect on what he had been three months before
and what he was now, to reflect how steadily he had been going
downhill, for every possibility of hope to be shattered.

Of late, in the loneliness in which he found himself, lying with his
face to the back of the sofa, a loneliness in the middle of a populous
town and of his numerous acquaintances and his family, a loneliness than which none more complete could be found anywhere—not
at the bottom of the sea, not deep down in the earth;—of late in this
fearful loneliness Ivan Ilych had lived only in imagination in the past.
One by one the pictures of his past rose up before him. It always
began from what was nearest in time and went back to the most
remote, to childhood, and rested there. If Ivan Ilych thought of the
stewed prunes that had been offered him for dinner that day, his
mind went back to the damp, wrinkled French plum of his childhood, of its peculiar taste and the flow of saliva when the stone was
sucked; and along with this memory of a taste there rose up a whole
series of memories of that period—his nurse, his brother, his playthings. 'I mustn't . . . it's too painful,' Ivan Ilych said to himself, and
he brought himself back to the present. The button on the back of the
sofa and the creases in the morocco. 'Morocco's dear, and doesn't
wear well; there was a quarrel over it. But the morocco was different,
and different too the quarrel when we tore father's portfolio and

were punished, and mamma bought us the tarts.' And again his mind rested on his childhood, and again it was painful, and he tried to drive it away and think of something else.

And again at that point, together with that chain of associations, quite another chain of memories came into his heart, of how his illness had grown up and become more acute. It was the same there, the further back the more life there had been. There had been both more that was good in life and more of life itself. And the two began to melt into one. 'Just as the pain goes on getting worse and worse, so has my whole life gone on getting worse and worse,' he thought. One light spot was there at the back, at the beginning of life, and then it kept getting blacker and blacker, and going faster and faster 'In inverse ratio to the square of the distance from death,' thought Ivan Ilych. And the image of a stone falling downwards with increasing velocity sank into his soul. Life, a series of increasing sufferings, falls more and more swiftly to the end, the most fearful sufferings. 'I am falling.' He shuddered, shifted himself, would have resisted, but he knew beforehand that he could not resist; and again, with eyes weary with gazing at it, but unable not to gaze at what was before him, he stared at the back of the sofa and waited, waited expecting that fearful fall and shock and dissolution. 'Resistance is impossible,' he said to himself. 'But if one could at least comprehend what it's for? Even that's impossible. It could be explained if one were to say that I hadn't lived as I ought. But that can't be alleged,' he said to himself, thinking of all the regularity, correctness, and propriety of his life. 'That really can't be admitted,' he said to himself, his lips smiling ironically as though someone could see his smile and be deceived by it. 'No explanation! Agony, death. . . . What for?'

XI

So passed a fortnight. During that fortnight an event occurred that had been desired by Ivan Ilych and his wife. Petrishchev made a formal proposal. This took place in the evening. Next day Praskovya Fyodorovna went in to her husband, revolving in her mind how to inform him of Fyodor Dmitryevich's proposal, but that night there had been a change for the worse in Ivan Ilych. Praskovya Fyodorovna found him on the same sofa, but in a different position. He was lying on his face, groaning, and staring straight before him with a fixed gaze.

She began talking of remedies. He turned his stare on her. She did not finish what she had begun saying; such hatred of her in particular was expressed in that stare.

'For Christ's sake, let me die in peace,' he said.

She would have gone away, but at that moment the daughter came in and went up to say good morning to him. He looked at his daughter just as at his wife, and to her inquiries how he was, he told her drily that they would soon all be rid of him. Both were silent, sat a little while, and went out.

'How are we to blame?' said Liza to her mother. 'As though we had done it! I'm sorry for papa, but why punish us?'

At the usual hour the doctor came. Ivan Ilych answered, 'Yes, no,' never taking his exasperated stare from him, and towards the end he said, 'Why, you know that you can do nothing, so let me be.'

'We can relieve your suffering,' said the doctor.

'Even that you can't do; let me be.'

The doctor went into the drawing-room and told Praskovya Fyodorovna that it was very serious, and that the only resource left them was opium to relieve his sufferings, which must be terrible. The doctor said his physical sufferings were terrible, and that was true; but even more terrible than his physical sufferings were his mental sufferings, and in that lay his chief misery.

His moral sufferings were due to the fact that during that night, as he looked at the sleepy, good-natured, broad-cheeked face of Gerasim, the thought had suddenly come into his head, 'What if in reality all my life, my conscious life, has been not the right thing?' The thought struck him that what he had regarded before as an utter impossibility, that he had spent his life not as he ought, might be the truth. It struck him that those scarcely detected impulses of struggle within him against what was considered good by persons of higher position, scarcely detected impulses which he had dismissed, that they might be the real thing, and everything else might be not the right thing. And his official work, and his ordering of his daily life and of his family, and these social and official interests,—all that might be not the right thing. He tried to defend it all to himself. And suddenly he felt all the weakness of what he was defending. And it was useless to defend it.

'But if it's so,' he said to himself, 'and I am leaving life with the consciousness that I have lost all that was given me, and there's no correcting it, then what?' He lay on his back and began going over his whole life entirely anew. When he saw the footman in the morning, then his wife, then his daughter, then the doctor, every movement they made, every word they uttered, confirmed for him the terrible truth that had been revealed to him in the night. In them he saw himself, saw all in which he had lived, and saw distinctly that it was all not the right thing; it was a horrible, vast deception that concealed both life and death. This consciousness intensified his physical agonies, multiplied them tenfold. He groaned and tossed from side to side and pulled at the covering over him. It seemed to him that it was stifling him and weighing him down. And for that he hated them.

They gave him a big dose of opium; he sank into unconsciousness; but at dinner-time the same thing began again. He drove them all away, and tossed from side to side.

His wife came to him and said, 'Jean, darling, do this for my sake' (for my sake?). 'It can't do harm, and it often does good. Why, it's nothing. And often in health people——'

He opened his eyes wide.

'What? Take the sacrament? What for? No. Besides . . .'

She began to cry.

'Yes, my dear? I'll send for our priest, he's so nice.'

'All right, very well,' he said.

When the priest came and confessed him he was softened, felt as it were a relief from his doubts, and consequently from his sufferings, and there came a moment of hope. He began once more thinking of the appendix and the possibility of curing it. He took the sacrament with tears in his eyes.

When they laid him down again after the sacrament for a minute, he felt comfortable, and again the hope of life sprang up. He began to think about the operation which had been suggested to him. 'To live, I want to live,' he said to himself. His wife came in to congratulate him; she uttered the customary words and added—

'It's quite true, isn't it, that you're better?'

Without looking at her, he said, 'Yes.'

Her dress, her figure, the expression of her face, the tone of her voice,—all told him the same: 'Not the right thing. All that in which you lived and are living is lying, deceit, hiding life and death away from you.' And as soon as he had formed that thought, hatred sprang up in him, and with that hatred agonising physical sufferings, and with these sufferings the sense of inevitable, approaching ruin. Something new was happening; there were twisting and shooting pains, and a tightness in his breathing.

The expression of his face as he uttered that 'Yes' was terrible. After uttering that 'Yes,' looking her straight in the face, he turned on to his face, with a rapidity extraordinary in his weakness, and shrieked—

'Go away, go away, let me be!'

XII

From that moment there began the scream that never ceased for three days, and was so awful that through two closed doors one could not hear it without horror. At the moment when he answered his wife he grasped that he had fallen, that there was no return, that the end had come, quite the end, while doubt was still as unsolved, still remained doubt.

'Oo! Oo—o! Oo!' he screamed in varying intonations. He had begun screaming, 'I don't want to!' and so had gone on screaming on the same vowel sound— oo!

All those three days, during which time did not exist for him, he was struggling in that black sack into which he was being thrust by an unseen resistless force. He struggled as the man condemned to death struggles in the hands of the executioner, knowing that he cannot save himself. And every moment he felt that in spite of all his efforts to struggle against it, he was getting nearer and nearer to what terrified him. He felt that his agony was due both to his being thrust into this black hole and still more to his not being able to get right into it. What hindered him from getting into it was the claim that his life had been good. That justification of his life held him fast and would not let him get forward, and it caused him more agony than all.

All at once some force struck him in the chest, in the side, and stifled his breathing more than ever; he rolled forward into the hole, and there at the end there was some sort of light. It had happened with him, as it had sometimes happened to him in a railway carriage, when he had thought he was going forward while he was going back, and all of a sudden recognised his real direction.

'Yes, it has all been not the right thing,' he said to himself, 'but that's no matter.' He could, he could do the right thing. 'What is the right thing?' he asked himself, and suddenly he became quiet.

This was at the end of the third day, two hours before his death. At that very moment the schoolboy had stealthily crept into his father's room and gone up to his bedside. The dying man was screaming and waving his arms. His hand fell on the schoolboy's head. The boy snatched it, pressed it to his lips, and burst into tears.

At that very moment Ivan Ilych had rolled into the hole, and caught sight of the light, and it was revealed to him that his life had not been what it ought to have been, but that that could still be set right. He asked himself, 'What is the right thing?'—and became quiet, listening. Then he felt someone was kissing his hand. He opened his eyes and glanced at his son. He felt sorry for him. His wife went up to him. He glanced at her. She was gazing at him with open mouth, the tears unwiped streaming over her nose and cheeks, a look of despair on her face. He felt sorry for her.

'Yes, I'm making them miserable,' he thought. 'They're sorry, but it will be better for them when I die.' He would have said this, but had not the strength to utter it. 'Besides, why speak, I must act,' he thought. With a glance to his wife he pointed to his son and said—

'Take away . . . sorry for him. . . . And you too . . .' He tried to say 'forgive,' but said 'forgo'[3] . . . and too weak to correct himself, shook his hand, knowing that He would understand whose understanding mattered.

And all at once it became clear to him that what had tortured him and would not leave him was suddenly dropping away all at once on both sides and on ten sides and on all sides. He was sorry for them, must act so that they might not suffer. Set them free and be free himself of those agonies. 'How right and how simple!' he thought. 'And the pain?' he asked himself. 'Where's it gone? Eh, where are you, pain?'

He began to watch for it.

'Yes, here it is. Well what of it, let the pain be.'

'And death. Where is it?'

He looked for his old accustomed terror of death, and did not find it. 'Where is it? What death?' There was no terror, because death was not either.

In the place of death there was light.

'So this is it!' he suddenly exclaimed aloud.

'What joy!'

To him all this passed in a single instant, and the meaning of that instant suffered no change after. For those present his agony lasted another two hours. There was a rattle in his throat, a twitching in his wasted body. Then the rattle and the gasping came at longer and longer intervals.

'It is over!' someone said over him.

He caught those words and repeated them in his soul.

'Death is over,' he said to himself. 'It's no more.'

He drew in a breath, stopped midway in the breath, stretched and died.

THE KREUTZER SONATA

CHAPTER I

"But I say unto you that every one that looketh on a woman to lust after her hath committed adultery with her already in his heart."—MATT. v. 28.

"The disciples say unto him, If the case of the man is so with his wife, it is not expedient to marry. But he said unto them, All men cannot receive this saying, but they to whom it is given. For there are some eunuchs, which were so born from their mother's womb: and there are some eunuchs, which were made eunuchs of men: and there be eunuchs, which have made themselves eunuchs for the kingdom of heaven's sake. He that is able to receive it, let him receive it.[1]"
—MATT. xix. 10–12.

It was early spring. We had been traveling for more than twenty-four hours. Passengers with tickets for more or less distant places had been entering and leaving our carriage, but there were four of us who had been on the train from the very start:—a weary-faced lady, neither beautiful nor young, who wore a hat and a semi-masculine paletot, and smoked cigarettes; her companion, a talkative man of forty, with neat, new luggage; and thirdly a rather short and very reserved gentleman not by any means old, but with curly hair prematurely turning gray, with very nervous motions, and with extraordinarily brilliant eyes which kept roving from object to object. He wore an old paletot with a lamb's-wool collar, made by an expensive tailor, and a high lamb's-wool hat. Under his paletot, when it was thrown open, were visible a *poddyovka*, or sleeveless kaftan, and a Russian embroidered shirt. The peculiarity of this gentleman consisted in the fact that he from time to time produced strange noises like a cough or like a laugh begun and broken off. This gentleman, during the whole journey, had carefully avoided all acquaintance and inter-course with the other passengers. If any of his neighbors spoke to him, he replied briefly and stiffly, and for the most part he either read or smoked, gazing out of the window, or else, getting his provisions out of his old sack, drank tea or ate luncheon.

It seemed to me that he was oppressed by his loneliness, and several times I was tempted to speak with him; but whenever our eyes met, as often happened, since we sat diagonally opposite each other, he turned away and devoted himself to his book or looked out of the window.

During one stop at a large station, just before the evening of our second day, this nervous gentleman left the carriage to get some hot water, and made himself some tea. The gentleman with the neat new luggage, a lawyer, as I afterward learned, went out also with the cigarette-smoking lady in the semi-masculine paletot, to drink tea in the station. During the absence of the gentleman and lady several new persons entered our carriage, and among them a tall, closely shaven, wrinkled old man, evidently a merchant, in a skunk-lined coat and a cloth cap with a huge vizor. This merchant sat down opposite the lawyer, and immediately entered into conversation with a young man, apparently a merchant's prikashchik, or manager, who entered the carriage at the same station.

I was sitting diagonally opposite, and while the train was stationary and no one was passing between us, I could hear snatches of their conversation.

The merchant at first explained that he was on his way to an estate of his which was situated only one station distant. Then, as usual, they began to talk about prices, about trade, and how Moscow does business at the present time; and then they discussed the Fair at Nizhni-Novgorod.

The merchant's clerk began to tell about the merrymaking at the Fair, of some rich merchant whom both of them knew; but the old man did not let him finish: he began to tell about the merrymakings which had taken place in former times at Kunavino, and which he himself had enjoyed. He was evidently proud of the share which he had taken in them, and with manifest delight he related how he and this same common acquaintance had once got drunk at Kunavino, and played such tricks that he had to tell about it in a whisper, whereat the clerk burst out in a hearty fit of laughter which filled the whole carriage, and the old man also laughed, displaying two yellow teeth.

Not expecting to hear anything interesting, I got up to go out on the platform till the train should start. At the door I met the lawyer and his lady, talking in a very animated manner as they walked.

"You won't have time," said the sociable lawyer. "The second bell will ring in a moment."

And in fact I had not even time to walk to the end of the carriage before the bell rang. When I got back to my place the lively conversation was still going on. The old merchant sat silent in front of them, sternly looking straight ahead, and occasionally expressing his disapprobation by chewing on his teeth.

"Whereupon she explained to her husband up and down"—the lawyer was saying with a smile as I passed them—"that she could not and, moreover, she would not live with him since. . . ."

And he proceeded to tell something more which I could not hear. Behind me came still other passengers, then came the conductor, followed by a guard on the run, and there was considerable noise for a time, so that I could not hear what they were talking about.

When it grew quieter the lawyer's voice was heard again; but the conversation had evidently gone over from a particular instance to general considerations. The lawyer was saying that the question of divorce was now occupying general attention in Europe, and that with us in Russia the phenomenon was appearing more and more frequently.

Noticing that his voice alone was heard, the lawyer cut his words short, and addressed himself to the old man.

"It didn't use to be so in old times; isn't that so?" he remarked, smiling pleasantly.

The old man was about to make some answer; but at this moment the train started, and, taking off his cap, he began to cross himself and to whisper a prayer. The lawyer, turning his eyes away, waited politely. Having finished his prayer and crossed himself thrice, the old man put on his cap and pulled it down, settling it in its place, and he began to speak.

"The same thing took place, sir, in old times, only less frequently," said he. "At the present time it can't help happening. People have grown cultured!"

The train, moving along more and more rapidly, thundered over the sleepers, and it was hard for me to hear; but it was interesting, and I took a seat nearer. My neighbor, the nervous, bright-eyed gentleman, was also evidently much interested, and listened, but without moving from his place.

"In what respect are we ill-educated?" asked the lady, with a scarcely perceptible smile. "Do you mean that it would be better for men and women to get married as they used to do in old times, when the bride and bridegroom never even saw each other?" she went on asking, replying after the fashion of many women, not to her neighbor's words, but to the words which she thought he would say.

"People did not know whether they would be able to love each other or not, but married whoever fell to their lot; yes, and often they were tortured their whole lives long! So you think that our old way was the best, do you?" she went on, addressing her discourse to me, and to the lawyer, and least of all to the old man with whom she was talking.

"We have already become very cultured," repeated the merchant, looking scornfully at the lady, and leaving her question unanswered.

"I should like to know how you explain the connection between culture and matrimonial quarrels," said the lawyer, with a scarcely perceptible smile.

The merchant was about to say something, but the lady interrupted him.

"No, that time has already passed," said she. But the lawyer checked her :—

"No, permit him to express his thought." . . .

"The absurdities of culture," said the old man, resolutely.

"People who do not love each other marry, and then they wonder that they get along inharmoniously," said the lady, hastily, glancing at the lawyer and then at me, and even at the clerk, who had got up in his seat and was standing with his elbow leaning on the back of the chair, and listening to the conversation with a smile. "You see animals only can be paired off in this way as the master may desire, but men and women have their own individual preferences and attachments," said the lady, evidently wishing to say something severe to the old merchant.

"When you speak thus, you speak to no purpose, madame," said the old man. "Animals are brutes, but man has a law."

"Well, how can one live with a man when there is no love?" insisted the lady, eager to express her opinion, which apparently seemed to her very novel.

"In former times they did not discuss this," said the old man, in a magisterial tone; "it is only a recent development. At any pretext the wife cries out: 'I will leave you.' Even among the peasantry this new method has come into fashion. 'Na,' says the muzhik's wife, 'here are your shirts and drawers, but I am going off with Vanka; his hair is curlier than yours.' Argument is no good. For a woman the first thing needed is fear."

The clerk looked at the lawyer and at the lady and at me, evidently repressing a smile, and ready either to laugh or to approve of the merchant's argument according as it was received by the company.

"Fear of what?" asked the lady.

"Why, of course, fear of her hu-us-band. . . . . That kind of fear."

"But the day for that sort of thing has gone by my good fellow," said the lady, with no little asperity.

"No, madame, the time for that can never go by. As Eve the woman was created out of the man's rib, so it will remain till the end of time," said the old man, and he nodded his head so sternly and triumphantly that the clerk instantly decided that the victory was on the merchant's side, and he burst out into a loud laugh.

"Yes, that is the way you men decide," said the lady, not yielding, and looking at us. "They give themselves full liberty, but you want to keep the woman in the terem. To you, of course, all things are permitted."

"No one gives any such permission, but it is a fact man does not make his family increase, but woman is a fragile vessel," suggested the merchant. The dictatorialness of the merchant's tone evidently impressed his hearers, and even the lady felt crushed, but still she would not give in.

"Yes, but I think you will agree that a woman is a human being, and has feelings as well as a man. Well, then, what is she going to do if she does not love her husband?"

"Not love her husband?" exclaimed the merchant, repeating her words in a savage tone, making a grimace with his lips and his eyebrows. "Never fear, she should come to love him."

This unexpected argument especially pleased the clerk, and he gave vent to a grunt of approbation.

"But that is not so, she may not come to love him," insisted the lady; "and if there is no love, then they ought not to be compelled to this."

"But if a woman is false to her husband, what then?" asked the lawyer.

"That is not to be supposed," said the old man; "he must look out for that."

"But if it does happen, what then? It has occurred.". . . .

"Yes, there are cases, but not among us," said the old man.

All were silent. The clerk changed his position, leaned forward a little more, and evidently wishing not to be left out of the conversation, began with a smile:—

"Well, there was a scandal arose in the house of a fine young fellow in our place. It was very hard to decide about it. It happened that the woman was very fond of amusements, and she began to play the devil; but her husband was a reasonable and progressive man. At first she flirted with a counting-house clerk. Her husband argued kindly with her; she would not stop. She did all sorts of dirty tricks and even stole his money. And he flogged her. What good did that do? She only acted worse. Then she had an intrigue with an unchristened Jew, if I may say so. What could he do? He turned her off entirely, and so he lives like a bachelor, and she has become a gadabout."

"That was because he was a fool," said the old man. "If at the very beginning he had not given her her head, but had given her a good sound berating, she would have been all right, I tell you. She must not have her own way at first. Don't trust a horse in the field, or your wife in your house."

At this moment the conductor came along to take up the tickets for the next station. The old man surrendered his.

"Yes," said he, "we've got to restrain the female sex betimes, or else everything will go to ruin."

"Yes, but you were just telling how you married men enjoyed yourselves at the fair at Kunavino," said I, unable to restrain myself.

"That was a personal matter," said the merchant, and he relapsed into silence.

When the whistle sounded the merchant got up, took his bag from under the seat, wrapped his coat round him, and, lifting his cap, went out to the platform.

CHAPTER II

As soon as the old man had gone out, several voices spoke up at once.

"An old style papa," exclaimed the clerk.

"The 'Domostroï' come to life," said the lady. "What savage notions of woman and marriage."

"Yes, indeed, we are still far from the European notions of marriage," said the lawyer.

"Well, the principal thing these men cannot understand," said the lady, "is that marriage without love is not marriage, that love alone consecrates marriage, and that the only true marriage is that which love consecrates."

The clerk listened and smiled, desiring to remember for future use as much as he could of the clever conversation.

In the midst of the lady's sentence, there was heard a sound just behind me like an interrupted laugh or a sob, and looking around we saw my neighbor, the bright-eyed, gray-haired, solitary gentleman, who during the conversation, which had evidently interested him, had unobtrusively drawn near us. He was standing with his hand resting on the back of the seat, and was evidently very much agitated; his face was red and the muscles of his cheek twitched.

"What is that love . . . . that love . . . . which consecrates marriage?" he asked, in a stammering voice.

The lady, seeing the agitated state of the speaker, tried to answer him as gently and circumstantially as possible.

"True love. It is that love between a man and a woman which makes marriage possible," said the lady.

"Yes, but what do you mean by true love," said the bright-eyed gentleman, smiling awkwardly and timidly.

"Every one knows what true love is," said the lady, evidently wishing to cut short her speech with him.

"But I don't know," said the gentleman. "You must define what you mean by it."

"Why?. . . . It is very simple," said the lady, but she hesitated. "Love . . . . love is the, is the exclusive preference which a man or woman feels for one person out of all the rest in the world," said she.

"A preference for how long a time? For a month or two months or half an hour?" asked the gray-haired man, and laughed.

"No, but excuse me, you are evidently not talking about the same thing."

"Yes, I am talking about the same thing."

"She says," interrupted the lawyer, and indicating the lady, "that marriage ought to result in the first place from an attachment, from love, if you will, and that if such a love actually exists, then only marriage furnishes of itself, so to speak, some consecration. Therefore, every marriage where there is no genuine attachment as a foundation—love, if you say so—has no moral obligation. Do I express your idea correctly?" said he, addressing the lady.

The lady by an inclination of her head expressed her concurrence with his interpretation of her idea.

"Therefore . . . ." the lawyer was about to continue, but the nervous gentleman, with his eyes all on fire, evidently restraining himself with difficulty, began, without allowing the lawyer to proceed:—

"No, I *am* speaking about the same thing, about the preference that one man or one woman has for one person above all others, and I simply ask, 'How long is this preference to last?' "

"How long? why, sometimes it lasts a whole lifetime," said the lady, shrugging her shoulders.

"Yes, but that is true only in novels, but never in real life. In real life this preference for one person rather than another may occasionally last for a year, more frequently it is measured by months, or even by weeks or days or hours," said he, evidently knowing that he was surprising every one by his opinion, and well satisfied with it.

"Oh, what are you saying?". . . . "No, excuse me!". . . . "Oh, no!" three of us exclaimed with one voice. Even the clerk uttered a disapproving grunt.

"Yes, I know," interrupted the gray-haired gentleman. "You are speaking of what is supposed to exist, but I am speaking of what does exist. Every man feels for every pretty woman what you call love."

"Oh, what you say is awful. Surely there exists among human beings that feeling which is called love, and which lasts not merely for months and years, but for whole lives!"

"No, I don't admit it. If it is granted even that a man may keep his preference for a given woman all his life, the woman in all probability will prefer someone else, and so it always has been in the world and always will be," said he; and, taking out a cigarette-case, he began to smoke.

"But it may be reciprocal," said the lawyer.

"No, it is impossible," he insisted, "just as impossible as that in a load of peas there should be two peas exactly alike, side by side. And over and above this improbability there is also the likelihood of satiety. That one or the other should love the same person a whole life long is as to say that a single candle would burn forever," said he, eagerly drawing in the smoke of his cigarette.

"But you are talking about carnal love; don't you admit that there is a love based on a unity of ideals, on a spiritual affinity?" asked the lady.

"Spiritual affinity! Unity of ideals!" repeated he, emitting his peculiar sound. "But in that case there is no reason why we should not sleep together,—excuse my brutality,—why, it is the very consequence of this unity of ideals that people go to bed together," said he, and he laughed nervously.

"But pardon me," said the lawyer, "what you say is contradicted by the facts. . . . . We see that marriage exists, that all the human race, or the majority of it, lives a married life, and many live honorably all their days under the marriage relation."

The gray-haired gentleman again laughed.

"You were just saying that marriage is founded on love, but when I expressed my doubt of the existence of love except the sentimental kind, you try to prove the existence of love by the fact that marriages exist. But marriages in our day are all falsehood."

"Oh, no, excuse me," exclaimed the lawyer; "I only say that marriages have always existed and still exist."

"Exist? Yes, but why do they exist? They have existed and exist for people who see in marriage something sacred—a sacrament which is entered into before God—for such people it exists. Among us, people get married, seeing nothing in marriage except copulation, and the result is either deception or violence. When it is deception it is easy to endure. Husband and wife only deceive people into believing that they are living a monogamous marriage, but they are really practising polygamy and polyandry. It is filthy, but still it is the fashion; but when, as happens oftener than otherwise, men take on themselves an external obligation to live together all their lives long,—and even from the second month they hate each other, desire to separate, and yet they go on living,—then results that terrible hell from which they try to escape by intoxication, by fighting duels, by killing and poisoning themselves and others," said he, talking more and more rapidly, and growing more and more excited. It was embarrassing.

"Yes, without doubt there are critical episodes in married life," said the lawyer, wishing to cut short this unseemly and exciting conversation.

"I imagine you have guessed who I am," said the gray-haired gentleman, quietly and with a certain appearance of calmness.

"No, I have not that pleasure."

"The pleasure will not be great. My name is Pozdnyshev; I am the man in whose life happened that critical episode to which you just hinted—the episode of a man killing his wife," said he, swiftly glancing at each one of us.

No one found anything to say, and we all kept silence.

"Well, it is immaterial," said he, emitting his peculiar grunt. "However, excuse me, I will not trouble you any more."

"Don't mention it," said the lawyer, himself not knowing exactly what he was saying.

But Pozdnyshev, not heeding him, quickly turned round and went back to his place. The gentleman talked in whispers with the lady. I sat down with Pozdnyshev and said nothing, as I was unable to think of anything to say to him. It was too dark to read, and so I shut my eyes and pretended that I was going to sleep.

Thus we rode in silence till we reached the next station. At that station the gentleman and lady were transferred to another carriage, concerning which they had arranged beforehand with the conductor. The merchant's superintendent got into a comfortable position on his sofa and went to sleep. Pozdnyshev kept smoking, and drank his tea, which he got boiling hot at the station.

When I opened my eyes and looked at him, he suddenly turned to me with an expression of resolution and exasperation:—

"Maybe it is disagreeable for you to be sitting with me, now that you know who I am. If that is so, I will leave you."

"Oh, not at all, I beg of you."

"Well, then, wouldn't you like some? Only it is rather strong."

And he poured me out some tea.

"They say . . . . but then they all lie . . . ." said he.

"What are you speaking about?" I asked.

"Always about the same thing—about 'love'—and what people mean by it. Don't you want to sleep?"

"Not at all."

"Then, if you would like, I will relate to you how I was led by this very same kind of love to do what I did."

"I should indeed, unless it would be painful for you."

"No, it is hard for me to hold my tongue. You drink your tea—or is it too strong for you?"

The tea was really like beer, but I drank a glass of it. At this moment the conductor came along. Pozdnyshev silently followed him with angry eyes, and did not begin until he had left the car.

CHAPTER III

"Well, then, I will tell you. But are you sure you would like to have me?"

I assured him that I was very eager to hear him. He remained silent, rubbed his face with his hands, and began:—

"If I tell you, I must begin at the very beginning, I must tell you how and why I got married, and what I was before I married.

"Up to the time of my marriage I lived as all men live; that is, all the men in my circle. I am a landed proprietor and a university graduate, and I have been marshal of the nobility. Up to the time of my marriage I lived as all men live,—a dissipated life; and, like all the young men of our circle, though living a dissipated life, I was persuaded that I was living as I ought. Regarding myself, I thought that I was a charming person, that I was a perfectly moral man. I was no vulgar seducer, I had no unnatural tastes, I did not make this sort of thing my chief object in life, as did many of my intimates; I indulged in dissipation only moderately, decently, for my health's sake;[2] I avoided such women as might, by the birth of a child, or by the force of attachment to me, entangle me. However, there may have been children and there may have been attachments; but I acted as if there was nothing of the sort, I not only considered this sort of thing moral, but I was proud of it."

He paused, emitted his peculiar sound, as he apparently always did when a new thought occurred to him.

"And precisely here is the chief viciousness of it all," he cried. "Depravity does not lie in anything physical; depravity does not imply any physical deformity; depravity, genuine depravity, consists in freeing oneself from the moral relations to women with whom you enter into physical relations. And this emancipation I arrogated to myself as a virtue. I remember how one time I tormented myself because I had not paid a woman, who apparently loved me and had given herself to me, and I was only rendered happy again when I sent her the money, so as to show her thereby that I did not consider myself morally bound to her. Do not nod your head as if you agreed with me," he suddenly cried. "You see I know that kind of trick. All of you, in the best circumstances, unless you are a rare exception, have just such views as I had then. Well, no matter, please excuse me," he went on. "But this is the whole trouble and it is awful! awful! awful!"

"What is awful?" I asked.

"The abyss of error in which we live in relation to women, and our relations to them. It is true I cannot talk with any calmness in regard to this, and the reason I cannot is that episode which took place in my life. But ever since that episode occurred, my eyes have been opened, and I have seen everything in an entirely different light—exactly the opposite—exactly the opposite."

He smoked his cigarette, and, leaning his elbows on his knees, went on talking again. In the darkness I could not see his face, but above the rattle and rumble of the train I could hear his suggestive, pleasant voice.

CHAPTER IV

"Yes, only by tormenting myself as I have, only by means of this have I learned where the root of the whole trouble is; have I learned what must be, and therefore have come to see the whole horror of what is.

"Now be kind enough to see, just here, how and when began that which led me to that episode of which I have spoken. It began when I was not quite sixteen years old. It happened when I was still in the gymnasium, and my oldest brother was a student in the first class. I had not known women at that time, but like all the unfortunate boys of our circle, I was by no means an innocent child. Two years before I had been corrupted by coarse boys; already woman, not any particular woman, but woman as a sweet something, woman, any woman—woman in her nakedness—had already begun to torment me. My solitudes were unchaste. I was tormented as ninety-nine per cent of our boys are tormented. I was horror-struck, I struggled, I prayed, and—I fell! I was already corrupted in my imagination and in my essence, but the final step had not yet been taken. I was ruined by myself, even before I had put my hands on another human being. But here a comrade of my brother, a gay young student, a so-called 'good fellow,'—in other words the greatest good-for-nothing possible,—who had already taught us to drink and to play cards, persuaded us after a drinking-bout to go there.*

"We went. My brother also had been innocent, and he fell the same night; and I, a boy of fifteen, polluted myself and accomplished the pollution of a woman, not at all understanding the enormity of what I was doing. You see I had never heard from any of my elders that what I was doing was wrong. And even now no one ever hears so. To be sure it is contained in the Ten Commandments, but the Ten Commandments seem to be used only in order to pass the priest's examination, and even then are not regarded as very important, not nearly so much so as the rule for the use of ut† in conditional sentences.

---

*Common way of referring to a brothel.
†In order that (Latin).

"Thus I had never heard a single one of my elders, whom I respected, say that this was wrong. On the contrary, I heard men whom I respected declare that it was a good thing. I heard them say that my struggles and sufferings would be relieved after that. I heard it, and I read it, and heard my elders say that it was good for the health; from my comrades I heard that there was merit, that there was gallantry, in such conduct. So that, as a rule, there is nothing to be anticipated from it except beneficial effects. Danger of disease? But even that you see is taken care of. A solicitous government looks out for that. It looks after and regulates the activity of houses of 'indulgence,' and makes lewdness safe for gymnasium students. And doctors for a consideration do the same. Thus it comes about. They affirm that lewdness is good for the health, they make a regular institution of lewdness. I know of mothers who see to it that their sons' health is regulated in this way. And Science follows them into the houses of 'indulgence.'"

"Why Science?" I asked.

"What are doctors? The priests of Science. Who corrupt young men, declaring that this thing is necessary for the health? They do.

"But it is certain that if one per cent of the energy that is employed in the cure of syphilis were expended in the eradication of lewdness, syphilis would long ago have become only a memory. But instead the energy is expended, not in the eradication of lewdness, but in the guaranteeing the safety of lewdness. Well, that is not the trouble. The trouble consists in this, that with me, as with nine out of ten, if not even more, not only of our class, but of all, even of the peasantry, the horrible fact exists that I fell, not by reason of yielding to a single temptation of the charm of any special woman—no, no special woman led me astray; but I fell because those immediately around me saw, in what was really a fall, some a lawful act, a regulator advantageous for the health, others, a most natural and not only simple, but even innocent, diversion for a young man.

"I did not even realize that this was a fall; I simply began to give myself up to those pleasures, to those necessities, which, as it was suggested to me, were peculiar to a certain degree of lewdness,— gave myself up to this form of dissipation just as I had begun to drink and to smoke. And yet there was something peculiar and pathetic in this first fall. I well remember how immediately, even before I left that room, a feeling of sadness, of deep sadness, came over me, so that I felt like weeping, weeping the loss of my innocence, for a forever sullied relationship to womanhood. Yes, the natural, simple relationship that I had enjoyed with women was for evermore impossible. Purity of relationship with any woman was at an end, and could never be again. I had become what is called a libertine. And to be a libertine is to be in a physical condition like that of a morphiomaniac, a drunkard, or a smoker. As the morphiomaniac, the drunkard, the smoker, is no longer a normal man, so a man who uses women for his own pleasure is no longer normal, but is a man forever spoiled—is a libertine. As the drunkard and the morphiomaniac can be instantly recognized by his face, by his actions, so it is with the rake. The libertine may restrain himself, may struggle with his inclinations, but his simple, pure, frank, and fraternal relations with woman are no longer possible. By the very way in which he looks at a young woman, and stares at her, the libertine is to be recognized. And I became a libertine, and I remained one, and that was my ruin.

CHAPTER V

"Yes, so it was. So it went further and further, and every kind of depravity ensued. My God! When I remember all my abominable actions in this particular, I am overwhelmed with horror. I also remember how my comrades used to laugh at my so-called innocence. And when you hear about our gilded youth, our officers, our young Parisians. . . .

"And all these gentlemen, and I, when we, libertines of thirty, having on our souls hundreds of the most varied and horrible crimes against woman, when we, rakes of thirty, come into the drawing-room or the ball-room, freshly washed, cleanly shaven, well-perfumed, in immaculate linen, in evening dress or uniform—what emblems of purity, how charming we are!. . . .

"Just think what ought to be and what is! It ought to be that when such a gentleman comes into the society of my sister, or my daughter, I, knowing about his life, what it is, should go to him, draw him quietly to one side, and say in a confidential whisper:—

" 'My dear fellow, you see I know exactly how you are living, how you are spending your nights and with whom. This is no place for you. Here are pure, innocent women and girls. Please go.'

"So it ought to be; but in reality, when such a gentleman makes his appearance, or when he dances with my sister or my daughter, clasping her in his arms, we rejoice if he is rich and well connected. Perhaps he honors my daughter after Rigulboche.* Even if traces of his disease still remain, it is of no consequence, the cure is easy nowadays. I know that some girls of the highest society have been given by their parents with enthusiasm to men affected with certain diseases. Oh, what rottenness! But the time is coming when this rottenness and falsehood will be cured."

Several times he emitted his strange noises and sipped his tea. His tea was terribly strong. There was no water at hand to weaken it. I was conscious that the two glasses which I had drunk had greatly excited my nerves. The tea also must have had a great effect on him, because he kept growing more and more excited. His voice kept growing louder and more energetic. He kept changing his position; at one moment he would pick up his hat, then he would put it on again; and his face kept strangely changing in the twilight in which we were sitting.

"Well, that was the way I lived until I was thirty years of age, never for a moment abandoning my intention of getting married and arranging for myself the most lofty and unsullied existence, and with this end in view I looked at every girl who came under observation," he continued. "I was soiled with the rottenness of lewdness, and at the same time I was looking round for a girl who by her purity might meet my demands. Many of them I instantly rejected on the ground that they were not sufficiently pure for me; at last I found one whom I thought worthy of me. She was one of the two daughters of a man in the government of Penza, who had formerly been very rich, but was at that time ruined. One evening, after we had been somewhere in a boat and were returning home by moonlight, and I was sitting next her and admiring her well-proportioned figure, clad in a jersey, and her curly locks, I suddenly made up my mind that she was the one. It

---

*Pejorative term for a cancan dancer, after the stage name of Margarita Bodelle, a Parisian dancer popular in the 1850s and 1860s.

seemed to me that evening that she understood everything I felt and thought, and I thought the most elevated thoughts. In reality it was simply the fact that her jersey was especially becoming to her and so were her curls, and that after I had spent a day in her immediate presence I wanted to be still closer to her.

"It is a marvelous thing how full of illusion is the notion that beauty is an advantage. A beautiful woman says all sorts of foolishness, you listen and you do not hear any foolishness, but what you hear seems to you wisdom itself. She says and does vulgar things, and to you it seems lovely. Even when she does not say stupid or vulgar things, but is simply beautiful, you are convinced that she is miraculously wise and moral.

"I returned home enthusiastic, and resolved that she was high above all moral perfection, and that she was therefore fit to be my wife; and the next day I made my proposal.

"See what an entanglement it was. Out of a thousand married men, not only in our rank, but unfortunately also in the people, there is scarcely one who, like Don Juan, would not have been married already not merely ten times, but even a hundred or a thousand times, before the marriage ceremony.

"It is true there are now, so I hear, and I believe it, some young men who live pure lives, feeling and knowing that this is no joke, but a serious matter.

"God help them! But in my time there was not one such out of ten thousand. And all know this and pretend that they do not know it. In all novels the feelings of the heroes, the ponds, the bushes around which they wander, are described in detail; but though their mighty love to some particular maiden is described, nothing is said about what the interesting hero was doing before, not a word about his frequenting 'houses of indulgence,' about his relations with chambermaids, cooks, and other women. . . . . Improper novels of this kind—if there are any—are not put into the hands of those who most of all need to know about these things—that is, young women.

"At first they pretend before young women that this form of dissipation, which fills half of the life of our cities, and of our villages also, does not exist at all.

"Afterward they become so accustomed to this hypocrisy that at last they come actually to believe that all of us are moral men and live in a moral world! Girls, poor things, really believe in this with perfect seriousness.

"Thus did my unhappy wife believe. I remember how, after I became engaged to her, I showed her my diary, in which she might learn as much as she would like, even though it were very little, of my past, and especially regarding the last intrigue in which I had been engaged; for she might hear about this from others, and so I felt it necessary to tell her.[3] I remember her horror, her despair, and disillusionment when she knew it all and realized what it meant. I saw that she was tempted to throw me over then. And why didn't she do it?". . . .

He emitted his peculiar sound, took another swallow of tea, and paused.

CHAPTER VI

"No, on the whole it is much better, ever so much better so," he cried. "I deserved it. But that is not the point. I mean that in this business the only persons deceived are the poor unfortunate girls.

"Their mothers certainly know this, their mothers know it as well as any one, because they have been told by their husbands. And they pretend that they believe in the purity of men, though in reality they do not at all. They know by what bait to catch men for themselves and for their daughters.

'But you see we men don't know, and we don't know because we don't want to know; but women know perfectly well that the most sublime, and as we call it the most poetic, love depends, not on moral qualities, but on physical proximity and then on the way of doing up the hair, the complexion, the cut of the gown. Ask an experienced coquette who has set herself the task of entrapping a man, which she would prefer to risk: being detected in falsehood, cruelty, even immorality, in the presence of the one whom she is trying to entice, or to appear before him in a badly made or unbecoming gown,—and every time she would choose the first. She knows that man merely lies when he talks about lofty feelings—all he wants is the body—and so he pardons all vulgarities, but he would never pardon an ugly, unbecoming, unfashionable costume. The coquette knows this consciously; every innocent girl knows this unconsciously, just as animals know it.

"Hence these abominable jerseys, these tournures, these naked shoulders, arms, and almost bosoms. Women, especially those that have been through the school of marriage, know very well that talk on the highest topics is all talk; but what man wants is the body, and everything which displays it in a deceptive but captivating light, and they act accordingly. If we should once forget that we are accustomed to this indecency which has become second nature, and look at the life of our upper classes as it really is, in all its shamelessness, it would appear like one luxurious 'house of indulgence.'

"Don't you agree with me? Excuse me, I will prove it to you," he repeated, not allowing me a chance to speak.

"You say that the women in our society live for other aims than the women in the 'houses of indulgence,' but I say that it is not so, and I will prove it to you. If people differ by their aims, by the internal contents of their lives, then this difference will be shown, also, externally, and externally they will be different. But look at these unhappy, these despised women, and then on the ladies of our highest social circles; the same decorations, the same fashions, the same perfumes, the same bare shoulders, arms, and bosoms, the same extravagant exhibition of the tournure, the same passion for precious stones, for costly, brilliant things, the same gayeties, dances and music and singing. The methods of allurement used by the ones are used by the others.

CHAPTER VII

"Yes, and I was captured by these jerseys and locks of hair and tournures.

"And it was very easy to capture me, because I had been brought up in those conditions in which young people, like cucumbers

under glass, are turned out in love. You see our too abundant and exciting food, coupled with a perfectly idle existence, is nothing else than a
systematic incitement to lust. You may be surprised or not, but it is so. I
myself have seen nothing of this sort of thing until recently, but now I
have seen it. This is the very thing that troubles me, that no one recognizes this, but every one says stupid things like the woman who just got
out.

"Yes; not far from where I live some muzhiks* were working this
spring on the railway. The ordinary fare of the peasantry is meager,—
bread, kvas,† onions; the muzhik is lively, healthy, and sound. He goes
to work on the railway, and his rations consist of kasha and one
pound of meat. But in repayment of this he gives back sixteen hours'
work, amounting to thirty poods,‡ carried on a wheelbarrow. And it
is always so with him."

"But we who eat daily two pounds of meat and game and fish and
all kinds of stimulating foods and drinks—how does that go? In sensual
excesses. If it goes that way, the safety-valve is open and all is satisfac-
tory; but cut off the safety-valve,—as I kept it covered temporarily,—
and immediately there will be an excitement which, coming through
the prism of our artificial life, is expressed in a love of the first water,
and is sometimes even platonic. And I fell in love as all young men do."

"And everything followed its course: transports[4] and emotions
and poetry. In reality, this love of mine was the result, on the one
side, of the activity of the mamasha and the dressmakers; on the
other, of the superfluity of stimulating food eaten by me in idleness.
Had there not been, on the one hand, excursions in boats, had there
not been dressmakers with close-fitting gowns, and the like, and had
my wife been dressed in some formless housedress, and stayed at
home, and had I, on the other hand, been a man in normal conditions, eating only as much food as I needed for my work, and had
my safety-valve been open,—but then it chanced to be temporarily
closed,—I should not have fallen in love, and there would not have
been any trouble.

---

*Peasant (Russian).
†Fermented grain beverage (Russian).
‡Russian unit of weight, approximately 36 pounds (16 kg).

CHAPTER VIII

"Well, so it went on. My rank and fortune and good clothes and excursions in boats did the business. Twenty times it does not succeed, but this time it succeeded like a trap. I am not jesting. You see, nowadays marriages are always arranged like traps. Do you see how natural it is? The girl has arrived at maturity, and must be married. What could be more simple when the girl is not a monster, and there are men who wish to get married? This is the way it used to be done. The girl has reached the right age; her parents arrange a marriage. Thus it has been done, thus it is done throughout the world; among the Chinese, the Hindus, the Muslims, and among the common Russian people; thus it is managed among at least ninety-nine per cent of the human race. It is only among a small one per cent, among us libertines and debauchees, that this custom has been found to be bad, and we have invented another. Now, what is this new way? It is this: the girls sit round, and the men come as at a bazaar and take their choice. And the girls wait and wonder, and have their own ideas, but they dare not say: 'Good fellow, take me,— no, me—not her, but me; look, what shoulders and all the rest.'

"And we, the men, walk by and stare at them and are satisfied. 'I know a thing or two, I am not caught.' They go by, they look, they are satisfied that this is all arranged for their special benefit. 'Look, don't get taken in—here's your chance!'"

"What is to be done, then?" I asked. "You would not have the young women make the offers, would you?"

"Well, I can't exactly say how; only if there is to be equality, then let it be equality. If it is discovered that the system of the go-between is humiliating, still this is a thousand times more so. Then the rights and chances were equal, but in our method the woman is either a slave in a bazaar, or the bait in the trap. You tell any mother or the girl herself the truth, that she is only occupied in husband-catching,— my God, what an insult! But the truth is they do this, and they have nothing else to do. And what is really dreadful is to see poor, and perfectly innocent, young girls engaged in doing this very thing. And again, it would not be so bad if it were only done openly, but it is all deception.

" 'Ah, the origin of species, how interesting it is! Ah, Lily is greatly interested in painting.'—And shall you be at the exhibition? How instructive! And the troïka rides and the theater and the symphony. Oh, how remarkable—'My Lily is crazy over music!' 'And why don't you share these views?' And then the boat rides. And always one thought:—'Take me, take my Lily. No, me!' 'Just try your luck!' Oh, vileness, oh, falsehood!" he concluded; and, swallowing the last of his tea, proceeded to gather together his cups and utensils.

CHAPTER IX

"Do you know," he began, while he was packing up his tea and sugar in his bag, "the dominance of women, which is the cause of the sufferings of the world, all proceeds from this?"

"How the dominance of women?" I asked. "All rights, the majority of rights, belong to men."

"Yes, yes, that is the very thing," he exclaimed, interrupting me. "That is the very thing I wanted to say to you, and that is just what explains the extraordinary phenomenon that on the one side it is perfectly true that woman is reduced to the lowest degree of humiliation; on the other, she is the queen. Just exactly as the Jews, by their pecuniary power, avenge themselves for their humiliation, so it is with women. 'Ah, you want us to be merely merchants; very well, we as merchants will get you under our feet,' say the Jews. 'Ah, you wish us to be merely the objects of sensuality; very well, we as objects of sensual pleasure will make you our slaves,' say the women. A woman's lack of rights does not consist in the fact that she cannot vote or sit as judge,—for rights are not embraced in any such activities,—but in the fact that in sexual intercourse she is not the equal of the man: she must have the right to enjoy the man or to keep him at a distance according to her fancy, she must be able to choose her husband according to her own desire, instead of being the one chosen.

"You say that this would be unbecoming; very good, then let the man cease to have these rights. Now the woman lacks the right which the man possesses. And now, in order to get back this right, she acts on the passions of man; by means of his passions, she subdues him so that, while ostensibly he chooses, she is really the one. And having once got hold of this means, she abuses it, and acquires a terrible power over men."

"Yes, but where is this special power?" I asked.

"Where? Everywhere, in everything. Go in any large city among the shops. Millions there. You could estimate the amount of human labor expended in them, but in ninety per cent of these shops what will you find intended for men? All the luxury of life is demanded and maintained by women. Reckon up all the factories. The vast proportion of them are manufacturing unprofitable adornments, such as carriages, furniture, trinkets, for women. Millions of men, generations of slaves, perish in the galley-slave work in factories merely for the caprice of women. Women, like tsaritsas, hold as prisoners in slavery and hard labor about ninety per cent of the human race. And all this because they have been kept down, deprived of their equal rights with men. And so they avenge themselves by acting on our passions, by ensnaring us in their nets. Yes, everything comes from that.

"Women have made of themselves such a weapon for attacking the senses of men, that a man cannot with any calmness be in a woman's company. As soon as a man approaches a woman, he falls under the influence of her deviltry, and grows foolish. And there always used to be something awkward and painful, when I saw a lady dressed in a ball-gown; but now it is simply terrible. I regard it as something dangerous for men and contrary to law, and I feel the impulse to call for the police, to summon protection from the peril, to demand that the dangerous object be removed and put out of sight.

"Yes, you are laughing," he cried, "but this is no joke at all. I am convinced that the time is coming and perhaps very soon when men will recognize this and will be amazed that a society could exist in which actions so subversive to social quietude were permitted as those adornments of their body, permitted to women of our circle and meant to appeal to the passions. It is exactly the same as if all kinds of traps should be placed along our promenades and roads—it is worse than that. Why should games of chance be forbidden, and women not be forbidden to dress in a way to appeal to the passions? It is a thousand times more dangerous."

CHAPTER X

"Now, then, you understand me. I was what is called 'in love.' I not only imagined her as absolute perfection, I also imagined myself at the time of my marriage as absolute perfection. You see there is no scoundrel who is not able by searching to find a scoundrel in some respects worse than himself, and who therefore would not find an excuse for pride and self-satisfaction. So it was with me: I was not marrying for money, it was not a question of advantage with me as it was with the majority of my acquaintances, who married either for money or connections: I was rich, she was poor. That is one thing. Another thing which afforded me reason for pride was the fact that, while other men married with the intention of continuing to live in the same polygamy as they had enjoyed up to the time of their marriage, I had firmly resolved to live after my marriage as a monogamist, and my pride had no bounds in consequence of this resolution. Yes, I was a frightful pig, but I imagined that I was an angel!

"The time between my betrothal and my marriage was not very long. But I cannot remember that period of my engagement without shame. How vile it was! You see love is represented as spiritual and not sensual. Well, if it is love, it is spiritual; if it is a spiritual communion, then this spiritual intercourse ought to be expressed in words, in conversations, in colloquies. There was nothing of this. It used to be awfully hard to talk when we were alone together. What a labor of Sisyphus it used to be! No sooner had we thought of something to say and said it, than we would have to be silent and it would be necessary to think of something else. There was nothing to talk about. Everything that might be said of the life awaiting us, our arrangements, our plans, had been said, and what was there more? You see, if we had been animals then we should have known that it was not expected of us to talk; but here, on the contrary, it was necessary to talk, but there was nothing to say because what really interested us could not be expressed in words.

"And, moreover, there was that abominable custom of eating bonbons, that coarse gluttony, that gormandizing on sweets, and all those vile preparations for marriage; discussions about rooms, apartments, beds, night-gowns, robes linen, and toilets. Now you will admit that, if marriages were arranged in accordance with the 'Domostroï,' as that old man said, then the cushions, the dowry, the bed, and all that sort of thing would be merely particulars corresponding with the sacrament. But among us, when out of ten men who go to the altar probably scarcely nine believe, not merely in the sacrament, but do not even believe that what they are doing is anything binding; when out of a hundred men there is scarcely one who has not been practically married before, and out of fifty not more than one who is not ready to deceive his wife on any convenient pretext; when the majority regard the going to the church as merely a special condition for the possession of a certain woman,—think what a terrible significance, in view of all this, all these details must have! It comes to be something in the nature of a sale. They sell the libertine the innocent girl, and they surround the sale with certain formalities.

CHAPTER XI

"That is the way all get married, and that is the way I got married, and the much-vaunted honeymoon began. What a vile name that is in itself!" he hissed spitefully. "I was making a tour of all the sights of Paris, and I went in to see the bearded woman and a water-dog. It seemed that the one was only a man décolleté, in a woman's gown, and the other was a dog fastened into a walrus-skin and swimming in a bath-tub full of water. The whole thing was very far from interesting; but when I left the place the showman conducted me out very obsequiously, and, addressing the public collected around the entrance, he pointed to me, and said:—

" 'Here, ask this gentleman if it is not worth looking at. Come in, come in, one franc apiece.' "

"I was ashamed to say that it was not worth looking at, and the showman evidently counted on that. So is it, undoubtedly, with those that have experienced all the vileness of the honeymoon, and do not dispel the illusions of others. I also refrained from dispelling any one's illusions. But now I do not see why one should not tell the truth. It even seems to me that it is essential to tell the truth about this. It was awkward, shameful, vile, pitiable, and, above all, it was wearisome, unspeakably wearisome. It was something analogous to what I experienced when I was learning to smoke, when I was sick at my stomach and salivated, and I swallowed it down and pretended that it was very pleasant. Just as from that, the delights of marriage, if there are any, will be subsequent; the husband must educate his wife in this vice, in order to procure any pleasure from it."

"Vice? What do you mean?" I asked. "Why, you are talking about one of the most natural of human functions!"

"Natural?" he exclaimed. "Natural? No, I will tell you that I have come to the conviction that it is not natural. Nay, it is perfectly unnatural. Ask children, ask an innocent young girl.

"You said 'natural.' "

"It is natural to eat. And it is agreeable, easy, and jolly, and not at all shameful, to eat; but this is vile and shameful and painful. No, it is not natural. And the pure maiden, I am convinced, will always hate it."

"But how," I asked, "how would the human race be perpetuated?"

"Well, why should not the human race perish?" he asked, with a touch of savage irony, as if he were expecting this unfair reply, as if he had heard it before. "Preach abstinence from procreation in the name of making it always possible for English lords to gormandize, and it will go! Preach abstinence from procreation in the name of giving a greater pleasure, it will go! But try to persuade people to refrain from procreation in the name of morality—ye fathers! what an outcry! The human race would not be extinguished, because an attempt was made to keep men from being swine. However, excuse me! this light is disagreeable to me; may I shade it?" he asked, pointing to the lamp.

I said that it was immaterial to me, and then—hastily, as in everything he did—he got up on the seat, and pulled down the woolen shade to the lamp.

"Nevertheless," said I, "if all men should adopt this for a law, the human race would be annihilated."

He did not immediately reply.

"You ask: 'How would the human race be perpetuated?' " said he, again taking his seat opposite me, and spreading his legs wide apart, and resting his elbows on his knees. "Why should it be continued—this human race of ours?" he exclaimed.

"Why do you ask such a question? Otherwise there would be no more of us."

"Well, why should there be?"

"What a question—why, to live, of course."

"But why should we live? If here is no other aim, if life was given only to perpetuate life, then there is no reason why we should live. And if this is so, then the Schopenhauers and Hartmanns,* and all the Buddhists as well, are perfectly right. Now, if there is a purpose in life, then it is clear that life ought to come to an end when that purpose is attained. This is the logic of it," said he, with evident agitation, and seeming to set a high value on his thought. "This is the logic of it. Observe: if the aim of mankind is happiness, goodness, love if you prefer; if the aim of mankind is what is said in the prophecies that all men are to unite themselves in universal love, that the spears are to be beaten into pruning-hooks and the like, then what stands in the way of the attainment of this aim? Human passions do! Of all passions, the most powerful and vicious and obstinate is sexual, carnal love; and so if passions are annihilated and with them the last and most powerful, carnal love, then the prophecy will be fulfilled, men will be united together, the aim of mankind will have been attained, and there would be no longer any reason for existence. As long as humanity exists, this ideal will be before it, and of course this is not the ideal of rabbits or of pigs, which is to propagate as rapidly as possible, and it is not the ideal of monkeys or of Parisians, which is to enjoy all the refinements of sexual passion, but it is the ideal of goodness attained by self-restraint and chastity. Toward this men are now striving, and always have striven. And see what results.

"It results that sexual love is the safety-valve. If the human race does not as yet attain this aim, it is simply because there are passions, and the strongest of them the sexual. But since there is sexual passion, a new generation comes along, and of course there is always the possibility that the aim may be attained by some succeeding generation. But as long as it is not attained, then there will be other generations until the aim is attained, until the prophecies are fulfilled, until all men are joined in unity. And then what would be the result?

---

*Reference to German philosophers Arthur Schopenhauer (1788–1860) and Eduard von Hartmann (1842–1906), both of whom considered questions of will.

"If it be granted that God created men for the attainment of a certain end, then He must have created them mortal, without sexual passion, or immortal. If they were mortal, but without sexual passion, then what would be the result?—this: that they would live without attaining their aim, and then would die, so that, to attain the aim, God would have to create new men. But if they were immortal, then let us suppose—although it is harder for those men to correct mistakes and approach perfection than it is for the new generations—let us suppose, I say, that they reached their goal after many thousand years; but then, why should they? What good would the rest of their lives be to them? It is better as it is!. . . .

"But perhaps you do not approve this form of expression, perhaps you are an evolutionist. Even then it comes to the same thing. The highest genus of animals, men, in order to get the advantage in the conflict with other creatures, must band together, like a hive of bees, and not propagate irregularly; must also, like the bees, nourish the sexless ones; in other words, must struggle toward continence, and never allow the kindling of the carnal lusts to which the whole arrangement of our life is directed."

He paused.

"Will the human race come to an end? Can any one who looks at the world as it is have the slightest doubt of it? Why, it is just as certain as death is certain. We find the end of the world inculcated in all the teachings of the Church, and in all the teachings of Science it is likewise shown to be inevitable.

CHAPTER XII

"In our society it is just exactly reversed: if a man has felt it incumbent on him to be continent during his bachelorhood, then always after he is married he feels it no longer necessary to restrain himself. You see, the wedding journeys, this retirement to solitude which young people with the sanction of their parents practise, are nothing else than a sanction for lewdness. But the moral law when it is broken brings its own punishment.

"In spite of all my endeavors to make my honeymoon a success, it was a failure. The whole time was merely vile, shameful, and tiresome. But very soon it became also painfully oppressive. This state of things began almost at the first. I think it was on the third or fourth day, I found my wife depressed, and I began to inquire what was the matter, began to put my arms around her, which I supposed was all she could possibly desire; but she pushed away my arm and burst into tears.

"What was it? She could not tell me. But she was depressed and down-hearted. Probably her highly wrought nerves whispered to her the truth as to the ignominy of our relations, but she could not tell me. I began to question her; she said something about being homesick for her mother. It seemed to me that this was not the truth. I tried to console her, but said nothing about her mother. I did not realize that she was simply bored, and that her mother was merely a pretext.

"But she immediately complained because I said nothing about her mother, as if I did not believe her. She told me that she could see I did not love her. I accused her of caprice, and immediately her face changed; in place of melancholy appeared exasperation, and she began in the bitterest terms to charge me with egotism and cruelty.

"I looked at her. Her whole face expressed the utmost coldness and hostility, almost hatred of me. I remember how alarmed I was on seeing this.

"'How is this? What does it mean?' I asked myself; 'love is the union of souls, and instead of this what have we here? Why, it cannot be, this is not she.'

"I did my best to soothe her, but I came up against such an insuperable wall of cold, venomous hostility that, before I had time to think, something like exasperation took possession of me also, and we said to each other a quantity of disagreeable words. The impression of this first quarrel was horrible. I called it a quarrel, but it was not a quarrel; it was really only the discovery of the gulf which was in reality between us. Our passionate love had worn itself out in the satisfaction of the senses, and therefore we remained facing each other as we really were, in other words, two egotists alien to each other, desirous each of getting the greatest possible pleasure out of the other!

"I called what took place between us a quarrel, but it was not a quarrel; it was only the consequence of the cessation of our sensuality, disclosing our actual relation to each other. I did not realize that this cold and hostile relationship was our normal relation. I did not understand this because this hostility, in the first weeks of our marriage, was very quickly hidden again from us by the rising of a newly distilled sensuality, that is to say, passionate love.

"And so I thought that we had quarreled and become reconciled, and that this would be the end of it. But in the very first month, during our honeymoon, very quickly came another period of satiety, and again we ceased to be necessary to each other, and another quarrel ensued. The second quarrel surprised me even more than the first. I said to myself:—

" 'Of course the first could not have been the result of chance, but had to be the result of necessity, and so with this, and there will be others.'

"The second quarrel surprised me the more because it proceeded from the most trivial cause—something pecuniary; but I never grudged money, and certainly could never have grudged any to my wife. I only remember that she made some remark of mine seem to be the expression of my desire to control her through money to which I claimed an exclusive right—something impossible, stupid, cowardly, and natural neither to her nor to me.

"I grew angry, and began to reproach her for her lack of delicacy; she returned the charge, and so it went on as before. And I perceived in her words, and in the expression of her face and her eyes, the same harsh, cold hostility as had surprised me the first time. I remember having quarreled with my brother, my friend, even my father; but never did there arise between us such a peculiar venomous anger as was manifested now. But after a short time our mutual reciprocal hatred concealed itself again under our passionate love, that is, our sensuality, and I once more cherished the notion that these two quarrels had been mistakes which might be rectified.

"But when the third and the fourth quarrel ensued, I came to believe that it was not a mere chance, but that it had to be, and that it would still be so, and I was horror-struck at what was before me. In this connection I was tormented by the horrible idea that I was the only person who had this misfortune, and that no other couple had any such experiences as I was having with my wife. I had not then found out that this is a common lot—that all men think, just as I did, that it is a misfortune exclusively peculiar to them, and so conceal this exclusive and shameful misfortune, not only from others but also from themselves, and are unwilling to acknowledge it.

"It began with us at the very first and kept on all the time, and grew more severe and more bitter. In the depths of my soul I from the very first felt that I was lost, that marriage had not turned out at all as I had expected, that it was not only not a happiness, but was something very oppressive; but, like all other men, I was not willing to acknowledge this—and I should not acknowledge it even now, had it not been for the sequel—and I concealed it not only from others, but even from myself.

"Now I am amazed that I did not recognize my real position. It might have been seen in the fact that our quarrels sprang from causes so trivial that afterward, when they were ended, it was impossible to remember what brought them about. Reason was not quick enough to sophisticate sufficient pretexts for the hostility that constantly existed between us.

"But still more amazing was the insufficiency of the pretexts for reconciliation. Occasionally it was a word, or an explanation, even tears, but sometimes . . . . oh, how shameful it is to remember it now! after the bitterest words exchanged, suddenly would come silence, glances, smiles, kisses, embraces!. . . . Fu! abomination. Why was it that I failed to see all the vileness of this even then?". . . .

CHAPTER XIII

Two passengers entered and began to settle themselves at the end of the carriage. He ceased speaking while they were taking their places, but as soon as they became quiet he went on with his story, never for an instant losing the thread of his thoughts.

"What is chiefly vile about this," he went on to say, "is that it is taken for granted in theory that love is something ideal and elevated; whereas, in practice, love is something low and swinish, which it is shameful and disgusting to speak of or remember. You see, it was not without reason that nature made it shameful and disgusting. But if it is shameful and disgusting, then it ought to be so much the more to be made known. But with us, on the contrary, people pretend that what is low and shameful and disgusting is beautiful and elevated.

"What were the first symptoms of my love? Why, these—that I gave myself up to animal excesses, not only not feeling any shame at it, but feeling a certain pride at the possibility of these animal excesses, not thinking either of her spiritual life or even of her physical life. I wondered what was the cause of our animosity to each other, but the thing was perfectly clear: this animosity was nothing else than the protest of human nature against the animal which was crushing it. I was amazed at our hatred of each other. But you see it could not have been otherwise. This hatred was nothing else than identical with the hatred felt by the accomplices in a crime, both for the instigation and for the accomplishment of the deed. What else was it than a crime, when she, poor thing, became pregnant within the first month and our swinish relations continued.

"You think that I am wandering from my story? Not at all. I am all the time relating to you how I killed my wife. . . . . At my trial I was asked why and how I killed her. . . . Fools! they think that I killed her with a dagger on the seventeenth of October. I did not kill her then, but long before. In exactly the same way they are all killing their wives now, all, all.". . . .

"How so?" I asked.

"It is something amazing that no one wishes to know what is so clear and evident—what doctors ought to know and to proclaim, but they hold their tongues. You see, it is really awfully simple! Men and women are like animals, and they are so created that after sexual union pregnancy begins, then suckling—a condition of things during which sexual union is dangerous both for the woman and for the child. The number of women and of men is about even: what does that signify? Of course it is clear. It does not require great wisdom to draw from these things the conclusion which animals also draw— that continence is necessary. But no! Science has gone so far as to discover certain corpuscles which run about in the blood, and all sorts of useless stupidities, but it cannot comprehend this yet. At least it is not rumored about that Science is saying this.

"And now for women there are only two methods of escape: one is by making monsters of themselves, by destroying or annihilating in themselves, according to the requirements of the case, the faculty of being women, that is to say, mothers, so that men may have no interruption of their enjoyment. The second escape is not an escape at all, but a simple, brutal, direct violation of the laws of nature. Such is constantly taking place in all so-called virtuous families, and it is this: the woman, in direct opposition to her nature, is obliged while bearing and nursing a child to be at the same time her husband's mistress, is obliged to be what no other animal ever permits. And she can't have the strength for it.

"Hence in our social sphere hysteria and nerves, and among the people women possessed. You have observed among girls, pure girls I mean, there is no such thing as 'possession'; it is only among peasant women and among women who live with their husbands. So it is with us. And it is exactly the same in Europe. All the hospitals are full of hysterical women, who have broken the laws of nature. And these possessed women and the patients of Charcot* are perfect cripples, and the world is full of half-crippled women. Only to think, what a mighty thing is taking place in a woman when she has conceived, or when she is nursing a baby. That which is growing is to continue ourselves, is to take our place. And this holy function is violated—for what? It is terrible to think about it. And yet they talk about the freedom; the rights, of women! It is just the same as if cannibals should feed up their prisoners for food, and at the same time talk, assert, that they were working for their freedom and rights."

All this was new, and surprised me.

"But what would you do?" I exclaimed. "If this came about, then a husband could have intercourse with his wife only once in two years; but a man . . . ."

"Yes, yes, a man must have it," said he, taking the words out of my mouth. "Again, the priests of Science support you in your views. Suggest to a man that vodka, tobacco, opium, are indispensable to him, and all that sort of thing will become indispensable to him. It means

---

*Jean-Martin Charcot (1825–1893), French neurologist and pioneer in the field of psychology.

that God did not understand what was needful, and that therefore, as
He did not ask advice of the magi, he arranged things badly. Pray
observe, the thing does not hang together. It is needful, it is indispensable, for a man to satisfy his carnal desires—so they decide; but
here comes in the question of conception and nursing babies, which
prevents the satisfaction of this necessity. How is the difficulty to be
overcome? How manage it? Why! go to the magi; they will arrange it.
They have thought it all out. Oh! when shall these magi be dethroned
from their deceptions? It is time! You see how far things have already
gone; men become mad and shoot themselves, and all from this one
cause. And how could it be otherwise? Animals seem to know that
their progeny perpetuate their kind, and they observe a certain law in
this respect. Only man has not the wisdom to know this, and does
not wish to know it. All he cares for is to have the greatest possible
pleasure. And who is he? he is the tsar of nature, he is man!

"Pray observe, animals enjoy intercourse only when there is to be
progeny, but the vile tsar of nature does it only for pleasure's sake,
and at any time; and, moreover, he idealizes this monkey-like business, and calls it the pearl of creation, love! And in the name of this
love, that is to say, this vileness, he destroys—what? one-half of the
human race! In the name of his gratifications he makes of all women,
who ought to be his coadjutors in the progress of humanity toward
truth and happiness, enemies instead! Look around and tell me who
everywhere acts as a hindrance to the progress of humanity—
women. And what makes them so? Nothing but this!

"Yes, yes," he repeated several times, and he began to shift his
position, to get out his cigarettes and to smoke, evidently desiring to
calm himself a little.

CHAPTER XIV

Thus I lived like a pig," he continued, in his former tone. "The
worst of it was that, while I was living this vile life, I imagined
that because I did not commit adultery with other women,
therefore I was leading a perfectly virtuous family life, that I was a

moral man, that I was in no manner to blame, but that if we had our quarrels she was to blame—her character!

"She was not to blame, of course. She was like all other women, like the majority. She had been educated in the way demanded by the position of women in our circle, and therefore as all women, without exception, belonging to the leisurely classes are educated and as they have to be educated.

"They talk nowadays about some new-fangled method of female education. All idle words: the training of women is exactly what it must be in view of the existent, sincere, and genuine notion of women universally held.

"And the education of women will always correspond to the notion of her held by men. Now we all know what that is, how men look on women: *Wein, Weib, und Gesang*,* and so it goes in the verses of the poets. Take all poetry, all painting, all sculpture, beginning with erotic verse and naked Venuses and Phrynes, and you will see that woman is an instrument of pleasure; such she is at Truba and at Grachevka† and at the finest ball. And mark the devil's subtlety: pleasure, satisfaction . . . . then let it be understood that it is merely pleasure, that woman is a sweet morsel. In the early days, knights boasted that they made divinities of women—apotheosized them, and at the same time they looked on them as the instruments of their pleasure. But nowadays men declare that they respect women, some relinquish their places to them, or pick up their handkerchiefs, others admit their rights to occupy all responsibilities, to take part in government and the like. They do all this, but their view of them is always the same, she is still the instrument of enjoyment, her body is the means of enjoyment. And she knows all that. It is just the same as slavery.

"Slavery is nothing else than the enjoyment by the few of the compulsory labor of the many. And in order that slavery may come to an end, people must cease desiring to take advantage of the compulsory labor of others, must consider it sinful or shameful. But while they take away, while they abolish, the external form of slavery, while they so arrange it that it is no longer possible to buy and sell slaves in the

---

*Wine, Woman, and Song (German).
†Red-light districts in Moscow.

market, and they believe and persuade themselves that slavery is abolished, they do not see and they do not wish to see that slavery still exists, for the reason that people, just the same as ever, like to profit by the labors of others, and consider it fair and honorable to do so. And as long as they consider this to be fair, there will always be men who will be stronger and keener than others, and will be able to do so.

"So it is with the emancipation of women. The slavery of woman consists in precisely this, that men desire to take advantage of her as an instrument of enjoyment, and consider it right to do so.

"Well, and now they emancipate woman, they give her all rights the same as to men, but they still continue to look on her as an instrument of enjoyment, and so they educate her with this end in view, both in childhood and by public opinion. But all the time she is just the same kind of a dissolute slave as before, and her husband is just the same kind of a dissolute slave-owner.

"They emancipate women in the colleges and in the law courts, but they look on her still as an object of enjoyment. Train her as she is trained among us, to regard herself in this light, and she will always remain a lower creature. Either she will, with the assistance of villainous doctors, prevent the birth of her offspring,—in other words, she will be a kind of prostitute, degrading herself, not to the level of a beast, but to the level of a thing; or she will be what she is, in the majority of cases, heart-sick, hysterical, unhappy, without the possibility of spiritual development.

"Gymnasia and universities cannot change this. It can be changed only by a change in the way men regard women, and the way women regard themselves. It can be changed only by woman coming to regard virginity as the highest condition, and not as it is now regarded, as a reproach and disgrace. Until this comes about, the ideal of every girl, whatever her education, will still remain that of attracting to herself as many men as possible, as many males as she can, in order that she may have a possibility of choice.

"The fact that one girl understands mathematics, and another can play on the harp, does not change this in the least. A woman is fortunate and attains all that she can desire when she obtains a husband, and therefore the chief task of woman is to learn how to bewitch him. So it has been, and so it will be. Just as this was characteristic of the maiden's life in our circle, so it continues to be even after she is married. In the maiden's life this was necessary for a choice; in the married woman's life it is needed for her ascendancy over her husband.

"The only thing which destroys this—curtails it for the time being—is the birth of children, and this is when she is not a monster; in other words, when she nurses her children. But here again the doctors interfere. In the case of my wife, although she wanted to suckle her first baby, and though she suckled the next five, the state of her health seemed precarious, and these doctors, who cynically undressed her and felt her all over,—for which service I was obliged to be grateful to them and to pay money,—these gentle doctors found that she ought not to nurse her child; and so she, this first time, was deprived of the sole means of saving herself from coquetry. She hired a wet-nurse; in other words, we took advantage of the poverty, needs, ignorance of another woman, decoyed her away from her own child to ours, and, in payment for this, gave her a head-dress with laces. But that is not the point. The point is that during this period of emancipation from bearing and nursing babies, the female coquetry, which had hitherto lain dormant, manifested itself in her with greater strength, while correspondingly in me there appeared with especial violence the pangs of jealousy, which unceasingly tore me during all my married life, as they cannot fail to tear all husbands who live with their wives as I lived with mine—that is to say, unnaturally.

CHAPTER XV

"During the whole course of my married life I never ceased to experience the pangs of jealousy, but there were periods when I suffered from them with especial acuteness; and one of these periods was after the birth of my first child, when the doctors forbade her to suckle it. I was especially jealous at this time; in the first place, because my wife suffered from that uneasiness characteristic of mothers, which is calculated to make an unreasonable interruption of the regular course of life; secondly, because when I saw how easily she renounced the moral responsibilities of a mother

I naturally, even though unconsciously, concluded that it would be equally easy for her to renounce the duties of a wife; the more so because she was perfectly healthy, and, notwithstanding the prohibition of the dear doctors, she nursed the other children, and nursed them excellently."

"But you don't seem to like doctors?" said I, for I had noticed a particularly bitter tone in his voice every time he mentioned them.

"This is not a matter of love or of hate. They ruined my life, as they have ruined, and will still continue to ruin, the lives of thousands, hundreds of thousands, of people; and I cannot help connecting cause and effect. I understand that they, like lawyers and others, must earn money to live on, and I would willingly give them a half of my income; and, if it were only realized what they were doing, every one else would also, I am convinced, give a half of his property on condition that they would not meddle with our family lives, and would never come near us. I have never collected any statistics, still I know of a dozen cases—a multitude of them—in which they have killed the unborn child, declaring that the mother would not live if the child were born; and yet afterward the mother was admirably fortunate in childbearing; and again they have killed the mother under the pretext of some operation or other. You see, no one reckons up these murders, just as no one ever reckoned the murders of the Inquisition, because it has been supposed that this was done for the benefit of humanity. It is impossible to count the crimes committed by them. But all these crimes are nothing compared to the moral corruption of materialism which they introduced into the world, especially through women.

"I say nothing about the fact that, if we should follow their prescription, then, thanks to the infection everywhere, in everything, people would have to separate instead of drawing closer together; they would have, according to the teachings of the doctors, to sit apart, and never let the atomizer, with carbolic acid, out of their mouths. . . . . Lately, however, they have discovered that even this is of no special use.

"But this is not to the point. The principal poison lies in the demoralization of the people, women especially.

"Today, it is no longer enough to say, 'You are living a bad life; live better.' You can't say that to yourself or to another man. But if you are living a bad life, then the cause for it lies in the abnormal state of the nervous functions, and the like. And you have to consult the doctors, and they prescribe for thirty-five kopeks' worth of medicine at the apothecaries, and you take it.

"You will grow even worse, then have to take new drugs and consult other doctors. An excellent dodge!

"But that is not to the point. I only say that she suckled the children admirably, and that the only thing that saved me from the pangs of jealousy was her bearing and nursing her children.

"If it had not been for that, the inevitable end would have come about earlier.

"The children saved me and her. During eight years she gave birth to five children, and all except the first she nursed herself."

"Where are your children now?" I asked.

"My children?" he repeated, with a startled look.

"Forgive me! perhaps this question caused you painful memories."

"No, it's of no consequence. My sister-in-law and her brother took charge of my children. They would not give them to me. You see I am a kind of insane man. I am going away from them now. I have seen them, but they won't give them to me. For if they did, I should educate them so that they should not be like their parents. But it is necessary that they should be the same. Well, what is to be done? I can understand why they should not give them to me, or trust me. And besides, I don't know as I should have the strength to bring them up. I think not. I am a ruin, a cripple! One thing I have . . . . I know. Yes, it is manifest that I know what it will be a long time before the rest of the world know.

"Yes, my children are alive, and are growing up to be just such savages as all the rest around them are. I have seen them—three times I have seen them. I can't do anything for them—not a thing. I am going now to my own place in the south; I have a little house and a little garden there.

"Yes, it will not be soon that people will know what I know. It will soon be easy to find out how much iron and what other metals there are in the sun and the stars; but what shall cure our swinishness, that is hard, awfully hard!

"You have listened to me, and even for that I am grateful.

CHAPTER XVI

"You just mentioned the children. There, again, what terrible lying goes on concerning children. Children are a divine benediction. Children are a delight. Now this is all a lie. All this used to be so, but now there is nothing of the sort, nothing at all. Children are a torment, and that is all. The majority of mothers feel so, and some of them do not hesitate to say so, up and down. Ask the greater number of the mothers of our circle,—people of means,— and they will tell you that from terror lest their children should sicken and die they do not wish to have children; if they are born, they do not wish to suckle them, lest they should grow too much attached to them and cause them sorrow. The delight which the child affords them by its beauty, its tiny little arms, its little feet, its whole body,—the satisfaction afforded is less than the agony of apprehension which they experience, I do not say from illness or the loss of the child, but from the mere apprehension of the possibility of illnesses and death. Having weighed the advantages and disadvantages, it seems to be disadvantageous, and therefore that it is not desirable, to have children. They say this openly, boldly, imagining that these sentiments grow out of their love to their children, good, praiseworthy feelings in which they take pride. They do not notice this: that by this reasoning they directly renounce love and assert their egoism. For them there is less pleasure from the charm of a child than suffering from apprehension for it, and therefore they don't desire a child which they would come to love. They do not sacrifice themselves for the beloved creature, but they sacrifice for themselves the beloved creature that is to be.

"It is clear that this is not love, but egoism. But it is not for me to criticize these mothers of well-to-do families for their egoism, when you think of all they endure from the health of their children in our modern fashionable life, thanks again to these same doctors. How well I remember even now our life and the conditions of our life during the first period of our marriage, when we had three or four young children, and she was absorbed with them! It fills me even now with horror.

"It was no kind of a life. It was a perpetual peril, rescue from it followed by new peril; then new and desperate endeavors, and then a new rescue—all the time as if we were on board a sinking ship. It sometimes seemed to me that this was done on purpose; that she was pretending to be troubled about her children so as to get the upper hand of me, so alluringly, so simply all questions were decided for her advantage. It seemed to me sometimes that all that she said and did in these circumstances was done on purpose. But no, she herself suffered terribly and kept tormenting herself about the children, and about the care of their health and about their illnesses. It was a torture for her and for me also. And it was impossible for her not to torment herself.

"You see her attachment to her children,—the animal instinct to nurse them, to fondle them, to protect them was in her as it is in the majority of women; but she had not what animals have—a freedom from imagination and reason. The hen has no fear of what may befall her chick, she knows nothing about the diseases which may come upon it, knows nothing of all those remedies which men imagine they can employ to keep away sickness and death. And for the hen the young ones are no torment. She does for her chicks what is natural and pleasant for her to do, and her young are a delight to her. When the chicken shows signs of sickness her duties are distinctly determined: she warms and nourishes it. And in doing this she knows that she is doing her duty. If the chicken dies, she does not ask herself why it died, where it has gone to, she cackles for a while, then stops and goes on living as before.

"But for our unhappy women and for my wife there was nothing of the kind. Then, besides the question of diseases and how to cure them, of how to educate them, how to develop them, she had heard from all sides and had read endlessly varied and contradictory rules: you must feed it this way, no not this way, but so; how to dress it, what to give it to drink, when to bathe it, when to put it to sleep, when to take it out to walk, ventilation,—in regard to all this, we— and she especially—learned new rules every week. Just as if children began to be born only yesterday! Why! some child was not fed quite properly, or wasn't bathed at the right time, and it fell ill, and it showed that we were to blame—that we had not done what we should have done. Even when children are well, they are a torment.

But when they fall ill, why then, of course, it is a perfect hell. It is presupposed that sickness may be cured and that there is such a science and there are such men—doctors, and that they know. Not that all know, but that the best of them do. And here is a sick child and it is requisite to get hold of this man, the very best of his profession, who can cure, and the child is saved; and if you don't get hold of this doctor, or if you don't live where this doctor lives, then the child is lost. And this belief was not exclusively confined to my wife, but it is the belief of all the women of her sphere, and on all sides she hears such talk as this:—

" 'Two of Yekaterina Semyonovna's children died because they did not call Ivan Zakharych in time, but Ivan Zakharych saved the life of Marya Ivanovna's oldest daughter; and here the Petrovich children were sent in time to different hotels by this doctor's advice, and so their lives were saved; but those that had not been isolated, died. And such and such a woman had a feeble child, and by the doctor's advice they took it South, and it lived. . . . .'

"How can one fail to torment oneself and grow excited all one's life long, when the life of her children, to whom she is devotedly attached, depends on her knowing in time what Ivan Zakharych will say about it? But no one knows what Ivan Zakharych will say—least of all himself, because he knows very well that he knows nothing at all and cannot give any help, and he only tergiversates at haphazard merely in order that people may not cease to believe in his knowledge.

"You see, if she had been simply an animal, she would not have tormented herself so; while if she had been a normal human being, then she would have had faith in God, she would have thought and spoken as true believers say:—

" 'God gave and God has taken and one can't escape from God.'*

"So our whole life with our children was no joy but a torment for her, and, therefore, for me also. How could we help tormenting ourselves? And she constantly did torment herself. It used to be that just as we were calming down from any scene of jealousy or a simple quarrel, and were planning to begin a new life, to read something

---

*Rough paraphrase from the biblical book of Job 1:21: "The Lord gave and the Lord has taken away; may the name of the Lord be praised" (King James Version).

and to do something, and had only got fairly started, word would suddenly be brought that Vasya was vomiting, that Masha had the dysentery, or that Andryusha had a rash—and the end of it was that we had no kind of a life. Where should we send, what doctor should we get, in which room should we isolate the patient? And then began the enemas, the taking of temperatures, the medicines, and the doctors. And this would scarcely be done with before something else would begin. There was no regular family life. But, as I have told you, there was a constant apprehension from real or fancied dangers. And that is the way it is in most families. In my family it was especially pronounced. My wife was affectionate and superstitious.

"Thus it was that the presence of children not only did not improve our life, but poisoned it. Moreover, the children gave us a new pretext for quarreling. From the time we began to have children, and the more in proportion as they grew up, the more frequently our children became the very means and object of our quarrels, not only the subject, but the very instrument of dissension; we, as it were, fought each other with our own children as weapons. Each of us had his own favorite child as a weapon of attack. I made more use of Vasya the eldest, and she of Liza. Later, when the children had begun to grow up, and their characters formed, it came about that they took sides with us according as we were able to attract them. They suffered terribly from this state of affairs, poor little things, but we in our incessant warfare had no time to think of them. The little girl was my special ally; the oldest boy, who resembled his mother and was her favorite, often seemed hateful to me.

CHAPTER XVII

"Well, thus we lived. Our relations grew more and more hostile, and at last it went so far that difference of views no longer produced enmity, but that enmity produced difference of views. Whatever she said I was ready in advance to disagree with her, and so it was with her.

"In the fourth year it was fairly admitted by both of us, though tacitly, that we could not understand each other—that we could not agree. We ceased to make any attempt to talk anything over to the end. In regard to the simplest things, especially the children, we each kept our own opinion unchangeably. As I now remember, the opinions which I advocated were not so precious in my sight that I could not give them up; but she had opposing notions, and to yield to them meant to yield to her. And this I could not do. Nor could she yield to me. She evidently counted herself always perfectly right toward me, and as for me, I was always a saint in my own eyes compared to her. When we were together we were almost reduced to silence, or to such conversations as I am convinced the beasts may carry on together:—'What time is it?'—'Is it bedtime?'—'What will you have for dinner today?'—'Where will you drive?'—'What is the news?'—'We must send for the doctor; Masha has a sore throat.'

"It required only to step a hair's width beyond this unendurably narrowing circle of conventional sentences in order to inspire a dissension,—skirmishes and expressions of hatred regarding the coffee, the table-cloth, the drive, the course of the game of bridge,—in fact, over trifles which could not have had the slightest importance for either of us. In me, at least, hatred of her boiled terribly. I often looked at her when she was drinking tea, waving her foot, or conveying her spoon to her mouth, sipping from it and swallowing the liquid, and I hated her for this very trifle as if it were the worst of crimes. I did not notice that these periods broke out in me with perfect regularity and uniformity, corresponding to the periods of what we called 'love.' A period of 'love'—then a period of hatred; an energetic period of passion, then a long period of hatred; a feebler manifestation of passion, then a briefer outbreak of hatred.

"We did not then comprehend that this love and hatred were one and the same animal passion, only with opposite poles. It would have been horrible to live in this way if we had realized our situation; but we did not realize it and did not see it. In this lie the salvation as well as the punishment of a man is that when he is living irregularly he may blind himself so as not to see the wretchedness of his situation.

"Thus it was with us. She endeavored to forget herself in strenuous and ever absorbing occupations,—her housekeeping, the arrangement of the furniture, dressing herself and the family, and the education and health of the children. I had my own affairs to attend to,—drinking, hunting, playing cards, going to my office. We were both busy all the time. We both felt that the busier we were the more annoyed we might be with each other.

" 'It is very well for you to make up such grimaces,' I would think, mentally addressing her. 'How you tormented me all night with your scenes. But I have a meeting to attend.'

" 'It is all very well for you,' she would not only think, but even say aloud, 'but the baby kept me awake all night long.'

"These new theories of hypnotism, mental diseases, hysteria, are all an absurdity—not a simple absurdity, but a vile and pernicious one. In regard to my wife, Charcot would have infallibly said that she was a victim of hysteria, and he would have said of me that I was abnormal, and probably he would have tried to cure us. But there was no disease to cure.

"Thus we lived in a continual mist, not cognizant of the situation in which we found ourselves. And if the catastrophy which overtook us had not occurred, I should have continued to live on till old age in the same way, and on my death-bed I should have even thought that I had lived a good life,—not remarkably good, but not at all a bad life,—like that of all other men. I should never have understood that abyss of unhappiness and that abominable falsehood in which I was floundering.

"We were like two convicts, fastened to one chain and hating each other, each poisoning the life of the other and striving not to recognize the fact. I did not then realize that ninety-nine per cent of married people live in the same hell as mine, and that it must infallibly be so. I did not then realize that it was true of others or true of myself.

"It is amazing what coincidences may be found in a regular and even in an irregular life. Thus when parents are beginning to find that they are making each other's lives unendurable, it becomes imperative that they go to the city for the better education of their children. And so it was we found it necessary to move to the city."

He stopped speaking, and twice gave vent to those strange sounds which this time were quite like repressed sobs. We were approaching a station.

"What time is it?" he asked.

I looked at my watch. It was two o'clock.

"Aren't you tired?" he asked.

"No; but are you not tired?"

"I am suffocating. Permit me, I will go out and get a drink of water."

And he got up and went staggering through the carriage.

I sat alone, cogitating over what he had told me, and I fell into such a brown study that I did not notice him when he returned through the other door.

CHAPTER XVIII

"Yes, I all the time wander from my story," he began; "I have pondered over it a good deal. I look on many things in a different way from what most do, and I want to talk it all out.

"Well, we began to live in the city. There a man may live a century and never dream that he has long ago died and rotted. One has no time to study himself—his time is wholly occupied: business, social relations, his health, art, the health of his children, and their education. Now he must receive calls from such and such people and must return them; now he must see this woman and hear some famous man or woman talk. You see, at any given moment there will be in the city surely one celebrity, and generally several, whom it is impossible for you to miss. Now you have to consult a doctor for yourself or for this one or that, then you have to see one of the tutors or the governess, and life is frittered away. Well, so it was we lived and suffered less from our life together. Moreover, we had at first the charming occupation of getting settled in a new city, in new quarters, and then again in traveling back and forth between the city and the country.

"Thus we lived one winter, and during the second winter the circumstance which I am going to relate took place, and though it seemed a trifling thing and attracted no attention, still it brought about all that succeeded.

"She became delicate in health, and the doctors forbade her to have any more children, and they taught her how to prevent it. This was repulsive to me. I had no patience with such an idea, but she with frivolous obstinacy insisted on having her own way, and I had to yield. The last justification of the swinish life—children—was taken away, and our life became viler than ever.

"To the muzhik, to the laboring man, children are a necessity; although it is hard for him to feed them, still he must have them and there the marital relations are justified. But to us, who already have children, more children are not a desideratum; they cause extra work, expense, further division of property—they are a burden.

"And therefore there is no justification for us of the swinish life. Either we artificially prevent the birth of children or we regard children as a misfortune,—as the consequence of carelessness, which is worse.

"There is no justification. But we have fallen morally so low that we do not see the need of any justification. The majority of men now belonging to the cultivated classes give themselves up to this form of debauchery without the slightest twinge of conscience.

"No one feels any conscientious scruples, because conscience is a non-existent quality except—if we may so say—the conscience of public opinion and of the criminal law. And in this respect neither the one nor the other is violated; no one has to bear the brunt of public scorn, for all do the same thing: both Marya Pavlovna and Ivan Zakharych. Why breed beggars or deprive oneself of the possibility of social life? . . . . or is there any reason to stand in awe of the criminal law or to fear it. Ugly peasant girls and soldiers' wives may throw their babies into ponds and wells, and they of course must go to prison, but all that sort of thing is done by us opportunely and neatly!

"Thus we lived two years. The means employed by the rascally doctors evidently began to take effect: physically she improved and she grew more beautiful, like the last beauty of the summer. She was conscious of this, and began to take care of herself. Her beauty became fascinating and disturbing to men. As she was in the prime of a woman of thirty and was no longer bearing children, she grew plump—stirring the passions. Even the sight of her made one uneasy. When she came among men she attracted all eyes. She was like a well-fed and bridled horse which had not been driven for some time and from which the bridle was taken off. There was no longer any restraint, as with ninety-nine per cent of our women. Even I felt this, and it was terrible to me."

CHAPTER XIX

He suddenly got up and sat down close by the window.

"Excuse me," he exclaimed, and looking out intently sat there for as much as three minutes. Then he sighed deeply and again sat down opposite me. His face had undergone a complete change, there came a piteous look into his eyes, and a strange sort of smile curved his lips.

"I had grown a little tired, but I will go on with my story. There is plenty of time left; it has not begun to grow light yet. Yes," he began again, after he had lighted a cigarette. "She grew plumper after she ceased to bear children, and her malady—the constant worriment over the children—began to disappear; it did not really disappear, but she, as it were, awoke from a drunken stupor; she began to remember, and she saw that there was a whole world, a divine world, with its joys about which she had entirely forgotten, but in which she did not know how to live—a divine world which she did not understand at all.

" 'How keep it from being wasted. Time is fleeting—it will not return.'

"Thus I imagined she thought or rather felt, and indeed it would have been impossible for it to be otherwise; she had been educated to believe that in this world there is only one thing worthy of any one's attention—love. She had become married, she had got some notion of what this love was, but it was very far from being what had been promised, from what she expected; she had undergone the loss of many illusions; she had borne many sufferings, and then that unexpected torment—so many children! This agony had worn her out. And now, thanks to the obliging doctors, she had found out that it was possible to avoid having children. She was glad of that, made the experiment, and began to live for the one thing which she knew about—for the sake of love. But the enjoyment of love with a husband who was consumed with the fiery passions of wrath and jealousy was not the kind she wanted. She began to picture to herself another, a more genuine, a newer kind of connection—at least that is what I imagine was the case. And so she began to look around, as if she were expecting something.

"I noticed it, and was correspondingly troubled. It kept all the time happening that she, talking as her habit was with me through the medium of others, that is to say, talking with strangers, but making her remarks for my ears, expressed herself boldly, never at all dreaming that she, an hour before, had said diametrically the opposite, and expressed herself half seriously to the effect that that maternal solicitude was a delusion, that there was no sense in sacrificing her life for her children, that she was still young and could still enjoy life. She really occupied herself less with her children, certainly with less of desperate solicitude; but she gave more and more attention to herself, occupied herself with her external appearance, although she tried to keep it secret; also with her pleasures and with her accomplishments. She once more enthusiastically took up her piano practice which hitherto she had entirely neglected. That was the beginning of the end."

He once more turned to the window his weary-looking eyes, but straightway, evidently making an effort to control himself, he proceeded:—

"Yes, that man appeared."

He hesitated, and twice produced through his nose his peculiar sounds. I saw that it was trying for him to mention that man, to recall him, even to allude to him. But he made an effort, and as it were breaking through the barrier which hindered him, he resolutely went on:—

"A vile fellow he was in my eyes, in my estimation. And not because he played an important part in my life, but because he was really vile. However, the fact that he was bad serves merely as a proof of how irresponsible she was. If it had not been he, it would have surely been someone else."

He again ceased speaking.

"Yes, he was a musician, a fiddler—not a professional musician, but half professional, half society man. His father was a landed proprietor, a neighbor of my father's. His father went to ruin, and his children—three of them were boys—all managed to make their way; only this one, the youngest, was intrusted to his godmother and sent to Paris. There he was sent to the Conservatoire, because he had a talent for music, and he was graduated as a fiddler and played in concerts. He was the man.". . . .

It was evident that he wished to say something harsh about him, but he restrained himself, and said, speaking rapidly:—

"Well, I don't know how he had lived up to that time, but that year he appeared in Russia and came to my house. . . . . He had almond-shaped, humid eyes, handsome, smiling lips, little waxed mustaches, the latest and most fashionable method of dressing his hair, an insipidly handsome face, such as women call 'not bad,' a slender build, though not ill-shaped, and with a largely developed behind such as they say characterize Hottentot women.[5] This it is said is musical! Slipping into familiarity, as far as was permitted him, but sensitive and always ready to stop short at the slightest resistance, with a regard to external appearances, and with that peculiar touch of Parisian elegance, caused by buttoned boots and bright-colored neckties and everything else which foreigners acquire in Paris, and which by their character of novelty always attract women. In his manners there was a factitious external gayety. A way, as you may know, of speaking about everything by means of hints and fragmentary allusions, as if the person with whom he was speaking knew all about it, and could fill out the missing links.

"Well, then, this man with his music was the cause of all the trouble. You see at the trial the whole affair was represented as having been caused by my jealousy. This was not so at all, that is to say, it was not exactly so; it was, and it was not. At the trial it was decided that I had been deceived and that I had committed the murder in defending my outraged honor,—so they called it in their language,—and on this ground I was acquitted. At the trial I did my best to explain my idea of it, but they understood that I had wished to rehabilitate my wife's honor.

"Her relations with that musician, whatever they were, did not have in my eyes that significance, nor in hers either. It simply had the significance I have already mentioned, that of my swinishness. All came from the fact that between us existed that terrible gulf, of which I have told you, that terrible tension of mutual hatred, whereby the first impulse was sufficient to precipitate the crisis. The quarrels between us, as time went on, became something awful and were remarkably striking, being mingled with intense animal passion.

"If he had not appeared, surely someone else would. If there had not been one pretext for jealousy, there would have been another. I insist upon it that all husbands living as I lived must either live wanton lives, or separate, or kill themselves or their wives as I did. If this does not occur in any given case, it is a rare exception. Why, before the end came, as I made it come, I was several times on the brink of suicide, and even she poisoned herself.

CHAPTER XX

"Yes, this happened not long before the crisis.

"We had been living in a sort of armistice, and there was no reason for it to be broken. Suddenly a conversation began, in which I remarked that a certain dog had received a medal at an exhibition. She said: —

" 'Not a medal, but honorable mention.'

"A dispute began. We began to reproach each other, skipping from subject to subject.

" 'Well, I knew that long ago; it was always so.'

" 'You said so and so.'

" 'No, I said thus and so.'

" 'Do you mean to say I lie?'

"There is a feeling that you are on the edge of a frightful quarrel, and that you will be tempted to kill yourself or her. You know that it will begin in an instant and you dread it like fire and you want to control yourself, but anger seizes on your whole being. She is in the same or in an even worse condition, and she deliberately puts a wrong construction on every word you say, giving it a false signification, and every word she speaks is steeped in poison; wherever she knows I am most sensitive, there she strikes. The farther it goes, the more portentous it grows. I cry: —

" 'Silence,' or the like.

"She rushes from the room and takes refuge in the nursery. I try to detain her so that I may say out my say and prove my position, and

I seize her by the arm. She pretends that I hurt her and screams:—

" 'Children, your father is striking me.'

"I cry:—

" 'Don't you lie!'

" 'And this is not the first time either,' she cries, or something to that effect.

"The children rush to her. She tries to calm them I say,—

" 'Don't pretend.'

"She says:—

" 'For you everything is pretense. You strike a woman and then say that she is pretending. Now I understand you. This is the very thing you want.'

"I shout:—

" 'Oh, if you were only dead!'

"I remember how horror-struck I was at those terrible words. I would never have believed myself capable of uttering such coarse, terrible words, and I am amazed that they leap forth from my mouth. I shout out those terrible words and rush into my library, sit down and smoke. I hear her go into the vestibule, preparing to go out. I ask:—

" 'Where are you going?'

"She makes no reply.

" 'Well, the devil go with her!' I say to myself, as I return to the library and again sit down and smoke. A thousand different plans of how to avenge myself on her and how to get rid of her, how to set everything to rights again and how to act as if nothing had taken place, go rushing through my brain.

"And as I sit and think, I smoke, smoke, smoke! I conceive the plan of running away from her, of hiding myself, of going to America. I actually go as far as to dream of getting rid of her, and I think how delightful it would be as soon as this is accomplished to make new ties with some beautiful woman, entirely new. I dream of getting rid of her by her dying or by securing a divorce, and I cogitate how this may be brought about. I see that my mind is wandering, that I am not thinking consecutively; but in order that I may not see that I am thinking the wrong kind of thoughts and am entirely at sea, I smoke.

"But life at home goes on. The governess comes and asks:—

" 'Where is madame? when will she be back?'

"The lackey asks:—

" 'Shall I serve tea?'

"I go into the dining-room. The children, especially the oldest one, Liza, who is already old enough to understand, look at me questioningly, disapprovingly. We silently drink our tea. Of her there is no sign. The whole evening passes; she does not come, and two thoughts mingle in my soul: wrath against her because she is tormenting me and all the children by her absence,—and yet, she will return in the end,—and fear that she will not come back, but will lay violent hands on herself.

"I should go out in search of her. But where to find her? At her sister's? But it would be stupid to go there with such an inquiry. Well, then, God go with her! if she wants to torment us, let her torment herself also. That is the very thing she would like. And next time she will be worse.

"But supposing she is not at her sister's, but has done something else—has even already laid hands on herself?

"Eleven o'clock, twelve o'clock. . . . . I will not go into the sleeping-room—it would be stupid to lie down there and wait alone, but I will lie down where I am. I try to occupy myself with some work, to write letters, to read; but I can't do anything. I sit alone in my library, I torment myself with apprehensions, I am full of anger, I listen. Three o'clock, four—no sign of her. I fall asleep just before morning. When I wake up, there is no sign of her.

"Everything in the house goes on as usual; but all are in a state of dubiety, and look questioningly and reproachfully at me, supposing that it is all my fault. And within me is still the same struggle—anger because she torments me, and anxiety about her.

"About eleven o'clock in the morning her sister comes as her envoy; and she begins in the usual way:—

" 'She is in a terrible state of mind. Now what does it all mean? Something must have happened.'

"I speak about the incompatibility of her temper, and I asseverate that I have done nothing.

" 'But you see that things cannot be allowed to go on in this way,' says she.

" 'It is all her affair, not mine,' I say. 'I shall not take the first step. If it be a separation, then let it be a separation.'

"My sister-in-law goes away without getting any satisfaction. I have spoken boldly that I would not take the first step; but as soon as she has gone, and I see the poor, frightened children, I am already prepared to take the first step. I should even be glad to do so, but I don't know how. Again I walk up and down and smoke, and after breakfast fortify myself with vodka and wine, and attain what I was unconsciously desirous of: I do not see the stupidity, the cowardice of my position.

"About three she returns. She meets me, but has nothing to say. I imagine that she has come to seek for a reconciliation, and I begin to tell her how I had been led on by her reproaches. She, with the same harsh, terribly harassed face, replies that she has not come to indulge in explanations, but to take the children away—that we cannot possibly live together.

"I begin to explain that I was not the one to blame, that it was she who had driven me out of my senses.

"She looks at me sternly, triumphantly, and then says:—

" 'Say no more, you will be sorry enough.'

"I reply that I cannot endure any comedy.

"Then she screams out something which I cannot comprehend and flees to her room. And she turns the key behind her; she has locked herself in. I knock; no answer, and full of wrath, I wait.

"At the end of half an hour Liza comes running in with tears in her eyes.

" 'What has happened?'

" 'I cannot hear mamma.'

"We go to her room. I press against the door with all my might. The bolt happens to be not wholly pushed in, and both halves of the door yield. I hasten to the bed. She is lying on it in an uncomfortable position in her petticoats and boots. On the table is an empty opium bottle. We bring her to consciousness. Tears and ultimate reconciliation. But it is no reconciliation; in the soul of each of us is the same old anger against each other, and an additional sense of exasperation for the pain which this quarrel has caused and which each blames the other for. But this trouble must be somehow ended, and life goes on in its old grooves. But in the same way such quarrels and even worse ones take place regularly all the time—now with a week's interval, now a month's interval, now every day, and it is always the same thing.

"One time I even applied for a foreign passport—the quarrel had lasted two days. But there ensued a semi-explanation, a semi-reconciliation, and I stayed.

CHAPTER XXI

"Such then were our relations when that man appeared. He came to Moscow—his name was Trukhachevsky—and he came to my house. It was in the morning. I received him. In former times we had been on familiar terms.[6] He endeavored, sometimes using the more formal, sometimes the more familiar, form of address, to keep on his old footing of thee and thou, but I quickly settled the question by using the formal 'you' and he immediately took the hint. Even at the first glance he impressed me unfavorably. But strangely enough some peculiar fatal power impelled me not to keep him at a distance, to send him away, but rather to draw him nearer to me. Why, what could have been simpler than to have talked coolly with him a few minutes, and to have said 'good morning' without introducing him to my wife?

"But no, I talked with him deliberately about his playing, and remarked that we had been told that he had given up playing the fiddle. He replied that on the contrary he was playing now more than ever before. He recalled the fact that I, too, had once played. I said that I had given up playing, but that my wife played very well. Wonderful thing! My relations to him that very first day, that very first hour of my meeting with him, were such as they could have been only after all that occurred subsequently. There was something strained in my relations with him; I noticed every word, every expression, said by him or myself, and attributed importance to them.

"I presented him to my wife. Immediately a conversation on music began between them, and he offered his services to practise with her. My wife, as was always the case with her at that later period of her life, was very elegant and fascinating, captivatingly beautiful. He evidently pleased her at first sight. Moreover, she was delighted with the prospect of having the gratification of playing with violin and piano, which she liked so much that she had once hired a fiddler from the theater, and her face expressed this pleasure. But as soon as she saw me, she instantly understood how I felt about it, and her expression changed, and our game of mutual deceit began. I smiled pleasantly, pretending it was very agreeable to me. He, looking at my wife as all immoral men look at pretty women, pretended that he was interested in nothing else but the topic of conversation, especially that part which did not interest him at all. She tried to seem indifferent, but my falsely smiling expression of jealousy, so well known to her, and his lecherous look evidently disturbed her. I saw that from his very first glance her eyes shone with peculiar brilliancy, and apparently as a consequence of my jealousy there passed between him and her something like an electrical shock, calling forth something like a uniformity in the expression of their eyes and their smiles. She blushed, he reddened. She smiled, he smiled. They talked about music, about Paris, about all sorts of trifles. He rose to take his leave, and stood smiling with his hat resting against his quivering thigh, and looked now at her, now at me, apparently waiting to see what we would do.

"I remember that moment especially because at that moment I might have refrained from inviting him to call again, and if I had, the trouble would not have happened. But I looked at him and her.

"'Do not think for an instant that I am jealous of you,' said I, mentally, to her, 'or that I am afraid of you,' said I, mentally, to him, and I invited him to come some evening and bring his fiddle and play with my wife. She looked at me in surprise, blushed, and as if startled, began to plead off, declaring that she did not play well enough. This refusal of hers irritated me still more, and I insisted on it with all the more vehemence. I remember the strange feeling I had as I looked at the back of his head and his white neck, strongly contrasting with his black hair which was combed back on both sides, as he left us with a springy gait like that of a bird. I cannot help acknowledging to myself that this man's presence was a torture to me.

"'It depends on me,' I said to myself, 'to act in such a way as never to see him again. But so to act would be equivalent to a confession that I fear him. No, I do not fear him; it would be too humiliating,' I said to myself. And there in the anteroom, knowing that my wife was listening to me, I insisted that he should come back that very evening and bring his fiddle with him. He promised that he would and took his departure.

"In the evening he came with his fiddle, and they played together. But for a long time the music did not go very well; we had not the pieces that he wanted, and those he had my wife could not play without preparation. I was very fond of music and sympathized with their playing, arranging the music-stand for him and turning over the leaves. They managed to play something—a few songs without words and a sonata by Mozart. He played excellently, and he had to the highest degree what is called 'temperament'—moreover, a delicate, noble art, entirely out of keeping with his character.

"He was, of course, far stronger than my wife, and he helped her and at the same time politely praised her playing. He behaved very well. My wife seemed interested only in the music, and was very simple and natural. Though I also pretended to be interested in the music, still, all the evening, I did not cease to be tortured by jealousy. From the first moment when his eyes fell on my wife I saw that the wild beast existing in them both, out of the reach of all the conditions of their position and the society in which they lived, was asking, 'Is it possible?' and answering its own question with a 'Yes, certainly it is.' I saw that he had never expected to find in my wife, in a society lady of Moscow, such a fascinating creature, and that he was delighted. Therefore there could be no doubt in his mind that she was harmonious with him. The whole question consisted in how the insufferable husband should not interfere with them. If I myself had been pure, I should not have understood this, but I, like the majority of men, had indulged in the same notions of women, until I was married, and therefore I could read his soul like a book.

"I was especially tormented by the fact that I could remark that her feelings and mine were in a state of constant irritation only occasionally interrupted by our habitual sensuality; while this man, both by his external elegance and by his novelty, by the fact that he was a stranger, but chiefly because of his indubitably great musical talent, by the proximity due to their playing together, by the influence produced by music, especially by a fiddle, on a very impressionable nature— all this, I say, made it inevitable that this man should please her, and more than that, that he should get a complete ascendancy over her, without the least hesitation, conquer, overwhelm, fascinate, enchain, and do with her whatever he willed. I could not help seeing that, and I suffered awfully. But in spite of this, or possibly in consequence of it, some force, against my will, compelled me to be especially polite and even affectionate to him. Whether I did this to show my wife, to show him, that I was not afraid of it, or whether I did it to deceive myself, I do not know; only I could not from the very first be natural with him. In order not to yield to my desire to kill him on the spot, I had to be friendly toward him. At dinner I treated him to expensive wines, I praised him for his playing and talked with him with a peculiarly affectionate smile, and invited him to dinner on the following Sunday, and to play again with my wife. I said I would ask some of my musical friends to hear him. And so it came to an end."

And Pozdnyshev, under the influence of powerful emotion, changed his position and emitted his peculiar sounds.

"It is strange what an effect the presence of that man had on me," he began once more, evidently making an effort to become calm.

"Two or three days after this I came home from an exhibition, and as I entered the vestibule I became conscious of a sudden feeling of oppression, exactly as if a stone had been rolled on my heart, and I could not explain it to myself. It was due to the fact that as I was passing through the vestibule I noticed something which reminded me of him. Only when I reached my library was I able to explain what it was, and I returned to the vestibule to verify it. Yes, I had not been mistaken, it was his cloak. A fashionable cloak, you know. Everything relating to him, although I could not explain the why and wherefore, I remarked with extraordinary attention. I asked if he was there, and the servant said 'yes.' I passed through the recitation-room, not the drawing-room, into the 'hall.' Liza, my daughter, was sitting with her book, and the nurse with the little girl was sitting at the table spinning a cover. The door into the 'hall' was closed, but I could hear the monotonous arpeggios and the sound of her voice and his. I listened, but could not decide what to do. Evidently the notes of the piano were played on purpose to drown out their words, perhaps their kisses. My God, what a storm arose in me! The mere thought of the wild beast which then awoke in me fills me with horror. My heart suddenly contracted, then stopped beating, and then it began to throb like a sledge-hammer.

"The chief feeling, as always in any outburst of anger, was pity for myself. 'Before the children, before the nurse,' I exclaimed inwardly. I must have been terrible to look at, because even Liza looked at me with frightened eyes.

"'What is there for me to do?' I asked myself. 'Shall I go in? I cannot, for God knows what I should do. But neither can I go away. The nurse is looking at me as if she understood my position. But I cannot go in.' I said this to myself and hurriedly opened the door.

"He was sitting at the piano and was playing those arpeggios with his large white fingers bent back. She was standing at one corner of the grand bending over an opened score. She was the first to see me or hear me and she looked at me. I know not whether she was startled or pretended not to be startled or really was not startled—at any rate, she did not show any agitation or even move, but merely blushed, but that was afterward.

"'How glad I am that you have come. We can't decide what to play next Sunday,' said she, in a tone which she would never have employed in addressing me when we were alone. That and the fact that she said 'we,' connecting herself and him, exasperated me. I silently bowed to him. He pressed my hand, and instantly, with a smile which seemed to me derisive, began to explain that he had brought some music for Sunday, but that they could not agree what to play; whether something difficult and classical, such as a Beethoven violin sonata, or some easy trifles. All this was so natural and simple that it was impossible to find any fault with it, and yet I was convinced that it was all a falsehood, that they had been planning how to deceive me.

"One of the most torturing conditions for jealous men—and all of us are jealous in our fashionable society—are certain social conventions whereby the greatest and most dangerous proximity is permitted to a man and a woman. People would simply make themselves ridiculous if they tried to prevent this proximity at balls, between doctors and their female patients, between artists, and especially musicians. Two people occupy themselves with the noblest of arts—music; in order to accomplish this a certain proximity is required, and this proximity has nothing reprehensible in it, and only a stupid, jealous husband could find anything undesirable in it. But meantime all know that precisely by means of these very occupations, especially by music, the largest part of the adultery committed in the ranks of our society is committed.

"I especially confused them by the confusion which I myself showed; it was long before I could speak a word. I was like an upturned bottle from which the water will not flow because it is too full. I wanted to heap abuses on him, to drive him away; but I felt that it was my duty to be friendly and affectionate to him again, and so I was. I pretended that I approved of everything, and once more I felt that strange impulse which compelled me to treat him with a friendliness proportioned to the torment which his presence caused me.

"I told him that I had great confidence in his taste and I advised her to do the same. He stayed just as long as it was required to do away with the disagreeable impression made by my sudden appearance with such a scared face, and after a silence he took his departure, pretending that they had now determined what they would play the next day. I was perfectly convinced that in comparison with what was really occupying them, the question as to what they should play was perfectly immaterial.

"I accompanied him with more than ordinary courtesy to the vestibule—how could one fail to treat courteously a man who had come on purpose to disturb my peace of mind and destroy the happiness of a whole family?—and I pressed his soft white hand with especial affection.

CHAPTER XXII

"That whole day I did not speak to her—I could not. Her proximity produced in me such hatred of her that I feared for myself. At dinner she asked me in the presence of the children when I was going away. My duties called me the following week to a meeting in my district. I told her when. She asked me if I needed anything for my journey. I did not say anything, and I sat in silence at the table, and silently went to my library. Of late she had got out of the habit of coming to my library, especially at that time of day. I was lying down in my library, and was angry enough. Suddenly her well-known steps were heard coming, and the terrible, ugly thought leaped to my brain that she, like Uriah's wife[7] had already committed the sin and wanted to hide it, and that was why she was coming to me at such an unseasonable hour.

"'Can it be that she is really coming to me?' I asked myself as I heard her approaching step.

"'If she is coming to me, then it means I am right.'

"And in my soul arose an ineffable hatred of her. Nearer, nearer came her steps.

"'Can it be that she is going by into the hall?'

"No, the door creaked and her tall, handsome figure appeared, and her face, her eyes, expressed timidity, and a desire to win my good-will, as I could easily see, and the significance of it I understood perfectly. I almost suffocated, so long I held my breath, and continuing to stare at her, I grasped my cigarette-case and began to smoke.

"'Now how can you? Someone comes to sit with you and you go to smoking;' and she sat down near me on the divan, and leaned up against me. I moved away, so as not to be in contact with her.

"'I see that you are vexed because I am going to play on Sunday,' said she.

"'Not in the least,' said I.

"'But can't I see that you are?'

"'Well, I congratulate you on your perspicacity. I see nothing except the fact that you behave like a coquette. To you all such kinds of vulgarity are pleasant, but to me they are horrible.'

"'There, now, if you are going to abuse me like a cab driver, then I will go.'

"'Go, then; but know that the honor of your family is not dear to you, neither are you dear to me—the devil take you—but the honor of the family is—'

"'Now, what do you mean?'

"'Get out of my sight! for God's sake, get out.'

"I know not whether she pretended that she did not comprehend, or really did not comprehend; but she only took offense, grew angry, and instead of leaving stood in the middle of the room.

"'You have become positively unendurable,' she began. 'You have such a disposition that not even an angel could get along with you.' And, as always, trying to wound me as keenly as possible, she reminded me of the way I had treated my sister. It had happened that one time I forgot myself and spoke some very harsh words to my sister; she knew about it and that it tormented me, and so she wounded me in that place.

"After that, nothing that you could do would surprise me," said she.

"'Yes, insult me, humiliate me, disgrace me, and make me out to blame,' said I, to myself, and suddenly a terrible anger against her seized me, such as I had never before experienced. For the first time I felt the impulse to express this anger with physical force. I leaped up and moved toward her; but at the instant that I sprang to my feet, I became conscious of my anger and asked myself, 'Is it well to give way to this impulse?' and immediately the answer came that it was, that this would serve to frighten her; and on the spot, instead of withstanding my wrath, I began to fan it to a greater heat, and to rejoice because it grew more and more intense in me.

"'Get out of here, or I will kill you,' I screamed, going closer to her and seizing her by the arm. In saying this I was conscious of raising my voice to a higher pitch, and I must have become terrible, because she became so frightened that she had not the strength to go, but merely stammered:—

"'Vasya, what is it, what is the matter with you?'

"'Go,' I cried, in a still louder tone. 'No one but you can drive me to madness. I won't be responsible for what I may do!'

"Having given free course to my madness I intoxicated myself with it, and I felt the impulse to do something extraordinary which should show the high-water mark of this madness of mine. I felt a terrible impulse to strike her, to kill her; but I knew that it was an impossibility, and therefore in order to give free course to my madness, I snatched up a paper-weight from the table, and shouting once more, 'Go!' I flung it down on the floor, near her. I aimed it carefully, so as to strike near her. Then she left the room, but remained standing in the doorway. And then while she was still looking—I did it so that she might see—I began to snatch up from the table various objects—the candlestick, the inkstand—and hurled them on the floor, still continuing to shout,—

"'Go, get out of my sight! I won't be responsible for what I may do.'

"She went, and I immediately ceased.

"In the course of an hour the nurse came and told me that my wife was suffering from hysterics. I went to her; she was sobbing and laughing, and could not speak a word and was trembling all over. She was not pretending, but was really ill. Toward morning she grew calm, and we had a reconciliation under the influence of that passion which we call 'love.'

"In the morning, after our reconciliation I confessed to her that I was jealous of Trukhachevsky. She was not in the least confused, and laughed in the most natural manner. So strange even to her seemed, as she said, the possibility of being drawn to such a man.

"'Is it possible that a respectable woman could feel anything for such a man beyond the pleasure which his music might afford? But if you wish, I am ready not to see him again. Even though all the guests are invited for Sunday, write him that I am ill, and that will be the end of it. Only one thing makes me indignant, and that is that any one could imagine, and especially he himself, that he is dangerous. I am too proud to permit myself to think of such a thing.'

"And evidently she was not prevaricating; she believed in what she was saying; she hoped by these words to evoke in herself scorn for him and to defend herself from him, but she did not succeed in this. Everything went against her, especially that cursed music.

"Thus the episode ended, and on Sunday the guests gathered and they played together again.

CHAPTER XXIII

"I think it is superfluous to remark that I was very ostentatious; there would not be any living in our general society if it were not for ostentation. Thus on that Sunday I took the greatest pains to arrange for our dinner and for the evening musicale. I myself ordered the things for dinner and invited the guests.

"At six o'clock the guests had arrived, and he also, in evening dress with diamonds shirt studs of bad taste. He was free and easy, made haste to answer all questions with a smile of sympathy and appreciation—you know what I mean, with that peculiar expression that signifies that everything you say or do is exactly what he expected. I remarked now with especial satisfaction everything about him calculated to give an unfavorable impression, because all this served to calm me, and prove that he stood in my wife's eyes on such a low level that, as she said, she could not possibly descend to it. I did not allow myself to be jealous. In the first place, I had already been through the pangs of that torment and needed rest; in the second place, I wanted to have faith in my wife's asseverations, and I did believe in them. But in spite of the fact that I was not jealous, still I was not at my ease with either of them, and during the dinner and the first half of the evening before the music began, I kept watching their motions and glances all the time.

"The dinner was like any dinner—dull and conventional. The music began rather early. Oh, how well I remember all the details of that evening. I remember how he brought his fiddle, opened the case, took off the covering which had been embroidered for him by some lady, took out the instrument and began to tune it. I remember how my wife sat with a pretendedly indifferent face under which I saw that she was hiding great diffidence,—the diffidence caused chiefly by distrust of her own ability,—how she took her seat at the grand piano with the same affected look and struck the usual *a*, which was followed by the pizzicato of the fiddle and the getting into tune. I remember how, then, they looked at each other, glanced at the audience, and then made some remark, and the music began. He struck the first chords. His face grew grave, stern, and sympathetic, and as he bent his head to listen to the sounds he produced, he placed his fingers cautiously on the strings. The piano replied. And it began.". . . .

Pozdnyshev paused and several times emitted his peculiar sounds. He started to speak again but snuffed through his nose and again paused.

"They played Beethoven's Kreutzer Sonata,"* he finally went on to say. "Do you know the first *presto*—You know it?" he cried. "U! U! U!. . . . That sonata is a terrible thing. And especially that movement. And music in general is a terrible thing. I cannot comprehend it. What is music? What does it do? And why does it have the effect it has? They say music has the effect of elevating the soul—rubbish! falsehood! It has its effect, it has a terrible effect,—I am speaking about its effect on me,—but not at all by elevating the soul. Its effect is neither to elevate nor to degrade, but to excite. How can I explain it to you? Music makes me forget myself, my actual position; it transports me into another state not my natural one; under the influence

---

*Also known as Sonata No. 9 in A major, Op. 47 (1803).

of music it seems to me that I feel what I do not really feel, that I understand what I do not really understand, that I can do what I can't do. I explain this by the fact that music acts like yawning or laughing; I am not sleepy but I yawn, looking at any one else who is yawning; I have nothing to laugh at, but I laugh when I hear others laugh.

"Music instantaneously transports me into that mental condition in which he who composed it found himself. I blend my soul with his, and together with him am transported from one mood to another; but why this is so I cannot tell. For instance, he who composed the Kreutzer Sonata—Beethoven—he knew why he was in that mood. That mood impelled him to do certain things, and therefore that mood meant something for him, but it means nothing for me. And that is why music excites and does not bring to any conclusion. Now they play a military march; the soldiers move forward under its strains, and the music accomplishes something; they play dance music and I dance, and the music accomplishes something; they perform a mass, I take the sacrament, again the music accomplishes its purpose. But in other cases there is only excitement, and it is impossible to tell what to do in this state of mind. And that is why music is so terrible, why it sometimes has such an awful effect. In China, music is regulated by government, and this is as it should be. Is it permissible that any one whatever shall hypnotize another person, or many persons, and then do with them what he pleases? And especially if this hypnotizer happens to be the first immoral man that comes along.

"And indeed it is a terrible means to place in any one's hands. For example, how could any one play this Kreutzer Sonata, the first *presto*, in a drawing-room before ladies dressed *décolletées?* To play that *presto* and then to applaud it, and then to eat ices and talk over the last bit of scandal? These things should be played only in certain grave, significant conditions, and only then when certain deeds corresponding to such music are to be accomplished: first play the music and perform that which this music was composed for. But to call forth an energy which is not consonant with the place or the time, and an impulse which does not manifest itself in anything, cannot fail to have a baneful effect. On me, at least, it had a horrible effect. It seemed to me that entirely new impulses, new possibilities, were revealed to me in myself, such as I had never dreamed of before.

"'This is the way I should live and think—not at all as I have lived and thought hitherto,' seemed to be whispered into my soul. What this new thing was I now knew I could not explain even to myself, but the consciousness of this new state of mind was very delightful. All those faces—his and my wife's among them—presented themselves in a new light.

"After the *allegro* they played the beautiful but rather commonplace and far from original *andante*, with the cheap variations and the weak *finale*. Then at the request of the guests they played other things, first an elegy by Ernst* and then various other trifles. All this was very good, but it did not produce on me a hundredth part of the impression which the first did. But all the music had the same background as the impression which the first produced.

"I felt gay and happy all the evening. I never saw my wife look as she did that evening: her gleaming eyes, her gravity and serenity of expression while she was playing, her perfectly melting mood, her tender, pathetic, and blissful smile, after they had finished playing; I saw it all, but attributed to it no significance other than that she was experiencing the same thing as I was; that before her, as before me, new and hitherto unexampled feelings were revealed, dimly rising in her consciousness. The evening was pronounced a great success, and when it was over the guests took their departure.

"Knowing that I was to be going to the district meeting in two days, Trukhachevsky, on bidding me farewell, said that he hoped that when he next came to Moscow he should have another pleasant evening like that. From this remark I was able to conclude that he did not deem it possible to visit my house during my absence, and that was agreeable to me. It seemed clear that as I should not return before his departure we should not meet again.

"For the first time I shook hands with him with genuine pleasure, and I thanked him for the gratification he had afforded us. He also bade my wife a final farewell, and their final farewell seemed to me most natural and proper. Everything was admirable. Both my wife and I were very well satisfied with the evening.

---

*Heinrich Wilhem Ernst (1814–1865), German violinist and composer.

CHAPTER XXIV

Two days later I started for my district, taking leave of my wife in the happiest and calmest frame of mind.

"In the district there was always a pile of work and a special life, a special little world. For two days I worked ten hours a day in my office. On the third day a letter from my wife was brought to me in the office. I read it then and there.

"She wrote about the children, about her uncle, about the nurse-girl, about the things she had bought, and mentioned as something perfectly commonplace the fact that Trukhachevsky had been to call, and had brought the music he had promised, and that he had offered to come and play again, but that she had declined.

"I did not remember that he had promised to bring any music. I had supposed that he had taken his final leave at that time, and so this gave me an unpleasant surprise. But I was so deeply engrossed in business that I could not stop to think it over, and it was not until evening, when I returned to my room, that I reread her letter.

"Besides the fact that Trukhachevsky had called again in my absence, the whole tone of the letter seemed to me unnatural. The frantic wild beast of jealousy roared in his cage and wanted to break forth; but I was afraid of this beast and I made haste to shut him up.

"'What a vile feeling this jealousy is,' I said to myself. 'What can be more natural than what she has written?'

"And I lay on my bed and tried to think of the business which I should have to attend to the next day. I never go to sleep very quickly during these sessions in a new place, but this time I dropped asleep almost immediately. But as you know it often happens, I suddenly felt something like an electric shock, and started up wide awake. As I woke, I woke with a thought of her, of my carnal love for her, and of Trukhachevsky, and how all had been accomplished between him and her. Horror and rage crushed my heart. But I tried to reason myself out of it.

"'What rubbish!' I exclaimed. 'There is not the slightest basis for any such suspicions. And how can I humiliate myself and her by harboring such horrible thoughts? Here is someone in the nature of a hired fiddler, with a reputation of being disreputable, and could a respectable woman, the mother of a family, my wife, suddenly fall a victim to such a man? What an absurdity.'

"That is what I argued on one side, but on the other, came these thoughts:—

"'How could it fail to be so? Why is it not the simplest and most comprehensible thing? Was it not for that I married her? Was it not for that I lived with her? Was it not that which makes me necessary to her? And would not therefore another man, this musician, be likewise necessary to her? He is an unmarried man, healthy,—I remember how lustily he crunched the gristle in the cutlet, and put the glass of wine to his red lips,—he is well-fed, sleek, and not only without principles, but evidently guided by the theory that it is best to take advantage of whatever pleasures present themselves. And between them is the tie of music; the subtle lust of the senses. What can restrain him? She? Yes, but who is she? She is as much of a riddle as she ever has been. I don't know her. I know her only as an animal; and nothing can restrain an animal, or is likely to.'

"Only at that instant I recalled their faces that evening after they had played the Kreutzer Sonata, and while they were performing some passionate piece,—I have forgotten what it was,—something sentimental to the degree of obscenity.

"'How could I have come away?' I asked myself, as I recalled their faces. 'Was it not perfectly evident that the fatal step was taken by them that evening, and was it not evident that even from that evening on, not only was there no bar between them, but that both of them—she especially—felt some sense of shame after what happened to them? I recalled with what a soft, pathetic, and blissful smile she wiped away the perspiration from her heated face, as I approached the piano. Even then they avoided looking at each other, and only at dinner when he poured her out some water did they look at each other, and timidly smile. I remembered with horror that glance which I had intercepted, and that almost imperceptible smile.

"'Yes, the fatal step has been taken,' said a voice within me; and instantly another voice seemed to say quite the contrary. 'You are crazy; this cannot be,' said this second voice.

"It was painful for me to lie there in the darkness. I lighted a match, and then it seemed to me terrible to be in that little room with its yellow wall-paper. I began to smoke a cigarette, and, as is always the case when one turns round in the same circle of irre-solvable contradictions, I smoked; and I smoked one cigarette after another, for the purpose of befogging my mind and not seeing the contradictions.

"I did not sleep all night, and at five o'clock, having made up my mind that I could remain no longer in such a state of tension, but would instantly go back, I got up, wakened the bell-boy who waited on me, and sent him after horses. I sent a note to the Session stating that I had been called back to Moscow on extraordinary business, and therefore begged them to let another member take my place. At eight o'clock I took my seat in the tarantas* and started."

CHAPTER XXV

The conductor came through the train, and noticing that our candle was almost burned out, extinguished it instead of put-ting in another. Out-of-doors it was beginning to grow light. Pozdnyshev ceased speaking and sighed heavily all the time the con-ductor was in the carriage. He proceeded with his story only when the conductor had taken his departure, and the only sound we could hear in the semi-darkness of the carriage was the rattle of the win-dows and regular snore of the merchant's clerk. In the twilight of the dawn I could not make out Pozdnyshev's face at all. I could only hear his passionate voice growing ever more and more excited:—

"I had to travel thirty-five versts† by tarantas and eight hours by rail. It was splendid traveling with horses. It was frosty autumnal weather with a brilliant sun,—you know that kind of weather when the tires leave their print on the slippery road. The roads were smooth, the light was dazzling, and the atmosphere was exhilarating. Yes, it was jolly traveling by tarantas. As soon as it grew light, and I was fairly on my way, my heart felt lighter.

---

*In English, tarantass, a low, four-wheeled carriage that is not particularly fancy.
†Russian unit of distance equivalent to 3,500 feet.

"As I looked at the horses, at the fields, at the persons I met, I forgot what my errand was. It sometimes seemed to me that I was simply out for a drive, and that there was nothing whatever to stir me so. And I felt particularly happy at thus forgetting myself. If by chance it occurred to me where I was bound, I said to myself:—

" 'Wait and see what will be; don't think about it now.'

"About half-way an event happened which delayed me, and still more tended to distract my attention; the tarantas broke down, and it was necessary to mend it. This break-down had a great significance because it caused me to reach Moscow at midnight instead of at five o'clock as we had expected, and home at one o'clock, for I missed the express, and was obliged to take a way train. The search for a cart, the mending of the tarantas, the settlement of the bill, tea at an inn, the conversation with the hostler,—all this served to divert me more and more. By twilight everything was ready, and I was on my way once more, and during the evening it was still pleasanter travel-ing than by day. There was a young moon, a slight touch of frost, the roads were still excellent, and so were the horses, the postilion was jolly, and so I traveled on and enjoyed myself, scarce thinking at all of what was awaiting me; or perhaps I enjoyed myself especially because I knew what was awaiting me, and I was having my last taste of the joys of life.

"But this calm state of mind, the power of controlling my feelings, came to an end as soon as I ceased traveling with the horses. As soon as I entered the railway carriage an entirely different state of things began. This eight-hour journey by rail was something horrible to me, and I shall never forget it as long as I live. Either because, as soon as I entered the carriage I vividly imagined myself as having already reached the end, or because railway travel has an exciting effect on people. As soon as I took my seat I had no longer any control over my imagination, which ceaselessly, with extraordinary vividness, began to bring up before me pictures kindling my jealousy; one after another they arose and always to the same effect: what had taken place during my absence, and how she had deceived me! I was on fire with indig-nation, wrath, and a peculiar sense of frenzy, caused by my humilia-tion, as I contemplated these pictures, and I could not tear myself away from them, could not help gazing at them, could not rub them out, could not help evoking them. And then the more I contemplated these

imaginary pictures the more I was convinced of their reality. The vividness with which these pictures presented themselves before me
seemed to serve as a proof of the actuality of what I imagined. A kind
of a devil, perfectly against my will, suggested and stimulated the most
horrible suggestions. A conversation I had once with Trukhachevsky's
brother occurred to me, and with a sort of enthusiasm I lacerated my
heart with this conversation, applying it to Trukhachevsky and my
wife.

"It had taken place long before, but it came back clearly to me. I
remember that once, Trukhachevsky's brother, in reply to a question
whether he ever went to certain houses, stated that no decent man
would ever go to such places, where there was danger of contracting
disease, and that it was vile and disgusting; one could always find
some society woman to serve his purpose. And now here was his
brother and he had found my wife!

" 'To be sure she is no longer young; she has a tooth missing on
one side of her mouth, her face is somewhat swollen,' I said, trying to
look from his standpoint. 'But what difference does that make? One
must take what one can get. Yes, he is conferring a favor on her to take
her as his mistress,' said I, to myself. 'Then besides, there is no danger
with her. . . . . No, it is impossible!' I exclaimed in horror. 'There is
no possibility of it, not the least, and there is not the slightest basis
for any such conjectures. Has she not told me that to her it was a
humiliating thought that I could be jealous of him. . . . . Yes, but she
is a liar, always a liar,' I would cry, and then begin the same thing over
again.

"There were only two passengers in my carriage; an old woman
with her husband, both of them very silent, and they got out at the
first stop, and I was left alone. I was like a wild beast in a cage; now I
would jump up and rush to the window, then staggering I would
walk back and forth through the aisle trying to make the train go
faster; but the carriage, with all its seats and its window-panes, shook
just exactly as ours is doing now." . . . .

And Pozdnyshev sprang to his feet and took a few steps and then
sat down again.

"Oh, I dread, I dread these railway carriages—they fill me with
horror—yes, I dread them awfully," he went on saying. "I said to
myself, 'I must think of something else. All right, let me think of the

landlord of the inn where I took tea. Well! Then before my eyes would arise the long-bearded innkeeper and his grandson, a boy about as old as my Vasya.

" 'My Vasya! He will see a musician kissing his mother. What will happen to his poor soul at the sight? But what will she care? She is in love.'

"And again would arise the same visions.

" 'No, no! Well I will think about the inspection of the hospital. Yesterday that sick man complained of the doctor. A doctor with mustaches just like Trukhachevsky's. . . . . And how brazenly he—they both deceived me, when he said that he was going away.' . . . .

"And again it would begin. Everything I thought of had some connection with them. I suffered awfully. My chief suffering lay in my ignorance, in the uncertainty of it all, in my question whether I ought to love her or hate her. These sufferings were so intense that I remember the temptation came into my mind with great fascination to go out on the track and throw myself under the train on the rails, and so end it. Then, at least, there would be no further doubt. The one thing that prevented me from doing so was my self-pity which was the immediate source of my hatred of her. Toward him, also, I had a strange feeling of hatred, and a consciousness of my humiliation and of his victory, but toward her my hatred was awful.

" 'It is impossible to put an end to myself and to leave her behind. I must do something to make her suffer, so that she may appreciate that I have suffered,' I said to myself.

"I got out at all the stations in order to divert my mind. At one station I noticed that people were drinking in the buffet, and I immediately fortified myself with vodka. Next me stood a Jew and he also was drinking. He spoke to me and that I might not be alone in my carriage I went with him into his third-class compartment, though it was filthy and full of smoke and littered with the husks of seeds. There I sat down next him, and he went on chatting and relating anecdotes. I listened to him, but did not take in what he said because I kept thinking of my own affairs. He noticed this and tried to attract my attention; then I got up and went back to my own carriage.

" 'I must think it all over again,' I said to myself, 'whether what I think is true and whether there is any foundation for my anguish.' I sat down, desiring calmly to think it over, but instantly in place of calm deliberation, the same tumult of thought began; in place of argument, pictures and figments of the imagination.

"'How often have I not tortured myself so,' I said to myself, for I remembered similar paroxysms of jealousy in times gone by, 'and then there was no ground for them. And so now, possibly, nay probably, I shall find her calmly sleeping; she will wake up and be glad to see me, and I shall be conscious both in her words and in her looks that nothing has taken place and that my suspicions were groundless. Oh! how delightful that would be!'

"'But no, this has been so too frequently and now it will be so no longer' said some inner voice, and once more it would begin anew. Ah! what a punishment was here! I should not take a young man to a syphilitic hospital to cure him of his passion for women, but into my own soul, and give him a glimpse of the fiends that were rending it. You see it was horrible that I claimed an undoubted absolute right to her body just as if it had been my own body, and at the same time I was conscious that I could not control that body of hers, that it was not mine, and that she had the power to dispose of it as she chose, and that she did not choose to dispose of it as I wished. I could not even do anything to her or to him. He, like Vanka the cellarer* before he was hanged, will sing a song of how he had kissed her on her sugary lips and the like. He would have the best of me. And with her I could do even less. If she had not yet done anything out of the way, but had it in mind to,—and I know that she did,—the case is still worse; it would be better to have it done with, so that I might know, so as to have this uncertainty settled.

"I could not tell what I desired. I desired her not to want what she could not help wanting. This was absolute madness.

---

*Recurring character in Russian folklore who seduces his master's wife.

CHAPTER XXVI

"At the next to the last station, when the conductor came along to take the tickets, I picked up my belongings and went out on the platform, and the consciousness of what was about to take place still further increased my agitation. I became cold, and my jaws trembled so that my teeth chattered. Mechanically I followed the crowd out of the station, engaged a cab driver, took my seat in his cab and drove away. As I drove along, glancing at the occasional pedestrians, at the dvorniks and the shadows cast by the street lamps and my cab, now in front and now behind, my mind seemed to be a blank. By the time we had driven half a verst from the station my feet became cold, and I remembered that I had removed my woolen stockings in the train and put them into my bag.

" 'Where is my bag? Have I brought it with me?'

"Yes, I had. 'But where is my wicker trunk?'

"Then I remembered that I had entirely forgotten about my baggage; but while I was thinking about it, I found my receipt and decided that it was not worth while to return for it, and so I drove home.

"In spite of my endeavors, I can never remember to this day what my state of mind was at that time,—what I thought, what I desired, I cannot tell. I only remember that I was conscious that something terrible and very vital in my life was in preparation. Whether this important event proceeded from the fact that I thought so or because I foreboded it, I do not know. Perhaps after what happened subsequently, all the preceding moments have taken on a gloomy shade in my recollection.

"I reached the doorstep. It was one o'clock. Several cab drivers were standing in front of the door waiting for fares in the light cast by the windows—the lighted windows were in our apartment, in the 'hall,' and the drawing-room. I made no attempt to explain to myself why our windows were still lighted so late at night, but still expectant of something dreadful about to happen, I mounted the steps and rang the bell. Yegor, the lackey, a good-natured, zealous, but extremely stupid fellow, answered it. The first thing that struck my eyes in the vestibule was a cloak hanging on a peg with other outside garments. I ought to have been surprised, but I was not, because it was what I expected.

" 'It is true,' I said to myself.

"When I asked Yegor who was there and he mentioned Trukhachevsky, I asked:—

" ' Is there any one else with them?' and he said:—

" 'No one.' I remember that in his reply, there was an intonation, as if he felt he was giving me a pleasure in dispelling my apprehension that any one else was there.

" 'It is true, it is true,' I seemed to say to myself.

" 'But the children?'

" 'Thank God, they are well. They have been asleep for a long time.'

"I could not breathe freely, nor could I prevent the trembling of my lower jaw.

"Yes, of course, it is not as I thought it might be; whereas formerly I imagined some misfortune and yet found everything all right, as usual, now it was not usual, now it was altogether what I had imagined and fancied that I only imagined, but it was now real. It was all . . . .

"I almost began to sob, but instantly a fiend suggested:—

" 'Shed tears, be sentimental; but they will calmly separate; there will be no proof, and you will be forever in doubt and torment.'

"Thereupon my self-pity vanished, and in its place came a strange feeling of gladness that my torture was now at an end, that I could punish her, could get rid of her, that I could give free course to my wrath. And I gave free course to my wrath—I became a wild beast, fierce and sly.

" 'No matter, no matter,' I said to Yegor, who was about to go to the drawing-room, 'attend to this instead: take a cab, and go as quickly as you can to the station for my luggage; here is the receipt. Off with you!'

"He went into the corridor to get his paletot. Fearing that he might disturb them, I accompanied him to his little room, and waited till he had got his things on. In the drawing-room, just through the wall, I could hear the sound of voices, and the clatter of knives and dishes. They were eating, and had not heard the bell.

" 'If only no one leaves the room now,' I said to myself.

"Yegor put on his paletot trimmed with astrakhan wool, and started. I let him out and shut the door behind him, and I felt a sense of dread at the idea of being left alone, of having to act instantly.

"How? I did not know as yet. All I knew was that all was ended, that there could be no longer any doubt as to her guilt, and that I should presently punish her, and put an end to my relations with her.

"Hitherto I had been troubled with vacillation, and I had said to myself: 'Maybe it is not so, maybe you are mistaken;' now this was at an end. Everything was now irrevocably decided. Clandestinely! alone with him! at night! This proved perfect forgetfulness of everything, or something even worse. Such audacity, such insolence, in crime was deliberately adopted in order that its very insolence might serve as a proof of innocence. All was clear, there could be no doubt! I was afraid of only one thing,—that they might escape, might invent some new deception, and deprive me of manifest proof, and the possibility of convincing myself. And so as to catch them as promptly as possible I went, not through the drawing-room, but through the corridor and the nursery, on my tiptoes, into the 'hall' where they were sitting.

"In the first nursery-room the boys were sound asleep; in the second nursery-room the nurse stirred, and was on the point of waking up; and I imagined to myself what she would think if she knew it all; and then such a sense of self-pity came over me at this thought that I could not restrain my tears, and in order not to wake the children I ran out, on my tiptoes, into the corridor and into my own room, flung myself down on my divan, and sobbed.

" 'I, an upright man . . . . I, the son of my own parents . . . . I, who have dreamed all my life of the happiness of family life . . . . I, a husband who have never been unfaithful to my wife! . . . . And here she, the mother of five children, and she is embracing a musician because he has red lips!

" 'No, she is not human. She is a bitch, a vile bitch! Next to the room where sleep her children, for whom, all her life, she has pretended to feel affection. And to write me what she wrote! And so insolently to throw herself into his arms! And how do I know? perhaps this same sort of thing has been taking place all the time! Who knows but the children whom I have always supposed to be mine may not have some lackey for their father!

" 'And if I had come home tomorrow she would have met me with her hair becomingly done up, and her graceful, indolent movements.' All the time I seemed to see her fascinating, abhorrent face . . . . 'and this wild beast of jealousy would have taken his position forever in my heart, and torn it. What will the nurse think? . . . . and Yegor? . . . . and poor Lizotchka? She already has her suspicions. And this brazen impudence, and this falsehood! . . . . And this animal sensuality which I know so well?' I said to myself.

"I tried to get up, but could not. My heart throbbed so that I could not stand on my legs.

"'Yes, I shall die of a stroke. She will have killed me. That is just what she wants! What would it be to her to kill me? Indeed, it would be quite too advantageous, and I will not bestow that gratification on her. Yes, here I am sitting, and yonder they are eating and talking together, and . . . .

"'Yes, in spite of the fact that she is no longer in her first youth, he will not despise her . . . . still, she is not bad-looking, and, what is the main thing, at least she is not dangerous for his precious health. Why, then, have I not strangled her already?' I asked myself, recalling that moment a week before when I drove her out of my library, and then smashed things. I had a vivid remembrance of the state of mind in which I was then; and not only had the remembrance, but I was conscious of the same necessity of striking, of destroying, as I had been conscious of before. I remember how I wanted to do something, and how all considerations except those that were necessary for action vanished from my mind. I came into the state of a wild animal, or rather, of a man under the influence of physical excitement in time of danger, when he acts definitely, deliberately, but without losing a single instant, and all the time with a single object in view.

CHAPTER XXVII

"The first thing I did was to take off my boots, and then, in my stocking feet, I went to the wall, where various weapons and daggers were hung up over the divan, and I took down a curved Damascus dagger, which had never been used, and was very keen. I drew it out of its sheath. I remember the sheath slipped down behind the divan, and I remember I said to myself:—

"'I must find it afterward or else it will get lost.' Then I took off my paletot which I had all the time been wearing and, gliding along in my stockings, I went there.[8]

"And stepping up stealthily, I suddenly threw open the door. I remember the expression of both of their faces. I remember that expression because it afforded me a tormenting pleasure—it was an expression of horror. That was the very thing I needed! I shall never forget the expression of despairing horror which came into their faces the first second when they saw me. He was seated, it seems, at the table, but when he saw me or heard me, he leaped to his feet and stood with his back against the sideboard. His face bore the one unmistakable expression of horror. On her face also was an expression of horror, but there was something else blended with it. If it had not been for that something else, maybe what happened would not have happened; but in the expression of her face there was, or so there seemed to me at the first instant, a look of disappointment, of annoyance that her pleasure in his love and her enjoyment with him were interrupted. It was as if she desired nothing else than to be left undisturbed in her present happiness. This expression and the other lingered but an instant on their faces. The expression of horror on his face instantly grew into a look, which asked the question: 'Is it possible to lie out of it or not? If it is possible, now is the time to begin. If not, then something else must be done—but what?'

"He looked questioningly at her. On her face the expression of annoyance and disappointment changed as it seemed to me when she looked at him into one of solicitude for him.

"I stood for an instant on the threshold holding the dagger behind my back.

"During that second he smiled, and in a voice so indifferent that it was ludicrous, he began:—

"'We have been having some music.'

"'Why! I was not expecting you,' she began at the same instant, adopting his tone.

"But neither he nor she finished their sentences. The very same madness which I had experienced a week before took possession of me. Once more I felt the necessity of destroying something, of using violence; once more I felt a transport of madness and I yielded to it. Neither finished what they were saying. The something else which he was afraid of began, and it swept away instantaneously all that they had to say.

"I threw myself on her, still concealing the dagger in order that he might not prevent me from striking her in the side under the breast. I had chosen the spot at the very beginning. The instant I threw myself on her he saw my design, and with an action which I never expected from him, he seized me by the arm and cried:—

" 'Think what you . . . . Help!'

"I wrenched away my arm, and without saying a word rushed at him. His eyes met mine; he suddenly turned as pale as a sheet, even to the lips, his eyes glittered with a peculiar light, and most unexpectedly to me he slipped under the piano and darted out of the door. I was just starting to rush after him when I was detained by a weight on my left arm. It was she! I tried to break away. She clung all the more heavily to my arm and would not let me go. This unexpected hindrance, the weight of her and her touch which was repulsive to me, still further inflamed my anger. I was conscious of being in a perfect frenzy and that I ought to be terrible, and I exulted in it. I drew back my left arm with all my might and struck her full in the face with my elbow. She screamed and let go my arm. I started to chase him, but remembered that it would be ridiculous for a man to chase his wife's lover in his stockings, and I did not want to be ridiculous, but I desired to be terrible.

"Notwithstanding the terrible frenzy in which I found myself, I never for an instant forgot the impression which I might produce on others, and this impression, even to a certain degree, governed me. I came back to her. She had fallen on a couch, and with her hand held up to her eyes, which I had bruised, was looking at me. In her face were such terror and hatred of me, her enemy, as a rat might show when the trap in which it had been caught was held up. At all events I could see nothing else in her face except terror and hatred of me. It was precisely the same terror and hatred which love to another would naturally evoke. But possibly I should have restrained myself and not done what I did if she had held her tongue. But she suddenly began to speak, and she seized my hand which held the dagger:—

" 'Come to your senses. What are you going to do? What is the matter with you? There has been nothing, no harm, I swear it.'

"I should have still delayed, but these last words, from which I drew exactly the opposite conclusion, that is, that my worst fears were realized, required an answer. And the answer had to correspond with the mood to which I had wrought myself up, which had gone on in a *crescendo* and was bound to reach its climax. Madness also has its laws.

" 'Do not lie, you wretch,' I cried, and with my left hand I seized her by the arm, but she tore herself away. Then, still clutching the dagger, I grasped her by the throat, pressed her over backward and began to strangle her. What a muscular throat she had! She grasped my hands with both hers, tearing them away from her throat, and I, as if I had been waiting for this opportunity, struck her with the dagger into the side under the ribs.

"When men say that in an attack of madness they don't remember what they did, it is all false, all nonsense. I remember every detail, and not for one second did I fail to remember. The more violently I kindled within me the flames of my madness, the more brightly burned the light of consciousness, so that I could not fail to see all that I did. I knew every second what I was doing. I cannot say that I knew in advance what I was going to do, but at the instant I did anything, and perhaps a little before I knew what I was up to, as if for the purpose of being able to repent, in order that I might say to myself: 'I might have stopped.' I knew that I struck below the ribs and that the dagger would penetrate. At the moment I was doing this, I knew that I was doing something, something awful, something which I had never done before and which would have awful consequences. But this consciousness flashed through my mind like lightning and was instantly followed by the deed. The deed made itself conscious with unexampled clearness. I felt and I remember the momentary resistance of her corset and of something else, and then the sinking of the blade into the soft parts of her body. She seized the dagger with her hands, wounding them, but she did not stop me.

"Afterward, in the prison, while a moral revolution was working itself out in me, I thought much about that moment—what I might have done, and I thought it all over. I remember that a second, only a second, before the deed was accomplished, I had the terrible consciousness that I was killing and had killed a woman—a defenseless woman—my wife. I recall the horror of this consciousness, and therefore I conclude—and indeed I dimly remember—that having plunged the dagger in, I immediately withdrew it, with the desire to remedy what I had done and to put a stop to it. I stood for a second motionless, waiting to see what would happen,—and whether I might undo what I had done.

"She sprang to her feet, and shrieked:—

" 'Nurse, he has killed me.'

"The nurse had heard the disturbance and was already on the threshold. I was still standing, expectant and irresolute. But at that instant the blood gushed from under her corset.

"Then only I realized that it was impossible to remedy it, and I instantly concluded that it was not necessary, that I myself did not wish to have it remedied, and that I had done the very thing I was in duty bound to do. I lingered until she fell and the nurse, with the exclamation 'Heavens,' rushed to her, and then I flung the dagger down and left the room.

" 'I must not get excited, I must know what I am doing,' said I to myself, looking neither at her nor at the nurse. The nurse screamed and called to the maid. I went along the corridor, and stopping to send the maid, I went to my room.

" 'What must I do now?' I asked myself, and instantly made up my mind. As soon as I reached my library I went directly to the wall and took down a revolver and contemplated it. It was loaded, and I laid it on the table. Then I picked up the sheath from behind the divan, and finally I sat down on the divan.

"I sat long in that attitude. My mind was without a thought, without a recollection. I heard some commotion there. I heard someone arrive, then someone else. Then I heard and saw Yegor bringing my luggage into my library. As if that would be useful to any one now.

" 'Have you heard what has happened?' I asked. 'Tell the porter to inform the police.'

"He said nothing, but went out. I got up, closed the door, got my cigarettes and matches, and began to smoke. I had not finished smoking my cigarette before drowsiness seized me and overcame me. I think I must have slept two hours. I remember I dreamed that she and I were friends, that we had quarreled, but had made it up, and that some trifle stood in our way; but still we were friends.

"A knock on the door awakened me.

" 'It is the police,' I thought as I woke; 'it seems I must have killed her. But maybe it is she herself and nothing has happened.'

"The knocking at the door was repeated. I did not answer, but kept trying to decide the question:—

" 'Had all that really taken place or not? . . . . Yes, it had.' I remembered the resistance of the corset and the sinking of the dagger, and a cold chill ran down my back.

" 'Yes, it is true. Yes, now I must have my turn,' said I to myself. But though I said this I knew I should not kill myself. Nevertheless, I got up and once more took the revolver into my hand. But strange as it may seem, I remember how many times before I had been near suicide, as, for instance, that very day on the railway train, and it had seemed to me very easy for the very reason that I thought that by that means I could fill her with consternation.

"Now I could not kill myself or think of such a thing. 'Why should I do it?' I asked myself; and there was no answer.

"The knocking still continued at the door.

" 'Yes, first I must find out who is knocking, I shall have time enough afterward . . . .'

"I laid the revolver down and covered it with a newspaper. Then I went to the door and drew back the bolt. It was my wife's sister, a worthy but stupid widow.

" 'Vasya, what does this mean?' she asked, and her ever ready tears began to gush forth.

" 'What do you want?' I asked harshly. I saw that this was entirely unnecessary and that I had no reason to be gruff with her, but I could not adopt any other tone.

" 'Vasya, she is dying. Ivan Zakharych says so.'

"Ivan Zakharych was her doctor, her adviser.

" 'Why, is he here?' I asked, and all my rage against her flamed up once more. 'Well, suppose she is.'

" 'Vasya, go to her. Oh, how horrible this is!' she exclaimed.

" 'Must I go to her?' was the question that arose in my mind, and I instantly decided that I must go, that probably when a husband had killed his wife as I had, he must always go to her, that it was the proper thing to do.

" 'If it is always done, then I must surely go,' I said to myself. 'Yes, if it is necessary to, I shall; I can still kill myself,' I reasoned in regard to my intention of blowing my brains out; and I followed her.

" 'Now there will be phrases and grimaces, but I will not let them affect me,' said I to myself.

" 'Wait,' said I to my sister. 'It is stupid to go without my boots, let me at least put on my slippers.'

CHAPTER XXVIII

"Another remarkable thing:—Once more as I left my room and went through the familiar rooms, once more arose the hope that nothing had taken place, but the odor of the vile medical appliances, iodoform, the carbolic acid, struck my senses.

"Yes, all was a reality. As I went though the corridor past the nursery I caught sight of Lizanka. She looked at me with frightened eyes. It seemed to me then that all five of the children were there and that all of them were looking at me.

"I went to the door and the chambermaid opened it from the inside and passed out. The first thing that struck my eyes was her light gray gown lying on a chair and all discolored with blood. She was lying on our double bed, on my own side of it,—for it was easier of access on that side, and her knees were raised. She was placed in a very sloping position on pillows alone, with her bed jacket unbuttoned. Something had been placed over the wound. The room was full of the oppressive odor of iodoform. I was more than all struck by her swollen face, black and blue,—part of her nose and under her eyes. It was the effect of the blow that I had given her with my elbow, when she was trying to hold me back. Her beauty had all vanished, and her appearance was decidedly repulsive to me. I paused on the threshold.

" 'Go to her, go,' said her sister.

" 'Yes, she probably wants to confess to me,' I thought. 'Shall I forgive her? Yes, she is dying and it is permissible to forgive her,' I said mentally, striving to be magnanimous.

"I went close to her. She with difficulty raised her eyes to me— one of them was blackened, and she said with difficulty, with pauses between the words:—

" 'You have had your way . . . . you have killed me.'

"And in her face, through her physical suffering and even the proximity of death, could be seen the old expression of cold animal hatred which I knew so well.

" 'The children . . . . anyway . . . . you shall not have. . . . She,' indicating her sister, 'will take them.'

"As to what was the principal thing for me—her guilt, her unfaithfulness, she did not consider it worth while to say a word.

" 'Yes . . . . delight yourself in what you have done.' said she, glancing at the door and sobbing. On the threshold stood her sister with the children. 'Oh, what have you done?'

"I looked at the children, at her bruised and discolored face, and for the first time forgot myself, my rights, my pride, for the first time recognized the human being in her. And so petty seemed all that had offended me, all my jealousy, and so significant the deed that I had done, that I had the impulse to bow down to her hand and to say, 'Forgive me,' but I had not the courage.

"She remained silent, closing her eyes, evidently too weak to speak further.

"Then her mutilated face was distorted with a frown. She feebly pushed me away.

" 'Why has all this taken place, why?'

" 'Forgive me,' I cried.

" 'Forgive? What nonsense! . . . . If only I had not to die!' she cried, raising herself up, and her deliriously flashing eyes were fastened on me.

" 'Yes, you have wreaked your will. I hate you. Aï! Oh,' she screamed, evidently out of her head, evidently afraid of something. 'Shoot, I am not afraid. . . . . Only kill us all. . . . . He has gone. . . . . He has gone.'

"The delirium continued to the very end. She did not recognize any one. On the same day at noon she died. Before that, at eight o'clock in the morning, I was arrested and taken to prison. And there, while I was confined for eleven months waiting for my trial, I had a chance to meditate on myself and my past life, and I came to understand it. On the third day I began to comprehend. On the third day they took me there."

He wanted to say something more, but not having the strength to hold back his sobs, he paused. Collecting his strength, he continued:—

"I began to comprehend only when I beheld her in her coffin." He sobbed, but immediately continued hastily:—

"Only when I beheld her dead face did I understand what I had done. I comprehended that I, I had killed her, that it was through me that she, who had been living, moving, warm, was now motionless, wax-like, and cold, and that there was no way of ever again making it right,—never, never again. He who has not lived through this cannot comprehend, U! U! U!" he cried several times, and said no more.

We sat a long time in silence. He sobbed and trembled before me. His face became pinched and long, and his mouth widened to its fullest extent.

"Yes," he said suddenly, "if I had known what I know now, then everything would have been entirely different. I would not have married her for . . . . I would not have married at all."

Again we were long silent.

"Well, good-by—Prostite."*

He turned from me and lay down on the seat, covering himself with his plaid.

At the station where I was to leave the train—it was eight o'clock in the morning—I went up to him to bid him farewell. Either he was asleep or was pretending to be sleeping; he did not move. I touched his hand. He uncovered himself, and it was plain that he had not been asleep.

"Proshchaïte—Farewell," said I, offering him my hand. He took it and almost smiled, but so piteously that I felt like weeping.

"Yes, good-by—Prostite," said he, repeating the very word with which he had closed his tale.

---

*"Prostite" (Russian) carries the double meaning of "forgive me" and "farewell."

The Caucases Region of Asia circa 1850

HADJI MURÁD

I

I was returning home by the fields. It was midsummer; the hay harvest was over, and they were just beginning to reap the rye. At that season of the year there is a delightful variety of flowers—red white and pink scented tufty clover; milk-white ox-eye daisies with their bright yellow centres and pleasant spicy smell; yellow honey-scented rape blossoms; tall campanulas with white and lilac bells, tulip-shaped; creeping vetch; yellow red and pink scabious; plantains with faintly-scented neatly-arranged purple, slightly pink-tinged blossoms; corn-flowers, bright blue in the sunshine and while still young, but growing paler and redder towards evening or when growing old; and delicate quickly-withering almond-scented dodder flowers. I gathered a large nosegay of these different flowers, and was going home, when I noticed in a ditch, in full bloom, a beautiful thistle plant of the crimson kind, which in our neighbourhood they call "Tartar," and carefully avoid when mowing—or, if they do happen to cut it down, throw out from among the grass for fear of pricking their hands. Thinking to pick this thistle and put it in the centre of my nosegay, I climbed down into the ditch, and, after driving away a velvety bumble-bee that had penetrated deep into one of the flowers and had there fallen sweetly asleep, I set to work to pluck the flower. But this proved a very difficult task. Not only did the stalk prick on every side—even through the handkerchief I wrapped round my hand—but it was so tough that I had to struggle with it for nearly five minutes, breaking the fibres one by one; and when I had at last plucked it, the stalk was all frayed, and the flower itself no longer seemed so fresh and beautiful. Moreover, owing to its coarseness and stiffness, it did not seem in place among the delicate blossoms of my nosegay. I felt sorry to have vainly destroyed a flower that looked beautiful in its proper place, and I threw it away.

"But what energy and tenacity! With what determination it defended itself, and how dearly it sold its life!" thought I to myself, recollecting the effort it had cost me to pluck the flower. The way

235

home led across black-earth fields that had just been ploughed up. I ascended the dusty path. The ploughed field belonged to a landed proprietor, and was so large that on both sides and before me to the top of the hill nothing was visible but evenly furrowed and moist earth. The land was well tilled, and nowhere was there a blade of grass or any kind of plant to be seen; it was all black. "Ah, what a destructive creature is man. . . . How many different plant-lives he destroys to support his own existence!" thought I, involuntarily looking round for some living thing in this lifeless black field. In front of me, to the right of the road, I saw some kind of little clump, and drawing nearer I found it was the same kind of thistle as that which I had vainly plucked and thrown away. This "Tartar" plant had three branches. One was broken, and stuck out like the stump of a mutilated arm. Each of the other two bore a flower, once red but now blackened. One stalk was broken and half of it hung down with a soiled flower at its tip. The other, though also soiled with black mud, still stood erect. Evidently a cartwheel had passed over the plant, but it had risen again and that was why, though erect, it stood twisted to one side, as if a piece of its body had been torn from it, its bowels had been drawn out, an arm torn off, and one of its eyes plucked out; and yet it stood firm and did not surrender to man, who had destroyed all its brothers around it. . . .

"What energy!" I thought. "Man has conquered everything, and destroyed millions of plants, yet this one won't submit." And I remembered a Caucasian episode of years ago, which I had partly seen myself, partly heard of from eye-witnesses, and in part imagined.

The episode, as it has taken shape in my memory and imagination, was as follows.

*   *   *   *   *

This happened towards the end of 1851.

On a cold November evening Hadji Murád rode into Makhmet, a hostile Chechen *aoul*, that was filled with the scented smoke of burning *kizyák*, and that lay some fifteen miles from Russian territory. The strained chant of the muezzin had just ceased, and through the clear mountain air, impregnated with *kizyák* smoke, above the lowing of the cattle and the bleating of the sheep that were dispersing among the *sáklyas* (which were crowded together like the cells of a honeycomb), could be clearly heard the guttural voices of disputing men, and sounds of women's and children's voices rising from near the fountain below.

This was Hadji Murád, Shamil's *naïb*, famous for his exploits, who used never to ride out without his banner, and was always accompanied by some dozens of *murids*,* who caracoled and showed off before him. Now, with one *murid* only, wrapped in hood and *búrka*, from under which protruded a rifle, he rode, a fugitive, trying to attract as little attention as possible, and peering with his quick black eyes into the faces of those he met on his way.

When he entered the *aoul*, Hadji Murád did not ride up the road leading to the open square, but turned to the left into a narrow side street; and on reaching the second *sáklya*, which was cut into the hillside, he stopped and looked round. There was no one under the penthouse in front; but on the roof of the *sáklya* itself, behind the freshly-plastered clay chimney, lay a man covered with a sheepskin. Hadji Murád touched him with the handle of his leather-plaited whip, and clicked his tongue. An old man rose from under the sheepskin. He had on a greasy old *beshmét* and a nightcap. His moist red eyelids had no lashes, and he blinked to get them unstuck. Hadji Murád, repeating the customary *"Selaam aleikum!"* uncovered his face. *"Aleikum, selaam!"* said the old man, recognising Hadji Murád and smiling with his toothless mouth; and rising up on his thin legs, he began thrusting his feet into the wooden-heeled slippers that stood by the chimney. Then he leisurely slipped his arms into the sleeves of his crumpled sheepskin, and going to the ladder that leant against the roof, he descended backwards. While he dressed, and as he climbed down, he kept shaking his head on its thin, shrivelled sunburnt neck, and mumbling something with his toothless mouth. As soon as he reached the ground he hospitably seized Hadji Murád's bridle and right stirrup; but the strong, active *murid* who accompanied Hadji Murád had quickly dismounted and, motioning the old man aside, took his place. Hadji Murád also dismounted and, walking with a slight limp, entered under the penthouse. A boy of fifteen, coming quickly out of the door, met him and wonderingly fixed his sparkling eyes, black as ripe sloes, on the new arrivals.

---

*A follower of Sufism, a movement within the Muslim religion.

"Run to the mosque and call your father," ordered the old man, as he hurried forward to open the thin, creaking door into the *sáklya* for Hadji Murád.

As Hadji Murád entered the outer door, a slight spare middle-aged woman in a yellow smock, red *beshmét*, and wide blue trousers came through an inner door carrying cushions.

"May thy coming bring happiness!" said she, and, bending nearly double, began arranging the cushions along the front wall for the guest to sit on.

"May thy sons live!" answered Hadji Murád, taking off his *búrka*, his rifle and his sword and handing them to the old man, who carefully hung the rifle and sword on a nail beside the weapons of the master of the house, which were suspended between two large basins that glittered against the clean clay-plastered and carefully whitewashed wall.

Hadji Murád adjusted the pistol at his back, came up to the cushions and, wrapping his Circassian coat closer round him, sat down. The old man squatted on his bare heels beside him, closed his eyes, and lifted his hands, palms upwards. Hadji Murád did the same; then, after repeating a prayer, they both stroked their faces, passing their hands downwards till the palms joined at the end of their beards.

"*Ne habar?*" asked Hadji Murád, addressing the old man. (That is, "Is there anything new?")

"*Habar yok*" ("nothing new"), replied the old man, looking with his lifeless red eyes not at Hadji Murád's face but at his breast. "I live at the apiary, and have only today come to see my son. . . . He knows."

Hadji Murád, understanding that the old man did not wish to say what he knew and what Hadji Murád wanted to know, slightly nodded his head and asked no more questions.

"There is no good news," said the old man. "The only news is that the hares keep discussing how to drive away the eagles; and the eagles tear first one and then another of them. The other day the Russian dogs burnt the hay in the Mitchit *aoul*. . . . May their faces be torn!" added he, hoarsely and angrily.

Hadji Murád's *murid* entered the room, his strong legs striding softly over the earthen floor. Retaining only his dagger and pistol, he shook off his *búrka*, rifle and sword as Hadji Murád had done, and hung them up on the same nails with his leader's weapons.

"Who is he?" asked the old man, pointing to the newcomer.

"My murid. Eldár is his name," said Hadji Murád.

"That is well," said the old man, and motioned Eldár to a place on a piece of felt beside Hadji Murád. Eldár sat down, crossing his legs, and fixing his fine ram-like eyes on the old man, who, having now started talking, was telling how their brave fellows had caught two Russian soldiers the week before, and had killed one and sent the other to Shamil in Vedén.

Hadji Murád heard him absently, looking at the door and listening to the sounds outside. Under the penthouse steps were heard, the door creaked, and Sado, the master of the house, came in. He was a man of about forty, with a small beard, long nose, and eyes as black, though not as glittering, as those of his fifteen-year-old son who had run to call him home, and who now entered with his father and sat down by the door. The master of the house took off his wooden slippers at the door, and pushing his old and much-worn cap on to the back of his head (which had remained unshaved so long that it was beginning to be overgrown with black hair), at once squatted down in front of Hadji Murád.

He too lifted his hands, palms upwards, as the old man had done, repeated a prayer, and then stroked his face downwards. Only after that did he begin to speak. He told how an order had come from Shamil to seize Hadji Murád, alive or dead; that Shamil's envoys had left only the day before; that the people were afraid to disobey Shamil's orders; and that therefore it was necessary to be careful.

"In my house," said Sado, "no one shall injure my kunák while I live; but how will it be in the open fields? . . . We must think it over."

Hadji Murád listened with attention and nodded approvingly. When Sado had finished he said,—

"Very well. Now we must send a man with a letter to the Russians. My murid will go, but he will need a guide."

"I will send brother Bata," said Sado. "Go and call Bata," he added, turning to his son.

The boy instantly bounded to his nimble feet as if he were on springs, and swinging his arms, rapidly left the sáklya. Some ten minutes later he returned with a sinewy, short-legged Chechen, burnt almost black by the sun, wearing a worn and tattered yellow Circassian coat with frayed sleeves, and crumpled black leggings.

Hadji Murád greeted the newcomer, and at once, and again without wasting a single word, asked,—

"Canst thou conduct my murid to the Russians?"

"I can," gaily replied Bata. "I can certainly do it. There is not another Chechen who would pass as I can. Another might agree to go, and might promise anything, but would do nothing; but I can do it!"

"All right," said Hadji Murád. "Thou wilt receive three for thy trouble," and he held up three fingers.

Bata nodded to show that he understood, and added that it was not money he prized, but that he was ready to serve Hadji Murád for the honour alone. Every one in the mountains knew Hadji Murád, and how he slew the Russian swine.

"Very well . . . . a rope should be long, but a speech short," said Hadji Murád.

"Well, then, I'll hold my tongue," said Bata.

"Where the river Argun bends by the cliff," said Hadji Murád, "there are two stacks in a glade in the forest—thou knowest?"

"I know."

"There my four horsemen are waiting for me," said Hadji Murád.

"Aye," answered Bata, nodding.

"Ask for Khan Mahomá. He knows what to do and what to say. Canst thou lead him to the Russian commander, Prince Vorontsóv?"

"I'll take him there."

"Take him, and bring him back again. Canst thou?"

"I can."

"Take him there, and return to the wood. I shall be there too."

"I will do it all," said Bata, rising, and putting his hands on his heart he went out.

Hadji Murád turned to his host when Bata had gone.

"A man must also be sent to Chekhi," he began, and took hold of one of the cartridge pouches of his Circassian coat, but immediately let his hand drop and became silent on seeing two women enter the sáklya.

One was Sado's wife—the thin middle-aged woman who had arranged the cushions for Hadji Murád. The other was quite a young girl, wearing red trousers and a green beshmét; a necklace of silver coins covered the whole front of her dress, and at the end of the not long but thick plait of hard black hair that hung between her thin shoulder-blades a silver rouble was suspended. Her eyes, as sloe black as those of her father and brother, sparkled brightly in her young face, which tried to be stern. She did not look at the visitors, but evidently felt their presence.

Sado's wife brought in a low round table, on which stood tea, pancakes in butter, cheese, *churek* (that is, thinly rolled out bread), and honey. The girl carried a basin, a ewer, and a towel.

Sado and Hadji Murád kept silent as long as the women, with their coin ornaments tinkling, moved softly about in their red soft-soled slippers, setting out before the visitors the things they had brought. Eldár sat motionless as a statue, his ram-like eyes fixed on his crossed legs, all the time the women were in the *sáklya*. Only after they had gone, and their soft footsteps could no longer be heard behind the door, did he give a sigh of relief.

Hadji Murád having pulled out a bullet that plugged one of the bullet-pouches of his Circassian coat, and having taken out a rolled-up note that lay beneath it, held it out, saying,—

"To be handed to my son."

"Where must the answer be sent?"

"To thee, and thou must forward it to me."

"It shall be done," said Sado, and placed the note in a cartridge-pocket of his own coat. Then he took up the metal ewer and moved the basin towards Hadji Murád.

Hadji Murád turned up the sleeves of his *beshmét* on his white muscular arms, and held out his hands under the clear cold water which Sado poured from the ewer. Having wiped them on a clean unbleached towel, Hadji Murád turned to the table. Eldár did the same. While the visitors ate, Sado sat opposite, and thanked them several times for their visit. The boy sat by the door, never taking his sparkling eyes off Hadji Murád's face, and smiled as if in confirmation of his father's words.

Though Hadji Murád had eaten nothing for more than twenty-four hours, he ate only a little bread and cheese; then, drawing out a small knife from under his dagger, he spread some honey on a piece of bread.

"Our honey is good," said the old man, evidently pleased to see Hadji Murád eating his honey. "This year, above all other years, it is plentiful and good."

"I thank thee," said Hadji Murád, and turned from the table. Eldár would have liked to go on eating, but he followed his leader's example, and, having moved away from the table, handed Hadji Murád the ewer and basin.

Sado knew that he was risking his life by receiving Hadji Murád in his house, as, after his quarrel with Shamil, the latter had issued a proclamation to all the inhabitants of Chechnya forbidding them to receive Hadji Murád on pain of death. He knew that the inhabitants of the *aoul* might at any moment become aware of Hadji Murád's presence in his house, and might demand his surrender; but this not only did not frighten Sado, but even gave him pleasure. He considered it his duty to protect his guest though it should cost him his life, and he was proud and pleased with himself because he was doing his duty.

"Whilst thou art in my house and my head is on my shoulders no one shall harm thee," he repeated to Hadji Murád.

Hadji Murád looked into his glittering eyes, and understanding that this was true, said with some solemnity,—

"Mayest thou receive joy and life!"

Sado silently laid his hand on his heart as a sign of thanks for these kind words.

Having closed the shutters of the *sáklya* and laid some sticks in the fireplace, Sado, in an exceptionally bright and animated mood, left the room and went into that part of his *sáklya* where his family all lived. The women had not yet gone to sleep, and were talking about the dangerous visitors who were spending the night in their guest-chamber.

II

At the advanced fort Vozdvízhensk, situated some ten miles from the *aoul* in which Hadji Murád was spending the night, three soldiers and a non-commissioned officer left the fortifications and went beyond the Shahgirínsk Gate. The soldiers, dressed as Caucasian soldiers used to be in those days, wore sheepskin coats and caps, and boots that reached above their knees, and they carried their cloaks tightly rolled up and fastened across their shoulders. Shouldering arms, they first went some five hundred paces along the road, and then turned off it and went some twenty paces to the right—the dead leaves rustling under their boots—till they reached the blackened trunk of a broken plane tree, just visible through the darkness. There they stopped. It was at this plane tree that an ambush party was usually placed.

The bright stars, that seemed to be running along the tree-tops while the soldiers were walking through the forest, now stood still, shining brightly between the bare branches of the trees.

"A good job it's dry," said the non-commissioned officer, Panóv, bringing down his long gun and bayonet with a clang from his shoulder, and placing it against the plane tree. The three soldiers did the same.

"Sure enough, I've lost it!" crossly muttered Panóv. "Must have left it behind, or I've dropped it on the way."

"What are you looking for?" asked one of the soldiers in a bright, cheerful voice.

"The bowl of my pipe. Where the devil has it got to?"

"Have you the stem?" asked the cheerful voice.

"Here's the stem."

"Then why not stick it straight into the ground?"

"Not worth bothering!"

"We'll manage that in a minute."

It was forbidden to smoke while in ambush, but this ambush hardly deserved the name. It was rather an outpost to prevent the mountaineers from bringing up a cannon unobserved and firing at the fort as they used to do. Panóv did not consider it necessary to forego the pleasure of smoking, and therefore accepted the cheerful soldier's offer. The latter took a knife from his pocket and dug with it a hole in the ground. Having smoothed this round, he adjusted the pipe-stem to it, then filled the hole with tobacco and pressed it down; and the pipe was ready. A sulphur match flared and for a moment lit up the broad-cheeked face of the soldier who lay on his stomach. The air whistled in the stem, and Panóv smelt the pleasant odour of burning tobacco.

"Fixed it up?" said he, rising to his feet.

"Why, of course!"

"What a smart chap you are, Avdéev! . . . As wise as a judge! Now then, lad."

Avdéev rolled over on his side to make room for Panóv, letting smoke escape from his mouth.

Panóv lay down prone, and, after wiping the mouthpiece with his sleeve, began to inhale.

When they had had their smoke the soldiers began to talk.

"They say the commander has had his fingers in the cash-box again," remarked one of them in a lazy voice. "He lost at cards, you see."

"He'll pay it back again," said Panóv.

"Of course he will! He's a good officer," assented Avdéev.

"Good! good!" gloomily repeated the man who had started the conversation. "In my opinion the company ought to speak to him. 'If you've taken the money, tell us how much and when you'll repay it.'"

"That will be as the company decides," said Panóv, tearing himself away from the pipe.

"Of course. 'The community is a strong man,'" assented Avdéev, quoting a proverb.

"There will be oats to buy and boots to get towards spring. The money will be wanted, and what if he's pocketed it?" insisted the dissatisfied one.

"I tell you it will be as the company wishes," repeated Panóv. "It's not the first time: he takes, and gives back."

In the Caucasus in those days each company chose men to manage its own commissariat. They received 6 roubles 50 kopeks a month per man from the treasury, and catered for the company. They planted cabbages, made hay, had their own carts, and prided themselves on their well-fed horses. The company's money was kept in a chest, of which the commander had the key; and it often happened that he borrowed from the chest. This had just happened again, and that was what the soldiers were talking about. The morose soldier, Nikítin, wished to demand an account from the commander, while Panóv and Avdéev considered it unnecessary.

After Panóv, Nikítin had a smoke; and then, spreading his cloak on the ground, sat down on it, leaning against the trunk of the plane tree. The soldiers were silent. Only far above their heads the crowns of the trees rustled in the wind. Suddenly, above this incessant low rustling, rose the howling whining weeping and chuckling of jackals.

"Hear those accursed creatures—how they caterwaul!"

"They're laughing at you because your mug's all on one side," remarked the high voice of another soldier, a Ükrainian.

All was silent again: only the wind swayed the branches, now revealing and now hiding the stars.

"I say, Panóv," suddenly asked the cheerful Avdéev, "do you ever feel dull?"

"Dull, why?" replied Panóv reluctantly.

"Well, I do feel dull . . . so dull sometimes that I don't know what I might not be ready to do to myself."

"There now!" was all Panóv replied.

"That time when I drank all the money, it was from dullness. It took hold of me . . . took hold of me till I thinks to myself, 'I'll just get blind drunk!' "

"But sometimes drinking makes it still worse."

"Yes, that's happened to me too. But what is one to do with one-self?"

"But what makes you feel so dull?"

"What, me? . . . Why, it's the longing for home."

"Is yours a wealthy home, then?"

"No, we weren't wealthy, but things went properly—we lived well." And Avdéev began to relate what he had already many times told to Panóv.

"You see, I went as a soldier of my own free will, instead of my brother," he said. "He has children. They were five in family, and I had only just married. Mother began begging me to go. So I thought, 'Well, maybe they will remember what I've done.' So I went to our proprietor . . . he was a good master, and he said, 'You're a fine fellow, go!' So I went instead of my brother."

"Well, that was right," said Panóv.

"And yet, will you believe me, Panóv, if I now feel so dull, it's chiefly because of that? 'Why did you go instead of your brother?' I say. 'He's now living like a king over there, while I have to suffer here;' and the more I think the worse I feel. . . . Seems it's just a piece of ill-luck!"

Avdéev was silent.

"Perhaps we'd better have another smoke," said he after a pause.

"Well then, fix it up!"

But the soldiers were not to have their smoke. Hardly had Avdéev risen to fix the pipe-stem in its place when above the rustling of the trees they heard footsteps along the road. Panóv took his gun, and pushed Nikítin with his foot.

Nikítin rose and picked up his cloak.

The third soldier, Bondarénko, rose also, and said,—

"And I have just dreamt such a dream, mates. . . ."

"Sh!" said Avdéev, and the soldiers held their breath, listening. The footsteps of men not shod in hard boots were heard approaching. Clearer and clearer through the darkness was heard a rustling of the fallen leaves and dry twigs. Then came the peculiar guttural tones of Chechen voices. The soldiers now not only heard, but saw two shadows passing through a clear space between the trees. One shadow was taller than the other. When these shadows had come in line with the soldiers, Panóv, gun in hand, stepped out on to the road, followed by his comrades.

"Who goes there?" cried he.

"Me, friendly Chechen," said the shorter one. This was Bata. "Gun, yok![2] . . . sword, yok!" said he, pointing to himself. "Prince, want!"

The taller one stood silent beside his comrade. He, too, was unarmed.

"He means he's a scout, and wants the colonel," explained Panóv to his comrades.

"Prince Vorontsóv . . . much want! Big business!" said Bata.

"All right, all right! We'll take you to him," said Panóv. "I say, you'd better take them," said he to Avdéev, "you and Bondarénko; and when you've given them up to the officer on duty come back again. Mind," he added, "be careful to make them keep in front of you!"

"And what of this?" said Avdéev, moving his gun and bayonet as though stabbing someone. "I'd just give a dig, and let the steam out of him!"

"What'll he be worth when you've stuck him?" remarked Bondarénko.

"Now, march!"

When the steps of the two soldiers conducting the scouts could no longer be heard, Panóv and Nikítin returned to their post.

"What the devil brings them here at night?" said Nikítin.

"Seems it's necessary," said Panóv. "But it's getting chilly," he added, and, unrolling his cloak, he put it on and sat down by the tree.

About two hours later Avdéev and Bondarénko returned.

"Well, have you handed them over?"

"Yes. They're not yet asleep at the colonel's—they were taken straight in to him. And do you know, mates, those shaven-headed lads are fine?" continued Avdéev. "Yes, really? What a talk I had with them!"

"Of course you'd talk," remarked Nikítin disapprovingly.

"Really, they're just like Russians. One of them is married. 'Marushka,' says I, 'bar?'³ 'Bar,' he says. Bondarénko, didn't I say 'bar?' 'Many bar?' 'A couple,' says he. A couple! Such a good talk we had! Such nice fellows!"

"Nice, indeed!" said Nikítin. "If you met him alone he'd soon let the guts out of you."

"It will be getting light before long," said Panóv.

"Yes, the stars are beginning to go out," said Avdéev, sitting down and making himself comfortable.

And the soldiers were again silent.

III

The windows of the barracks and of the soldiers' houses had long been dark in the fort; but there was still light in the windows of the best house there.

In it lived Prince Simon Mikhailovich Vorontsóv,¹ commander of the Kurín Regiment, an imperial aide-de-camp, and son of the commander-in-chief. Vorontsóv lived with his wife, Mary Vasílevna, a famous Petersburg beauty, and lived in this little Caucasian fort more luxuriously than any one had ever lived there before. To Vorontsóv, and especially to his wife, it seemed that they were not only living a very modest life, but one full of privations; while to the inhabitants of the place their luxury was surprising and extraordinary.

Now at midnight, in the spacious drawing-room with its carpeted floor, its rich curtains drawn across the windows, at a card table lit by four candles, sat the hosts and their visitors, playing cards. One of the players was Vorontsóv himself: a long-faced, fair-haired colonel, wearing the initials and gold cords of an aide-de-camp. His partner— a graduate of Petersburg University, whom the Princess Vorontsóv had lately had sent out as tutor to her little son (born of her first marriage)—was a shaggy young man of gloomy appearance. Against them played two officers: one a broad and red-faced man, Poltorát- sky, a company commander, who had exchanged out of the guards; and the other, the regimental adjutant, a man with a cold expression on his handsome face, who sat very straight on his chair.

The princess, Mary Vasílevna, the large-built large-eyed and black- browed beauty, sat beside Poltorátsky (her crinoline touching his legs) and looked over his cards. In her words, her looks, and her smile, in her perfume and in every movement of her body, there was something that reduced Poltorátsky to obliviousness of everything except a consciousness of her nearness; and he made blunder after blunder, trying his partner's temper more and more.

"No . . . that's too bad! You've again wasted an ace," said the regi- mental Adjutant, flushing all over, as Poltorátsky threw out an ace.

Poltorátsky uncomprehendingly—as though he had just awoke— turned his kindly, wide-set black eyes towards the dissatisfied Adjutant.

"Do forgive him!" said Mary Vasílevna, smiling. "There, you see? Didn't I tell you so?" she went on, turning to Poltorátsky.

"But that's not at all what you said," replied Poltorátsky, smiling.

"Wasn't it?" she replied, also smiling; and this answering smile excited and delighted Poltorátsky to such a degree that he blushed crimson, and seizing the cards began to shuffle.

"It isn't your turn to deal," said the Adjutant sternly, and with his white ringed hand he himself began to deal as though he only wished to get rid of the cards as quickly as possible.

The Prince's valet entered the drawing-room, and announced that the officer on duty wanted the Prince.

"Excuse me, gentlemen," said the Prince, speaking Russian with an English accent. "Will you take my place, Marie?"

"Do you all agree?" asked the Princess, rising quickly and lightly to her full height, rustling with her silks, and smiling the radiant smile of a happy woman.

"I always agree to everything," replied the Adjutant, very pleased that the Princess—who could not play at all—was now going to play against him.

Poltorátsky only spread out his hands and smiled.

The rubber was nearly finished when the Prince returned to the drawing-room. He came back animated and very pleased.

"Do you know what I propose?"

"What is it?"

"Let us have some champagne."

"I am always ready for that," said Poltorátsky.

"Why not? We shall be delighted!" said the Adjutant.

"Vasíly! bring some!" said the Prince.

"What did they want you for?" asked Mary Vasílevna.

"It was the officer on duty, and another man."

"Who? What about?" asked Mary Vasílevna quickly.

"I mustn't say," said Vorontsóv, shrugging his shoulders.

"You mustn't say!" repeated Mary Vasilevna. "We'll see about that."

When the champagne was brought, each of the visitors drank a glass; and, having finished the game and settled the scores, they began to take their leave.

"Is it your company that's ordered to the forest tomorrow?" the Prince asked Poltorátsky as they said good-bye.

"Yes, mine . . . why?"

"Oh, then we'll meet tomorrow," said the Prince, slightly smiling.

"Very pleased," replied Poltorátsky, not quite understanding what Vorontsóv was saying to him, and preoccupied only by the thought that he would in a minute be pressing Mary Vasílevna's hand.

Mary Vasílevna, according to her wont, not only firmly pressed his hand, but shook it vigorously; and again reminding him of his mistake in playing diamonds, she gave him what appeared to Poltorátsky to be a delightful affectionate and meaning smile.

Poltorátsky went home in an ecstatic condition only to be understood by people like himself who, having grown up and been educated in society, meet a woman belonging to their own circle after months of isolated military life, and, moreover, a woman like the Princess Vorontsóv.

When he reached the little house in which he and his comrade lived he pushed the door, but it was locked. He knocked, but still the door was not opened. He felt vexed, and began banging the door with his foot and his sword. Then he heard a sound of footsteps, and Vovílo—a domestic serf belonging to Poltorátsky—undid the cabin-hook which fastened the door.

"What do you mean by locking yourself in, blockhead?"

"But how is it possible, sir . . . ?"

"You're tipsy again! I'll show you how 'it is possible!'" and Poltorátsky was about to strike Vovílo, but changed his mind. "Well, go to the devil! . . . Light a candle."

"In a minute."

Vovílo was really tipsy. He had been drinking at the Name's-Day party of the ordnance-sergeant. On returning home he began comparing his life with that of the latter, Iván Petróvich. Iván Petróvich had a salary, was married, and hoped in a year's time to get his discharge.

Vovílo had been taken "up" when a boy; that is, he had been taken into his owner's household service; and now he was already over forty, was not married, and lived a campaigning life with his harum-scarum young master. He was a good master, who seldom struck him; but what kind of a life was it? "He promised to free me when we return from the Caucasus, but where am I to go with my freedom? . . . It's a dog's life!" thought Vovílo; and he felt so sleepy that, afraid lest someone should come in and steal something, he fastened the hook of the door and fell asleep.

     *   *   *   *   *

Poltorátsky entered his bedroom, which he shared with his comrade Tikhonov.

"Well, have you lost?" asked Tikhonov, waking up.

"As it happens, I've not. I've won seventeen roubles, and we drank a bottle of Cliquot!"

"And you've looked at Mary Vasílevna?"

"Yes, and I've looked at Mary Vasílevna," repeated Poltorátsky.

"It will soon be time to get up," said Tikhonov. "We are to start at six."

"Vovílo!" shouted Poltorátsky, "see that you wake me up properly tomorrow at five!"

"How's one to wake you, if you fight?"

"I tell you you're to wake me! Do you hear?"

"All right." Vovílo went out, taking Poltorátsky's boots and clothes with him. Poltorátsky got into bed, and smiling, smoked a cigarette and put out his candle. In the dark he saw before him the smiling face of Mary Vasílevna.

*　　　*　　　*　　　*　　　*

The Vorontsóvs did not go to bed at once. When the visitors had left, Mary Vasílevna went up to her husband, and standing in front of him, said severely,—

"Eh bien! Vous allez me dire ce que c'est."

"Mais, ma chère."

"Pas de 'ma chère'! C'était un émissaire, n'est ce pas?"

"Quand même, je ne puis pas vous le dire."

"Vous ne pouvez pas? Alors, c'est moi qui vais vous le dire!"

"Vous?"

"It was Hadji Murád, wasn't it?" said Mary Vasílevna, who had for some days past heard of the negotiations, and thought that Hadji Murád himself had been to see her husband. Vorontsóv could not altogether deny this, but disappointed her by saying that it was not Hadji Murád himself but only an emissary to announce that Hadji Murád would come to meet him next day, at the spot where a wood-cutting expedition had been arranged.

In the monotonous life of the fortress, the young Vorontsóvs—both husband and wife—were glad of this occurrence; and when, after speaking of the pleasure the news would give his father, they went to bed, it was already past two o'clock.

I V

After the three sleepless nights he had passed flying from the murids Shamil sent to capture him, Hadji Murád fell asleep as soon as Sado, having bid him good-night, had gone out of the sáklya. He slept fully dressed, with his head on his hand, his elbow sinking deep into the red down-cushions his host had arranged for him.

At a little distance, by the wall, slept Eldár. He lay on his back, his strong young limbs stretched out so that his high chest with the black cartridge-pouches sewn into the front of his white Circassian coat was higher than his freshly-shaven blue-gleaming head, which had rolled off the pillow and was thrown back. His upper lip, on which a little soft down was just appearing, pouted like a child's, now contracting and now expanding, as though he were sipping something. He, like Hadji Murád, slept with pistol and dagger in his belt. The sticks in the grate burnt low, and a nightlight in the niche in the wall gleamed faintly.

In the middle of the night the floor of the guest-chamber creaked, and Hadji Murád immediately rose, putting his hand to his pistol. Sado entered treading softly on the earthen floor.

"What is it?" asked Hadji Murád, as if he had not been asleep at all.

"We must think," replied Sado, squatting down in front of him. "A woman from her roof saw you arrive, and told her husband; and now the whole *aoul* knows. A neighbour has just been to tell my wife that the Elders have assembled in the mosque, and want to detain you."

"I must be off!" said Hadji Murád.

"The horses are saddled," said Sado, quickly leaving the *sáklya*.

"Eldár!" whispered Hadji Murád; and Eldár, hearing his name, and above all his master's voice, leapt to his feet, setting straight his cap.

Hadji Murád donned his weapons and then his *búrka*. Eldár did the same; and they both went silently out of the *sáklya* into the penthouse. The black-eyed boy brought their horses. Hearing the clatter of hoofs on the hard beaten road, someone stuck his head out of the door of a neighbourng *sáklya*, and, clattering with his wooden shoes, a man ran up the hill towards the mosque. There was no moon, but the stars shone brightly in the black sky, so that the outlines of the *sáklya* roofs could be seen in the darkness, and rising above the other buildings, the mosque with its minarets in the upper part of the village. From the mosque came a hum of voices.

Hadji Murád, quickly seizing his gun, placed his foot in the narrow stirrup, and, silently and easily throwing his body across, swung himself on to the high cushion of the saddle.

"May God reward you!" he said, addressing his host, while his right foot felt instinctively for the stirrup, and with his whip he lightly touched the lad who held his horse, as a sign that he should let go. The boy stepped aside; and the horse, as if it knew what it had to do, started at a brisk pace down the lane towards the principal street.

Eldár rode behind him. Sado in his sheepskin followed almost running, swinging his arms, and crossing now to one side and now to the other of the narrow side-street. At the place where the streets met, first one moving shadow and then another appeared in the road.

"Stop . . . who's that? Stop!" shouted a voice, and several men blocked the path.

Instead of stopping, Hadji Murád drew his pistol from his belt, and increasing his speed rode straight at those who blocked the way. They separated, and Hadji Murád without looking round started down the road at a swift canter. Eldár followed him at a sharp trot. Two shots cracked behind them, and two bullets whistled past without hitting either Hadji Murád or Eldár. Hadji Murád continued riding at the same pace, but having gone some three hundred yards, he stopped his slightly panting horse, and listened.

In front of him, lower down, gurgled rapidly running water. Behind him, in the *aoul*, cocks crowed, answering one another. Above these sounds he heard behind him the approaching tramp of horses, and the voices of several men. Hadji Murád touched his horse and rode on at an even pace. Those behind him galloped and soon overtook him. They were some twenty mounted men, inhabitants of the *aoul*, who had decided to detain Hadji Murád, or at least to make a show of detaining him in order to justify themselves in Shamil's eyes. When they came near enough to be seen in the darkness, Hadji Murád stopped, let go his bridle, and with an accustomed movement of his left hand unbuttoned the cover of his rifle, which he drew forth with his right. Eldár did the same.

"What do you want?" cried Hadji Murád. "Do you wish to take me! . . . Take me, then!" and he raised his rifle. The men from the *aoul* stopped, and Hadji Murád, rifle in hand, rode down into the ravine. The mounted men followed him, but did not draw any nearer. When Hadji Murád had crossed to the other side of the ravine, the men shouted to him that he should hear what they had to say. In reply he fired his rifle and put his horse to a gallop. When he reined it in, his pursuers were no longer within hearing, and the crowing of the cocks could also no longer be heard; only the murmur of the water in the forest sounded more distinctly, and now and then came the cry of an owl. The black wall of forest appeared quite close. It was in this forest that his murids awaited him.

On reaching it Hadji Murád paused, and drawing much air into his lungs, he whistled and then listened silently. The next minute he was answered by a similar whistle from the forest. Hadji Murád turned from the road and entered it. When he had gone about a hundred paces, he saw among the trunks of the trees a bonfire, and the shadows of some men sitting round it, and, half lit-up by the firelight, a hobbled horse which was saddled. Four men were seated by the fire.

One of them rose quickly, and coming up to Hadji Murád took hold of his bridle and stirrup. This was Hadji Murád's sworn brother, who managed his household affairs for him.

"Put out the fire," said Hadji Murád, dismounting.

The men began scattering the pile, and trampling on the burning branches.

"Has Bata been here?" asked Hadji Murád, moving towards a búrka that was spread on the ground.

"Yes, he went away long ago, with Khan Mahomá."

"Which way did they go?"

"That way," answered Khanéfi, pointing in the opposite direction to that from which Hadji Murád had come.

"All right," said Hadji Murád, and unslinging his rifle he began to load it.

"We must take care—I have been pursued," said Hadji Murád to a man who was putting out the fire.

He was Gamzálo, a Chechen. Gamzálo approached the búrka, took up a rifle that lay on it wrapped in its cover, and without a word went to that side of the glade from which Hadji Murád had come.

Eldár, when he had dismounted, took Hadji Murád's horse; and having reined up both horses' heads high, tied them to two trees. Then he shouldered his rifle, as Gamzálo had done, and went to the other side of the glade. The bonfire was extinguished, the forest no longer looked so black as before, and in the sky the stars shone, though but faintly.

Lifting his eyes to the stars, and seeing that the Pleiades had already risen half-way up the sky, Hadji Murád calculated that it must be long past midnight, and that his nightly prayer was long overdue. He asked Khanéfi for a ewer (they always carried one in their packs), and putting on his búrka he went to the water.

Having taken off his shoes and performed his ablutions, Hadji

Murád stepped on to the *búrka* with bare feet, and then squatted down on his calves, and having first placed his fingers in his ears and closed his eyes, he turned to the south and recited the usual prayer.

When he had finished he returned to the place where the saddle-bags lay, and sitting down on the *búrka* he leant his elbows on his knees and bowed his head, and fell into deep thought.

Hadji Murád always had great faith in his own fortune. When planning anything he felt in advance firmly convinced of success, and fate smiled on him. It was so, with a few rare exceptions, during the whole course of his stormy military life; and so he hoped it would be now. He pictured to himself how—with the army Vorontsóv would place at his disposal—he would march against Shamil and take him prisoner, and revenge himself on him; and how the Russian Tsar would reward him, and he would again rule over not only Avaria, but also over the whole of Chechnya, which would submit to him.[2] With these thoughts he fell asleep before he was aware of it.

He dreamt how he and his brave followers rushed at Shamil, with songs and with the cry, "Hadji Murád is coming!" and how they seized him and his wives, and he heard the wives crying and sobbing. He woke up. The song, *Lya-il-allysha*, and the cry, "Hadji Murád is coming!" and the weeping of Shamil's wives, was the howling weeping and laughter of jackals that awoke him. Hadji Murád lifted his head, glanced at the sky which seen between the trunks of the trees was already getting light in the east, and inquired after Khan Mahomá of a *murid* who sat at some distance from him. On hearing that Khan Mahomá had not yet returned, Hadji Murád again bowed his head and fell asleep at once.

He was awakened by the merry voice of Khan Mahomá, returning from his mission with Bata. Khan Mahomá at once sat down beside Hadji Murád, and told him how the soldiers had met them and had led them to the Prince himself; and how pleased the Prince was, and how he promised to meet them in the morning, where the Russians would be felling trees beyond the Mitchík, in the Shalín glade. Bata interrupted his fellow-envoy to add details of his own.

Hadji Murád asked particularly for the words with which Vorontsóv had answered his offer to go over to the Russians; and Khan Mahomá and Bata replied with one voice that the Prince promised to receive Hadji Murád as a guest, and to act so that it should be well for him.

Then Hadji Murád questioned them about the road, and when Khan Mahomá assured him that he knew the way well, and would conduct him straight to the spot, Hadji Murád took out some money and gave Bata the promised three roubles; and he ordered his men to take out of the saddle-bags his gold-ornamented weapons and his turban, and to clean themselves up so as to look well when they arrived among the Russians.

While they cleaned their weapons, harness and horses, the stars faded away; it became quite light, and an early morning breeze sprang up.

V

Early in the morning, while it was still dark, two companies, carrying axes and commanded by Poltorátsky, marched six miles beyond the Shahgirínsk Gate, and having thrown out a line of sharpshooters, set to work to fell trees as soon as the day broke. Towards eight o'clock the mist which had mingled with the perfumed smoke of the hissing and crackling damp green branches on the bonfires began to rise, and the wood-fellers—who till then had not seen five paces off, but had only heard one another—began to see both the bonfires and the road through the forest, blocked with fallen trees. The sun now appeared like a bright spot in the fog, and now again was hidden.

In the glade, some way from the road, Poltorátsky, and his subaltern Tikhonov, two officers of the 3rd Company, and Baron Freze, an ex-officer of the Guards who had been reduced to the ranks for a duel, a fellow-student of Poltorátsky's at the Cadet College, were sitting on drums. Bits of paper that had contained food, cigarette stumps, and empty bottles lay scattered round the drums. The officers had had some vódka, and were now eating, and drinking porter. A drummer was uncorking their third bottle.

Poltorátsky, although he had not had enough sleep, was in that peculiar state of elation and kindly careless gaiety which he always felt when he found himself among his soldiers and with his comrades, where there was a possibility of danger.

The officers were carrying on an animated conversation, the subject of which was the latest news: the death of General Sleptsóv. None of them saw in this death that most important moment of a life—its termination and return to the source whence it sprang—but they only saw in it the valour of a gallant officer, who rushed at the mountaineers sword in hand and desperately hacked them.

Though all of them—and especially those who had been in action—knew and could not help knowing that never in those days in the Caucasus, nor in fact anywhere, nor at any time, did such hand-to-hand hacking as is always imagined and described take place (or if hacking with swords and bayonets ever does take place, it is only those who are running away that get hacked), that fiction of hand-to-hand fighting endowed them with the calm pride and cheerfulness with which they sat on drums (some with a jaunty air, others on the contrary in a very modest pose), drank and joked without troubling about death, which might overtake them at any moment as it had overtaken Sleptsóv. And, as if to confirm their expectations, in the midst of their talk, they heard to the left of the road the pleasing stirring sound of a rifle-shot; and a bullet, merrily whistling somewhere in the misty air, flew past and crashed into a tree.

"Hullo!" exclaimed Poltorátsky in a merry voice; "why, that's at our line. . . . There now, Kóstya," and he turned to Freze, "now's your chance. Go back to the company. I will lead the whole company to support the cordon, and we'll arrange a battle that will be simply delightful . . . and then we'll make a report."

Freze jumped to his feet and went at a quick pace towards the smoke-enveloped spot where he had left his company.

Poltorátsky's little Kabardá[3] dapple-bay was brought to him, and he mounted and drew up his company, and led it in the direction whence the shots were fired. The outposts stood on the skirts of the forest, in front of the bare descending slope of a ravine. The wind was blowing in the direction of the forest, and not only was it possible to see the slope of the ravine, but the opposite side of it was also distinctly visible. When Poltorátsky rode up to the line, the sun came out from behind the mist; and on the other side of the ravine, by the outskirts of a young forest, at the distance of a quarter of a mile, a few horsemen became visible. They were the Chechens who had pursued

Hadji Murád and wanted to see him meet the Russians. One of them fired at the line. Several soldiers fired back. The Chechens retreated, and the firing ceased.

But when Poltorátsky and his company came up, he nevertheless gave orders to fire; and scarcely had the word been passed, when along the whole line of sharpshooters started the incessant, merry, stirring rattle of our rifles, accompanied by pretty dissolving cloudlets of smoke. The soldiers, pleased to have some distraction, hastened to load, and fired shot after shot. The Chechens evidently caught the feeling of excitement, and leaping forward one after another, fired a few shots at our men. One of these shots wounded a soldier. It was that same Avdéev who had lain in ambush the night before.

When his comrades approached him he was lying prone, holding his wounded stomach with both hands, and rocking himself with a rhythmic motion, moaned softly. He belonged to Poltorátsky's company, and Poltorátsky, seeing a group of soldiers collected, rode up to them.

"What is it, lad? Been hit?" said Poltorátsky. "Where?"

Avdéev did not answer.

"I was just going to load, your honour, when I heard a click," said a soldier who had been with Avdéev; "and I look, and see he's dropped his gun."

"Tut, tut, tut!" Poltorátsky clicked his tongue. "Does it hurt much, Avdéev?"

"It doesn't hurt, but it stops me walking. A drop of vódka now, your honour!"

Some vódka (or rather the spirits drunk by the soldiers in the Caucasus) was found, and Panóv, severely frowning, brought Avdéev a can-lid full. Avdéev tried to drink it, but immediately handed back the lid.

"My soul turns against it," he said. "Drink it yourself."

Panóv drank up the spirit.

Avdéev raised himself, but sank back at once. They spread out a cloak and laid him on it.

"Your honour, the colonel is coming," said the sergeant-major to Poltorátsky.

"All right. Then will you see to him?" said Poltorátsky; and, flourishing his whip, he rode at a fast trot to meet Vorontsóv.

Vorontsóv was riding his thoroughbred English chestnut gelding, and was accompanied by the adjutant, a Cossack, and a Chechen interpreter.

"What's happening here?" asked Vorontsóv.

"Why, a skirmishing party attacked our advanced line," Poltorátsky answered.

"Come, come; you've arranged the whole thing yourself!"

"Oh no, Prince, not I," said Poltorátsky with a smile; "they pushed forward of their own accord."

"I hear a soldier has been wounded?"

"Yes, it's a great pity. He's a good soldier."

"Seriously?"

"Seriously, I believe . . . in the stomach."

"And do you know where I am going?" Vorontsóv asked.

"I don't."

"Can't you guess?"

"No."

"Hadji Murád has surrendered, and we are now going to meet him."

"You don't mean to say so?"

"His envoy came to me yesterday," said Vorontsóv, with difficulty repressing a smile of joy. "He will be waiting for me at the Shalín glade in a few minutes. Place sharpshooters as far as the glade, and then come and join me."

"I understand," said Poltorátsky, lifting his hand to his cap, and rode back to his company. He led the sharpshooters to the right himself, and ordered the sergeant-major to do the same on the left side.

The wounded Avdéev had meanwhile been taken back to the fort by some of the soldiers.

On his way back to rejoin Vorontsóv, Poltorátsky noticed behind him several horsemen who were overtaking him. In front, on a white-maned horse, rode a man of imposing appearance. He wore a turban, and carried weapons with gold ornaments. This man was Hadji Murád. He approached Poltorátsky and said something to him in Tartar. Raising his eyebrows, Poltorátsky made a gesture with his arms to show that he did not understand, and smiled. Hadji Murád gave him smile for smile, and that smile struck Poltorátsky by its child-like kindliness. Poltorátsky had never expected to see the terrible mountain chief look like that. He expected to see a morose, hard-featured man; and here was a vivacious person, whose smile was so kindly that Poltorátsky felt as if he were an old acquaintance. He had but one peculiarity: his eyes, set wide apart, gazed from under their black brows attentively, penetratingly and calmly into the eyes of others.

Hadji Murád's suite consisted of five men. Among them was Khan Mahomá, who had been to see Prince Vorontsóv that night. He was a rosy, round-faced fellow, with black lashless eyes and a beaming expression, full of the joy of life. Then there was the Avar Khanéfi, a thick-set, hairy man, whose eyebrows were joined. He was in charge of all Hadji Murád's property, and led a stud-bred horse which carried tightly-packed saddle-bags. Two men of the suite were particularly striking. The first was a Lesgian:[4] a youth, broad-shouldered, but with a waist as slim as a woman's, a brown beard just appearing on his face, and beautiful ram-like eyes. This was Eldár. The other, Gamzálo, was a Chechen, blind in one eye, without eyebrows or eyelashes, with a short red beard, and a scar across his nose and face. Poltorátsky pointed out to Hadji Murád, Vorontsóv, who had just appeared on the road. Hadji Murád rode to meet him, and, putting his right hand on his heart, said something in Tartar, and stopped. The Chechen interpreter translated.

"He says, 'I surrender myself to the will of the Russian Tsar. I wish to serve him,' he says. 'I wished to do so long ago, but Shamil would not let me.'"

Having heard what the interpreter said, Vorontsóv stretched out his hand in its wash-leather glove to Hadji Murád. Hadji Murád looked at it hesitatingly for a moment, and then pressed it firmly, again saying something, and looking first at the interpreter and then at Vorontsóv.

"He says he did not wish to surrender to any one but you, as you are the son of the Sirdar, and he respects you much."

Vorontsóv nodded to express his thanks. Hadji Murád again said something, pointing to his suite.

"He says that these men, his henchmen, will serve the Russians as well as he."

Vorontsóv turned towards them, and nodded to them too. The merry, black-eyed, lashless Chechen, Khan Mahomá, also nodded, and said something which was probably amusing, for the hairy Avar drew his lips into a smile, showing his ivory-white teeth. But the red-haired Gamzálo's one red eye just glanced at Vorontsóv and then was again fixed on the ears of his horse.

When Vorontsóv and Hadji Murád with their retinues rode back to the fort, the soldiers, released from the lines, gathered in groups and made their own comments.

"What a number of souls the damned fellow has destroyed! And now see what a fuss they will make of him!"

"Naturally. He was Shamil's right hand, and now—no fear!"

"Still there's no denying it! he's a fine fellow—a regular *dzhigit!*"*

"And the red one? The red one squints at you like a beast!"

"Ugh! He must be a hound!"

They had all specially noticed the red one. Where the wood-felling was going on, the soldiers nearest to the road ran out to look. Their officer shouted to them, but Vorontsóv stopped him.

"Let them have a look at their old friend."

"You know who that is?" asked Vorontsóv, turning to the nearest soldier, and speaking the words slowly with his English accent.

"No, your Excellency."

"Hadji Murád. . . . Heard of him?"

"How could we help it, your Excellency? We've beaten him many a time!"

"Yes, and we've had it hot from him, too."

"Yes, that's right, your Excellency," answered the soldier, pleased to be talking with his chief.

Hadji Murád understood that they were speaking about him, and smiled brightly with his eyes.

Vorontsóv, in the most cheerful mood, returned to the fort.

---

*Skilled warrior on horseback (Tatar).

Young Vorontsóv was much pleased that it was he, and not any one else, who had succeeded in winning over and receiving Hadji Murád—next to Shamil Russia's chief and most active enemy. There was just one unpleasant thing about it: General Meller-Zakomélsky was in command of the army in Vozdvízhensk, and the whole affair ought to have been carried out through him; and as Vorontsóv had done everything himself without reporting it, there might be some unpleasantness; and this thought somewhat interfered with his satisfaction. On reaching his house he entrusted Hadji Murád's henchmen to the regimental adjutant, and himself showed Hadji Murád into the house.

Princess Mary Vasílevna, elegantly dressed and smiling, and her little son, a handsome curly-headed, six-year-old boy, met Hadji Murád in the drawing-room. The latter placed his hands on his heart, and through the interpreter—who had entered with him—said with solemnity that he regarded himself as the Prince's kunák, since the Prince had brought him into his own house; and that a kunák's whole family was as sacred as the kunák himself.

Hadji Murád's appearance and manners pleased Mary Vasílevna; and the fact that he flushed when she held out her large white hand to him, inclined her still more in his favour. She invited him to sit down; and having asked him whether he drank coffee, had some served up. He, however, declined it when it came. He understood a little Russian, but could not speak it. When something was said which he could not understand he smiled, and his smile pleased Mary Vasílevna, just as it had pleased Poltorátsky. The curly-headed, keen-eyed little boy (whom his mother called Búlka) standing beside her did not take his eyes off Hadji Murád, whom he had always heard spoken of as a great warrior.

Leaving Hadji Murád with his wife, Vorontsóv went to his office to do what was necessary about reporting the fact of Hadji Murád's having come over to the Russians. When he had written a report to the general in command of the left flank—General Kozlóvsky—at Grózny, and a letter to his father, Vorontsóv hurried home, afraid that his wife might be vexed with him for forcing on her this terrible stranger, who had to be treated in such a way that he should not take offence, and yet not too kindly. But his fears were needless. Hadji Murád was sitting in an armchair with little Búlka, Vorontsóv's step-son, on his knee; and with bent head was listening attentively to the interpreter, who was translating to him the words of the laughing Mary Vasílevna. Mary Vasílevna was telling him that if every time a kunák admired anything of his he made him a present of it, he would soon have to go about like Adam . . .

When the Prince entered, Hadji Murád rose at once, and surprising and offending Búlka by putting him off his knee, changed the playful expression of his face to a stern and serious one; and he only sat down again when Vorontsóv had himself taken a seat.

Continuing the conversation, he answered Mary Vasílevna by telling her that it was a law among his people that anything your kunák admired must be presented to him.

"Thy son, kunák!" he said in Russian, patting the curly head of the boy, who had again climbed on his knee.

"He is delightful, your brigand!" said Mary Vasílevna, to her husband in French. "Búlka has been admiring his dagger, and he has given it to him."

Búlka showed the dagger to his father. "C'est un objet de prix!" added she.

"Il faudra trouver l'occasion de lui faire cadeau," said Vorontsóv.

Hadji Murád, his eyes turned down, sat stroking the boy's curly head and saying: "Dzhigit, dzhigit!"

"A beautiful, beautiful dagger," said Vorontsóv, half drawing out the sharpened blade, which had a ridge down the centre. "I thank thee!"

"Ask him what I can do for him," he said to the interpreter.

The interpreter translated, and Hadji Murád at once replied that he wanted nothing, but that he begged to be taken to a place where he could say his prayers.

Vorontsóv called his valet, and told him to do what Hadji Murád desired.

As soon as Hadji Murád was alone in the room allotted to him his face altered. The pleased expression, now kindly and now stately, vanished, and a look of anxiety showed itself. Vorontsóv had received him far better than Hadji Murád had expected. But the better the reception the less did Hadji Murád trust Vorontsóv and his officers. He feared everything: that he might be seized, chained, and sent to Siberia, or simply killed; and therefore he was on his guard. He asked Eldár, when the latter entered his room, where his murids had been put, and whether their arms had been taken from them, and where the horses were. Eldár reported that the horses were in the Prince's stables; that the men had been placed in a barn; that they retained their arms, and that the interpreter was giving them food and tea.

Hadji Murád shook his head in doubt; and after undressing he said his prayers, and told Eldár to bring him his silver dagger. He then dressed, and, having fastened his belt, sat down with his legs on the divan to await what might befall him.

At four in the afternoon the interpreter came to call him to dine with the Prince.

At dinner he hardly ate anything, except some pilau, to which he helped himself from the very part of the dish from which Mary Vasílevna had helped herself.

"He is afraid we shall poison him," Mary Vasílevna remarked to her husband. "He has helped himself from the place where I took my helping." Then, instantly turning to Hadji Murád, she asked him through the interpreter when he would pray again. Hadji Murád lifted five fingers and pointed to the sun. "Then it will soon be time," and Vorontsóv drew out his watch and pressed a spring. The watch struck four and one quarter. This evidently surprised Hadji Murád, and he asked to hear it again, and to be allowed to look at the watch.

"Voilà l'occasion! Donnez lui la montre," said the Princess to her husband.

Vorontsóv at once offered the watch to Hadji Murád.

The latter placed his hand on his breast and took the watch. Several times he touched the spring, listened, and nodded his head approvingly.

After dinner, Meller-Zakomélsky's aide-de-camp was announced.

The aide-de-camp informed the Prince that the General, having heard of Hadji Murád's arrival, was highly displeased that this had not been reported to him, and required Hadji Murád to be brought to him without delay. Vorontsóv replied that the General's command should be obeyed; and through the interpreter he informed Hadji Murád of these orders, and asked him to go to Meller with him.

When Mary Vasílevna heard what the aide-de-camp had come

about, she at once understood that unpleasantness might arise between her husband and the General, and decided, in spite of all her husband's attempts to dissuade her, to go with him and Hadji Murád.

"*Vous feriez bien mieux de rester—c'est mon affaire, non pas la vôtre . . .*"

"*Vous ne pouvez pas m'empêcher d'aller voir madame la générale!*"

"You could go some other time."

"But I wish to go now!"

There was no help for it, so Vorontsóv agreed; and they all three went.

When they entered, Meller with sombre politeness conducted Mary Vasílevna to his wife, and told his aide-de-camp to show Hadji Murád into the waiting-room, and not to let him out till further orders.

"Please . . ." he said to Vorontsóv, opening the door of his study and letting the Prince enter before him.

Having entered the study, he stopped in front of the Prince and said, without offering him a seat,—

"I am in command here, and therefore all negotiations with the enemy must be carried on through me! Why did you not report to me the fact of Hadji Murád's having come over?"

"An emissary came to me and announced Hadji Murád's wish to capitulate only to me," replied Vorontsóv, growing pale with excitement, expecting some rude expression from the angry general, and at the same time becoming infected with his anger.

"I ask you why I was not informed?"

"I intended to do so, Baron, but . . ."

"You are not to address me as 'Baron,' but as 'Your Excellency'!" And here the Baron's pent-up irritation suddenly broke out, and he uttered all that had long been boiling in his soul.

"I have not served my sovereign twenty-seven years in order that men who began their service yesterday, relying on family connections, should give orders under my very nose about matters that do not concern them!"

"Your Excellency, I request you will not say things that are incorrect!" interrupted Vorontsóv.

"I am saying what is correct, and I won't allow . . ." said the General, still more irritably.

But at that moment Mary Vasílevna entered, rustling with her skirts, and followed by a little modest-looking lady, Meller-Zakomélsky's wife.

"Come, come, Baron! Simon did not wish to displease you," began Mary Vasílevna.

"I am not speaking about that, Princess . . ."

"Well, you know, let's leave all that! . . . You know, 'A bad peace is better than a good quarrel!' . . . Oh dear, what am I saying?" and she laughed.

The angry General capitulated to the enchanting laugh of the beauty. A smile hovered under his moustache.

"I confess I was wrong," said Vorontsóv, "but—"

"Well, and I too got rather carried away," said Meller, and held out his hand to the Prince.

Peace was re-established, and it was decided to leave Hadji Murád for the present at Meller's, and then to send him to the commander of the left flank.

Hadji Murád sat in the next room, and though he did not understand what was said, he understood what it was necessary for him to understand—namely, that they were quarrelling about him, and that his desertion of Shamil was a matter of immense importance to the Russians, and that therefore not only would they not exile him or kill him, but that he would be able to demand much from them. He also understood that though Meller-Zakomélsky was the commanding-officer, he had not as much influence as his subordinate Vorontsóv; and that Vorontsóv was important and Meller-Zakomélsky unimportant; and therefore, when Meller-Zakomélsky sent for him and began to question him, Hadji Murád bore himself proudly and ceremoniously, saying that he had come from the mountains to serve the White Tsar, and would give account only to his Sirdar, meaning the commander-in-chief, Prince Vorontsóv, in Tiflis.

VII

The wounded Avdéev was taken to the hospital—a small wooden building roofed with boards, at the entrance of the fort—and was placed on one of the empty beds in the common ward. There were four patients in the ward: one, ill with typhus and in high fever, another, pale, with dark shadows under his eyes, who had ague and was just expecting another attack, and yawned continually; and two more who had been wounded in a raid three weeks before: one in the hand—he was up—and the other in the shoulder; the latter was sitting on a bed. All of them, except the typhus patient, surrounded and questioned the newcomer, and those who had brought him.

"Sometimes they fire as if it were peas they were spilling over you, and nothing happens . . . and this time only about five shots were fired," related one of the bearers.

"Each gets what fate sends!"

"Oh!" groaned Avdéev loudly, trying to master his pain when they began to place him on the bed; but he stopped groaning when he was on it, and only frowned and moved his feet continually. He held his hands over his wound and looked fixedly before him.

The doctor came, and gave orders to turn the wounded man over, to see whether the bullet had passed out behind.

"What's this?" the doctor asked, pointing to the large white scars that crossed one another on the patient's back and loins.

"That was done long ago, your honour!" replied Avdéev, with a groan.

They were the scars left by the flogging Avdéev had received for the money he drank.

Avdéev was again turned over, and the doctor long probed in his stomach, and found the bullet, but failed to extract it. He put a dressing on the wound, and having stuck plaster over it went away. During the whole time the doctor was probing and bandaging the wound Avdéev lay with clenched teeth and closed eyes, but when the doctor had gone he opened them and looked around as though amazed. His eyes were turned to the other patients and to the surgeon's orderly, but he seemed to see not them, but something else that surprised him.

His friends, Panóv and Serógin, came in; but Avdéev continued to lie in the same position, looking before him with surprise. It was long before he recognised his comrades, though his eyes gazed straight at them.

"I say, Peter, have you no message to send home?" said Panóv.

Avdéev did not answer, though he was looking Panóv in the face.

"I say, haven't you any orders to send home?" again repeated Panóv, touching Avdéev's cold large-boned hand.

Avdéev seemed to come to.

"Ah! . . . Panóv!"

"Yes, here. . . . I've come! Have you nothing for home? Serógin would write a letter."

"Serógin . . ." said Avdéev, moving his eyes with difficulty towards Serógin, "will you write? . . . Well then, write so: 'Your son,' say, 'Peter, has given orders that you should live long. He envied his brother' . . . I told you about that today . . . 'and now he is himself glad. Don't worry him. . . . Let him live. God grant it him. I am glad!' Write that."

Having said this he was long silent, with his eyes fixed on Panóv.

"And did you find your pipe?" he suddenly asked. Panóv did not reply.

"Your pipe . . . your pipe! I mean, have you found it?" Avdéev repeated.

"It was in my bag."

"That's right! . . . Well, and now give me a candle. . . . I am going to die," said Avdéev.

Just then Poltorátsky came in to inquire after his soldier.

"How goes it, my lad! Badly?" said he.

Avdéev closed his eyes and shook his head negatively. His broad-cheeked face was pale and stern. He did not reply, but again said to Panóv,—

"Bring a candle. . . . I am going to die."

A wax taper was placed in his hand, but his fingers would not bend, so it was placed between them, and was held up for him.

Poltorátsky went away, and five minutes later the orderly put his ear to Avdéev's heart and said that all was over.

Avdéev's death was described in the following manner in the report sent to Tiflis,—

"23rd Nov.—Two companies of the Kurín regiment advanced from the fort on a wood-felling expedition. At midday a considerable number of mountaineers suddenly attacked the wood-fellers. The sharp-shooters began to retreat, but the 2nd Company charged with the bayonet and overthrew the mountaineers. In this affair two privates were slightly wounded and one killed. The mountaineers lost about a hundred men killed and wounded.

VIII

On the day Peter Avdéev died in the hospital at Vozdvízhensk, his old father, the wife of the brother in whose place he had enlisted, and that brother's daughter—who was already approaching womanhood and almost of age to get married—were threshing oats on the hard-frozen threshing floor.

The day before, there had been a heavy fall of snow followed towards morning by a severe frost. The old man woke when the cocks were crowing for the third time, and seeing the bright moonlight through the frozen window-panes, got down from the oven-top, put on his boots, his sheepskin coat and cap, and went out to the threshing-floor. Having worked there for a couple of hours, he returned to the hut and awoke his son and the women. When the younger woman and the girl came to the threshing-floor they found it ready swept, a wooden shovel sticking in the dry white snow, and beside it birch brooms with the twigs upwards, and two rows of oat-sheaves laid ears to ears in a long line the whole length of the clean threshing-floor. They choose their flails and started threshing, keeping time with their triple blows. The old man struck powerfully with his heavy flail, breaking the straw; the girl struck the ears from above with measured blows; and his daughter-in-law turned the oats over with her flail.

The moon had set, dawn was breaking, and they were finishing the line of sheaves when Akím, the eldest son, in his sheepskin and cap, joined the threshers.

"What are you lazing about for?" shouted his father to him, pausing in his work and leaning on his flail.

"The horses had to be seen to."

" 'Horses seen to!' " the father repeated, mimicking him. "The old woman will look after them. . . . Take your flail! You're getting too fat, you drunkard!"

"Have you been standing me treat?" muttered the son.

"What?" said the old man, frowning sternly and missing a stroke.

The son silently took a flail, and they began threshing with four flails.

"Trak, tapatam . . . trak, tapatam . . . trak . . ." came down the old man's heavy flail after the three others.

"Why, you've got a nape like a goodly gentleman! . . . Look here, my trousers have hardly anything to hang on!" said the old man, omitting his stroke and only swinging his flail in the air, so as not to get out of time.

They had finished the row, and the women began removing the straw with rakes.

"Peter was a fool to go in your stead. They'd have knocked the nonsense out of you in the army; and he was worth five of such as you at home!"

"That's enough, father," said the daughter-in-law, as she threw aside the binders that had come off the sheaves.

"Yes, feed the six of you, and get no work out of a single one! Peter used to work for two. He was not like . . ."

Along the trodden path from the house came the old man's wife, the frozen snow creaking under the new bark shoes she wore over her tightly-wound woollen leg-bands. The men were shovelling the unwinnowed grain into heaps, the woman and the girl sweeping up what remained.

"The Elder has been, and orders everybody to go and work for the master, carting bricks," said the old woman. "I've got breakfast ready. . . . Come along, won't you?"

"All right. . . . Harness the roan and go," said the old man to Akím, "and you'd better look out that you don't get me into trouble, as you did the other day! . . . One can't help regretting Peter!"

"When he was at home you used to scold him," retorted Akím. "Now he's away you keep nagging at me."

"That shows you deserve it," said his mother in the same angry tones. "You'll never be Peter's equal."

"Well, all right," said the son.

" 'All right,' indeed! You've drunk the meal, and now you say 'all right!' "

"Let bygones be bygones!" said the daughter-in-law.

The disagreements between father and son had begun long ago—almost from the time Peter went as a soldier. Even then the old man felt that he had parted with an eagle for a cuckoo. It is true that according to right—as the old man understood it—a childless man had to go in place of a family man. Akím had four children, and Peter had none; but Peter was a worker like his father, skilful, observant, strong, enduring, and above all, industrious. He was always at work. If he happened to pass by where people were working he lent a helping hand, as his father would have done, and took a turn or two with the scythe, or loaded a cart, or felled a tree, or chopped some wood. The old man regretted his going away, but there was no help for it. Conscription in those days was like death. A soldier was a severed branch; and to think about him at home was to tear one's heart uselessly. Only occasionally, to prick his elder son, the father mentioned him, as he had done that day. But his mother often thought of her younger son, and she had long—for more than a year now—been asking her husband to send Peter a little money, to which the old man made no reply.

The Kúrenkovs were a well-to-do family, and the old man had some savings hidden away; but he would on no account have consented to touch what he had laid by. Now, however, his old woman, having heard him mention their younger son, made up her mind again to ask him to send him at least a rouble after selling the oats. This she did. As soon as the young people had gone to work for the proprietor, and the old folk were left alone together, she persuaded him to send Peter a rouble out of the oats-money.

So when ninety-six bushels of the winnowed oats had been packed on to three sledges, lined with sacking carefully pinned together at the top with wooden skewers, she gave her old man a letter written at her dictation by the church clerk; and the old man promised when he got to town to enclose a rouble, and to send it off to the right address.

The old man, dressed in a new sheepskin with a homespun cloak over it, his legs wrapped round with warm white woollen leg-bands, took the letter, placed it in his wallet, said a prayer, got into the front sledge, and drove to town. His grandson drove in the last sledge. When he reached the town the old man asked the innkeeper to read the letter to him, and he listened to it attentively and approvingly.

In her letter Peter's mother first sent him her blessing, then greetings from everybody, and the news of his godfather's death; and at the end she added that Aksínya (Peter's wife) had not wished to stay with them, but had gone into service, where they heard she was living well and honestly. Then came a reference to that present of a rouble; and finally, in her own words, what the old woman, with tears in her eyes and yielding to her sorrow, had dictated and the church clerk had taken down exactly, word for word:—

"One thing more, my darling child, my sweet dove, my own Peterkin! I have wept my eyes out lamenting for thee, thou light of my eyes. To whom hast thou left me? . . ." At this point the old woman had sobbed and wept, and said: "That will do !" So the words stood in the letter; but it was not fated that Peter should receive the news of his wife's having left home, nor the present of the rouble, nor his mother's last words. The letter with the money in it came back with the announcement that Peter had been killed in the war, defending his Tsar, his Fatherland, and the Orthodox Faith. That is how the army clerk expressed it.

The old woman, when this news reached her, wept for as long as she could spare time, and then set to work again. The very next Sunday she went to church, and had a requiem chanted, and Peter's name entered among those for whose souls prayers were to be said; and she distributed bits of holy bread to all the good people, in memory of Peter the servant of God.

Aksínya, the soldier's widow, also lamented loudly when she heard of her beloved husband's death, with whom she had lived but one short year. She regretted her husband, and her own ruined life; and in her lamentations mentioned Peter's brown locks and his love, and the sadness of her life with her little orphaned Vánka; and bitterly reproached Peter for having had pity on his brother, but none on her— obliged to wander among strangers!

But in the depth of her soul Aksínya was glad of her husband's death.

She was pregnant by the shopman in whose service she was living; and no one would now have a right to scold her, and the shopman could marry her as, when he was persuading her to yield, he had said he would.

IX

Michael Seménovich Vorontsóv, being the son of the Russian ambassador, had been educated in England, and possessed a European education quite exceptional among the higher Russian officials of his day. He was ambitious, gentle, and kind in his manner with inferiors, and a finished courtier with superiors. He did not understand life without power and submission. He had obtained all the highest ranks and decorations, and was looked upon as a clever commander, and even as the conquerer of Napoleon at Krásnoye.

In 1852 he was over seventy, but was still quite fresh, moved briskly, and above all was in full possession of a facile refined and agreeable intellect, which he used to maintain his power and to strengthen and spread his popularity. He possessed large means—his own and his wife's (*née* Countess Branítsky)—and received an enormous salary as viceroy; and he spent a great part of his means on building a palace and laying out a garden on the south coast of the Crimea.

On the evening of 4th December 1852 a courier's *troyka* drew up before his palace in Tiflis. A tired officer, black with dust, whom General Kozlóvsky had sent with the news of Hadji Murád's surrender to the Russians, went stretching the stiffened muscles of his legs past the sentinel, and entered the wide porch. It was six o'clock, and Vorontsóv was just going in to dinner, when he was informed of the arrival of the courier. Vorontsóv received him at once, and was therefore a few minutes late for dinner.

When he entered the drawing-room, the thirty persons invited to dine, sitting beside the Princess Elizabeth Ksavérevna Vorontsóv, or standing in groups by the windows, turned their faces towards him. Vorontsóv was dressed in his usual black military coat, with shoulder-straps but no epaulets, and wore the White Cross of the Order of St. George at his neck.

His clean-shaven, foxlike face smiled pleasantly as, screwing up his eyes, he surveyed the assembly. Entering with quick, soft steps he apologised to the ladies for being late, greeted the men, and approaching the Princess Manana Orbelyáni—a tall, fine, handsome woman of Oriental type about forty-five years of age—he offered her his arm to take her in to dinner. The Princess Elizabeth Ksavérevna Vorontsóv herself gave her arm to a red-haired general with bristly moustaches, who was visiting Tiflis. A Georgian Prince offered his arm to the Princess Vorontsóv's friend, the Countess Choiseuil; Dr. Andréevsky, the aide-de-camp, and others, with ladies or without, followed these first couples. Footmen in livery and knee-breeches drew back and replaced the guests' chairs when they sat down, while the major-domo ceremoniously ladled out steaming soup from a silver tureen.

Vorontsóv took his place in the centre of one side of the long table, and his wife sat opposite, with the General on her right. On the Prince's right sat his lady, the beautiful Orbelyáni; and on his left was a graceful, dark, red-cheeked Georgian woman, glittering with jewels and incessantly smiling.

"*Excellentes, chère amie!*" replied Vorontsóv to his wife's inquiry about what news the courier had brought him. "*Simon a eu de la chance!*" And he began to tell aloud, so that every one could hear, the striking news (for him alone not quite unexpected, because negotiations had long been going on) that the bravest and most famous of Shamil's officers, Hadji Murád, had come over to the Russians, and would in a day or two be brought to Tiflis.

Everybody—even the young aides-de-camp and officials who sat at the far ends of the table, and who had been quietly laughing at something among themselves—became silent and listened.

"And you, General, have you ever met this Hadji Murád?" asked the Princess of her neighbour, the carroty General with the bristly moustaches, when the Prince had finished speaking.

"More than once, Princess."

And the General went on to tell how Hadji Murád, after the mountaineers had captured Gergebel in 1843, had fallen upon General

Pahlen's detachment and killed Colonel Zolotúkhin almost before their very eyes.

Vorontsóv listened to the General and smiled amiably, evidently pleased that the latter had joined in the conversation. But suddenly Vorontsóv's face assumed an absent-minded and depressed expression.

The General, having started talking, had begun to tell of his second encounter with Hadji Murád.

"Why, it was he, if your Excellency will please remember," said the General, "who arranged the ambush that attacked the rescue party in the 'Biscuit' expedition."

"Where?" asked Vorontsóv, screwing up his eyes.

What the brave General spoke of as the "rescue," was the affair in the unfortunate Dargo campaign in which a whole detachment, including Prince Vorontsóv who commanded it, would certainly have perished had it not been rescued by the arrival of fresh troops. Every one knew that the whole Dargo campaign under Vorontsóv's command—in which the Russians lost many killed and wounded and several cannon—had been a shameful affair; and therefore, if any one mentioned it in Vorontsóv's presence, they only did so in the aspect in which Vorontsóv had reported it to the Tsar: as a brilliant achievement of the Russian army. But the word "rescue" plainly indicated that it was not a brilliant victory, but a blunder costing many lives. Everybody understood this, and some pretended not to notice the meaning of the General's words, others nervously waited to see what would follow, while a few exchanged glances and smiled. Only the carroty General with the bristly moustaches noticed nothing, and, carried away by his narrative, quietly replied,—

"At the rescue, your Excellency."

Having started on his favourite theme the General recounted circumstantially how Hadji Murád had so cleverly cut the detachment in two, that if the rescue party had not arrived (he seemed to be particularly fond of repeating the word "rescue") not a man in the division would have escaped, because. . . . The General did not finish his story, for Manana Orbelyáni, having understood what was happening, interrupted him by asking if he had found comfortable quarters in Tiflis. The General, surprised, glanced at everybody all round, and saw his aides-de-camp from the end of the table looking fixedly and significantly at him, and suddenly he understood! Without replying to the Princess's question he frowned, became silent, and began hurriedly eating, without chewing, the delicacy that lay on his plate, both the appearance and taste of which completely mystified him.

Everybody felt uncomfortable, but the discomfort of the situation was relieved by the Georgian Prince—a very stupid man, but an extraordinarily refined and artful flatterer and courtier—who sat on the other side of the Princess Vorontsóv. Without seeming to have noticed anything, he began to relate how Hadji Murád had carried off the widow of Akhmet Khan of Mekhtulí.

"He came into the village at night, seized what he wanted, and galloped off again with the whole party."

"Why did he want that particular woman?" asked the Princess.

"Oh, he was her husband's enemy, and pursued him, but could never once succeed in meeting him right up to the time of his death, so he revenged himself on the widow."

The Princess translated this into French to her old friend the Countess Choiseuil, who sat next to the Georgian Prince.

"*Quelle horreur!*" said the Countess, closing her eyes and shaking her head.

"Oh, no!" said Vorontsóv, smiling. "I have been told that he treated his captive with chivalrous respect and afterwards released her."

"Yes, for a ransom!"

"Well, of course. But, all the same, he acted honourably."

These words of the Prince's set the tone for the further conversation. The courtiers understood that the more importance was attributed to Hadji Murád the better pleased the Prince would be.

"The man's audacity is amazing. A remarkable man!"

"Why, in 1849, he dashed into Temir Khan Shurá, and plundered the shops in broad daylight."

An Armenian sitting at the end of the table, who had been in Temir Khan Shurá at the time, related the particulars of that exploit of Hadji Murád's.

In fact, only Hadji Murád was talked about during the whole dinner.

Everybody in succession praised his courage, his ability, and his magnanimity. Someone mentioned his having ordered twenty-six prisoners to be slain; but that too was met by the usual rejoinder, "What's to be done? *À la guerre, comme à la guerre!*"

"He is a great man."

"Had he been born in Europe he might have been another Napoleon," said the stupid Georgian prince with a gift of flattery.

He knew that every mention of Napoleon was pleasant to Vorontsóv, who wore the White Cross at his neck as a reward for having defeated him.

"Well, not Napoleon, perhaps, but a gallant cavalry general, if you like," said Vorontsóv.

"If not Napoleon, then Murat."*

"And his name is Hadji Murád!"

"Hadji Murád has surrendered, and now there'll be an end to Shamil also," someone remarked.

"They feel that now"—this "now" meant under Vorontsóv—"they can't hold out," remarked another.

"*Tout cela est grâce à vous!*" said Manana Orbelyáni.

Prince Vorontsóv tried to moderate the waves of flattery which began to flow over him. Still, it was pleasant, and in the best of spirits he led his lady back into the drawing-room.

After dinner, when coffee was being served in the drawing-room, the Prince was particularly amiable to everybody, and going up to the General with the red bristly moustaches, he tried to appear not to have noticed his blunder.

Having made a round of the visitors, he sat down to the card table. He only played the old-fashioned game of ombre. The Prince's partners were the Georgian Prince, an Armenian General (who had learnt the game of ombre from Prince Vorontsóv's valet, and the fourth was Dr. Andréevsky, a man remarkable for the great influence he exercised.

Placing beside him his gold snuff-box, with a portrait of Alexander I. on the lid, the Prince tore open a pack of highly-glazed cards, and was going to spread them out when his Italian valet, Giovanni, brought him a letter on a silver tray.

"Another courier, your Excellency."

Vorontsóv laid down the cards, excused himself, opened the letter, and began to read.

---

*Pun on the name of Napoleon's marshal Joachim Murat (1767–1815).

The letter was from his son, who described Hadji Murád's surrender, and his own encounter with Meller-Zakomélsky.

The Princess came up and inquired what their son had written.

"It's all about the same matter. . . . *Il a eu quelques désagréments avec le commandant de la place. Simon a eu tort.* . . . But 'All's well that ends well,'" he added in English, handing the letter to his wife; and turning to his respectfully waiting partners, he asked them to draw cards.

When the first round had been dealt, Vorontsóv did what he was in the habit of doing when in a particularly pleasant mood: with his white, wrinkled old hand he took out a pinch of French snuff, carried it up to his nose, and released it.

X

When, next day, Hadji Murád appeared at the Prince's palace, the waiting-room was already full of people. Yesterday's General with the bristly moustaches was there in full uniform, with all his decorations, having come to take leave. There was the commander of a regiment who was in danger of being court-martialled for misappropriating commissariat money; and there was a rich Armenian (patronised by Doctor Andréevsky) who wanted to get from the Government a renewal of his monopoly for the sale of vódka. There, dressed in black, was the widow of an officer who had been killed in action. She had come to ask for a pension, or for free education for her children. There was a ruined Georgian Prince in a magnificent Georgian costume, who was trying to obtain for himself some confiscated church property. There was an official with a large roll of paper containing a new plan for subjugating the Caucasus. There was also a Khan, who had come solely to be able to tell his people at home that he had called on the Prince.

They all waited their turn, and were one by one shown into the Prince's cabinet and out again by the aide-de-camp, a handsome, fair-haired youth.

When Hadji Murád entered the waiting-room with his brisk

though limping step all eyes were turned towards him, and he heard his name whispered from various parts of the room.

He was dressed in a long white Circassian coat over a brown *beshmét* trimmed round the collar with fine silver lace. He wore black leggings and soft shoes of the same colour, which were stretched over his instep as tight as gloves. On his head he wore a high cap, draped turban-fashion—that same turban for which, on the denunciation of Akhmet Khan, he had been arrested by General Klügenau, and which had been the cause of his going over to Shamil.

Hadji Murád stepped briskly across the parquet floor of the waiting-room, his whole slender figure swaying slightly in consequence of his lameness in one leg, which was shorter than the other. His eyes, set far apart, looked calmly before him and seemed to see no one.

The handsome aide-de-camp, having greeted him, asked him to take a seat while he went to announce him to the Prince; but Hadji Murád declined to sit down, and, putting his hand on his dagger, stood with one foot advanced, looking contemptuously at all those present.

The Prince's interpreter, Prince Tarkhánov, approached Hadji Murád and spoke to him. Hadji Murád answered abruptly and unwillingly. A Kumýk Prince, who was there to lodge a complaint against a police official, came out of the Prince's room, and then the aide-de-camp called Hadji Murád, led him to the door of the cabinet, and showed him in.

Vorontsóv received Hadji Murád standing beside his table. The white old face of the commander-in-chief did not wear yesterday's smile, but was rather stern and solemn.

On entering the large room, with its enormous table and great windows with green venetian blinds, Hadji Murád placed his small sunburnt hands on that part of his chest where the front of his white coat overlapped, and, having lowered his eyes, began without hurrying to speak in Tartar distinctly and respectfully, using the Kumýk dialect, which he spoke well.

"I put myself under the powerful protection of the great Tsar and of yourself," said he, "and promise to serve the White Tsar in faith and truth to the last drop of my blood, and I hope to be useful to you in the war with Shamil, who is my enemy and yours."

Having heard the interpreter out, Vorontsóv glanced at Hadji Murád, and Hadji Murád glanced at Vorontsóv.

The eyes of the two men met, and expressed to each other much that could not have been put into words, and that was not at all what the interpreter said. Without words they told each other the whole truth. Vorontsóv's eyes said that he did not believe a single word Hadji Murád was saying, and that he knew he was and always would be an enemy to everything Russian, and had surrendered only because he was obliged to. Hadji Murád understood this, and yet continued to give assurances of his fidelity. His eyes said, "That old man ought to be thinking of his death, and not of war; but though old he is cunning, and I must be careful." Vorontsóv understood this also, but nevertheless he spoke to Hadji Murád in the way he considered necessary for the success of the war.

"Tell him," said Vorontsóv, "that our sovereign is as merciful as he is mighty, and will probably at my request pardon him and take him into his service. . . . Have you told him?" he asked, looking at Hadji Murád. . . . "Until I receive my master's gracious decision, tell him I take it on myself to receive him and to make his sojourn among us pleasant."

Hadji Murád again pressed his hands to the centre of his chest, and began to say something with animation.

"He says," the interpreter translated, "that before, when he governed Avaria in 1839, he served the Russians faithfully, and would never have deserted them had his enemy, Akhmet Khan, wishing to ruin him, not calumniated him to General Klügenau."

"I know, I know," said Vorontsóv (though, if he had ever known, he had long forgotten it). "I know," said he, sitting down and motioning Hadji Murád to the divan that stood beside the wall. But Hadji Murád did not sit down. Shrugging his powerful shoulders as a sign that he could not make up his mind to sit in the presence of so important a man, he went on, addressing the interpreter,—

"Akhmet Khan and Shamil are both my enemies. Tell the Prince that Akhmet Khan is dead, and I cannot revenge myself on him; but Shamil lives, and I will not die without taking vengeance on him," said he, knitting his brows and tightly closing his mouth.

"Yes, yes; but how does he want to revenge himself on Shamil?" said Vorontsóv quietly to the interpreter. "And tell him he may sit down."

Hadji Murád again declined to sit down; and, in answer to the question, replied that his object in coming over to the Russians was to help them to destroy Shamil.

"Very well, very well," said Vorontsóv; "but what exactly does he wish to do? . . . Sit down, sit down!"

Hadji Murád sat down, and said that if only they would send him to the Lesghian line, and would give him an army, he would guarantee to raise the whole of Daghestan, and Shamil would then be unable to hold out.

"That would be excellent. . . . I'll think it over," said Vorontsóv.

The interpreter translated Vorontsóv's words to Hadji Murád.

Hadji Murád pondered.

"Tell the Sirdar one thing more," Hadji Murád began again: "That my family are in the hands of my enemy, and that as long as they are in the mountains I am bound, and cannot serve him. Shamil would kill my wife and my mother and my children if I went openly against him. Let the Prince first exchange my family for the prisoners he has, and then I will destroy Shamil or die!"

"All right, all right," said Vorontsóv. "I will think it over. . . . Now let him go to the chief of the staff, and explain to him in detail his position, intentions, and wishes."

Thus ended the first interview between Hadji Murád and Vorontsóv.

That evening, at the new theatre, which was decorated in Oriental style, an Italian opera was performed. Vorontsóv was in his box when the striking figure of the limping Hadji Murád wearing a turban appeared in the stalls. He came in with Lóris-Mélikov, Vorontsóv's aide-de-camp, in whose charge he was placed, and took a seat in the front row. Having sat through the first act with Oriental, Mohammedan dignity, expressing no pleasure, but only obvious indifference, he rose and looking calmly round at the audience went out, drawing to himself everybody's attention.

The next day was Monday, and there was the usual evening party at the Vorontsóvs'. In the large brightly-lighted hall a band was playing, hidden among trees. Young and not very young women, in dresses displaying their bare necks arms and breasts, turned round and round in the embrace of men in bright uniforms. At the buffet footmen in red swallowtail coats and wearing shoes and knee-breeches, poured out champagne and served sweetmeats to the ladies. The "Sirdar's" wife also, in spite of her age, went about half-dressed among the visitors, affably smiling, and through the interpreter said a few amiable words to Hadji Murád, who glanced at the visitors with the same indifference he had shown yesterday in the theatre. After the hostess, other half-naked women came up to him, and all of them shamelessly stood before him and smilingly asked him the same question: How he liked what he saw? Vorontsóv himself, wearing gold epaulets and gold shoulder-knots, with his white cross and ribbon at his neck, came up and asked him the same question, evidently feeling sure, like all the others, that Hadji Murád could not help being pleased at what he saw. Hadji Murád replied to Vorontsóv, as he had replied to them all, that among his people nothing of the kind was done, without expressing an opinion as to whether it was good or bad that it was so.

Here at the ball Hadji Murád tried to speak to Vorontsóv about buying out his family; but Vorontsóv, pretending he had not heard him, walked away; and Lóris-Mélikov afterwards told Hadji Murád that this was not the place to talk about business.

When it struck eleven Hadji Murád, having made sure of the time by the watch the Vorontsóvs had given him, asked Lóris-Mélikov whether he might now leave. Lóris-Mélikov said he might, though it would be better to stay. In spite of this Hadji Murád did not stay, but drove in the phaeton placed at his disposal to the quarters that had been assigned to him.

XI

On the fifth day of Hadji Murád's stay in Tiflis, Lóris-Mélikov, the Viceroy's aide-de-camp, came to see him at the latter's command.

"My head and my hands are glad to serve the Sirdar," said Hadji Murád with his usual diplomatic expression, bowing his head and putting his hands to his chest. "Command me!" said he, looking amiably into Lóris-Mélikov's face.

Lóris-Mélikov sat down in an arm-chair placed by the table, and Hadji Murád sank on to a low divan opposite, and resting his hands on his knees, bowed his head and listened attentively to what the other said to him.

Lóris-Mélikov, who spoke Tartar fluently, told him that though the

Prince knew about his past life, he yet wanted to hear the whole story from himself.

"Tell it me, and I will write it down and translate it into Russian, and the Prince will send it to the Emperor."

Hadji Murád remained silent for a while (he never interrupted any one, but always waited to see whether his collocutor had not something more to say). Then he raised his head, shook back his cap, and smiled the peculiar childlike smile that had captivated Mary Vasílevna.

"I can do that," said he, evidently flattered by the thought that his story would be read by the Emperor.

"Thou must tell me" (nobody is addressed as "you" in Tartar) "everything, deliberately, from the beginning," said Lóris-Mélikov, drawing a notebook from his pocket.

"I can do that, only there is much—very much—to tell! Many events have happened!" said Hadji Murád.

"If thou canst not do it all in one day, thou wilt finish it another time," said Lóris-Mélikov.

"Shall I begin at the beginning?"

"Yes, at the very beginning . . . where thou wast born, and where thou didst live."

Hadji Murád's head sank, and he sat in that position for a long time. Then he took a stick that lay beside the divan, drew a little knife with ivory gold-inlaid handle, sharp as a razor, from under his dagger, and started whittling the stick with it and speaking at the same time.

"Write: Born in Tselméss, a small *aoul*, 'the size of an ass's head,' as we in the mountains say," he began. "Not far from it, about two cannon-shots, lies Khunzákh, where the Khans lived. Our family was closely connected with them.

"My mother, when my eldest brother Osman was born, nursed the eldest Khan, Abu Nutsal Khan. Then she nursed the second son of the Khan, Umma Khan, and reared him; but Akhmet, my second brother, died; and when I was born and the Khansha bore Bulách Khan, my mother would not go as wet-nurse again. My father ordered her to, but she would not. She said: 'I should again kill my own son; and I will not go.' Then my father, who was passionate, struck her with a dagger, and would have killed her had they not rescued her from him. So she did not give me up, and later on she composed a song . . . but I need not tell that.

"Well, so my mother did not go as nurse," he said, with a jerk of his head, "and the Khansha took another nurse, but still remained fond of my mother; and mother used to take us children to the Khansha's palace, and we played with her children, and she was fond of us.

"There were three young Khans: Abu Nutsal Khan, my brother Osman's foster-brother; Umma Khan, my own sworn brother; and Bulách Khan, the youngest—whom Shamil threw over the precipice. But that happened later.

"I was about sixteen when *murids* began to visit the *aouls*. They beat the stones with wooden scimitars, and cried, 'Muslims, *Ghazavát!*'* The Chechens all went over to Muridism, and the Avars began to go over, too. I was then living in the palace like a brother of the Khans. I could do as I liked, and I became rich. I had horses and weapons and money. I lived for pleasure and had no care, and went on like that till the time when Kazi-Mulla, the Imám, was killed and Hamzád succeeded him. Hamzád sent envoys to the Khans to say that if they did not join the *Ghazavát* he would destroy Khunzákh.

"This needed consideration. The Khans feared the Russians, but were also afraid to join in the Holy War. The old Khansha sent me with her second son, Umma Khan, to Tiflis, to ask the Russian commander-in-chief for help against Hamzád. The commander-in-chief at Tiflis was Baron Rosen. He did not receive either me or Umma Khan. He sent word that he would help us, but did nothing. Only his officers came riding to us and played cards with Umma Khan. They made him drunk with wine, and took him to bad places; and he lost all he had to them at cards. His body was as strong as a bull's, and he was as brave as a lion, but his soul was weak as water. He would have gambled away his last horses and weapons if I had not made him come away.

"After visiting Tiflis my ideas changed, and I advised the old Khansha and the Khans to join the *Ghazavát*. . . ."

"What made you change your mind?" asked Lóris-Mélikov. "Were you not pleased with the Russians?"

---

*Uprising, military campaign, or struggle (Tatar); used here as a call to arms.

Hadji Murád paused.

"No, I was not pleased," he answered decidedly, closing his eyes. "And there was also another reason why I wished to join the *Ghazavát*."

"What was that?"

"Why, near Tselméss the Khan and I encountered three murids, two of whom escaped, but the third one I shot with my pistol.

"He was still alive when I approached to take his weapons. He looked up at me, and said, 'Thou hast killed me. . . . I am happy; but thou art a Muslim, young and strong. Join the *Ghazavát*! God wills it!'"

"And did you join it?"

"I did not, but it made me think," said Hadji Murád, and he went on with his tale.

"When Hamzád approached Khunzákh we sent our Elders to him to say that we would agree to join the *Ghazavát* if the Imám would send a learned man to us to explain it to us. Hamzád had our Elders' moustaches shaved off, their nostrils pierced, and cakes hung to their noses; and in that condition he sent them back to us.

"The Elders brought word that Hamzád was ready to send a Sheik to teach us the *Ghazavát*, but only if the Khansha sent him her youngest son as a hostage. She took him at his word, and sent her youngest son, Bulách Khan. Hamzád received him well, and sent to invite the two elder brothers also. He sent word that he wished to serve the Khans as his father had served their father. . . . The Khansha was a weak, stupid and conceited woman, as all women are when they are not under control. She was afraid to send away both sons, and sent only Umma Khan. I went with him. We were met by murids about a mile before we arrived, and they sang and shot and caracoled around us; and when we drew near, Hamzád came out of his tent and went up to Umma Khan's stirrup and received him as a Khan. He said,—

"'I have not done any harm to thy family, and do not wish to do any. Only do not kill me, and do not prevent my bringing the people over to the *Ghazavát*, and I will serve you with my whole army, as my father served your father! Let me live in your house, and I will help you with my advice, and you shall do as you like!'

"Umma Khan was slow of speech. He did not know how to reply, and remained silent. Then I said that if this was so, let Hamzád come to Khunzákh, and the Khansha and the Khans would receive him with honour. . . . But I was not allowed to finish—and here I first encountered Shamil, who was beside the Imám. He said to me,—

" 'Thou hast not been asked. . . . It was the Khan!'

"I was silent, and Hamzád led Umma Khan into his tent. Afterwards Hamzád called me and ordered me to go to Khunzákh with his envoys. I went. The envoys began persuading the Khansha to send her eldest son also to Hamzád. I saw there was treachery, and told her not to send him; but a woman has as much sense in her head as an egg has hair. She ordered her son to go. Abu Nutsal Khan did not wish to. Then she said, 'I see thou art afraid!' Like a bee, she knew where to sting him most painfully. Abu Nutsal Khan flushed, and did not speak to her any more, but ordered his horse to be saddled. I went with him.

"Hamzád met us with even greater honour than he had shown Umma Khan. He himself rode out two rifle-shot lengths down the hill to meet us. A large party of horsemen with their banners followed him, and they too sang, shot, and caracoled.

"When we reached the camp, Hamzád led the Khan into his tent, and I remained with the horses. . . .

"I was some way down the hill when I heard shots fired in Hamzád's tent. I ran there, and saw Umma Khan lying prone in a pool of blood, and Abu Nutsal was fighting the murids. One of his cheeks had been hacked off, and hung down. He supported it with one hand, and with the other stabbed with his dagger at all who came near him. I saw him strike down Hamzád's brother, and aim a blow at another man; but then the murids fired at him and he fell."

Hadji Murád stopped, and his sunburnt face flushed a dark red, and his eyes became bloodshot.

"I was seized with fear, and ran away."

"Really? . . . I thought thou never wast afraid," said Lóris-Mélikov.

"Never after that. . . . Since then I have always remembered that shame, and when I recalled it I feared nothing!"

XII

"But enough! It is time for me to pray," said Hadji Murád, drawing from an inner breast-pocket of his Circassian coat Vorontsóv's repeater watch and carefully pressing the spring. The repeater struck twelve and a quarter. Hadji Murád listened with his head on one side, repressing a childlike smile.

"*Kunák* Vorontsóv's present," he said, smiling.

"It is a good watch," said Lóris-Mélikov. "Well then, go thou and pray, and I will wait."

"*Yakshí.* Very well," said Hadji Murád, and went to his bedroom.

Left by himself, Lóris-Mélikov wrote down in his notebook the chief things Hadji Murád had related; and then lighting a cigarette, began to pace up and down the room. On reaching the door opposite the bedroom, he heard animated voices speaking rapidly in Tartar. He guessed that the speakers were Hadji Murád's *murids*, and, opening the door, he went in to them.

The room was impregnated with that special leathery acid smell peculiar to the mountaineers. On a *búrka* spread out on the floor sat the one-eyed red-haired Gamzálo, in a tattered greasy *beshmét*, plaiting a bridle. He was saying something excitedly, speaking in a hoarse voice; but when Lóris-Mélikov entered he immediately became silent, and continued his work without paying any attention to him.

In front of Gamzálo stood the merry Khan Mahomá, showing his white teeth, his black lashless eyes glittering, saying something over and over again. The handsome Eldár, his sleeves turned up on his strong arms, was polishing the girths of a saddle suspended from a nail. Khanéfi, the principal worker and manager of the household, was not there; he was cooking their dinner in the kitchen.

"What were you disputing about?" asked Lóris-Mélikov, after greeting them.

"Why, he keeps on praising Shamil," said Khan Mahomá, giving his hand to Lóris-Mélikov. "He says Shamil is a great man, learned, holy, and a *dzhigit*."

"How is it that he has left him and still praises him?"

"He has left him, and still praises him," repeated Khan Mahomá, his teeth showing and his eyes glittering.

"And does he really consider him a saint?" asked Lóris-Mélikov.

"If he were not a saint the people would not listen to him," said Gamzálo rapidly.

"Shamil is no saint, but Mansur was!" replied Khan Mahomá. "He was a real saint. When he was Imám the people were quite different. He used to ride through the *aouls*, and the people used to come out and kiss the hem of his coat and confess their sins and vow to do no evil. Then all the people—so the old men say—lived like saints: not drinking, nor smoking, nor neglecting their prayers, and forgave one another their sins, even when blood had been spilt. If any one then found money or anything, he tied it to a stake and set it up by the roadside. In those days God gave the people success in everything—not as now."

"In the mountains they don't smoke or drink now," said Gamzálo.

"Your Shamil is a *lámorey*," said Khan Mahomá, winking at Lóris-Mélikov. (*Lámorey* was a contemptuous term for a mountaineer.)

"Yes, *lámorey* means mountaineer," replied Gamzálo. "It is in the mountains that the eagles dwell."

"Smart fellow. Well hit!" said Khan Mahomá with a grin, pleased at his adversary's apt retort.

Seeing the silver cigarette-case in Lóris-Mélikov's hand, Khan Mahomá asked for a cigarette; and when Lóris-Mélikov remarked that they were forbidden to smoke, he winked with one eye and jerking his head in the direction of Hadji Murád's bedroom replied that they could do it as long as they were not seen. He at once began smoking— not inhaling—and pouting his red lips awkwardly as he blew out the smoke.

"That is wrong!" said Gamzálo severely, and left the room for a time.

Khan Mahomá winked after him, and, while smoking, asked Lóris-Mélikov where he could best buy a silk *beshmét* and a white cap.

"Why; hast thou so much money?"

"I have enough," replied Khan Mahomá with a wink.

"Ask him where he got the money," said Eldár, turning his handsome smiling face towards Lóris-Mélikov.

"Oh, I won it!" said Khan Mahomá quickly; and related how, walking in Tiflis the day before, he had come upon a group of men— Russians and Armenians—playing at *orlyánka* (a kind of heads-and-tails). The stake was a large one: three gold pieces and much silver. Khan Mahomá at once saw what the game consisted in, and, jingling the coppers he had in his pocket, he went up to the players and said he would stake the whole amount.

"How couldst thou do it? Hadst thou so much?" asked Lóris-Mélikov.

"I had only twelve kopeks," said Khan Mahomá, grinning.

"Well, but if thou hadst lost?"

"Why, look here!" said Khan Mahomá, pointing to his pistol.

"Wouldst thou have given that?"

"Why give it? I should have run away, and if any one had tried to stop me I should have killed him—that's all!"

"Well, and didst thou win?"

"Aye, I won it all, and went away!"

Lóris-Mélikov quite understood what sort of men Khan Mahomá and Eldár were. Khan Mahomá was a merry fellow, careless and ready for any spree. He did not know what to do with his superfluous vitality. He was always gay and reckless, and played with his own and other people's lives. For the sake of that sport with life, he had now come over to the Russians, and for the same sport he might go back to Shamil tomorrow.

Eldár was also quite easy to understand. He was a man entirely devoted to his murshíd; calm, strong, and firm.

The red-haired Gamzálo was the only one Lóris-Mélikov did not understand. He saw that that man was not only loyal to Shamil, but felt an insuperable aversion contempt repugnance and hatred for all Russians; and Lóris-Mélikov could therefore not understand why he had come over to the Russians. It occurred to him that, as some of the higher officials suspected, Hadji Murád's surrender, and his tales of hatred against Shamil, might be a fraud; and that perhaps he had surrendered only to spy out the Russians' weak spots, that—after escaping back to the mountains—he might be able to direct his forces accordingly. Gamzálo's whole person strengthened this suspicion.

"The others, and Hadji Murád himself, know how to hide their intentions; but this one betrays them by his open hatred," thought he.

Lóris-Mélikov tried to speak to him. He asked whether he did not feel dull. "No, I don't!" he growled hoarsely, without stopping his work, and he glanced at Lóris-Mélikov out of the corner of his one eye. He replied to all Lóris-Mélikov's other questions in a similar manner.

While Lóris-Mélikov was in the room, Hadji Murád's fourth murid, the Avar Khanéfi, came in; a man with a hairy face and neck, and a vaulted chest as rough as though overgrown with moss. He was strong, and a hard worker; always engrossed in his duties, and, like Eldár, unquestionably obedient to his master.

When he entered the room to fetch some rice, Lóris-Mélikov stopped him and asked where he came from, and how long he had been with Hadji Murád.

"Five years," replied Khanéfi. "I come from the same *aoul* as he. My father killed his uncle, and they wished to kill me," he said calmly, looking from beneath his joined eyebrows straight into Lóris-Mélikov's face. "Then I asked them to adopt me as a brother."

"What do you mean by 'adopt as a brother?' "

"I did not shave my head nor cut my nails for two months, and then I came to them. They let me in to Patimát, his mother, and she gave me the breast and I became his brother."

Hadji Murád's voice could be heard from the next room, and Eldár, immediately answering his call, promptly wiped his hands and went with large strides into the drawing-room.

"He asks thee to come," said he, coming back.

Lóris-Mélikov gave another cigarette to the merry Khan Mahomá, and went into the drawing-room.

XIII

W hen Lóris-Mélikov entered the drawing-room, Hadji Murád received him with a bright face.

"Well, shall I continue?" he asked, sitting down comfortably on the divan.

"Yes, certainly," said Lóris-Mélikov. "I have been in to have a talk with thy henchmen. . . . One is a jolly fellow!" he added.

"Yes, Khan Mahomá is a frivolous fellow," said Hadji Murád.

"I liked the young handsome one."

"Ah, that's Eldár. He's young, but firm—made of iron!"

They were silent for a while.

"So I am to go on?"

"Yes, yes!"

"I told thee how the Khans were killed. . . . Well, having killed them, Hamzád rode into Khunzákh and took up his quarters in their palace. The Khansha was the only one of the family left alive. Hamzád sent for her. She reproached him, so he winked to his murid, Aseldár, who struck her from behind and killed her."

"Why did he kill her?" asked Lóris-Mélikov.

"What could he do? . . . Where the fore legs have gone, the hind legs must follow! He killed off the whole family. Shamil killed the youngest son—threw him over a precipice. . . .

"Then the whole of Avaria surrendered to Hamzád. But my brother and I would not surrender. We wanted his blood for the blood of the Khans. We pretended to yield, but our only thought was how to get his blood. We consulted our grandfather, and decided to await the time when he would come out of his palace, and then to kill him from an ambush. Someone overheard us and told Hamzád, who sent for grandfather, and said, 'Mind, if it be true that thy grandsons are planning evil against me, thou and they shall hang from one rafter. I do God's work, and cannot be hindered. . . . Go, and remember what I have said!'

"Our grandfather came home and told us.

"Then we decided not to wait, but to do the deed on the first day of the feast in the mosque. Our comrades would not take part in it, but my brother and I remained firm.

"We took two pistols each, put on our búrkas, and went to the mosque. Hamzád entered the mosque with thirty murids. They all had drawn swords in their hands. Aseldár, his favourite murid (the one who had cut off the head of the Khansha) saw us, shouted to us to take off our búrkas, and came towards me. I had my dagger in my hand, and I killed him with it and rushed at Hamzád; but my brother Osman had already shot him. He was still alive, and rushed at my brother dagger in hand, but I gave him a finishing blow on the head. There were thirty murids, and we were only two. They killed my brother Osman, but I kept them at bay, leapt through the window, and escaped.

"When it was known that Hamzád had been killed, all the people rose. The murids fled; and those of them who did not flee were killed."

Hadji Murád paused, and breathed heavily.

"That was all very well," he continued, "but afterwards everything was spoilt.

"Shamil succeeded Hamzád. He sent envoys to me to say that I should join him in attacking the Russians, and that if I refused he would destroy Khunzákh and kill me.

"I answered that I would not join him, and would not let him come to me. . . ."

"Why didst thou not go with him?" asked Lóris-Mélikov.

Hadji Murád frowned, and did not reply at once.

"I could not. The blood of my brother Osman and of Abu Nutsal Khan was on his hands. I did not go to him. General Rosen sent me an officer's commission, and ordered me to govern Avaria. All this would have been well, but that Rosen appointed as Khan of Kazi-Kumúkh, first Mahómet-Murza, and afterwards Akhmet Khan, who hated me. He had been trying to get the Khansha's daughter, Sultanetta, in marriage for his son, but she would not give her to him, and he believed me to be the cause of this. . . . Yes, Akhmet Khan hated me and sent his henchmen to kill me, but I escaped from them. Then he calumniated me to General Klügenau. He said that I told the Avars not to supply wood to the Russian soldiers; and he also said that I had donned a turban—this one—" and Hadji Murád touched his turban— "and that this meant that I had gone over to Shamil. The General did not believe him, and gave orders that I should not be touched. But when the General went to Tiflis, Akhmet Khan did as he pleased. He sent a company of soldiers to seize me, put me in chains, and tied me to a cannon.

"So they kept me six days," he continued. "On the seventh day they untied me and started to take me to Temir-Khan-Shurá. Forty soldiers with loaded guns had me in charge. My hands were tied, and I knew that they had orders to kill me if I tried to escape.

"As we approached Mansooha the path became narrow, and on the right was an abyss about a hundred and twenty yards deep. I went to the right—to the very edge. A soldier wanted to stop me, but I jumped down and pulled him with me. He was killed outright, but I, as you see, remained alive.

"Ribs, head, arms, and leg—all were broken! I tried to crawl, but grew giddy and fell asleep. I awoke, wet with blood. A shepherd saw me, and called some people who carried me to an *aoul*. My ribs and head healed, and my leg too, only it has remained short," and Hadji Murád stretched out his crooked leg. "It still serves me, however, and that is well," said he.

"The people heard the news, and began coming to me. I recovered, and went to Tselméss. The Avars again called on me to rule over them," said Hadji Murád, with tranquil, confident pride, "and I agreed."

He quickly rose, and taking a portfolio out of a saddle-bag, drew out two discoloured letters and handed one of them to Lóris-Mélikov. They were from General Klügenau. Lóris-Mélikov read the first letter, which was as follows,—

"Lieutenant Hadji Murád, thou hast served under me, and I was satisfied with thee, and considered thee a good man.

"Recently Akhmet Khan informed me that thou art a traitor, that thou hast donned a turban, and hast intercourse with Shamil, and that thou hast taught the people to disobey the Russian Government. I ordered thee to be arrested and brought before me, but thou fledst. I do not know whether this is for thy good or not, as I do not know whether thou art guilty or not.

"Now hear me. If thy conscience is pure, if thou art not guilty in anything towards the great Tsar, come to me; fear no one. I am thy defender. The Khan can do nothing to thee; he is himself under my command, so thou hast nothing to fear."

Klügenau added that he always kept his word and was just, and he again exhorted Hadji Murád to appear before him.

When Lóris-Mélikov had read this letter, Hadji Murád, before handing him the second one, told him what he had written in reply to the first.

"I wrote that I wore a turban, not for Shamil's sake, but for my soul's salvation; that I neither wished nor could go over to Shamil, because he was the cause of my father's, my brothers', and my relations' deaths; but that I could not join the Russians because I had been dishonoured by them. (In Khunzákh, while I was bound, a scoundrel sh—on me; and I could not join your people until that man was killed.) But, above all, I feared that liar, Akhmet Khan.

"Then the General sent me this letter," said Hadji Murád, handing Lóris-Mélikov the other discoloured paper.

"Thou hast answered my first letter, and I thank thee," read Lóris-

Mélikov. "Thou writest that thou art not afraid to return, but that the insult done thee by a certain Giaour* prevents it; but I assure thee that the Russian law is just, and that thou shalt see him who dared to offend thee punished before thine eyes. I have already given orders to investigate the matter.

"Hear me, Hadji Murád! I have a right to be displeased with thee for not trusting me and my honour; but I forgive thee, for I know how suspicious mountaineers are in general. If thy conscience is pure, if thou hast put on a turban only for thy soul's salvation, then thou art right, and mayst look me and the Russian Government boldly in the eyes. He who dishonoured thee shall, I assure thee, be punished; and thy property shall be restored to thee, and thou shalt see and know what Russian law is. And besides, we Russians look at things differently, and thou has not sunk in our eyes because some scoundrel has dishonoured thee.

"I myself have consented to the Gimrints† wearing turbans; and I regard their actions in the right light; and therefore I repeat that thou hast nothing to fear. Come to me with the man by whom I am sending thee this letter. He is faithful to me, and is not the slave of thy enemies but is the friend of a man who enjoys the special favour of the Government."

Further on Klügenau again tried to persuade Hadji Murád to come over to him.

"I did not believe him," said Hadji Murád when Lóris-Mélikov had finished reading, "and did not go to Klügenau. The chief thing for me was to revenge myself on Akhmet Khan; and that I could not do through the Russians. Then Akhmet Khan surrounded Tselméss, and wanted to take me or kill me. I had too few men, and could not drive him off; and just then came an envoy with a letter from Shamil, promising to help me to defeat and kill Akhmet Khan, and making me ruler over the whole of Avaria. I considered the matter for a long time, and then went over to Shamil; and from that time have fought the Russians continually."

Here Hadji Murád related all his military exploits, of which there were very many, and some of which were already familiar to Lóris-Mélikov. All his campaigns and raids had been remarkable for the

*Infidel.
†People from Gimry, the Avar village where Shamil was born.

extraordinary rapidity of his movements and the boldness of his attacks, which were always crowned with success.

"There never was any friendship between me and Shamil," said Hadji Murád at the end of his story, "but he feared me and needed me. But it so happened that I was asked who should be Imám after Shamil, and I replied: 'He will be Imám whose sword is sharpest!'

"This was told to Shamil, and he wanted to get rid of me. He sent me into Tabasarán. I went, and captured a thousand sheep and three hundred horses; but he said I had not done the right thing, and dismissed me from being *Naïb*, and ordered me to send him all the money. I sent him a thousand gold pieces. He sent his *murids*, and they took from me all my property. He demanded that I should go to him; but I knew he wanted to kill me, and I did not go. Then he sent to take me. I resisted, and went over to Vorontsóv. Only I did not take my family. My mother, my wives, and my son are in his hands. Tell the Sirdar that as long as my family is in Shamil's power, I can do nothing."

"I will tell him," said Lóris-Mélikov.

"Take pains, do try! . . . What is mine is thine, only help me with the Prince! I am tied up, and the end of the rope is in Shamil's hands," said Hadji Murád, concluding his story.

XIV

On 20th December Vorontsóv wrote as follows to Chernyshóv, the Minister of War. The letter was in French,—

"I did not write to you by the last post, dear Prince, as I wished first to decide what we should do with Hadji Murád, and for the last two or three days I have not been feeling quite well.

"In my last letter I informed you of Hadji Murád's arrival here. He reached Tiflis on the 8th, and next day I made his acquaintance; and during the following seven or eight days I have spoken to him and have considered what use we can make of him in the future, and especially what we are to do with him at present; for he is much concerned about the fate of his family, and with every appearance of perfect frankness says that while they are in Shamil's hands he is paralysed and cannot render us any service, nor show his gratitude for the friendly reception and forgiveness we have extended to him.

"His uncertainty about those dear to him makes him feverish; and the persons I have appointed to live with him assure me that he does not sleep at night, hardly eats anything, prays continually, and asks only to be allowed to ride out accompanied by several Cossacks—the sole recreation and exercise possible for him, and made necessary to him by lifelong habit. Every day he comes to me to know whether I have any news of his family, and to ask me to have all the prisoners in our hands collected and offered to Shamil in exchange for them. He would also give a little money. There are people who would let him have some for the purpose. He keeps repeating to me: 'Save my family, and then give me a chance to serve you' (preferably, in his opinion, on the Lesgian line) 'and if within a month I do not render you great service, punish me as you think fit.' I reply that to me all this appears very just; and that many persons among us would even not trust him so long as his family remains in the mountains and are not in our hands as hostages; and that I will do everything possible to collect the prisoners on our frontier; that I have no power under our laws to give him money for the ransom of his family in addition to the sum he may himself be able to raise, but that I may perhaps find some other means of helping him. After that I told him frankly that in my opinion Shamil would not in any case give up the family, and that Shamil might tell him so straight out and promise him a full pardon and his former posts, but threaten, if Hadji Murád did not return, to kill his mother, wives, and six children; and I asked him whether he could say frankly what he would do if he received such an announcement from Shamil. Hadji Murád lifted his eyes and arms to heaven, and said that everything is in God's hands, but that he would never surrender to his foe; for he is certain Shamil would not forgive him, and he would therefore not have long to live. As to the destruction of his family, he did not think Shamil would act so rashly: firstly, to avoid making him a yet more desperate and dangerous foe; and secondly, because there were many people, and even very influential people, in Dagestan, who would dissuade Shamil from such a course. Finally, he repeated several times that whatever God might decree for him in the future, he was at present interested in nothing but his family's ransom; and he implored me, in God's name, to help him, and to allow him to return to the neighbourhood of the Chechnya, where he could, with the help and consent of our commanders, have some intercourse with his family, and regular news of their condition, and of the best means to liberate them. He said that many people, and even some Naïbs in that part of the enemy's territory, were more or less attached to him; and that among the whole of the population already subjugated by Russia, or neutral, it would be easy with our help to establish relations very useful for the attainment of the aim which gives him no peace day or night, and the attainment of which would set him at ease and make it possible for him to act for our good and to win our confidence.

"He asks to be sent back to Grózny with a convoy of twenty or thirty picked Cossacks, who would serve him as a protection against foes and us as a guarantee of his good faith.

"You will understand, dear Prince, that I have been much perplexed by all this; for, do what I will, a great responsibility rests on me. It would be in the highest degree rash to trust him entirely; yet in order to deprive him of all means of escape we should have to lock him up, and in my opinion that would be both unjust and impolitic. A measure of that kind, the news of which would soon spread over the whole of Dagestan, would do us great harm by keeping back those (and there are many such) who are now inclined more or less openly to oppose Shamil, and who are keenly watching to see how we treat the Imám's bravest and most adventurous officer, now that he has found himself obliged to place himself in our hands. If we treat Hadji Murád as a prisoner, all the good effect of the situation will be lost. Therefore I think that I could not act otherwise than as I have done, though at the same time I feel that I may be accused of having made a great mistake if Hadji Murád should take it into his head again to escape. In the service, and especially in a complicated situation such as this, it is difficult, not to say impossible, to follow any one straight path without risking mistakes, and without accepting responsibility; but once a path seems to be the right one, I must follow it, happen what may.

"I beg of you, dear Prince, to submit this to his Majesty the Emperor for his consideration; and I shall be happy if it pleases our most august monarch to approve my action.

"All that I have written above, I have also written to Generals Zavodóvsky and Kozlóvsky, to guide the latter when communicating direct with Hadji Murád, whom I have warned not to act or go anywhere without Kozlóvsky's consent. I also told him that it would be all the better for us if he rode out with our convoy, as otherwise Shamil might spread a rumour that we were keeping him prisoner; but at the same time I made him promise never to go to Vozdvízhensk, because my son, to whom he first surrendered and whom he looks upon as his kunák (friend), is not the commander of that place, and some unpleasant misunderstanding might easily arise. In any case, Vozdvízhensk lies too near a thickly populated, hostile settlement; while for the intercourse with his friends which he desires, Grózny is in all respects suitable.

"Besides the twenty chosen Cossacks who, at his own request, are to keep close to him, I am also sending Captain Lóris-Mélikov with him—a worthy excellent and highly-intelligent officer who speaks Tartar, and knows Hadji Murád well, and apparently enjoys his full confidence. During the ten days Hadji Murád has spent here, he has, however, lived in the same house with Lieutenant-Colonel Prince Tarkhanov, who is in command of the Shoushín District, and is here on business connected with the service. He is a truly worthy man whom I trust entirely. He also has won Hadji Murád's confidence, and through him alone—as he speaks Tartar perfectly—we have discussed the most delicate and secret matters. I have consulted Tarkhanov about Hadji Murád, and he fully agrees with me that it was necessary either to act as I have done, or to put Hadji Murád in prison and guard him in the strictest manner (for if we once treat him badly, he will not be easy to hold), or else to remove him from the country altogether. But these two last measures would not only destroy all the advantage accruing to us from Hadji Murád's quarrel with Shamil, but would inevitably check any growth of the present insubordination and possible future revolt of the people against Shamil's power. Prince Tarkhanov tells me he himself has no doubt of Hadji Murád's truthfulness, and that Hadji Murád is convinced that Shamil will never forgive him, but would have him executed in spite of any promise of forgiveness. The only thing Tarkhanov has noticed in his intercourse with Hadji Murád that might cause any anxiety, is his attachment to his religion. Tarkhanov does not deny that Shamil might influence Hadji Murád from that side. But as I have already said, he will never persuade Hadji Murád that he will not take his life sooner or later, should the latter return to him.

"This, dear Prince, is all I have to tell you about this episode in our affairs here."

XV

The report was despatched from Tiflis on 24th December 1851, and on New Year's Eve a courier, having overdriven a dozen horses and beaten a dozen drivers bloody, delivered it to Prince Chernyshóv, who at that time was Minister of War; and on 1st January 1852 Chernyshóv, among other papers, took Vorontsóv's report to the Emperor Nicholas.

Chernyshóv disliked Vorontsóv because of the general respect in which the latter was held, and because of his immense wealth; and also because Vorontsóv was a real aristocrat, while Chernyshóv after all was a *parvenu*; but especially because the Emperor was particularly well disposed towards Vorontsóv. Therefore at every opportunity Chernyshóv tried to injure Vorontsóv.

When he had last presented a report about Caucasian affairs, he had succeeded in arousing Nicholas's displeasure against Vorontsóv because—through the carelessness of those in command—almost the whole of a small Caucasian detachment had been destroyed by the mountaineers. He now intended to present the steps taken by Vorontsóv in relation to Hadji Murád in an unfavourable light. He wished to suggest to the Emperor that Vorontsóv always protected and even indulged the natives, to the detriment of the Russians; and that he had acted unwisely in allowing Hadji Murád to remain in the Caucasus, for there was every reason to suspect that he had only come over to spy on our means of defence; and that it would therefore be better to transport him to Central Russia, and make use of him only after his family had been rescued from the mountaineers and it had become possible to convince ourselves of his loyalty.

Chernyshóv's plan did not succeed, merely because on that New Year's Day Nicholas was in particularly bad spirits, and out of perversity would not have accepted any suggestion whatever from any one, and least of all from Chernyshóv, whom he only tolerated—regarding him as indispensable for the time being, but looking upon him as a blackguard; for Nicholas knew of his endeavours at the trial of the Decembrists to secure the conviction of Zachary Chernyshóv and of his attempt to obtain Zachary's property for himself. So, thanks to Nicholas's ill temper, Hadji Murád remained in the Caucasus; and his circumstances were not changed as they might have been had Chernyshóv presented his report at another time.

*   *   *   *   *

It was half-past nine o'clock when, through the mist of the cold morning (the thermometer showed 13 degrees Fahrenheit below zero) Chernyshóv's fat, bearded coachman, sitting on the box of a small sledge (like the one Nicholas drove about in) with a sharp-angled cushion-shaped azure velvet cap on his head, drew up at the entrance of the Winter Palace, and gave a friendly nod to his chum, Prince Dolgorúky's coachman—who, having brought his master to the palace, had himself long been waiting outside, in his big coat with the thickly wadded skirts, sitting on the reins and rubbing his numbed hands together. Chernyshóv had on a long, large-caped cloak, with a fluffy collar of silver beaver, and a regulation three-cornered hat with cocks' feathers. He threw back the bearskin apron of the sledge, and carefully disengaged his chilled feet, on which he had no goloshes (he prided himself on never wearing any). Clanking his spurs with an air of bravado, he ascended the carpeted steps and passed through the hall door, which was respectfully opened for him by the porter, and entered the hall. Having thrown off his cloak, which an old Court lackey hurried forward to take, he went to a mirror and carefully removed the hat from his curled wig. Looking at himself in the mirror, he arranged the hair on his temples and the tuft above his forehead with an accustomed movement of his old hands, and adjusted his cross, the shoulder-knots of his uniform, and his large-initialled epaulets; and then went up the gently-ascending carpeted stairs, his not very reliable old legs feebly mounting the shallow steps. Passing the Court lackeys in gala livery, who stood obsequiously bowing, Chernyshóv entered the waiting-room. A newly appointed aide-de-camp to the Emperor, in a shining new uniform, with epaulets shoulder-knots and a still fresh rosy face, a small black moustache, and the hair on his temples brushed towards his eyes (Nicholas's fashion) met him respectfully.

Prince Vasíly Dolgorúky, Assistant-Minister of War, with an expression of *ennui* on his dull face—which was ornamented with similar whiskers, moustaches, and temple tufts brushed forward like Nicholas's—greeted him.

"*L'empereur?*" said Chernyshóv, addressing the aide-de-camp, and looking inquiringly towards the door leading to the cabinet.

"*Sa majesté vient de rentrer*," replied the aide-de-camp, evidently enjoying the sound of his own voice, and, stepping so softly and steadily that had a tumbler of water been placed on his head none of it would have been spilt, he approached the noiselessly opening door and, his whole body evincing reverence for the spot he was about to visit, he disappeared.

Dolgorúky meanwhile opened his portfolio to see that it contained the necessary papers, while Chernyshóv, frowning, paced up and down to restore the circulation in his numbed feet, and thought over what he was about to report to the Emperor. He was near the door of the cabinet when it opened again, and the aide-de-camp, even more radiant and respectful than before, came out and with a gesture invited the minister and his assistant to enter.

The Winter Palace had been rebuilt after the fire some considerable time before this; but Nicholas was still occupying rooms in the upper story. The cabinet in which he received the reports of his ministers and other high officials, was a very lofty apartment with four large windows. A big portrait of the Emperor Alexander I hung on the front wall. Between the windows stood two bureaux. By the walls stood several chairs. In the middle of the room was an enormous writing-table, with an arm-chair before it for Nicholas, and other chairs for those to whom he gave audience.

Nicholas sat at the table in a black coat with shoulder-straps but no epaulets, his enormous body—of which the overgrown stomach was tightly laced in—was thrown back, and he gazed at the newcomers with fixed, lifeless eyes. His long, pale face, with its enormous receding forehead between the tufts of hair which were brushed forward and skilfully joined to the wig that covered his bald patch, was specially cold and stony that day. His eyes, always dim, looked duller than usual; the compressed lips under his upturned moustaches, and his fat freshly-shaven cheeks—on which symmetrical sausage-shaped bits of whiskers had been left—supported by the high collar, and his chin which also pressed upon it, gave to his face a dissatisfied and even irate expression. The cause of the bad mood he was in was fatigue. The fatigue was due to the fact that he had been to a masquerade the night before, and while walking about as was his wont, in his Horse Guards' uniform with a bird on the helmet, among the public which crowded round and timidly made way for his enormous, self-assured figure, he again met the mask who at the previous masquerade, by her whiteness, her beautiful figure, and her tender voice had aroused his senile sensuality. She had then disappeared, after promising to meet him at the next masquerade.

At yesterday's masquerade she had come up to him, and he had not let her go again, but had led her to the box specially kept ready for that purpose, where he could be alone with her. Having arrived in silence at the door of the box, Nicholas looked round to find the attendant, but he was not there. Nicholas frowned, and pushed the door open himself, letting the lady enter first.

"*Il y a quelqu'un!*" said the mask, stopping short.

The box actually was occupied. On the small velvet-covered sofa sat, close together, an Uhlan officer and a pretty, curly-haired, fair young woman in a domino, who had removed her mask. On catching sight of the angry figure of Nicholas, drawn up to its full height, the fair-haired woman quickly covered her face with her mask; but the Uhlan officer, rigid with fear, without rising from the sofa, gazed at Nicholas with fixed eyes.

Used as he was to the terror he inspired in people, that terror always pleased Nicholas, and by way of contrast he sometimes liked to astound those who were plunged in terror by addressing kindly words to them. He did so on this occasion.

"Well, friend!" said he to the officer, rigid with fear, "you are younger than I, and might give up your place to me."

The officer jumped to his feet, and growing pale and then red and bending almost double, he followed his partner silently out of the box, and Nicholas remained alone with his lady.

She proved to be a pretty, twenty-year old virgin, the daughter of a Swedish governess. She told Nicholas how, when quite a child, she had fallen in love with him from his portraits; how she adored him, and made up her mind to attract his attention at any cost. Now she had succeeded, and wanted nothing more—so she said.

The girl was taken to the place where Nicholas usually had rendezvous with women, and there he spent more than an hour with her.

When he returned to his room that night and lay on the hard narrow bed about which he prided himself, and covered himself with the cloak which he considered to be (and spoke of as being) as famous as Napoleon's hat, it was long before he could fall asleep. He thought now of the frightened and elated expression on that girl's fair face, and now of the full, powerful shoulders of his regular mistress, Nelídova, and he compared the two. That profligacy in a married man was a bad thing did not once enter his head; and he would have been greatly surprised had any one censured him for it. Yet, though convinced that he had acted properly, some kind of unpleasant after-taste remained behind, and to stifle that feeling he began to dwell on a thought that always tranquillised him—the thought of his own greatness.

Though he fell asleep very late, he rose before eight, and after attending to his toilet in the usual way—rubbing his big well-fed body all over with ice—and saying his prayers (repeating those he had been used to from childhood—the prayer to the Virgin, the Apostles' Creed, and the Lord's Prayer, without attaching any kind of meaning to the words he uttered), he went out through the smaller portico of the palace on to the embankment, in his military cloak and cap.

On the embankment he met a student in the uniform of the School of Jurisprudence, who was as enormous as himself. On recognising the uniform of that School, which he disliked for its freedom of thought, Nicholas frowned; but the stature of the student, and the painstaking manner in which he drew himself up and saluted, ostentatiously sticking out his elbow, mollified Nicholas's displeasure.

"Your name?" said he.

"Polosátov, your Imperial Majesty."

". . . fine fellow!"

The student continued to stand with his hand lifted to his hat.

Nicholas stopped.

"Do you wish to enter the army?"

"Not at all, your Imperial Majesty."

"Blockhead!" And Nicholas turned away and continued his walk, and began uttering aloud the first words that came into his head.

"Kopervine . . . Kopervine—" he repeated several times (it was the name of yesterday's girl). "Horrid . . . horrid—" He did not think what he said, but stifled his feelings by listening to it.

"Yes, what would Russia do without me?" said he, feeling his former dissatisfaction returning; "yes, what would—not Russia alone, but Europe be, without me?" and calling to mind the weakness and stupidity of his brother-in-law, the King of Prussia, he shook his head.

As he was returning to the small portico, he saw the carriage of Helena Pávlovna, with a red-liveried footman, approaching the Saltykóv entrance of the palace.

Helena Pávlovna was to him the personification of that futile class of people who discussed not merely science and poetry, but even the ways of governing men: imagining that they could govern themselves better than he, Nicholas, governed them! He knew that however much he crushed such people, they reappeared again and again; and he recalled his brother, Michael Pávlovich, who had died not long before. A feeling of sadness and vexation came over him, and with a dark frown he again began whispering the first words that came into his head. He only ceased doing this when he re-entered the palace.

On reaching his apartments he smoothed his whiskers and the hair on his temples and the wig on his bald patch, and twisted his moustaches upwards in front of the mirror; and then went straight to the cabinet in which he received reports.

He first received Chernyshóv, who at once saw by his face, and especially by his eyes, that Nicholas was in a particularly bad humour that day; and knowing about the adventure of the night before, he understood the cause. Having coldly greeted Chernyshóv and invited him to sit down, Nicholas fixed on him a lifeless gaze. The first matter Chernyshóv reported upon was a case, which had just been discovered, of embezzlement by commissariat officials; the next was the movement of troops on the Prussian frontier; then came a list of rewards to be given at the New Year to some people omitted from a former list; then Vorontsóv's report about Hadji Murád; and lastly some unpleasant business concerning an attempt by a student of the Academy of Medicine on the life of a professor.

Nicholas heard the report of the embezzlement silently, with compressed lips, his large white hand—with one ring on the fourth finger—stroking some sheets of paper, and his eyes steadily fixed on Chernyshóv's forehead and on the tuft of hair above it.

Nicholas was convinced that everybody stole. He knew he would have to punish the commissariat officials now, and decided to send them all to serve in the ranks; but he also knew that this would not prevent those who succeeded them from acting in the same way. It was a characteristic of officials to steal, and it was his duty to punish them for doing so; and tired as he was of that duty he conscientiously performed it.

"It seems there is only one honest man in Russia!" said he.

Chernyshóv at once understood that this one honest man was Nicholas himself, and smiled approvingly.

"It looks like it, your Imperial Majesty," said he.

"Leave it—I will give a decision," said Nicholas, taking the document and putting it on the left side of the table.

Then Chernyshóv reported about the rewards to be given, and about moving the army on the Prussian frontier.

Nicholas looked over the list and struck out some names; and then briefly and firmly gave orders to move two divisions to the Prussian frontier. Nicholas could not forgive the King of Prussia for granting a Constitution to his people after the events of 1848, and therefore, while expressing most friendly feelings to his brother-in-law in letters and conversation, he considered it necessary to keep an army near the frontier in case of need. He might want to use these troops to defend his brother-in-law's throne if the people of Prussia rebelled (Nicholas saw a readiness for rebellion everywhere) as he had used troops to suppress the rising in Hungary a few years previously. Another reason why troops were wanted, was to give more weight and influence to the advice he gave to the King of Prussia.

"Yes—what would Russia be like now, if it were not for me?" he again thought.

"Well, what else is there?" said he.

"A courier from the Caucasus," said Chernyshóv, and he reported what Vorontsóv had written about Hadji Murád's surrender.

"Dear me!" said Nicholas. "Well, it's a good beginning!"

"Evidently the plan devised by your Majesty begins to bear fruit," said Chernyshóv.

This approval of his strategic talents was particularly pleasant to

Nicholas, because, though he prided himself on those talents, at the bottom of his heart he knew that they did not really exist; and he now desired to hear more detailed praise of himself.

"How do you mean?" he asked.

"I understand it this way—that if your Majesty's plans had been adopted long ago, and we had moved forward steadily though slowly, cutting down forests and destroying the supplies of food, the Caucasus would have been subjugated long ago. I attribute Hadji Murád's surrender entirely to his having come to the conclusion that they can hold out no longer."

"True," said Nicholas.

Although the plan of a gradual advance into the enemy's territory by means of felling forests and destroying the food supplies was Ermólov's and Velyamínov's plan, and was quite contrary to Nicholas's own plan of seizing Shamil's place of residence and destroying that nest of robbers— which was the plan on which the Dargo expedition in 1845 (that cost so many lives) had been undertaken—Nicholas nevertheless also attributed to himself the plan of a slow advance and a systematic felling of forests and devastation of the country. It would seem that to believe that the plan of a slow movement by felling forests and destroying food supplies was his own, necessitated the hiding of the fact that he had insisted on quite contrary operations in 1845. But he did not hide it, and was proud of the plan of the 1845 expedition, and also of the plan of a slow advance—though evidently the two were contrary to one another. Continual brazen flattery from everybody round him, in the teeth of obvious facts, had brought him to such a state that he no longer saw his own inconsistencies or measured his actions and words by reality logic or even by simple common sense; but was quite convinced that all his orders, however senseless unjust and mutually contradictory they might be, became reasonable just and mutually accordant simply because he gave them. His decision in the case next reported to him—that of the student of the Academy of Medicine—was of that senseless kind.

The case was as follows: A young man who had twice failed in his examinations was being examined a third time, and when the examiner again would not pass him, the young man, whose nerves were deranged, considering this to be an injustice, in a paroxysm of fury seized a penknife from the table and, rushing at the professor, inflicted on him several trifling wounds.

"What's his name?" asked Nicholas.

"Bzhezóvsky."

"A Pole?"

"Of Polish descent, and a Roman Catholic," answered Chernyshóv.

Nicholas frowned. He had done much evil to the Poles. To justify that evil he had to be certain that all Poles were rascals, and he considered them to be such, and hated them accordingly in proportion to the evil he had done to them.

"Wait a little," he said, closing his eyes and bowing his head.

Chernyshóv, having more than once heard Nicholas say so, knew that when the Emperor had to take a decision, it was only necessary for him to concentrate his attention for a few moments, and the spirit moved him, and the best possible decision presented itself, as though an inner voice had told him what to do. He was now thinking how most fully to satisfy the feeling of hatred against the Poles which this incident had stirred up within him; and the inner voice suggested the following decision. He took the report and in his large handwriting wrote on its margin, with three orthographical mistakes:

"Diserves deth, but, thank God, we have no capitle punishment, and it is not for me to introduce it. Make him run the gauntlet of a thousand men twelve times.—Nicholas."

He signed, adding his unnaturally huge flourish.

Nicholas knew that twelve thousand strokes with the regulation rods were not only certain death with torture, but were a superfluous cruelty, for five thousand strokes were sufficient to kill the strongest man. But it pleased him to be ruthlessly cruel, and it also pleased him to think that we have abolished capital punishment in Russia.

Having written his decision about the student, he pushed it across to Chernyshóv.

"There," he said, "read it."

Chernyshóv read it, and bowed his head as a sign of respectful amazement at the wisdom of the decision.

"Yes, and let all the students be present on the drill ground at the punishment," added Nicholas.

"It will do them good! I will abolish this revolutionary spirit, and will tear it up by the roots!" he thought.

"It shall be done," replied Chernyshóv; and after a short pause he straightened the tuft on his forehead and returned to the Caucasian report.

"What do you command me to write in reply to Prince Vorontsóv's despatch?"

"To keep firmly to my system of destroying the dwellings and food supplies in Chechnya, and to harass them by raids," answered Nicholas.

"And what are your Majesty's commands with reference to Hadji Murád?" asked Chernyshóv.

"Why, Vorontsóv writes that he wants to make use of him in the Caucasus."

"Is it not dangerous?" said Chernyshóv, avoiding Nicholas's gaze. "Prince Vorontsóv is, I'm afraid, too confiding."

"And you—what do you think?" asked Nicholas sharply, detecting Chernyshóv's intention of presenting Vorontsóv's decision in an unfavourable light.

"Well, I should have thought it would be safer to deport him to Central Russia."

"You would have thought!" said Nicholas ironically. "But I don't think so, and agree with Vorontsóv. Write to him accordingly."

"It shall be done," said Chernyshóv, rising and bowing himself out.

Dolgorúky also bowed himself out, having during the whole audience only uttered a few words (in reply to a question from Nicholas) about the movement of the army.

After Chernyshóv Nicholas received Bíbikov, General-Governor of the Western Provinces. Having expressed his approval of the measures taken by Bíbikov against the mutinous peasants who did not wish to accept the Orthodox Faith, he ordered him to have all those who did not submit tried by court-martial. That was equivalent to sentencing them to run the gauntlet. He also ordered the editor of a newspaper to be sent to serve in the ranks of the army for publishing information about the transfer of several thousand State peasants to the Imperial estates.

"I do this because I consider it necessary," said Nicholas, "and I will not allow it to be discussed."

Bíbikov saw the cruelty of the order concerning the Uniate peasants, and the injustice of transferring State peasants (the only free peasants in Russia in those days) to the Crown, which meant making them serfs of the Imperial family. But it was impossible to express dissent. Not to agree with Nicholas's decisions would have meant the loss of that brilliant position which it had cost Bíbikov forty years to attain, and which he now enjoyed; and he therefore submissively bowed his dark head (already touched with grey) to indicate his submission and his readiness to fulfil the cruel, insensate and dishonest supreme will.

Having dismissed Bíbikov, Nicholas, with a sense of duty well fulfilled, stretched himself, glanced at the clock, and went to get ready to go out. Having put on a uniform with epaulets Orders and a ribbon, he went out into the reception hall, where more than a hundred persons—men in uniforms and women in elegant low-necked dresses, all standing in the places assigned to them—awaited his arrival with agitation.

He came out to them with a lifeless look in his eyes, his chest expanded, his stomach bulging out above and below its bandages; and feeling everybody's gaze tremulously and obsequiously fixed upon him, he assumed an even more triumphant air. When his eyes met those of people he knew, remembering who was who, he stopped and addressed a few words to them, sometimes in Russian and sometimes in French, and transfixing them with his cold glassy eye, listened to what they said.

Having received all the New Year congratulations, he passed on to church. God, through His servants the priests, greeted and praised Nicholas just as worldly people did; and weary as he was of these greetings and praises, Nicholas duly accepted them. All this was as it should be, because the welfare and happiness of the whole world depended on him; and though the matter wearied him, he still did not refuse the universe his assistance.

When at the end of the service the magnificently arrayed deacon, his long hair crimped and carefully combed, began the chant *Many Years*, which was heartily caught up by the splendid choir, Nicholas looked round and noticed Nelídova, with her fine shoulders, standing by a window, and he decided the comparison with yesterday's girl in her favour.

After Mass he went to the Empress and spent a few minutes in the bosom of his family, joking with the children and with his wife. Then, passing through the Hermitage, he visited the Minister of the Court, Volkónsky, and among other things ordered him to pay out of a special fund a yearly pension to the mother of yesterday's girl. From there he went for his customary drive.

Dinner that day was served in the Pompeian Hall. Besides the younger sons of Nicholas and Michael, there were also invited Baron Lieven, Count Rjévsky, Dolgorúky, the Prussian Ambassador, and the King of Prussia's aide-de-camp.

While waiting for the appearance of the Emperor and Empress, an interesting conversation took place between Baron Lieven and the Prussian Ambassador concerning the disquieting news from Poland.

"*La Pologne et le Caucase, ce sont les deux cautères de la Russie,*" said Lieven. "*Il nous faut 100,000 hommes à peu près, dans chaqu'un de ces deux pays.*"

The Ambassador expressed a fictitious surprise that it should be so.

"*Vous dites, la Pologne——*" began the Ambassador.

"*Oh oui, c'était un coup de maître de Metternich, de nous en avoir laissé l'embarras. . . .*"

At this point the Empress, with her trembling head and fixed smile, entered, followed by Nicholas.

At dinner Nicholas spoke of Hadji Murád's surrender, and said that the war in the Caucasus must now soon come to an end in consequence of the measures he was taking to limit the scope of the mountaineers, by felling their forests and by his system of erecting a series of small forts.

The Ambassador, having exchanged a rapid glance with the aide-de-camp—to whom he had only that morning spoken about Nicholas's unfortunate weakness for considering himself a great strategist—warmly praised this plan, which once more demonstrated Nicholas's great strategic ability.

After dinner Nicholas drove to the ballet, where hundreds of women marched round in tights and scant clothing. One of them specially attracted him, and he had the German ballet master sent for, and gave orders that a diamond ring should be presented to her.

The next day, when Chernyshóv came with his report, Nicholas again confirmed his order to Vorontsóv—that now that Hadji Murád had surrendered, the Chechens should be more actively harassed than ever, and the cordon round them tightened.

Chernyshóv wrote in that sense to Vorontsóv; and another courier, overdriving more horses and bruising the faces of more drivers, galloped to Tiflis.

XVI

In obedience to this command of Nicholas, a raid was immediately made in Chechnya that same month, January 1852.

The detachment ordered for the raid consisted of four infantry battalions, two companies of Cossacks, and eight guns. The column marched along the road, and on both sides of it in a continuous line, now mounting, now descending, marched *Jägers* in high boots, sheepskin coats and tall caps, with rifles on their shoulders and cartridges in their belts.

As usual when marching through a hostile country, silence was observed as far as possible. Only occasionally the guns jingled, jolting across a ditch, or an artillery horse, not understanding that silence was ordered, snorted or neighed, or an angry commander shouted in a hoarse subdued voice to his subordinates that the line was spreading out too much, or marching too near or too far from the column, Only once was the silence broken, when, from a bramble patch between the line and the column, a gazelle with a white breast and grey back jumped out, followed by a ram of the same colour with small backward-curving horns. Doubling up their forelegs at each big bound they took, the beautiful and timid creatures came so close to the column that some of the soldiers rushed after them, laughing and shouting, intending to bayonet them, but the gazelles turned back, slipped through the line of *Jägers*, and, pursued by a few horsemen and the company's dogs, fled like birds to the mountains.

It was still winter, but towards noon, when the column (which had started early in the morning) had gone three miles, it had risen high enough and was powerful enough to make the men quite hot, and its rays were so bright that it was painful to look at the shining steel of the bayonets, or at the reflections—like little suns—on the brass of the cannons.

The clear rapid stream the detachment had just crossed lay behind, and in front were tilled fields and meadows in the shallow valleys. Further in front were the dark mysterious forest-clad hills, with crags rising beyond them, and further still, on the lofty horizon, were the ever-beautiful ever-changing snowy peaks that played with the light like diamonds.

In a black coat and tall cap, shouldering his sword, at the head of the 5th Company marched Butler, a tall handsome officer who had recently exchanged from the Guards. He was filled with a buoyant sense of the joy of living, and also of the danger of death, and with a wish for action, and the consciousness of being part of an immense whole directed by a single will. This was the second time he was going into action, and he thought how in a moment they would be fired at, and that he would not only not stoop when the shells flew overhead, nor heed the whistle of the bullets, but would even carry his head more erect than before, and would look round at his comrades and at the soldiers with smiling eyes, and would begin to talk in a perfectly calm voice about quite other matters.

The detachment turned off the good road on to a little-used one that crossed a stubbly maize field, and it was drawing near the forest when—they could not see whence—with an ominous whistle, a shell flew past amid the baggage wagons, and tore up the ground in the field by the roadside.

"It is beginning," said Butler, with a bright smile to a comrade who was walking beside him.

And so it was. After the shell, from under the shelter of the forest appeared a thick crowd of mounted Chechens with banners. In the midst of the crowd could be seen a large green banner, and an old and very far-sighted sergeant-major informed the short-sighted Butler that Shamil himself must be there. The horsemen came down the hill and appeared to the right, at the highest part of the valley nearest the detachment, and began to descend. A little general in a thick black coat and tall cap rode up to Butler's company on his ambler, and ordered him to the right to encounter the descending horsemen. Butler quickly led his company in the direction indicated, but before he reached the valley he heard two cannon shots behind him. He looked round: two clouds of grey smoke had risen above two cannons and were spreading along the valley. The mountaineer's horsemen—who had evidently not expected to meet artillery—retired. Butler's company began firing at them, and the whole ravine was filled with the smoke of powder. Only higher up, above the ravine, could the mountaineers be seen hurriedly retreating, though still firing back at the Cossacks who pursued them. The company followed the mountaineers further, and on the slope of a second ravine they came in view of an *aoul*.

Following the Cossacks, Butler with his company entered the *aoul* at a run. None of its inhabitants were there. The soldiers were ordered to burn the corn and the hay, as well as the *sáklyas*, and the whole *aoul* was soon filled with pungent smoke, amid which the soldiers rushed about, dragging out of the *sáklyas* what they could find, and above all catching and shooting the fowls the mountaineers had not been able to take away with them.

The officers sat down at some distance beyond the smoke, and lunched and drank. The sergeant-major brought them some honey-combs on a board. There was no sign of any Chechens, and early in the afternoon the order was given to retreat. The companies formed into a column behind the *aoul*, and Butler happened to be in the rear-guard. As soon as they started Chechens appeared, and, following the detachment, fired at it.

When the detachment came out into an open space, the mountaineers pursued it no further. Not one of Butler's company had been wounded, and he returned in a most happy and energetic mood. When, after fording the same stream it had crossed in the morning, the detachment spread over the maize fields and the meadows, the singers of each company came forward, and songs filled the air.

"Very diff'rent, very diff'rent, Jägers are, Jägers are!" sang Butler's singers, and his horse stepped merrily to the music. Trezórka, the shaggy grey dog of the company, with his tail curled up, ran in front with an air of responsibility, like a commander. Butler felt buoyant calm and joyful. War presented itself to him as consisting only in his exposing himself to danger and to possible death, and thereby gaining rewards and the respect of his comrades here, as well as of his friends in Russia. Strange to say, his imagination never pictured the other aspect of war: the death and wounds of the soldiers officers and mountaineers. To retain this poetic conception he even unconsciously avoided looking at the dead and wounded. So that day, when we had three dead and twelve wounded, he passed by a corpse lying on its back, and only saw with one eye the strange position of the waxen hand and a dark red spot on the head, and did not stop to look. The hillsmen appeared to him only as mounted *dzhigits*, from whom one had to defend oneself.

"You see, my dear sir," said his major in an interval between two songs, "it's not as with you in Petersburg—'Eyes right! Eyes left!'

Here we have done our job; and now we go home, and Másha will set a pie and some nice cabbage soup before us. That's life; don't you think so?—Now then! *As the Dawn was Breaking!*" he called for his favourite song.

There was no wind, the air was fresh and clear, and so transparent that the snow hills nearly a hundred miles away seemed quite near, and in the intervals between the songs the regular sound of the footsteps and the jingle of the guns was heard as a background on which each song began and ended. The song that was being sung in Butler's company was composed by a cadet in honour of the regiment, and went to a dance tune. The chorus was, "Very diff'rent, very diff'rent, Jägers are, Jägers are!"

Butler rode beside the officer next in command above him, Major Petróv, with whom he lived; and he felt he could not be thankful enough to have exchanged from the Guards and come to the Caucasus. His chief reason for exchanging was that he had lost all he had at cards, and was afraid that if he remained there he would be unable to resist playing, though he had nothing more to lose. Now all this was over, his life was quite changed, and was such a pleasant and brave one! He forgot that he was ruined, and forgot his unpaid debts. The Caucasus, the war, the soldiers, the officers, those tipsy brave good-natured fellows, and Major Petróv himself, all seemed so delightful that sometimes it appeared too good to be true that he was not in Petersburg—in a room filled with tobacco-smoke, turning down the corners of cards and gambling, hating the holder of the bank, and feeling a dull pain in his head—but was really here in this glorious region among these brave Caucasians.

The Major and the daughter of a surgeon's orderly, formerly known as Másha, but now generally called by the more respectful name of Mary Dmítrievna, lived together as man and wife. Mary Dmítrievna was a handsome fair-haired very freckled childless woman of thirty. Whatever her past may have been, she was now the major's faithful companion, and looked after him like a nurse—a very necessary matter, since the Major often drank himself into oblivion.

When they reached the fort everything happened as the Major had foreseen. Mary Dmítrievna gave him, Butler, and two other officers of the detachment who had been invited, a nourishing and tasty dinner, and the Major ate and drank till he was unable to speak, and then went off to his room to sleep.

Butler, tired but contented, having drunk rather more Chikhír wine than was good for him, went to his bedroom, and hardly had he time to undress before, placing his hand under his handsome curly head, he fell into a sound, dreamless, and unbroken sleep.

XVII

The *aoul* which had been destroyed was that in which Hadji Murád had spent the night before he went over to the Russians. Sado, with his family, had left the *aoul* on the approach of the Russian detachment; and when he returned he found his *sáklya* in ruins—the roof fallen in, the door and the posts supporting the penthouse burned, and the interior filthy. His son, the handsome, brighteyed boy who had gazed with such ecstasy at Hadji Murád, was brought dead to the mosque on a horse covered with a *búrka*. He had been stabbed in the back with a bayonet. The dignified woman who had served Hadji Murád when he was at the house now stood over her son's body, her smock torn in front, her withered old breasts exposed, her hair down; and she dug her nails into her face till it bled, and wailed incessantly. Sado, with pickaxe and spade, had gone with his relatives to dig a grave for his son. The old grandfather sat by the wall of the ruined *sáklya*, cutting a stick and gazing solidly in front of him. He had only just returned from the apiary. The two stacks of hay there had been burnt; the apricot and cherry trees he had planted and reared were broken and scorched; and, worse still, all the beehives and bees were burnt. The wailing of the women and of the little children who cried with their mothers, mingled with the lowing of the hungry cattle, for whom there was no food. The bigger children did not play, but followed their elders with frightened eyes. The fountain was polluted, evidently on purpose, so that the water could not be used. The mosque was polluted in the same way, and the Mullah and his assistants were cleaning it out. No one spoke of hatred of the Russians. The feeling experienced by all the Chechens, from the youngest to the oldest, was stronger than hate. It was not hatred, for they did not regard those Russian dogs as human beings; but it was such repulsion, disgust, and perplexity at the senseless cruelty of these creatures, that the desire to exterminate them—like the desire to exterminate rats, poisonous spiders, or wolves—was as natural an instinct as that of self-preservation.

The inhabitants of the *aoul* were confronted by the choice of remaining there and restoring with frightful effort what had been produced with such labour and had been so lightly and senselessly destroyed, facing every moment the possibility of a repetition of what had happened, or—contrary to their religion and despite the repulsion and contempt they felt—to submit to the Russians. The old men prayed, and unanimously decided to send envoys to Shamil, asking him for help. Then they immediately set to work to restore what had been destroyed.

XVIII

On the morning after the raid, not very early, Butler left the house by the back porch, meaning to take a stroll and a breath of fresh air before breakfast, which he usually had with Petróv. The sun had already risen above the hills, and it was painful to look at the brightly lit-up white walls of the houses on the right side of the street; but then, as always, it was cheerful and soothing to look to the left, at the dark receding ascending forest-clad hills, and at the dim line of snow peaks which as usual pretended to be clouds. Butler looked at these mountains, inhaled deep breaths and rejoiced that he was alive, and that it was just he himself that was alive, and that he lived in this beautiful place.

He was also rather pleased that he had behaved so well in yesterday's affair, both during the advance and especially during the retreat, when things were pretty hot; and he was also pleased to remember how on their return after the raid Másha (or Mary Dmítrievna), Petróv's mistress, had treated them at dinner, and had been particularly nice and simple with everybody, but specially kind—as he thought—to him.

Mary Dmítrievna, with her thick plait of hair, her broad shoulders, her high bosom, and the radiant smile on her kindly freckled face, involuntarily attracted Butler, who was a strong young bachelor; and it even seemed to him that she wanted him; but he considered that that would be wrong towards his good-natured simple-hearted comrade, and he maintained a simple respectful attitude towards her, and was pleased with himself for so doing.

He was thinking of this when his meditations were disturbed by the tramp of many horses' hoofs along the dusty road in front of him, as if several men were riding that way. He looked up, and saw at the end of the street a group of horsemen coming towards him at a walk. In front of a score of Cossacks, rode two men: one in a white Circassian coat, with a tall turban on his head; the other, an officer in the Russian service, dark, with an aquiline nose, and much silver on his uniform and weapons. The man with the turban rode a fine chestnut horse with mane and tail of a lighter shade, a small head, and beautiful eyes. The officer's was a large handsome Karabákh horse. Butler, a lover of horses, immediately recognised the great strength of the first horse, and stopped to learn who these people were.

The officer addressed him. "This the house of commanding officer?" he asked, his foreign accent and his words betraying his foreign origin.

Butler replied that it was. "And who is that?" he added, coming nearer to the officer and indicating the man with the turban.

"That, Hadji Murád. He come here to stay with the commander," said the officer.

Butler knew about Hadji Murád, and about his having come over to the Russians; but he had not at all expected to see him here in this little fort. Hadji Murád gave him a friendly look.

"Good day, *kotkildy*," said Butler, repeating the Tartar greeting he had learnt.

"*Saubul!*" (Be well!) replied Hadji Murád, nodding. He rode up to Butler and held out his hand, from two fingers of which hung his whip.

"Are you the chief?" he asked.

"No, the chief is in here. I will go and call him," said Butler, addressing the officer; and he went up the steps and pushed the door. But the door of the visitors' entrance—as Mary Dmítrievna called it—was locked; and as it still remained closed after he had knocked, Butler went round to the back door. He called his orderly, but received no reply; and finding neither of the two orderlies, he went into the kitchen, where Mary Dmítrievna—flushed, with a kerchief tied round her head, and her sleeves rolled up on her plump white arms—was rolling pastry, white as her hands, and cutting it into small pieces to make pies of.

"Where have the orderlies gone to?" asked Butler.

"Gone to drink," replied Mary Dmítrievna. "What do you want?"

"To have the front door opened. You have a whole horde of mountaineers in front of your house. Hadji Murád has come!"

"Invent something else!" said Mary Dmítrievna, smiling.

"I am not joking, he is really waiting by the porch!"

"Is it really true?" said she.

"Why should I want to deceive you? Go and see; he's just at the porch!"

"Dear me, here's a go!" said Mary Dmítrievna, pulling down her sleeves, and putting up her hand to feel whether the hairpins in her thick plait were all in order. "Then I will go and wake Iván Matveich."

"No, I'll go myself. And you, Bondarénko, go and open the door," said he to Petróv's orderly, who had just appeared.

"Well, so much the better!" said Mary Dmítrievna, and returned to her work.

When he heard that Hadji Murád had come to his house, Iván Matveich Petróv, the Major, who had already heard that Hadji Murád was in Grózny, was not at all surprised; and sitting up in bed he made a cigarette, lit it, and began to dress, loudly clearing his throat, and grumbling at the authorities who had sent "that devil" to him.

When he was ready, he told his orderly to bring him some medicine. The orderly knew that "medicine" meant vódka, and brought some.

"There is nothing so bad as mixing," muttered the Major, when he had drunk the vódka and taken a bite of rye bread. "Yesterday I drank a little Chikhír, and now I have a headache. . . . Well, I'm ready," said he, and went to the parlour, into which Butler had already shown Hadji Murád and the officer who accompanied him.

The officer handed the Major orders from the commander of the Left Flank, to the effect that he should receive Hadji Murád, and should allow him to have intercourse with the mountaineers through spies, but was on no account to let him leave the fort without a convoy of Cossacks.

Having read the order, the Major looked intently at Hadji Murád, and again scrutinised the paper. After passing his eyes several times from one to the other in this manner, he at last fixed them on Hadji Murád and said:

"*Yakshí, Bek; yakshí!*" (Very well, sir, very well!) Let him stay here, and tell him I have orders not to let him out—and that what is commanded is sacred! Well, Butler, where do you think we'd better lodge him? Shall we put him in the office?"

Butler had not time to answer before Mary Dmítrievna—who had come from the kitchen and was standing in the doorway—said to the Major,—

"Why? Keep him here! We will give him the guest chamber and the storeroom. Then at any rate he will be within sight," said she, glancing at Hadji Murád; but meeting his eyes she turned quickly away.

"Well, you know, I think Mary Dmítrievna is right," said Butler.

"Now then, now then; get away! Women have no business here," said the Major, frowning.

During the whole of this discussion, Hadji Murád sat with his hand on the hilt of his dagger, and a faint smile of contempt on his lips. He said it was all the same to him where he lodged, and that he wanted nothing but what the Sirdar had permitted—namely to have communication with the mountaineers; and that he therefore wished that they should be allowed to come to him.

The Major said this should be done, and asked Butler to entertain the visitors till something could be got for them to eat, and their rooms could be prepared. Meantime he himself would go across to the office, to write what was necessary, and to give some orders.

Hadji Murád's relations with his new acquaintances were at once very clearly defined. From the first he was repelled by, and felt contempt for, the Major, to whom he always behaved very haughtily. Mary Dmítrievna, who prepared and served up his food, pleased him particularly. He liked her simplicity, and especially the—to him—

foreign type of beauty, and he was influenced by the attraction she felt towards him and unconsciously conveyed. He tried not to look at her or speak to her; but his eyes involuntarily turned towards her and followed her movements. With Butler, from their first acquaintance, he immediately made friends, and talked much and willingly with him about his life, telling him of his own, and communicating to him the news the spies brought him of his family's condition; and even consulting him about how he ought to act.

The news he received through the spies was not good. During the first four days of his stay in the fort they came to see him twice, and both times brought bad news.

XIX

Hadji Murád's family had been removed to Vedenó soon after his desertion to the Russians, and were there kept under guard, awaiting Shamil's decision. The women: his old mother Patimát, and his two wives with their five little children, were kept under guard in the *sáklya* of the officer, Ibrahim Raschid; while Hadji Murád's son, Yusúf, a youth of eighteen, was put in prison: that is, into a pit more than seven feet deep, together with seven criminals who like himself were awaiting a decision as to their fate.

The decision was delayed, because Shamil was away on a campaign against the Russians.

On 6 January 1852, he returned to Vedenó, after a battle in which, according to the Russians, he had been vanquished, and had fled to Vedenó; but in which, according to him and all the *murids*, he had been victorious, and had repulsed the Russians. In this battle he himself fired his rifle—a thing he seldom did—and, drawing his sword, would have charged straight at the Russians, had not the *murids* who accompanied him held him back. Two of them were killed on the spot, at Shamil's side.

It was noon when Shamil—surrounded by a party of *murids* who caracoled around him, firing their rifles and pistols and continually singing *Lya illyah il Allah!*—rode up to his place of residence.

All the inhabitants of the large *aoul* were in the street or on their roofs to meet their ruler; and as a sign of triumph they also fired off rifles and pistols. Shamil rode a white arab steed, which pulled at its bit as it approached the house. The horse's equipment was of the simplest, without gold or silver ornaments, a delicately worked red leather bridle with a stripe down the middle, metal cup-shaped stirrups, and a red saddle-cloth showing a little from under the saddle. The Imám wore a brown cloth cloak, lined with black fur showing at the neck and sleeves, and was tightly girded round his thin long waist with a black strap which held a dagger. On his head he wore a tall cap with flat crown and black tassel; round it was wound a white turban, one end of which hung down on his neck. He wore green slippers and black leggings, trimmed with plain braid.

In fact, the Imám wore nothing bright—no gold or silver—and his tall erect powerful figure, clothed in garments without any ornaments, surrounded by murids with gold and silver on their clothes and weapons, produced on the people just the impression and influence that he desired and knew how to produce. His pale face, framed by a closely-trimmed reddish beard, with his small eyes always screwed up, was as immovable as though hewn out of stone. As he rode through the *aoul* he felt the gaze of a thousand eyes turned eagerly on him, but his eyes looked at no one.

Hadji Murád's wives had come out into the penthouse with the rest of the inmates of the *sáklya*, to see the Imám's entry. Only Patimát, Hadji Murád's old mother did not go out, but remained sitting on the floor of the *sáklya* with her grey hair down, her long arms encircling her thin knees, blinking with her scorching black eyes as she watched the dying embers in the fireplace. She, like her son, had always hated Shamil; and now she hated him more than ever, and did not wish to see him. Neither did Hadji Murád's son see Shamil's triumphal entry. Sitting in his dark and fetid pit, he only heard the firing and singing, and endured tortures such as can only be felt by the young who are full of vitality and deprived of freedom. He only saw his unfortunate dirty and exhausted fellow prisoners—embittered, and for the most part filled with hatred of one another. He now passionately envied those who, enjoying fresh air and light and freedom, caracoled on fiery steeds around their chief, shooting and heartily singing: *Lya illyah il Allah!*

When he had crossed the *aoul*, Shamil rode into the large courtyard adjoining the inner court where his seraglio was. Two armed Lesgians met him at the open gates of this outer court, which was crowded with people. Some had come from distant parts about their own affairs; some had come with petitions; and some had been summoned by Shamil to be tried and sentenced. As Shamil rode in, all respectfully saluted the Imám with their hands on their breasts. Some knelt down and remained on their knees while he rode across the court from the outer to the inner gates. Though he recognised among the people who waited in the court many whom he disliked, and many tedious petitioners who wanted his attention, Shamil passed them all with the same immovable stony expression on his face, and having entered the inner court, dismounted at the penthouse in front of his apartment, to the left of the gate. He was worn out, mentally rather than physically, with the strain of the campaign—for in spite of the public declaration that he had been victorious, he knew very well that his campaign had been unsuccessful; that many Chechen *aouls* had been burnt down and ruined, and that the unstable and fickle Chechens were wavering, and those nearest the border line were ready to go over to the Russians.

All this oppressed him, and had to be dealt with; but at that moment Shamil did not wish to think at all. He only desired one thing: rest, and the delights of family life, and the caresses of his favourite wife, the eighteen-year-old, black-eyed, quick-footed Aminal, who at that very moment was close at hand behind the fence that divided the inner court and separated the men's from the women's quarters (Shamil felt sure she was there with his other wives, looking through a chink in the fence while he dismounted), but not only was it impossible for him to go to her, he could not even lie down on his feather cushions and rest from his fatigues, but had first of all to perform the mid-day rites, for which he had just then not the least inclination, but which—as the religious leader of the people—he could not omit, and which moreover, were as necessary to him himself as his daily food. So he performed his ablutions and said his prayers, and summoned those who were waiting for him.

The first to enter was Jemal Eddin, his father-in-law and teacher, a tall grey-haired good-looking old man, with a beard white as snow and a rosy red face. He said a prayer, and began questioning Shamil about the incidents of the campaign, and telling him what had happened in the mountains during his absence.

Among events of many kinds—murders connected with blood feuds, cattle-stealing, people accused of disobeying the Tarikát (smoking and drinking wine)—Jemal Eddin related how Hadji Murád had sent men to bring his family over to the Russians, but that this had been detected, and the family had been brought to Vedéno, where they were kept under guard and awaited the Imám's decision. In the next room, the guest-chamber, the Elders were assembled to discuss all these affairs, and Jemal Eddin advised Shamil to finish with them and let them go that same day, as they had already been waiting three days for him.

After eating his dinner—served to him in his room by Zeidát, a dark sharp-nosed disagreeable-looking woman, whom he did not love but who was his eldest wife—Shamil passed into the guest-chamber.

The six old men who made up his Council—white, grey, or red-bearded, with tall caps on their heads, some with turbans and some without, wearing new *beshméts* and Circassian coats girdled with straps to which hung their daggers—rose to greet him on his entrance. Shamil towered a head above them all. He, as well as all the others, lifted his hands, palms upwards, closed his eyes and recited a prayer, and then stroked his face downwards with both hands, uniting them at the end of his beard. Having done this, they all sat down, Shamil on a larger cushion than the others, and discussed the various cases before them.

In the case of the criminals, the decisions were given according to the Shariah; two were sentenced to have a hand cut off for stealing; one man to be beheaded for murder; and three were pardoned. Then they came to the principal business—how to stop the Chechens from going over to the Russians. To counteract that tendency, Jemal Eddin drew up the following proclamation:—

"I wish you eternal peace with God the Almighty!

"I hear that the Russians flatter you and invite you to surrender to them. Do not believe them, and do not surrender, but endure. If ye be not rewarded for it in this life, ye shall receive your reward in the life to come. Remember what happened before, when they took your arms from you! If God had not brought you to reason then, in 1840, ye would now be soldiers, and your wives would no longer wear trousers and would be dishonoured.

"Judge of the future by the past. It is better to die in enmity with the Russians than to live with the Unbelievers. Endure for a little while, and I will come with the Koran and the sword, and will lead you against the enemy. But now I strictly command you not only to entertain no intention, but not even a thought of submitting to the Russians!"

Shamil approved this proclamation, signed it, and had it sent out.

After this business they considered Hadji Murád's case. This was of the utmost importance to Shamil. Although he did not wish to admit it, he knew that if Hadji Murád, with his agility boldness, and courage had been with him, what had now happened in Chechnya would not have occurred. It would therefore be well to make it up with Hadji Murád, and again have the benefit of his services; but as this was not possible, it would never do to allow him to help the Russians; and therefore he must be enticed back and killed. They might accomplish this either by sending a man to Tiflis who would kill him there, or by inducing him to come back, and then killing him. The only means of doing the latter was by making use of his family, and especially his son, whom, as Shamil knew, Hadji Murád loved passionately. Therefore they must act through the son.

When the councillors had talked all this over, Shamil closed his eyes and sat silent.

The councillors knew that this meant that he was listening to the voice of the Prophet, who spoke to him and told him what to do.

After five minutes of solemn silence Shamil opened his eyes, and narrowing them more than usual, said,—

"Bring Hadji Murád's son to me."

"He is here," replied Jemal Eddin; and in fact Yusúf, Hadji Murád's son, thin pale tattered and evil-smelling, but still handsome in face and figure, with black eyes that burnt like his grandmother Patimát's, was already standing by the gate of the outside court, waiting to be called in.

Yusúf did not share his father's feelings towards Shamil. He did not know all that had happened in the past, or if he knew it, not having lived through it, he still did not understand why his father was so obstinately hostile to Shamil. To him, who wanted only one thing—

to continue living the easy loose life that as the Naïb's son he had led in Khunzákh—it seemed quite unnecessary to be at enmity with Shamil. Out of defiance and a spirit of contradiction to his father, he particularly admired Shamil, and shared the ecstatic adoration with which he was regarded in the mountains. With a peculiar feeling of tremulous veneration for the Imám, he now entered the guest-chamber. As he stopped by the door he met the steady gaze of Shamil's half-closed eyes. He paused for a moment, and then approached Shamil and kissed his large, long-fingered hand.

"Thou art Hadji Murád's son?"

"I am, Imám."

"Thou knowest what he has done?"

"I know, Imám, and deplore it."

"Canst thou write?"

"I was preparing myself to be a Mullah—"

"Then write to thy father that if he will return to me now, before the Feast of Bairam, I will forgive him, and everything shall be as it was before; but if not, and if he remains with the Russians—" and Shamil frowned sternly, "I will give thy grandmother, thy mother, and the rest, to the different *aouls*, and thee I will behead!"

Not a muscle of Yusúf's face stirred, and he bowed his head to show that he understood Shamil's words.

"Write that, and give it to my messenger."

Shamil ceased speaking, and looked at Yusúf for a long time in silence.

"Write that I have had pity on thee and will not kill thee, but will put out thine eyes as I do to all traitors! . . . Go!"

While in Shamil's presence Yusúf appeared calm; but when he had been led out of the guest-chamber he rushed at his attendant, snatched the man's dagger from its sheath, and wished to stab himself; but he was seized by the arms, bound, and led back to the pit.

That evening at dusk, after he had finished his evening prayers, Shamil put on a white fur-lined cloak, and passed out to the other side of the fence where his wives lived, and went straight to Aminal's room; but he did not find her there. She was with the older wives. Then Shamil, trying to remain unseen, hid behind the door and stood waiting for her. But Aminal was angry with him because he had given some silk stuff to Zeidát, and not to her. She saw him come out and go into her room looking for her, and she purposely kept away. She stood a long time at the door of Zeidát's room, softly laughing at Shamil's white figure that kept coming in and out of her room.

Having waited for her in vain, Shamil returned to his own apartments when it was already time for the midnight prayers.

XX

Hadji Murád had been a week in the Major's house at the fort. Although Mary Dmítrievna quarrelled with the shaggy Khanéfi (Hadji Murád had only brought two of his murids, Khanéfi and Eldár, with him) and had turned him out of her kitchen—for which he nearly killed her—she evidently felt a particular respect and sympathy for Hadji Murád. She now no longer served him his dinner, having handed over that duty to Eldár, but she seized every opportunity of seeing him and rendering him service. She always took the liveliest interest in the negotiations about his family, knew how many wives and children he had, and their ages; and each time a spy came to see him, she inquired as best she could into the results of the negotiations.

Butler during that week had become quite friendly with Hadji Murád. Sometimes the latter came to Butler's room; sometimes Butler went to Hadji Murád's. Sometimes they conversed by the help of the interpreter; and sometimes got on as best they could with signs and especially with smiles.

Hadji Murád had evidently taken a fancy to Butler. This could be gathered from Eldár's relations with the latter. When Butler entered Hadji Murád's room, Eldár met him with a pleased smile, showing his glittering teeth, and hurried to put down a cushion for him to sit on, and to relieve him of his sword if he was wearing one.

Butler also got to know and became friendly with the shaggy Khanéfi, Hadji Murád's sworn brother. Khanéfi knew many mountain songs, and sang them well. To please Butler, Hadji Murád often made Khanéfi sing, choosing the songs which he considered best. Khanéfi had a high tenor voice, and sang with extraordinary clearness and expression. One of the songs Hadji Murád specially liked, impressed Butler by its solemnly mournful tone, and he asked the interpreter to translate it.

The subject of the song was the very blood-feud that had existed between Khanéfi and Hadji Murád. It ran as follows:—

> "The earth will dry on my grave,
>   Mother, my Mother!
> And thou wilt forget me,
> And over me rank grasses wave,
>   Father, my Father!
> Nor wilt thou regret me!
> When tears cease thy dark eyes to lave,
>   Sister, dear Sister!
> No more will grief fret thee!
>
> "But thou my Brother the Elder, wilt never forget,
>   With vengeance denied me!
> And thou, my Brother the Younger, wilt ever regret,
>   Till thou liest beside me!
>
> "Hotly thou camest, O death-bearing ball that I
>   spurned,
>   For thou wast my Slave!
> And thou, black earth, that battle-steed trampled and
>   churned,
>   Wilt cover my grave!
>
> "Cold art Thou, O Death, yet I was thy Lord and thy
>   Master!
> My body sinks fast to earth; my Soul to Heaven flies
>   faster."

Hadji Murád always listened to this song with closed eyes, and when it ended on a long gradually dying note he always remarked in Russian,—

"Good song! Wise song!"

After Hadji Murád's arrival and Butler's intimacy with him and his murids, the poetry of the energetic life of the mountains took a still stronger hold on Butler. He procured for himself a beshmét, a Circassian coat and leggings, and imagined himself a mountaineer living the life those people lived.

On the day of Hadji Murád's departure, the Major invited several officers to see him off. They were sitting, some at the table where Mary Dmítrievna was pouring out tea, some at another table on which stood vódka Chikhír and light refreshments, when Hadji Murád, dressed for the journey, came limping with soft rapid footsteps into the room.

They all rose and shook hands with him. The Major offered him a seat on the divan, but Hadji Murád thanked him and sat down on a chair by the window.

The silence that followed his entrance did not at all abash him. He looked attentively at all the faces and fixed an indifferent gaze on the tea-table with the samovar and refreshments. Petróvsky, a lively officer who now met Hadji Murád for the first time, asked him through the interpreter whether he liked Tiflis.

"Alya!" he replied.

"He says, 'Yes,'" translated the interpreter.

"What did he like there?"

Hadji Murád said something in reply.

"He liked the theatre best of all."

"And how did he like the ball at the house of the Commander-in-chief?"

Hadji Murád frowned. "Every nation has its own customs! Our women do not dress in such a way," said he, glancing at Mary Dmítrievna.

"Well, didn't he like it?"

"We have a proverb," said Hadji Murád to the interpreter, "'The dog gave meat to the ass, and the ass gave hay to the dog, and both went hungry,'" and he smiled. "It's own customs seem good to each nation."

The conversation went no further. Some of the officers took tea; some, other refreshments. Hadji Murád accepted the tumbler of tea offered him, and put it down before him.

"Won't you have cream and a bun?" asked Mary Dmítrievna, offering them to him.

Hadji Murád bowed his head.

"Well, I suppose it is good-bye!" said Butler, touching his knee. "When shall we meet again!"

"Good-bye, good-bye!" said Hadji Murád with a smile, in Russian. "*Kunák bulug.*—Strong *kunák* to thee! Time—*ajia*—go!" and he jerked his head in the direction in which he had to go.

Eldár appeared in the doorway carrying some large white thing across his shoulder and a sword in his hand. Hadji Murád beckoned him to himself, and Eldár came with his big strides and handed him a white *búrka* and the sword. Hadji Murád rose, took the *búrka*, threw it over his arm, and, saying something to the interpreter, handed it to Mary Dmítrievna.

The interpreter said, "He says thou hast praised the *búrka*, so accept it."

"Oh, why?" said Mary Dmítrievna, blushing.

"It is necessary. *Adat* it is," said Hadji Murád.

"Well, thank you," said Mary Dmítrievna, taking the *búrka*. "God grant that you rescue your son," added she. "*Ulan yakshi,*" said she. "Tell him that I wish him success in releasing his son."

Hadji Murád glanced at Mary Dmítrievna, and nodded his head approvingly. Then he took the sword from Eldár and handed it to the Major. The Major took it, and said to the interpreter,—

"Tell him to take my chestnut gelding. I have nothing else to give him."

Hadji Murád waved his hand in front of his face to show that he did not want anything and would not accept it. Then, pointing first to the mountains and then to his heart, he went out.

Every one followed him as far as the door. The officers who remained inside the room drew the sword from its scabbard, examined its blade, and decided that it was a real Gurda.

Butler accompanied Hadji Murád to the porch, and then something very unexpected occurred which might have ended fatally for Hadji Murád, had it not been for his quick observation, determination, and agility.

The inhabitants of the Kumúkh *aoul*, Tash-Kichu, which friendly to the Russians, greatly respected Hadji Murád, and had often come to the fort merely to look at the famous *Naïb*. They had sent messengers to him three days previously to ask him to visit their mosque on the Friday. But the Kumúkh princes who lived in Tash-Kichu hated Hadji Murád because there was a blood feud between them; and on hearing of this invitation they announced to the people that they would not allow him to enter the mosque. The people became excited, and a fight occurred between them and the princes' supporters. The Russian authorities pacified the mountaineers and sent word to Hadji Murád not to go to the mosque.

Hadji Murád did not go, and every one supposed that the matter was settled.

But at the very moment of his departure, when he came out into the porch before which the horses stood waiting, Arslán Khan—one of the Kumúkh princes and an acquaintance of Butler's and of the Major's—rode up to the house.

When he saw Hadji Murád he snatched a pistol from his belt and aimed at him; but before he could fire, Hadji Murád—in spite of his lameness—rushed down from the porch like a cat towards Arslán Khan, who fired and missed.

Seizing Arslán Khan's horse by the bridle with one hand, Hadji Murád drew his dagger with the other and shouted something to him in Tartar.

Butler and Eldár both ran at once towards the enemies, and caught them by the arms. The Major, who had heard the shot, also came out.

"What do you mean by it, Arslán—starting such a horrid business on my premises?" said he, when he heard what had happened. "It's not right, friend! 'To the foe in the field, you need not yield!'—but to start this kind of slaughter in my place—!"

Arslán Khan, a little man with black moustaches, got off his horse, pale and trembling, looked angrily at Hadji Murád, and went into the house with the Major. Hadji Murád, breathing heavily and smiling, returned to the horses.

"Why did he want to kill him?" Butler asked the interpreter.

"He says it is a law of theirs," the interpreter translated Hadji Murád's reply. "Arslán must avenge a relation's blood, and so he tried to kill him."

"And supposing he overtakes him on the road?" asked Butler.

Hadji Murád smiled.

"Well, if he kills me it will prove that such is Allah's will. . . . Good-bye," he said again in Russian, taking his horse by the withers. Glancing round at everybody who had come out to see him off, his eyes rested kindly on Mary Dmítrievna.

"Good-bye, my lass," said he to her. "I thank you."

"God help you—God help you to rescue your family!" repeated Mary Dmítrievna.

He did not understand her words, but felt her sympathy for him, and nodded to her.

"Mind, don't forget your kunák," said Butler.

"Tell him I am his true friend and will never forget him," answered Hadji Murád to the interpreter; and in spite of his short leg he swung himself lightly and quickly, barely touching the stirrup, into the high saddle, automatically feeling for his dagger and adjusting his sword. Then, with that peculiarly proud look with which only a Caucasian hillsman sits his horse—as though he were one with it—he rode away from the Major's house. Khanéfi and Eldár also mounted, and having taken a friendly leave of their hosts and of the officers, they rode off at a trot, following their murshíd.

As usual after any one's departure, those who remained behind began to discuss them.

"Plucky fellow! Didn't he rush at Arslán Khan like a wolf! His face quite changed!"

"But he'll be up to tricks—he's a terrible rogue, I should say," remarked Petróvsky.

"God grant there were more Russian rogues of such a kind!" suddenly put in Mary Dmítrievna with vexation. "He has lived a week with us, and we have seen nothing but good from him. He is courteous wise and just," she added.

"How did you find that out?"

"Well, I did find it out!"

"She's quite smitten," said the Major, who had just entered the room; "and that's a fact!"

"Well, and if I am smitten? What's that to you? But why run him down if he's a good man? Though he's a Tartar, he's still a good man!"

"Quite true, Mary Dmítrievna," said Butler; "and you're quite right to take his part!"

XXI

Life in our advanced forts in the Chechen lines went on as usual. Since the events last narrated there had been two alarms when the companies were called out, and militiamen galloped about; but both times the mountaineers who had caused the excitement got away; and once at Vozdvízhensk they killed a Cossack, and succeeded in carrying off eight Cossack horses that were being watered. There had been no further raids since the one in which the *aoul* was destroyed; but an expedition on a large scale was expected in consequence of the appointment of a new Commander of the Left Flank, Prince Baryátinsky.[5] He was an old friend of the Viceroy's, and had been in command of the Kabardá Regiment. On his arrival at Grózny as commander of the whole Left Flank, he at once mustered a detachment to continue to carry out the Tsar's commands as communicated by Chernyshóv to Vorontsóv. The detachment mustered at Vozdvízhensk left the fort, and took up a position towards Kurín. The troops were encamped there, and were felling the forest. Young Vorontsóv lived in a splendid cloth tent, and his wife, Mary Vasílevna, often came to the camp and stayed the night. Baryátinsky's relations with Mary Vasílevna were no secret to any one, and the officers who were not in the aristocratic set, and the soldiers, abused her in coarse terms—for her presence in camp caused them to be told off to lie in ambush at night. The mountaineers were in the habit of bringing guns within range and firing shells at the camp. The shells generally missed their aim, and therefore at ordinary times no special measures were taken to prevent such firing; but now, men were placed in ambush to hinder the mountaineers from injuring or frightening Mary Vasílevna with their cannons. To have to be always lying in ambush at night to save a lady from being frightened, offended and annoyed them; and therefore the soldiers, as well as the officers not admitted to the higher society, called Mary Vasílevna bad names.

Butler, having obtained leave of absence from his fort, came to the camp to visit some old messmates from the cadet corps and fellow-officers of the Kurín regiment, who were serving as adjutants and orderly-officers. When he first arrived he had a very good time. He put up in Poltorátsky's tent, and there met many acquaintances who gave him a hearty welcome. He also called on Vorontsóv whom he knew slightly, having once served in the same regiment with him. Vorontsóv received him very kindly, introduced him to Prince Baryátinsky, and invited him to the farewell dinner he was giving in honour of General Kozlóvsky, who, until Baryátinsky's arrival, had been in command of the Left Flank.

The dinner was magnificent. Special tents were erected in a line, and along the whole length of them a table was spread, as for a dinner-party, with dinner-services and bottles. Everything recalled life in the guards in Petersburg. Dinner was served at two o'clock. In the middle on one side sat Kozlóvsky; on the other, Baryátinsky. At Kozlóvsky's right and left hand sat the Vorontsóvs, husband and wife. All along the table on both sides sat the officers of the Kabardá and Kurín regiments. Butler sat next to Poltorátsky, and they both chatted merrily and drank with the officers around them. When the roast was served and the orderlies had gone round and filled the champagne glasses, Poltorátsky, with real anxiiety, said to Butler,—

"Our Kozlóvsky will disgrace himself!"

"Why?"

"Why, he'll have to make a speech, and what good is he at that? . . . Yes, it's not as easy as capturing entrenchments under fire! And with a lady beside him, too, and these aristocrats!"

"Really it's painful to look at him," said the officers to one another. And now the solemn moment had arrived. Baryátinsky rose and lifting his glass addressed a short speech to Kozlóvsky. When he had finished, Kozlóvsky—who always had a trick of using the word "how" superfluously—rose and stammeringly began,—

"In compliance with the august will of his Majesty, I am leaving you—parting from you, gentlemen," said he. "But consider me as always remaining among you. The truth of the proverb, how 'One man in the field is no warrior,' is well known to you, gentlemen. . . . Therefore, how every reward I have received . . . how all the benefits showered on me by the great generosity of our sovereign the Emperor . . . how all my position—how my good name . . . how everything decidedly . . . how . . ." (here his voice trembled) ". . . how I am indebted to you for it, to you alone, my friends!" The wrinkled face puckered up still more, he gave a sob, and tears came into his eyes. "How from my heart I offer you my sincerest, heartfelt gratitude!"

Kozlóvsky could not go on, but turned round and began to embrace the officers. The Princess hid her face in her handkerchief. The Prince blinked, with his mouth drawn awry. Many of the officers' eyes grew moist, and Butler, who had hardly known Kozlóvsky, could also not restrain his tears. He liked all this very much.

Then followed other toasts. Baryátinsky's, Vorontsóv's, the officers', and the soldiers' healths were drunk, and the visitors left the table intoxicated with wine and with the military elation to which they were always so prone. The weather was wonderful, sunny and calm, and the air fresh and bracing. On all sides bonfires crackled and songs resounded. It might have been thought that everybody was celebrating some joyful event. Butler went to Poltorátsky's in the happiest most emotional mood. Several officers had gathered there, and a card-table was set. An Adjutant started a bank with a hundred roubles. Two or three times Butler left the tent with his hand gripping the purse in his trousers-pocket; but at last he could resist the temptation no longer, and despite the promise he had given to his brother and to himself not to play, he began to bet. Before an hour was past, very red, perspiring, and soiled with chalk, he sat with both elbows on the table and wrote on it—under cards bent for "corners" and "transports"—the figures of his stakes. He had already lost so much that he was afraid to count up what was scored against him. But he knew without counting that all the pay he could draw in advance, added to the value of his horse, would not suffice to pay what the Adjutant, a stranger to him, had written down against him. He would still have gone on playing, but the Adjutant sternly laid down the cards he held in his large clean hands, and added up the chalked figures of the score of Butler's losses. Butler, confused, began to make excuses for being unable to pay the whole of his debt at once; and said he would send it from home. When he said this he noticed that everybody pitied him, and that they all—even Poltorátsky—avoided meeting his eye. That was his last evening there. He need only have refrained from playing, and gone to the Vorontsóvs who had invited him, and all would have been well, thought he; but now it was not only not well, but terrible.

Having taken leave of his comrades and acquaintances he rode home and went to bed, and slept for eighteen hours as people usually sleep after losing heavily. From the fact that he asked her to lend him fifty kopeks to tip the Cossack who had escorted him, and from his sorrowful looks and short answers, Mary Dmítrievna guessed that he had lost at cards, and she reproached the Major for having given him leave of absence.

When he woke up at noon next day and remembered the situation he was in, he longed again to plunge into the oblivion from which he had just emerged; but it was impossible. Steps had to be taken to repay the four hundred and seventy roubles he owed to the stranger. The first step he took was to write to his brother, confessing his sin and imploring him, for the last time, to lend him five hundred roubles on the security of the mill that they still owned in common. Then he wrote to a stingy relative, asking her to lend him five hundred roubles at whatever rate of interest she liked. Finally he went to the Major, knowing that he—or rather Mary Dmítrievna—had some money, and asked him to lend him five hundred roubles.

"I'd let you have them at once," said the Major, "but Másha won't! These women are so close-fisted—who the devil can understand them? . . . And yet you must get out of it somehow, devil take him! . . . Hasn't that brute the canteen-keeper something?"

But it was no use trying to borrow from the canteen-keeper; so that Butler's salvation could only come from his brother or from his stingy relative.

XXII

Not having attained his aim in Chechnya, Hadji Murád returned to Tiflis and went every day to Vorontsóv's; and whenever he could obtain audience he implored the Viceroy to gather together the mountaineer prisoners and to exchange them for his family. He said that unless that were done his hands were tied and he could not serve the Russians and destroy Shamil, as he desired to do. Vorontsóv vaguely promised to do what he could, but put it off, saying that he would decide when General Argutínsky reached Tiflis and he could talk the matter over with him.

Then Hadji Murád asked Vorontsóv to allow him to go to live for a while in Nukhá, a small town in Transcaucasia, where he thought he could better carry on negotiations about his family with Shamil and with the people who were attached to himself. Moreover, Nukhá being a Muslim town, had a mosque where he could more conveniently perform the rites of prayer demanded by the Muslim law. Vorontsóv wrote to Petersburg about it, but meanwhile gave Hadji Murád permission to go to Nukhá.

For Vorontsóv and the authorities in Petersburg, as well as for most Russians acquainted with Hadji Murád's history, the whole episode presented itself as a lucky turn in the Caucasian war, or simply as an interesting event. For Hadji Murád, on the other hand, it was (especially latterly) a terrible crisis in his life. He had escaped from the mountains partly to save himself, partly out of hatred of Shamil; and difficult as this flight had been, he had attained his object and for a time was glad of his success, and really devised a plan to attack Shamil; but the rescue of his family—which he had thought would be easy to arrange—had proved more difficult than he expected.

Shamil had seized the family and kept them prisoners, threatening to hand the women over to the different *aouls*, and to blind or kill the son. Now Hadji Murád had gone to Nukhá intending to try, by the aid of his adherents in Dagestan, to rescue his family from Shamil by force or by cunning. The last spy who had come to see him in Nukhá informed him that the Avars devoted to him were preparing to capture his family and to come over to the Russians with them; but that there were not enough of them, and they could not risk making the attempt in Vedenó where the family was at present imprisoned, but could only do it if the family were moved from Vedenó to some other place: in which case they promised to rescue them on the way.

Hadji Murád sent word to his friends that he would give three thousand roubles for the liberation of his family.

At Nukhá a small house of five rooms was assigned to Hadji Murád near the mosque and the Khan's palace. The officers in charge of him, his interpreter, and his henchmen stayed in the same house. Hadji Murád's life was spent in the expectation and reception of messengers from the mountains, and in rides he was allowed to take in the neighbourhood.

On 24th April, returning from one of these rides, Hadji Murád learnt that during his absence an official had arrived from Tiflis, sent by Vorontsóv. In spite of his longing to know what message the official had brought him, Hadji Murád, before going into the room where the officer in charge and the official were waiting, went to his bedroom and repeated his noonday prayer. When he had finished he came out into the room which served him as drawing and reception room. The official who had come from Tiflis, Councillor Kiríllov, informed Hadji Murád of Vorontsóv's wish that he should come to Tiflis on the 12th, to meet General Argutínsky.

"*Yakshí!*" said Hadji Murád angrily. The councillor did not please him. "Have you brought money?"

"I have," answered Kiríllov.

"For two weeks now," said Hadji Murád, holding up first both hands and then four fingers. "Give here!"

"We'll give it you at once," said the official, getting his purse out of his travelling-bag. "What does he want with the money?" he went on in Russian, thinking Hadji Murád would not understand. But Hadji Murád understood, and glanced angrily at Kiríllov. While getting out the money the councillor, wishing to begin a conversation with Hadji Murád in order on his return to have something to tell Prince Vorontsóv, asked through the interpreter whether Hadji Murád was not feeling dull there. Hadji Murád glanced contemptuously out of the corner of his eye at the fat unarmed little man dressed as a civilian, and did not reply. The interpreter repeated the question.

"Tell him that I cannot talk with him! Let him give me the money!" and having said this, Hadji Murád sat down at the table ready to count the money.

When Kiríllov had got out the money and arranged it in seven piles of ten gold pieces each (Hadji Murád received five gold pieces daily) and pushed them towards Hadji Murád, the latter poured the gold into the sleeve of his Circassian coat, rose, and quite unexpectedly slapped Councillor Kiríllov on his bald pate, and turned to go.

The councillor jumped up and ordered the interpreter to tell Hadji Murád that he must not dare to behave like that to him, who held a rank equal to that of colonel! The officer in charge confirmed this, but Hadji Murád only nodded to signify that he knew, and left the room.

"What is one to do with him?" said the officer in charge. "He'll stick his dagger into you, that's all! One cannot talk with those devils! I see that he is getting exasperated."

As soon as it began to grow dusk, two spies with hoods covering their faces up to their eyes, came to him from the hills. The officer in charge led them to Hadji Murád's room. One of them was a fleshy swarthy Tavlinian; the other, a thin old man. The news they brought was not cheering for Hadji Murád. His friends who had undertaken to rescue his family, now definitely refused to do so, being afraid of Shamil—who threatened to punish with the most terrible tortures any one who helped Hadji Murád. Having heard the messengers, Hadji Murád sat with his elbows on his crossed legs, and bowing his turbaned head, remained silent a long time.

He was thinking, and thinking resolutely. He knew that he was now considering the matter for the last time, and that it was necessary to come to a decision. At last he raised his head, gave each of the messengers a gold piece, and said: "Go!"

"What answer will there be?"

"The answer will be as God pleases. . . . Go!"

The messengers rose and went away, and Hadji Murád continued to sit on the carpet, leaning his elbows on his knees. He sat thus a long time, and pondered.

"What am I to do? To take Shamil at his word and return to him?" he thought. "He is a fox and will deceive me. Even if he did not deceive me, it would still be impossible to submit to that red liar. It is impossible . . . because now that I have been with the Russians he will not trust me," thought Hadji Murád; and he remembered a Tavlinian fable about a falcon who had been caught and lived among men, and afterwards returned to his own kind in the hills. He returned, but wearing jesses with bells; and the other falcons would not receive him. "Fly back to where they hung those silver bells on thee!" said they. "We have no bells and no jesses." The falcon did not want to leave his home, and remained; but the other falcons did not wish to let him stay there, and pecked him to death.

"And they would peck me to death in the same way," thought Hadji Murád. "Shall I remain here and conquer Caucasia for the Russian Tsar, and earn renown, titles, riches?"

"That could be done," thought he, recalling his interviews with Vorontsóv, and the flattering things the Prince had said. "But I must decide at once, or Shamil will destroy my family."

That night Hadji Murád remained awake, thinking.

XXIII

By midnight his decision had been formed. He had decided that he must fly to the mountains, and with the Avars still devoted to him must break into Vedenó, and either die or rescue his family. Whether after rescuing them he would return to the Russians or escape to Khunzákh and fight Shamil, he had not made up his mind. All he knew was that first of all he must escape from the Russians into the mountains; and he at once began to carry out his plan.

He drew his black wadded *beshmét* from under his pillow, and went into his henchmen's room. They lived on the other side of the hall. As soon as he entered the hall, the outer door of which stood open, he was at once enveloped by the dewy freshness of the moonlit night and his ears were filled by the whistling and trilling of several nightingales in the garden by the house.

Having crossed the hall, Hadji Murád opened the door of his henchmen's room. There was no light in the room, but the moon in its first quarter shone in at the window. A table and two chairs were standing on one side of the room; and four of Hadji Murád's henchmen were lying on carpets or on *búrkas* on the floor. Khanéfi slept outside with the horses. Gamzálo heard the door creak, rose, turned round, and saw Hadji Murád. On recognising him he lay down again. But Eldár, who lay beside him, jumped up and began putting on his *beshmét*, expecting his master's orders. Khan Mahomá and Bata slept on. Hadji Murád put down the *beshmét* he had brought on the table, and it hit the table with a dull sound. This was caused by the gold sewn up in it.

"Sew these in too," said Hadji Murád, handing Eldár the gold pieces he had that day received. Eldár took them, and at once went into the moonlight, drew a small knife from under his dagger, and started unstitching the lining of the *beshmét*. Gamzálo raised himself and sat up with his legs crossed.

"And you, Gamzálo, tell the fellows to examine the rifles and pistols and to get the ammunition ready. Tomorrow we shall go far," said Hadji Murád.

"We have bullets and powder; everything shall be ready," replied Gamzálo, and roared out something incomprehensible. He understood why Hadji Murád had ordered the rifles to be loaded. From the first he had desired only one thing—to slay and stab as many Russians as possible, and to escape to the hills; and this desire had increased day by day. Now at last he saw that Hadji Murád also wanted this, and he was satisfied.

When Hadji Murád went away, Gamzálo roused his comrades, and all four spent the rest of the night examining their rifles pistols flints and accoutrements; replacing what was damaged, sprinkling fresh powder on to the pans, and stoppering packets filled with powder measured for each charge with bullets wrapped in oiled rags, sharpening their swords and daggers and greasing the blades with tallow.

Before daybreak Hadji Murád again came out into the hall to get some water for his ablutions. The songs of the nightingales that had burst into ecstasy at dawn sounded even louder and more incessant than they had done before, while from his henchmen's room, where the daggers were being sharpened, came the regular squeaking and rasping of iron against stone.

Hadji Murád got himself some water from a tub, and was already at his own door when, above the sound of the grinding, he heard from his murids' room the high tones of Khanéfi's voice singing a familiar song. Hadji Murád stopped to listen. The song told of how a dzhigit, Hamzád, with his brave followers captured a herd of white horses from the Russians, and how a Russian prince followed him beyond the Térek and surrounded him with an army as large as a forest; and then the song went on to tell how Hamzád killed the horses, and, with his men entrenched behind this gory bulwark, fought the Russians as long as they had bullets in their rifles, daggers in their belts, and blood in their veins. But before he died Hamzád saw some birds flying in the sky and cried to them,—

> "Fly on, ye winged ones, fly to our homes!
> Tell ye our mothers, tell ye our sisters,
> Tell the white maidens, fighting we died
> For Ghazavát! Tell them our bodies
> Never shall lie and rest in a tomb!
> Wolves shall devour and tear them to pieces,
> Ravens and vultures pluck out our eyes."

With that the song ended, and at the last words, sung to a mournful air, the merry Bata's vigorous voice joined in with a loud shout of "*Lya-il lyakha-il' Allakh!*" finishing with a shrill shriek. Then all was quiet again, except for the *tchut, tchuk, tchuk, tchuk* and whistling of the nightingales from the garden, and from behind the door the even grinding, and now and then the whizz, of iron sliding quickly along the whetstone.

Hadji Murád was so full of thought that he did not notice how he tilted his jug till the water began to pour out. He shook his head at himself, and re-entered his room. After performing his morning ablutions he examined his weapons and sat down on his bed. There was nothing more for him to do. To be allowed to ride out, he would have to get permission from the officer in charge; but it was not yet daylight, and the officer was still asleep.

Khanéfi's song reminded him of another song, the one his mother had composed just after he was born: the song addressed to his father, that Hadji Murád had mentioned to Lóris-Mélikov.

> "Thy sword of Damascus-steel tore my white bosom;
> But close on it laid I my own little boy;
> In my hot-streaming blood him I laved; and the wound
> Without herbs or specifics was soon fully healed.
> As I, facing death, remained fearless, so he,
> My boy, my *dzhigit*, from all fear shall be free!"

He remembered how his mother put him to sleep beside her under a cloak, on the roof of their *sáklya*, and how he asked her to let him see the place on her side where the wound had left a scar. Hadji Murád seemed to see his mother before him—not wrinkled, grey-haired, with gaps between her teeth, as he had lately left her, but young handsome and so strong that she carried him in a basket on her back across the mountains to her father's when he was a heavy five-year-old boy. He also recalled his grandfather, wrinkled and grey-bearded, and how the old man hammered silver with his sinewy hands, and made him say his prayers.

He thought of the fountain at the foot of the hill, whither, holding to her wide trousers, he went with his mother to fetch water. He

remembered the lean dog that used to lick his face, and he recalled
with special vividness the peculiar smell of sour milk and smoke in
the shed where his mother took him with her when she went to milk
the cows or scald the milk. He remembered how she shaved his head
for the first time, and how surprised he was to see his round blue-
gleaming head reflected in the brightly-polished brass basin that
hung against the wall.

And the recollection of himself as a little child reminded him of
his beloved son, Yusúf, whose head he himself had shaved for the first
time; and now this Yusúf was a handsome young *dzhigit*. He pictured
him as he was when last he saw him. It was on the day that Hadji
Murád left Tselméss. His son brought him his horse and asked to be
allowed to accompany him. Yusúf was ready dressed and armed, and
led his own horse by the bridle. His rosy handsome young face and
the whole of his tall slender figure (he was taller than his father)
breathed of daring, youth, and the joy of life. The breadth of his
shoulders, though he was so young, the very wide youthful hips, the
long slender waist, and the strength of his long arms, the power flex-
ibility and agility of all his movements had always rejoiced Hadji
Murád, who admired his son.

"Thou hadst better stay. Thou wilt be alone at home now. Take care
of thy mother and thy grandmother," said Hadji Murád. And he
remembered the spirited and proud look and the flush of pleasure with
which Yusúf had replied that as long as he lived no one should injure
his mother or grandmother. All the same Yusúf had mounted and
accompanied his father as far as the stream. There he turned back, and
since then Hadji Murád had not seen his wife, his mother, or his son.
And it was this son whose eyes Shamil wished to put out! Of what
would be done to his wife, Hadji Murád did not wish to think.

These thoughts so excited him that he could not sit still any
longer. He jumped up and went limping quickly to the door, opened
it, and called Eldár. The sun had not yet risen, but it was already quite
light. The nightingales were still singing.

"Go, and tell the officer that I want to go out riding; and saddle
the horses," said he.

XXIV

Butler's only consolation all this time was the poetry of warfare, to which he gave himself up not only during his hours of service, but also in private life. Dressed in his Circassian costume he rode and swaggered about, and twice went into ambush with Bogdanovich, though neither time did they discover or kill any one. This closeness to and friendship with Bogdanovich, famed for his courage, seemed pleasant and warlike to Butler. He had paid his debt, having borrowed the money of a Jew at an enormous rate of interest—that is to say, he had only postponed his difficulties without solving them. He tried not to think of his position, and to find oblivion not only in the poetry of warfare, but also in wine. He drank more and more every day, and day by day grew morally weaker. He was now no longer the chaste Joseph he had been towards Mary Dmítrievna, but on the contrary began courting her grossly, but to his surprise, met with a strong and decided repulse which put him to shame.

At the end of April there arrived at the fort a detachment with which Baryátinsky intended to effect an advance right through Chechnya, which had till then been considered impassable. In that detachment were two companies of the Kabardá regiment, and according to the Caucasian custom these were treated as guests by the Kurín companies. The soldiers were lodged in the barracks, and were treated not only to supper, consisting of buckwheat-porridge and beef, but also to vódka. The officers shared the quarters of the Kurín officers, and as usual those in residence gave the newcomers a dinner, at which the regimental singers performed, and which ended up with a drinking-bout. Major Petróv, very drunk and no longer red but ashy pale, sat astride a chair, and drawing his sword, hacked at imaginary foes, alternately swearing and laughing, now embracing someone and now dancing to the tune of his favourite song.

> "Shamil, he began to riot
> In the days gone by;
> Try, ry, rataty,
> In the years gone by!"

Butler was there, too. He tried to see the poetry of warfare in this also; but in the depth of his soul he was sorry for the Major. To stop him however was quite impossible; and Butler, feeling that the fumes were mounting to his own head, quietly left the room and went home.

The moon lit up the white houses and the stones on the road. It was so light that every pebble, every straw, every little heap of dust was visible. As he approached the house, Butler met Mary Dmítrievna with a shawl over her head and neck. After the rebuff she had given him, Butler had avoided her, feeling rather ashamed; but now, in the moonlight and after the wine he had drunk, he was pleased to meet her, and wished again to make up to her.

"Where are you off to?" he asked.

"Why, to see after my old man," she answered pleasantly. Her rejection of Butler's advances was quite sincere and decided, but she did not like his avoiding her as he had done lately.

"Why bother about him? He'll soon come back."

"But will he?"

"If he doesn't, they'll bring him."

"Just so. . . . That's not right, you know! . . . But you think I'd better not go?"

"No, don't. We'd better go home."

Mary Dmítrievna turned back and walked beside him. The moon shone so brightly that round the shadows of their heads a halo seemed to move along the road. Butler was looking at this halo and making up his mind to tell her that he liked her as much as ever, but he did not know how to begin. She waited to hear what he would say. So they walked on in silence almost to the house, when some horsemen appeared from round the corner. They were an officer with an escort.

"Who's that coming now?" said Mary Dmítrievna, stepping aside. The moon was behind the rider, so that she did not recognise him until he had almost come up to Butler and herself. It was Peter Nikoláevich Kámenev, an officer who had formerly served with the Major, and whom Mary Dmítrievna therefore knew.

"Is that you, Peter Nikoláevich?" said she, addressing him.

"It's me," said Kámenev. "Ah, Butler, how d'you do? . . . Not asleep yet? Having a walk with Mary Dmítrievna! You'd better look out, or the Major will give it you. . . . Where is he?"

"Why, there. . . . Listen!" replied Mary Dmítrievna, pointing in the direction whence came the sounds of a *tulumbas* and of songs. "They're on the spree."

"How's that? Are your people having a spree on their own?"

"No; some officers have come from Hasav-Yurt, and they are being entertained."

"Ah, that's good! I shall be in time. . . . I just want the Major for a moment."

"On business?" asked Butler.

"Yes, just a little business matter."

"Good or bad?"

"It all depends. . . . Good for us, but bad for some people," and Kámenev laughed.

By this time they had reached the Major's house.

"Chikhirév," shouted Kámenev to one of his Cossacks, "come here!"

A Don Cossack rode up from among the others. He was dressed in the ordinary Don Cossack uniform, with high boots and a mantle, and carried saddle-bags behind.

"Well, take the thing out," said Kámenev, dismounting.

The Cossack also dismounted, and took a sack out of his saddle-bag. Kámenev took the sack from him, and put his hand in.

"Well, shall I show you a novelty? You won't be frightened, Mary Dmítrievna?"

"Why should I be frightened?" she replied.

"Here it is!" said Kámenev, taking out a man's head, and holding it up in the light of the moon. "Do you recognise it?"

It was a shaven head with salient brows, black short-cut beard and moustaches, one eye open and the other half-closed. The shaven skull was cleft, but not right through, and there was congealed blood in the nose. The neck was wrapped in a blood-stained towel. Notwithstanding the many wounds on the head, the blue lips still bore a kindly childlike expression.

Mary Dmítrievna looked at it, and without a word turned away and went quickly into the house.

Butler could not tear his eyes from the terrible head. It was the head of that very Hadji Murád with whom he had so recently spent his evenings in such friendly intercourse.

"How's that? Who has killed him?" he asked.

"Wanted to give us the slip, but was caught," said Kámenev, and he gave the head back to the Cossack, and went into the house with Butler.

"He died like a hero," said Kámenev.

"But however did it all happen?"

"Just wait a bit. When the Major comes I will tell you all about it. That's what I am sent for. I take it round to all the forts and *aouls* and show it."

The Major was sent for, and he came back accompanied by two other officers as drunk as himself, and began embracing Kámenev.

"And I have brought you Hadji Murád's head," said Kámenev.

"No? . . . Killed?"

"Yes; wanted to escape."

"I always said he would bamboozle them! . . . And where is it? The head, I mean. . . . Let's see it."

The Cossack was called, and brought in the bag with the head. It was taken out, and the Major looked at it long with drunken eyes.

"All the same, he was a fine fellow," said he. "Let me kiss him!"

"Yes, it's true. It was a valiant head," said one of the officers.

When all had looked at it, it was returned to the Cossack, who put it in his bag, trying to let it bump against the floor as gently as possible.

"I say, Kámenev, what speech do you make when you show the head?" asked an officer.

"No! . . . Let me kiss him. He gave me a sword!" shouted the Major.

Butler went out into the porch.

Mary Dmítrievna was sitting on the second step. She looked round at Butler, and at once turned angrily away again.

"What's the matter, Mary Dmítrievna?" asked he.

"You're all cutthroats! . . . I hate it! You're cutthroats, really," and she got up.

"It might happen to any one," remarked Butler, not knowing what to say. "That's war."

"War? War, indeed! . . . Cutthroats and nothing else. A dead body should be given back to the earth, and they're grinning at it there! . . . Cutthroats, really," she repeated, as she descended the steps and entered the house by the back door.

Butler returned to the room, and asked Kámenev to tell them in detail how the thing had occurred.

And Kámenev told them.

This is what had happened.

XXV

Hadji Murád was allowed to go out riding in the neighbourhood of the town, but never without a convoy of Cossacks. There was only half a troop of them altogether in Nukhá, ten of whom were employed by the officers, so that if ten were sent out with Hadji Murád (according to the orders received) the same men would have had to go every other day. Therefore, after ten had been sent out the first day, it was decided to send only five in future, and Hadji Murád was asked not to take all his henchmen with him. But on 25th April he rode out with all five. When he mounted, the commander, noticing that all five henchmen were going with him, told him that he was forbidden to take them all; but Hadji Murád pretended not to hear, touched his horse, and the commander did not insist.

With the Cossacks rode a non-commissioned officer, Nazárov, who had received the Cross of St. George for bravery. He was a young healthy brown-haired lad, as fresh as a rose. He was the eldest of a poor family belonging to the sect of Old Believers, had grown up without a father, and had maintained his old mother, three sisters, and two brothers.

"Mind, Nazárov, keep close to him!" shouted the commander.

"All right, your honour!" answered Nazárov, and rising in his stirrups and adjusting the rifle that hung at his back, he started his fine large roan gelding at a trot. Four Cossacks followed him: Ferapontov, tall and thin, a regular thief and plunderer (he it was who had sold gunpowder to Gamzálo); Ignátov, a sturdy peasant who boasted of his strength, was no longer young, and had nearly completed his service; Míshkin, a weakly lad at whom everybody laughed; and the young fair-haired Petrakóv, his mother's only son, always amiable and jolly.

The morning had been misty, but it cleared up later on, and the opening foliage, the young virgin grass, the sprouting corn and the ripples of the rapid river just visible to the left of the road, all glittered in the sunshine.

Hadji Murád rode slowly along, followed by the Cossacks and by his henchmen. They rode out along the road beyond the fort at a walk. They met women carrying baskets on their heads, soldiers driving carts, and creaking wagons drawn by buffaloes. When he had gone about a mile and a half, Hadji Murád touched up his white Kabardá horse, which started at an amble that obliged the henchmen and Cossacks to ride at a quick trot to keep up with him.

"Ah, he's got a fine horse under him," said Ferapontov. "If only he were still an enemy I'd soon bring him down."

"Yes, mate. Three hundred roubles were offered for that horse in Tiflis."

"But I can get ahead of him on mine," said Nazárov.

"You get ahead? A likely thing!"

Hadji Murád kept increasing his pace.

"Hey, *kunák*, you mustn't do that. Steady!" cried Nazárov, starting to overtake Hadji Murád.

Hadji Murád looked round, said nothing, and continued to ride at the same pace.

"Mind, they're up to something, the devils!" said Ignátov. "See how they are tearing along."

So they rode for the best part of a mile in the direction of the mountains.

"I tell you it won't do!" shouted Nazárov.

Hadji Murád did not answer, and did not look round, but only increased his pace to a gallop.

"Humbug! You'll not get away!" shouted Nazárov, stung to the quick. He gave his big roan gelding a cut with his whip, and rising in his stirrups and bending forward, flew full speed in pursuit of Hadji Murád.

The sky was so bright, the air so clear, and life played so joyously in Nazárov's soul as, becoming one with his fine strong horse, he flew along the smooth road behind Hadji Murád, that the possibility of anything sad or dreadful happening never occurred to him. He rejoiced that with every step he was gaining on Hadji Murád.

Hadji Murád judged by the approaching tramp of the big horse behind him that he would soon be overtaken, and seizing his pistol with his right hand, with his left he began slightly to rein in his Kabardá horse, which was excited by hearing the tramp of hoofs behind it.

"You mustn't, I tell you!" shouted Nazárov, almost level with Hadji Murád, and stretching out his hand to seize the latter's bridle. But before he reached it a shot was fired.—"What are you doing?" screamed Nazárov, catching hold of his breast. "At them, lads!" he exclaimed, and he reeled and fell forward on his saddle-bow.

But the mountaineers were beforehand in taking to their weapons, and fired their pistols at the Cossacks and hewed at them with their swords.

Nazárov hung on the neck of his horse, which careered round his comrades. The horse under Ignátov fell, crushing his leg, and two of the mountaineers, without dismounting, drew their swords and hacked at his head and arms. Petrakóv was about to rush to his comrades' rescue, when two shots—one in the back and the other in his side—stung him, and he fell from his horse like a sack.

Míshkin turned round and galloped off towards the fortress. Khanéfi and Bata rushed after him, but he was already too far away and they could not catch him. When they saw that they could not overtake him, they returned to the others.

Petrakóv lay on his back, his stomach ripped open, his young face turned to the sky, and while dying he gasped for breath like a fish.

Gamzálo having finished off Ignátov with his sword, gave a cut to Nazárov too, and threw him from his horse. Bata took their cartridge-pouches from the slain. Khánefi wished to take Nazárov's horse, but Hadji Murád called out to him to leave it, and dashed forward along the road. His murids galloped after him, driving away Nazárov's horse that tried to follow them. They were already among rice fields more than six miles from Nukhá when a shot was fired from the tower of that place to give the alarm.

*　　　*　　　*　　　*　　　*

"Oh, good Lord! Oh, dear me! Dear me! What have they done?" cried the commander of the fort, seizing his head with his hands, when he heard of Hadji Murád's escape. "They've done for me! They've let him escape, the villains!" cried he, listening to Míshkin's account.

An alarm was raised everywhere, and not only the Cossacks of the place were sent after the fugitives, but also all the militia that could be mustered from the pro-Russian *aouls*. A thousand roubles reward was offered for the capture of Hadji Murád alive or dead, and two hours after he and his followers had escaped from the Cossacks more than two hundred mounted men were galloping after the officer in charge to find and capture the runaways.

After riding some miles along the highroad, Hadji Murád checked his panting horse, which, wet with perspiration, had turned from white to grey.

To the right of the road could be seen the *sáklyas* and minarets of the *aoul* Benerdzhík, on the left lay some fields, and beyond them the river. Although the way to the mountains lay to the right, Hadji Murád turned in the opposite direction, to the left, assuming that his pursuers would be sure to go to the right; while he, abandoning the road, would cross the Alazán and would come out on to the highroad on the other side, where no one would expect him, and would ride along it to the forest, and then, after recrossing the river, would make his way to the mountains.

Having come to this conclusion, he turned to the left. But it proved impossible to reach the river. The rice-field which had to be crossed had just been flooded, as is always done in spring, and had become a bog in which the horses' legs sank above their pasterns. Hadji Murád and his henchmen turned, now to the left, now to the right, hoping to find drier ground; but the field they happened to be in had been equally flooded all over, and was now saturated with water. The horses drew their feet out of the sticky mud into which they sank, with a pop like that of a cork drawn from a bottle, and stopped, panting, after every few steps. They struggled in this way so long that it began to grow dusk, and they had still not reached the river. To their left lay a patch of higher ground overgrown with shrubs, and Hadji Murád decided to ride in among these clumps and remain there till night to rest their worn-out horses and let them graze. The men themselves ate some bread and cheese that they had brought with them. At last night came on and the moon that had been shining at first, hid behind the hill, and it became dark. There were a great many nightingales in that neighbourhood, and there were two of them in these shrubs. As long as Hadji Murád and his men were making a noise among the bushes the nightingales had been silent, but when the people became still, the birds again began to call to one another and to sing.

Hadji Murád, awake to all the sounds of night, listened to them involuntarily, and their trills reminded him of the song about Hamzád which he had heard the night before when he went to get water. He might now at any moment find himself in the position in which Hamzád had been. He fancied that it would be so, and suddenly his soul became serious. He spread out his búrka and performed his ablutions, and scarcely had he finished before a sound was heard approaching their shelter. It was the sound of many horses' feet plashing through the bog.

The keen-sighted Bata ran out to one edge of the clump, and peering through the darkness saw black shadows, which were men on foot and on horseback. Khanéfi discerned a similar crowd on the other side. It was Kargánov, the military commander of the district, with his militia.

"Well, then, we shall fight like Hamzád," thought Hadji Murád.

When the alarm was given, Kargánov, with a troop of militiamen and Cossacks, had rushed off in pursuit of Hadji Murád; but he had been unable to find any trace of him. He had already lost hope, and was returning home, when towards evening he met an old man and asked him if he had seen any horsemen about. The old man replied that he had. He had seen six horsemen floundering in the rice-field, and then had seen them enter the clump where he himself was getting wood. Kargánov turned back, taking the old man with him; and seeing the hobbled horses, he made sure that Hadji Murád was there. In the night he surrounded the clump, and waited till morning to take Hadji Murád alive or dead.

Having understood that he was surrounded, and having discovered an old ditch among the shrubs, Hadji Murád decided to entrench himself in it, and to resist as long as strength and ammunition lasted. He told this to his comrades, and ordered them to throw up a bank in front of the ditch; and his henchmen at once set to work to cut down branches, dig up the earth with their daggers, and to make an entrenchment. Hadji Murád himself worked with them.

As soon as it began to grow light the commander of the militia troop rode up to the clump and shouted,—

"Hey! Hadji Murád, surrender! We are many, and you are few!"

In reply came the report of a rifle, a cloudlet of smoke rose from the ditch, and a bullet hit the militiaman's horse, which staggered under him and began to fall. The rifles of the militiamen, who stood at the outskirt of the clump of shrubs, began cracking in their turn, and their bullets whistled and hummed, cutting off leaves and twigs and striking the embankment, but not the men entrenched behind it. Only Gamzálo's horse, that had strayed from the others, was hit in the head by a bullet. It did not fall, but breaking its hobbles and rushing among the bushes it ran to the other horses, pressing close to them, and watering the young grass with its blood. Hadji Murád and his men fired only when any of the militiamen came forward, and rarely missed their aim. Three militiamen were wounded, and the others, far from making up their minds to rush the entrenchment, retreated further and further back, only firing from a distance and at random.

So it continued for more than an hour. The sun had risen to about half the height of the trees, and Hadji Murád was already thinking of leaping on his horse and trying to make his way to the river, when the shouts were heard of many men who had just arrived. These were Hadji Aga of Mekhtulí with his followers. There were about two hundred of them. Hadji Aga had once been Hadji Murád's *kunák*, and had lived with him in the mountains, but he had afterwards gone over to the Russians. With him was Akhmet Khan, the son of Hadji Murád's old enemy.

Like Kargánov, Hadji Aga began by calling to Hadji Murád to surrender, and Hadji Murád answered as before with a shot.

"Swords out, lads!" cried Hadji Aga, drawing his own; and a hundred voices were raised of men who rushed shrieking in among the shrubs.

The militiamen ran in among the shrubs, but from behind the entrenchment came the crack of one shot after another. Some three men fell, and the attackers stopped at the outskirts of the clump and also began firing. As they fired they gradually approached the entrenchment, running across from behind one shrub to another. Some succeeded in getting across; others fell under the bullets of Hadji Murád or of his men. Hadji Murád fired without missing; Gamzálo too, rarely wasted a shot, and shrieked with joy every time he saw that his bullet had hit its aim. Khan Mahomá sat at the edge of the ditch singing "Il lyakha il Allah!" and fired leisurely, but often missed. Eldár's whole body trembled with impatience to rush dagger in hand at the enemy, and he fired often and at random, constantly looking round at Hadji Murád and stretching out beyond the entrenchment. The shaggy Khanéfi, with his sleeves rolled up, did the duty of a servant even here. He loaded the guns which Hadji Murád and Kahn Mahomá passed to him, carefully driving home with a ramrod the bullets wrapped in greasy rags, and pouring dry powder out of the powder-flask on to the pans. Bata did not remain in the ditch as the others did, but kept running to the horses, driving them away to a safer place, and, shrieking incessantly, fired without using a prop for his gun. He was the first to be wounded. A bullet entered his neck, and he sat down spitting blood and swearing. Then Hadji Murád was wounded, the bullet piercing his shoulder. He tore some cotton wool from the lining of his *beshmét*, plugged the wound with it, and went on firing.

"Let us fly at them with our swords!" said Eldár for the third time, and he looked out from behind the bank of earth, ready to rush at the enemy; but at that instant a bullet struck him, and he reeled and fell backwards on to Hadji Murád's leg. Hadji Murád glanced at him. His beautiful ram's eyes gazed intently and seriously at Hadji Murád. His mouth, the upper lip pouting like a child's, twitched without opening. Hadji Murád drew his leg away from under him and continued firing.

Khanéfi bent over the dead Eldár and began taking the unused ammunition out of the cartridge-cases of his coat.

Khan Mahomá meanwhile continued to sing, loading leisurely and firing. The enemy ran from shrub to shrub, hallooing and shrieking, and drawing ever nearer and nearer.

Another bullet hit Hadji Murád in the left side. He lay down in the ditch, and again pulled some cotton wool out of his *beshmét* and plugged the wound. This wound in the side was fatal, and he felt that he was dying. Memories and pictures succeeded one another with extraordinary rapidity in his imagination. Now he saw the powerful Abu Nutsal Khan as, dagger in hand and holding up his severed cheek, he rushed at his foe; then he saw the weak, bloodless old Vorontsóv, with his cunning white face, and heard his soft voice; and then he saw his own son Yusúf, his wife Sofiát, and then the pale, red-bearded face of his enemy Shamil with half-closed eyes. All these images passed through his mind without evoking any feeling within him: neither pity nor anger nor any kind of desire; everything seemed so insignificant in comparison with what was beginning, or had already begun, within him.

Yet his strong body continued the thing that he had commenced. Gathering together his last strength, he rose from behind the bank, fired his pistol at a man who was just running towards him, and hit him. The man fell. Then Hadji Murád got quite out of the ditch, and, limping heavily, went dagger in hand straight at the foe.

Some shots cracked, and he reeled and fell. Several militiamen with triumphant shrieks rushed towards the fallen body. But the body that seemed to be dead, suddenly moved. First the uncovered bleeding shaven head rose; then, with hands holding to the trunk of the tree, the body rose. He seemed so terrible that those who were running towards him stopped short. But suddenly a shudder passed through him; he staggered away from the tree and fell on his face, stretched out at full length, like a thistle that had been mown down, and he moved no more.

He did not move, but still he felt.

When Hadji Aga, who was the first to reach him, struck him on the head with a large dagger, it seemed to Hadji Murád that someone was striking him with a hammer, and he could not understand who was doing it, or why. That was his last consciousness of any connection with his body. He felt nothing more, and his enemies kicked and hacked at what had no longer anything in common with him.

Hadji Aga placed his foot on the back of the corpse, and with two blows cut off the head, and carefully—not to soil his shoes with blood—rolled it away with his foot. Crimson blood spurted from the arteries of the neck, and black blood flowed from the head, soaking the grass.

Kargánov and Hadji Aga and Akhmet Khan and all the militiamen gathered together—like sportsmen round a slaughtered animal—near the bodies of Hadji Murád and his men (Khanéfi, Khan Mahomá, and Gamzálo were bound), and amid the powder-smoke which hung over the bushes, they triumphed in their victory.

The nightingales, that had hushed their songs while the firing lasted, now started their trills once more: first one quite close, then others in the distance.

  *   *   *   *   *

It was of this death that I was reminded by the crushed thistle in the midst of the ploughed field.

ENDNOTES

"Family Happiness"

1. (p. 14) *'like Mash—Marya Alexandrovna'*: Russian names consist of a given name, a patronymic based on the father's name ending in -ovich or -ich or -ych for males and -ovna or -evna for females, and a surname. The use of the given name and a patronymic indicates a degree of polite formality between adults. Greater familiarity or intimacy is indicated by the use of the first name or a diminutive of the first name without the patronymic. When writing about characters in these works, one might use the first name (for example, Ivan), first name and patronymic (Ivan Ilych), or the surname (Golovin), but never the patronymic alone (Ilych)—a form of address that expresses familiarity between, for instance, a landowner and an elderly house servant.

2. (p. 24) *Lieutenant Strelski . . . Alfred . . . Eleonora*: These names resemble those used in sentimental romance novels of the time.

3. (p. 42) *'I was just meaning to call thee so . . . I feel thee quite mine'*: Russian employs a familiar form of address (corresponding to "thee" and "thou") that is used among family members and persons on intimate terms or by adults addressing children, and a formal form of the second person pronoun (corresponding to "you") used by adults who would also refer to each other using the first name and patronymic. The two main characters here are marking a new stage of intimacy by changing from "Marya Alexandrovna," "Sergei Mikhailych," and "you" to "Masha," "Sergei," and "thou/thee."

4. (p. 48) *This duty of solemnly presiding before the sacred shrine of the samovar . . . was for a long while a source of confusion to me*: A samovar has a large chamber in which water is traditionally heated by coals from below; a smaller pot containing strong, concentrated tea usually rests on top of the larger chamber to stay warm. When the water is heated, it is mixed in individual glasses with the stronger tea to taste. Each glass rests in a metal base with a handle that stays cool, though the glass itself is hot.

"The Death of Ivan Ilych"

1. (p. 89) *where their game of 'bridge' was to be that evening*: The game described here is vint, a form of whist believed to be the immediate precursor of modern auction bridge. The name means "screw" and derives from the

357

fact that the play proceeds in a circle around the table. Frequently portrayed in the works of Tolstoy, Chekhov, and others as a decadent bourgeois pastime, *vint* rapidly disappeared from Russia after the Revolution of 1917 but survived as *skruuvi* in Finland, which had been a Russian possession.

2. (p. 95) *He was the son of an official . . . be dismissed*: Peter the Great established a system of corresponding military, civil, and judiciary ranks, or *chin*, in 1722. The plight of the petty functionary (*chinovnik*) attempting to improve his rank is a comnon theme in nineteenth-century Russian works, such as Aleksandr Pushkin's "The Station Master" and Nikolai Gogol's "The Overcoat," which would in turn inspire modernists like Franz Kafka, Jean-Paul Sartre, and Samuel Beckett in the twentieth century.

3. (p. 143) *He tried to say 'forgive,' but said 'forgo'*: Ivan Ilych means to say "*prosti*," which means "forgive (me)," but instead says "*propusti*," meaning literally "let (me) pass." The translator has translated *propusti* as "forgo" to convey a sense of the mispronunciation in Russian.

"The Kreutzer Sonata"

1. (p. 147) *For there are some eunuchs . . . let him receive it*: The final passage of the epigraph—from the Bible, Matthew 19:10–12—was central to the Russian religious sect known as the *skoptsi* ("eunuchs"), who were first described in legal documents in the late eighteenth century and practiced various forms of celibacy, including castration. The skoptsi were arrested and deported to Siberia at various points during the nineteenth century. The sect experienced a revival in growth in the 1870s and continued to be of sufficient legal concern that this line was censored from early printings of "The Kreutzer Sonata" and therefore does not appear in some translations.

2. (p. 157) *"for my health's sake"*: Tolstoy here refers to a medical view originating in France that men needed sexual release with a certain frequency for the maintenance of good sexual health, and that pornography and prostitution might be generally legalized toward this end. He criticizes the notion directly in his "Afterword to *The Kreutzer Sonata*," published some months after the story appeared, and elsewhere in his writings.

3. (p. 164) *"I showed her my diary . . . I felt necessary to tell her"*: In *Anna Karenina* Levin makes a similar confession to Kitty before they are married, as did Tolstoy to his own wife-to-be, Sophia Behrs.

4. (p. 166) *transports*: The Russian here, *vostorgi*, evokes the emblematic sentimental expression "wild delight" (*dikii vostorgi*) that appears in "Family Happiness."

5. (p. 196) *"A largely developed behind such as they say characterize Hottentot women"*: This is an allusion to the "Hottentot Venus," a Khoi-Khoi woman from South Africa named Saartjie Baartman who was brought to England in 1810 and exhibited as a sexual oddity for her large, protruding buttocks, pendulous breasts, and enlarged vulva. She died in 1814 in France at age twenty-five, and her genitalia, brain, and skeleton were preserved for exhibit at the Musée de l'Homme in Paris.

6. (p. 201) *"In former times we had been on familiar terms"*: See endnote 3, p. 42.

7. (p. 206) *"She, like Uriah's wife"*: The reference is to the story of Bathsheba in the Bible, 2 Samuel 11. Bathsheba, the wife of Uriah, sleeps with King David and conceives. At David's prompting she attempts to conceal the adultery from her husband by seducing him, but Uriah refuses her and is killed at David's behest.

8. (p. 224) *"I went there"*: Note that the euphemism for a brothel—there— is now used to refer to the scene where Pozdnyshev's wife and Trukhachevsky are sitting.

"Hadji Murád"

1. (p. 247) *Prince Simon Mikhailovich Vorontsóv*: Vorontsóv and Poltorátsky, like most of the officers and persons of rank, including Hadji Murád, Shamil, and other Caucasian leaders, are real historical figures. Poltorátsky's memoir was one of Tolstoy's primary sources for "Hadji Murád," as was the published record of Count Lóris-Mélikov's conversations with Hadji Murád, described in chapters XI–XIII.

2. (p. 255) *He would again rule over not only Avaria . . . would submit to him*: In 1864 the Russians made an incursion into Avaria, a Muslim region in the northeastern Caucasus and took control from the native Khan.

3. (p. 257) *Plotorátsky's little Kabardá*: Kabardá, now incorporated into what is known as the Kabardino-Balkar Republic, is in the northern Caucasus and at the time Tolstoy wrote the story had long been aligned with the Russians.

4. (p. 260) *The first was a Lesgian*: The Lesgians are Muslims from southeast Dagestan and the adjacent border region of Azerbaijan.

5. (p. 332) *Prince Baryátinsky*: Prince Alexandr Ivanovich Baryátinski (1814–1879) ultimately captured Shamil in 1859 after twenty-five years of resistance, ending the major portion of the fighting in the Caucasus in this period. Tolstoy had met Baryátinski during his service in Sevastopol.

INSPIRED BY THE DEATH OF IVAN
ILYCH AND OTHER STORIES

Music

"The Kreutzer Sonata" has a notable pedigree, having been inspired by a great work and inspiring other great works in turn. Tolstoy based his story on what is perhaps Beethoven's best-known sonata for violin and piano, No. 9 in A major, Op. 47 (1803). The composer wrote the work for George Augustus Polgreen Bridgetower, a celebrated violin virtuoso of Ethiopian and British ancestry who had a unique playing style. The two premiered the sonata in Vienna, with Bridgetower adding a flourish to the final presto movement. (Beethoven was delighted with the improvement, one of the few instances in which he allowed anyone to change his work.) The piece was an immediate success, but Beethoven and Bridgetower soon found themselves competing for the same woman's affections. So Beethoven dedicated the work to Rodolphe Kreutzer, an influential composer and violinist, and it became known as the "Kreutzer." Ironically, Rodolphe Kreutzer was not at all taken with Beethoven's composition.

Thirty-four years after Tolstoy wrote "The Kreutzer Sonata," the Czech composer Leoš Janáček based his String Quartet No. 1 (1923) on the story, composing it in a single autumn week. "Note after note fell smoldering from my pen," wrote the composer, whose personal life smoldered as passionately as his music: Janáček, then sixty-nine, was secretly in love with a woman thirty-eight years his junior, Kamila Stosslova. He met Stosslova in 1917, and his infatuation with her inspired everything he composed subsequently, though both were married and living in different cities. Janáček's adoration of Kamila lives on in the more than seven hundred letters he wrote to her. String Quartet No. 1 presents the events of Tolstoy's novella and its themes; the two violins are clearly rivals, an increasing tempo foretells disaster, and in a plaintive fourth movement the husband reflects upon his actions and empathizes with his dead wife.

Film

Tolstoy's stories have also inspired numerous filmmakers, and cinematic versions of "The Death of Ivan Ilych," "Hadji Murád," and "The Kreutzer Sonata" have been produced in countries as diverse as Japan, America, Germany, Czechoslovakia, Mexico, Argentina, Italy, and, of course, Russia. Notable adaptations include *The White Warrior,* directed by Richard Freda and based on "Hadji Murád" (1961), and *Sonata* (1991), an interactive film installation by Grahame Weinbren that combines "The Kreutzer Sonata," the biblical story of Judith, and the works of Sigmund Freud.

Another innovative Tolstoy adaptation is *Ivans xtc. (To Live and Die in Hollywood),* directed by Bernard Rose (2000). The film is the story of hotshot Hollywood agent Ivan Beckman, played by Danny Huston, the son of filmmaker John Huston. Beckman's life is a parade of cocaine, call girls, and vicious industry posturing—a modern analogue to the hollowness Tolstoy's Ivan recognizes in his life at its end. The film's treatment of human frailty and the inability to comprehend the weight of mortality makes it a standout in contemporary cinema and an homage to the influence of Tolstoy.

COMMENTS & QUESTIONS

In this section, we aim to provide the reader with an array of perspectives on the text, as well as questions that challenge those perspectives. The commentary has been culled from sources as diverse as reviews contemporaneous with the work, letters written by the author, literary criticism of later generations, and appreciations written throughout the works' history. Following the commentary, a series of questions seeks to filter Leo Tolstoy's The Death of Ivan Ilych and Other Stories *through a variety of points of view and bring about a richer understanding of these enduring works.*

Comments

FYODOR DOSTOEVSKY

I like Leo Tolstoy a lot but, in my opinion, he will not write much.
　　　　　　　—from a letter to A. N. Maykov (January 18, 1856)

NORTH AMERICAN REVIEW

["The Death of Ivan Ilych"] is the latest work of that celebrated religious enthusiast, and in it he has carried the grotesque to its uttermost point. As usual, it is pessimistic; but it has some of the pleasant touches that make his little story, "Katia," so charming and true to life. Nevertheless, it is a *danse macabre*, headed by a skeleton. Tolstoi's personality actually possesses Ivan Ilyitch and dissects the qualities of that awful fear of death which comes to each man, at one time or another, forcing on him a sense of his helplessness. Ilyitch cannot see, feel, or hear what the terrible It is. It is death; he knows that; he is in its grasp; the whole world united cannot save him, and slowly but surely the relentless and unseen force loosens his hands from the hold they have on earth. The keenness and pitilessness of psychological analysis makes one shiver as if one had been present at a delicate bit of dissection done by a skillful surgeon. The dance of death begins in Ivan's household almost before his eyes, full of questions and remorseful fears, are closed. "Ivan Ilyitch" is the first novel Tolstoi has written in ten years. It was supposed that the peculiar ethics he had adopted were opposed to his further continuance in the art of novel-writing. The appearance of "The Death of Ivan Ilyitch" puts aside this supposition, and also the other, that his philosophical and theological meditations—culminating in the famous "My Religion"—had destroyed his interest in human life as a subject for artistic study. American readers may wonder why Russian novelists seem to bend all their energies toward increasing the gloomy tendency of the Russian nation under its present conditions. "Ivan Ilyitch" will increase that wonder.

—August 1887

NORTH AMERICAN REVIEW

The story of Hadji Murád was written by Tolstoy during his illness of 1901–02, and it is not one of his great stories. Done at a time when he was not at all well and unable to work on *What Is Religion?*—a book that he really had at heart—the tale is bald and meager. Only one who made a special study of Tolstoy and wanted to know his mind in all its phases would find it readable. His point of view is there, his sincerity, his intensity, but very little of his literary art. The tale is really only a first draft or outline of a book.

—June 1912

AYLMER MAUDE

"I am writing to you specially to say how glad I have been to be your contemporary, and to express my last and sincere request. My friend, return to literary activity! That gift came to you from whence comes all the rest . . . Great writer of our Russian land, listen to my wish!"

So wrote Turgénev on his deathbed to Tolstoy, when the latter, absorbed in religious struggles and studies, had for five years produced no work of art save one short story.

Nor was it long before the wish was realised, for three years later Tolstoy was writing "The Death of Iván Ilyitch."

—from his preface to Hadji Murád (1912)

VIRGINIA WOOLF

Again and again we share Masha's feelings in *Family Happiness*. One shuts one's eyes to escape the feeling of pleasure and fear. Often it is pleasure that is uppermost. In this very story there are two descriptions, one of a girl walking in a garden at night with her lover, one of a newly married couple prancing down their drawing-room, which so convey the feeling of intense happiness that we shut the book to feel it better. But always there is an element of fear which makes us, like Masha, wish to escape from the gaze which Tolstoy fixes on us. Is it the sense, which in real life might harass us, that such happiness as he describes is too intense to last, that we are on the edge of disaster? Or is it not that the very intensity of our pleasure is somehow questionable and forces us to ask, with Pozdnyshev in the *Kreutzer Sonata*, 'But why live?' Life dominates Tolstoy as the soul dominates Dostoevsky.

—from *The Common Reader* (1925)

Questions

1. Do these four works have in common a theme, a perspective on human character, a sensibility, a method? Or are these elements different in each case?

2. What is the point of telling the sad tale of Ivan Ilych's death? When precisely does his process of dying begin?

3. If you were going to make a movie out of "Hadji Murád," what would you emphasize? Which would be your big scenes? Could a movie be made that would not in crucial ways betray Tolstoy's novella?

4. On the basis of these stories could you write an essay on Tolstoy's view of the relations between the sexes or his view of marriage? Could Tolstoy reconcile the idea of motherhood with the possibility of female sexual desire? How would you sum up these views?

5. "The Kreutzer Sonata" created an uproar when it was published, and the Czar Alexander III had to be persuaded to relax the official censorship on its behalf. Was the uproar justified? Can the novella still shock? If not, why not?

FOR FURTHER READING

Russian Literature and History

Riasanovsky, Nicholas Valentine. *A History of Russia.* New York: Oxford University Press, 1963.

Terras, Victor, ed. *Handbook of Russian Literature.* New Haven, CT: Yale University Press, 1985.

Biographical and Critical Studies

Bayley, John. *Tolstoy and the Novel.* 1966. Reprint with a new preface: Chicago: University of Chicago Press, 1988.

Berlin, Isaiah. *The Hedgehog and the Fox: An Essay on Tolstoy's View of History.* 1953. New York: Simon and Schuster, 1986.

Christian, R. F., ed. *Tolstoy's Letters.* 2 vols. New York: Charles Scribner's Sons, 1978.

———. *Tolstoy's Diaries.* 2 vols. New York: Charles Scribner's Sons, 1985.

Gustafson, Richard F. *Leo Tolstoy, Resident and Stranger: A Study in Fiction and Theology.* Princeton, NJ: Princeton University Press, 1986.

Layton, Susan. *Russian Literature and Empire: Conquest of the Caucasus from Pushkin to Tolstoy.* Cambridge and New York: Cambridge University Press, 1994.

Mandelker, Amy. *Framing "Anna Karenina": Tolstoy, the Woman Question, and the Victorian Novel.* Columbus: Ohio State University Press, 1993.

Orwin, Donna T. *Tolstoy's Art and Thought, 1847–1880.* Princeton, NJ: Princeton University Press, 1993.

Shklovsky, Victor. *Lev Tolstoy.* Translated by Olga Shartse. Moscow: Progress Publishers, 1978.

Silbajoris, Rimvydas. *Tolstoy's Aesthetics and His Art.* Columbus, OH: Slavica Publishers, 1991.

Simmons, Ernest J. *Leo Tolstoy.* New York: Vintage, 1960.

Wasiolek, Edward. *Tolstoy's Major Fiction.* Chicago: University of Chicago Press, 1978.

Wilson, A. N. *Tolstoy.* New York: W. W. Norton, 1988.

Other Works Cited in the Introduction

Dobrolyubov, N. A. "What Is Oblomovitis?" In *Selected Philosophical Essays*, translated by J. Fineberg. Moscow: Foreign Languages Publishing House, 1956.

Goncharov, Ivan Aleksandrovich. *Oblomov*. Translated by David Magarshack. 1859. New York: Penguin, 1967.

Tolstoy, Leo. *Anna Karenina*. Translated by Constance Garnett; introduction and notes by Amy Mandelker. New York: Barnes and Noble Classics, 2003.

————. *War and Peace*. Second edition. Translated by Louise and Aylmer Maude; edited by George Gibian. Norton Critical Edition. New York: W. W. Norton, 1996.

————. *What Is Art?* Translated by Aylmer Maude; introduction by Vincent Tomas. Indianapolis, IN: Bobbs-Merrill, Liberal Arts Press, 1960.

Adventures of Huckleberry Finn	Mark Twain	1-59308-112-X	$5.95
The Adventures of Tom Sawyer	Mark Twain	1-59308-139-1	$5.95
The Aeneid	Vergil	1-59308-237-1	$8.95
Aesop's Fables		1-59308-062-5	$7.95
The Age of Innocence	Edith Wharton	1-59308-143-X	$7.95
Alice's Adventures in Wonderland and Through the Looking-Glass	Lewis Carroll	1-59308-015-8	$7.95
Anna Karenina	Leo Tolstoy	1-59308-027-1	$8.95
The Arabian Nights	Anonymous	1-59308-281-9	$9.95
The Art of War	Sun Tzu	1-59308-017-4	$7.95
The Autobiography of an Ex-Colored Man and Other Writings	James Weldon Johnson	1-59308-289-4	$5.95
The Awakening and Selected Short Fiction	Kate Chopin	1-59308-113-8	$6.95
Billy Budd and The Piazza Tales	Herman Melville	1-59308-253-3	$7.95
The Brothers Karamazov	Fyodor Dostoevsky	1-59308-045-X	$11.95
The Call of the Wild and White Fang	Jack London	1-59308-200-2	$6.95
Candide	Voltaire	1-59308-028-X	$6.95
The Canterbury Tales	Geoffrey Chaucer	1-59308-080-8	$10.95
A Christmas Carol, The Chimes and The Cricket on the Hearth	Charles Dickens	1-59308-033-6	$6.95
The Collected Oscar Wilde		1-59308-310-6	$10.95
The Collected Poems of Emily Dickinson		1-59308-050-6	$5.95
The Complete Sherlock Holmes, Vol. I	Sir Arthur Conan Doyle	1-59308-034-4	$9.95
The Complete Sherlock Holmes, Vol. II	Sir Arthur Conan Doyle	1-59308-040-9	$9.95
Confessions	Saint Augustine	1-59308-259-2	$6.95
The Count of Monte Cristo	Alexandre Dumas	1-59308-151-0	$9.95
Don Quixote	Miguel de Cervantes	1-59308-046-8	$9.95
Dracula	Bram Stoker	1-59308-114-6	$6.95
Emma	Jane Austen	1-59308-152-9	$6.95
Essays and Poems by Ralph Waldo Emerson		1-59308-076-X	$8.95
The Essential Tales and Poems of Edgar Allan Poe		1-59308-064-6	$8.95
Ethan Frome and Selected Stories	Edith Wharton	1-59308-090-5	$6.95
Fairy Tales	Hans Christian Andersen	1-59308-260-6	$9.95
Founding America: Documents from the Revolution to the Bill of Rights	Jefferson, et al.	1-59308-230-4	$12.95
Frankenstein	Mary Shelley	1-59308-115-4	$6.95
Great American Short Stories: From Hawthorne to Hemingway	Various	1-59308-086-7	$9.95
The Great Escapes: Four Slave Narratives	Various	1-59308-294-0	$6.95
Great Expectations	Charles Dickens	1-59308-116-2	$6.95
Grimm's Fairy Tales	Jacob and Wilhelm Grimm	1-59308-056-5	$9.95
Gulliver's Travels	Jonathan Swift	1-59308-132-4	$5.95
Heart of Darkness and Selected Short Fiction	Joseph Conrad	1-59308-123-5	$5.95
The Idiot	Fyodor Dostoevsky	1-59308-058-1	$7.95
The Importance of Being Earnest and Four Other Plays	Oscar Wilde	1-59308-059-X	$7.95
The Inferno	Dante Alighieri	1-59308-051-4	$9.95
Jane Eyre	Charlotte Brontë	1-59308-117-0	$7.95

(continued)

Jude the Obscure	Thomas Hardy	1-59308-035-2	$6.95
The Jungle	Upton Sinclair	1-59308-118-9	$7.95
The Last of the Mohicans	James Fenimore Cooper	1-59308-137-5	$7.95
Les Liaisons Dangereuses	Pierre Choderlos de Laclos	1-59308-240-1	$8.95
Little Women	Louisa May Alcott	1-59308-108-1	$7.95
Lost Illusions	Honoré de Balzac	1-59308-315-7	$9.95
Main Street	Sinclair Lewis	1-59308-386-6	$9.95
Mansfield Park	Jane Austen	1-59308-154-5	$5.95
The Metamorphosis and Other Stories	Franz Kafka	1-59308-029-8	$6.95
Moby-Dick	Herman Melville	1-59308-018-2	$10.95
My Ántonia	Willa Cather	1-59308-202-9	$6.95
Narrative of Sojourner Truth		1-59308-293-2	$6.95
The Odyssey	Homer	1-59308-009-3	$7.95
Oliver Twist	Charles Dickens	1-59308-206-1	$6.95
The Origin of Species	Charles Darwin	1-59308-077-8	$9.95
Paradise Lost	John Milton	1-59308-095-6	$8.95
Persuasion	Jane Austen	1-59308-130-8	$5.95
The Picture of Dorian Gray	Oscar Wilde	1-59308-025-5	$6.95
A Portrait of the Artist as a Young Man and Dubliners	James Joyce	1-59308-031-X	$7.95
Pride and Prejudice	Jane Austen	1-59308-201-0	$6.95
The Prince and Other Writings	Niccolò Machiavelli	1-59308-060-3	$5.95
The Red Badge of Courage and Selected Short Fiction	Stephen Crane	1-59308-119-7	$4.95
Republic	Plato	1-59308-097-2	$7.95
Robinson Crusoe	Daniel Defoe	1-59308-360-2	$6.95
The Scarlet Letter	Nathaniel Hawthorne	1-59308-207-X	$5.95
The Secret Agent	Joseph Conrad	1-59308-305-X	$8.95
Selected Stories of O. Henry		1-59308-042-5	$7.95
Sense and Sensibility	Jane Austen	1-59308-125-1	$5.95
Siddhartha	Hermann Hesse	1-59308-379-3	$7.95
The Souls of Black Folk	W. E. B. Du Bois	1-59308-014-X	$5.95
The Strange Case of Dr. Jekyll and Mr. Hyde and Other Stories	Robert Louis Stevenson	1-59308-131-6	$6.95
A Tale of Two Cities	Charles Dickens	1-59308-138-3	$5.95
Three Theban Plays	Sophocles	1-59308-235-5	$7.95
Thus Spoke Zarathustra	Friedrich Nietzsche	1-59308-278-9	$8.95
The Time Machine and The Invisible Man	H. G. Wells	1-59308-388-2	$6.95
Treasure Island	Robert Louis Stevenson	1-59308-247-9	$6.95
The Turn of the Screw, The Aspern Papers and Two Stories	Henry James	1-59308-043-3	$5.95
Uncle Tom's Cabin	Harriet Beecher Stowe	1-59308-121-9	$7.95
Vanity Fair	William Makepeace Thackeray	1-59308-071-9	$8.95
Walden and Civil Disobedience	Henry David Thoreau	1-59308-208-8	$6.95
The War of the Worlds	H. G. Wells	1-59308-362-9	$5.95
Ward No. 6 and Other Stories	Anton Chekhov	1-59308-003-4	$7.95
Wuthering Heights	Emily Brontë	1-59308-128-6	$5.95

ℬ

BARNES & NOBLE CLASSICS

If you are an educator and would like to receive an
Examination or Desk Copy of a Barnes & Noble Classics edition,
please refer to Academic Resources on our website at
WWW.BN.COM/CLASSICS
or contact us at
BNCLASSICS@BN.COM

All prices are subject to change.